Sat 6/8

A GATHERING LIGHT

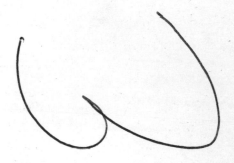

A GATHERING LIGHT

Jennifer Donnelly

BLOOM**21**SBURY

First published ...on ...sbury Publi...ing Plc

...are, London W1D 3QT

T... ...ublished in 2007

First publish... ...U... by Harcourt Brace Inc.

Text copy... ...nifer Donnelly 2003
Introduction c... ...Jeanette Winterson 200...

The moral rig... ...hor has been asserted

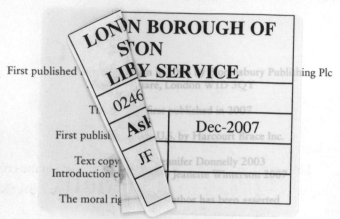

A CIP catalogue record for this book is available from the British Library

ISBN 9780747589969

10 9 8 7 6 5 4 3 2 1

Printed in Great Britain by Clays Ltd, St Ives plc

www.bloomsbury.com/jenniferdonnelly
www.jenniferdonnelly.com

The paper this book is printed on is certified by the © Forest Stewardship
Council 1996 A.C. (FSC). It is ancient-forest friendly.
The printer holds FSC chain of custody SGS-COC-2061

FSC
Mixed Sources
Product group from well-managed
forests and other controlled sources

Cert no. SGS-COC-2061
www.fsc.org
© 1996 Forest Stewardship Council

Introduction
Jeanette Winterson

A woman's body is dragged out of a lake.

The young girl Mattie, watching this, runs to make coffee and find a blanket, but it is too late for coffee and blankets, because the woman in Big Moose Lake is dead.

The day before, this strange sad figure, Grace Brown had given Mattie a bundle of letters and begged her to burn them. Mattie, working in a tourist hotel, is used to odd requests from guests, but this one feels different, because her own life is caught up in the struggle, the sadness, and the loss.

Mattie's mother has been dead four years, and her father has had to harden with the times, which are tough enough for raising children and working a farm. There is no tenderness in Mattie's life, only scraping by, and making do, and secretly saving a few cents when she can, to buy an exercise book to write in.

Matttie is not used to kind words, but words themselves are the things that give her hope. She loves reading, loves books, loves to write her own stories and poems, as though she could write her life again, and change it.

At school, Mattie is lucky to have a teacher, Miss Wilcox, who encourages her to try for a scholarship and get to college in

New York City. Miss Wilcox was at college there herself, and she is something of a dangerous eccentric in the tight-knit, hard-up farming and logging community in the North Woods at the turn of the century. Miss Wilcox is a woman with wider horizons than the sun setting over the lake, beautiful though that is, and it is she who first shows Mattie the struggle between what ordinary life has to offer, and the life someone could make for themselves, if they wanted it badly enough.

A *Gathering Light* isn't about simple choices between a two-bit town and the bright lights; Mattie falls in love at home, with a handsome son-of-the soil boy, who wants to marry her and farm with her, in much the same way that his family has done for generations. What he offers is a genuine life, although cynically given, because he is more in love with Mattie's father's farmland than with Mattie herself, but it is a life she could choose. The story does not underestimate the pull of ordinariness; staying near home, settling down, meeting someone to care about, doing the things that come naturally, and finding satisfaction there. Mattie likes animals and the land – she lives in her body as well as in her head, so for her the choices are not simple. And she loves her father too, and recognises how hard he works to put food on the table and keep his family together.

The refusal of simplicity gives this story its edge. There is no black and white; there are all the colours of the heart.

What is so well done is Mattie's growing awareness of these many colours. When she accuses her teacher, Miss Wilcox, of oversimplifying, in the way that novels sometimes oversimplify, Miss Wilcox tells her to write it the way it is – to put in all the difficulty and the pain, but never to refuse life.

When Mattie sees Grace Brown dead, and reads her love letters to the man who turns out to have murdered her, Mattie realises that whatever choice you make, right or wrong, you have to choose for life. Death ends all possibility; there are no more choices.

As she looks around her, she realises there is such a thing as dying before you have even lived.

The morning she slips out of the hotel and away to the railway station, leaving letters of her own behind for those she loves, she knows she is not walking towards the cliché of a happy ending, but towards the conscious choice of a new beginning. Whatever she is doing, she is doing it for herself, wherever it leads, because words have made a bridge she has to cross.

Grace Brown's letters, the pages of the novels Miss Wilcox has given her, the poems Miss Wilcox has written herself, the words that Mattie looks up every day in the battered dictionary – these words have become the struts and planks and piers of the bridge that she must cross.

Her heart is bursting with 'grief and fear and joy'. The complexity can't be bleached out – it comes with the colours of life. In the end, it may be intensity, vividness, that is the choice, and nothing so simple as happiness. This book has a happy ending, not because everything is resolved, but because it isn't. At the end of the book, life begins.

For Megan,
who escaped from the enchanted forest

And if the many sayings of the wise
Teach of submission I will not submit
But with a spirit all unreconciled
Flash an unquenched defiance to the stars.

ADELAIDE CRAPSEY
Saranac Lake, 1913

A
Gathering
Light

*W*hen summer comes to the North Woods, time slows down. And some days it stops altogether. The sky, gray and lowering for much of the year, becomes an ocean of blue, so vast and brilliant you can't help but stop what you're doing—pinning wet sheets to the line maybe, or shucking a bushel of corn on the back steps— to stare up at it. Locusts whir in the birches, coaxing you out of the sun and under the boughs, and the heat stills the air, heavy and sweet with the scent of balsam.

As I stand here on the porch of the Glenmore, the finest hotel on all of Big Moose Lake, I tell myself that today—Thursday, July 12, 1906—is such a day. Time has stopped, and the beauty and calm of this perfect afternoon will never end. The guests up from New York, all in their summer whites, will play croquet on the lawn forever. Old Mrs. Ellis will stay on the porch until the end of time, rapping her cane on the railing for more lemonade. The children of doctors and lawyers from Utica, Rome, and Syracuse will always run through the woods, laughing and shrieking, giddy from too much ice cream.

I believe these things. With all my heart. For I am good at telling myself lies.

Until Ada Bouchard comes out of the doorway and slips her hand into mine. And Mrs. Morrison, the manager's wife, walks right by us, pausing at the top of the steps. At any other time, she'd scorch our ears for standing idle; now she doesn't seem to even know we're here. Her arms cross over her chest. Her eyes, gray and troubled, fasten on the dock. And the steamer tied alongside it.

"That's the *Zilpha*, ain't it, Mattie?" Ada whispers. "They've been dragging the lake, ain't they?"

I squeeze her hand. "I don't think so. I think they were just looking along the shoreline. Cook says they probably got lost, that couple. Couldn't find their way back in the dark and spent the night under some pines, that's all."

"I'm scared, Mattie. Ain't you?"

I don't answer her. I'm not scared, not exactly, but I can't explain how I feel. Words fail me sometimes. I have read most every one in the *Webster's International Dictionary of the English Language,* but I still have trouble making them come when I want them to.

Right now I want a word that describes the feeling you get—a cold, sick feeling deep down inside—when you know something is happening that will change you, and you don't want it to, but you can't stop it. And you know, for the first time, for the very first time, that there will now be a *before* and an *after,* a *was* and a *will be.* And that you will never again be quite the same person you were.

I imagine it's the feeling Eve had as she bit into the

2

apple. Or Hamlet when he saw his father's ghost. Or Jesus as a boy, right after someone sat him down and told him his pa wasn't a carpenter after all.

What is the word for that feeling? For knowledge and fear and loss all mixed together? *Frisdom? Dreadnaciousness? Malbominance?*

Standing on that porch, under that flawless sky, with bees buzzing lazily in the roses and a cardinal calling from the pines so sweet and clear, I tell myself that Ada is a nervous little hen, always worrying when there's no cause. Nothing bad can happen at the Glenmore, not on such a day as this.

And then I see Cook running up from the dock, ashen and breathless, her skirts in her hands, and I know that I am wrong.

"Mattie, open the parlor!" she shouts, heedless of the guests. "Quick, girl!"

I barely hear her. My eyes are on Mr. Crabb, the *Zilpha*'s engineer. He is coming up the path carrying a young woman in his arms. Her head lolls against him like a broken flower. Water drips from her skirt.

"Oh, Mattie, look at her. Oh, jeezum, Mattie, look," Ada says, her hands twisting in her apron.

"*Sssh,* Ada. She got soaked, that's all. They got lost on the lake and . . . and the boat tipped and they swam to shore and she . . . she must've fainted."

"Oh, dear Lord," Mrs. Morrison says, her hands coming up to her mouth.

"Mattie! Ada! Why are you standing there like a pair

of jackasses?" Cook wheezes, heaving her bulky body up the steps. "Open the spare room, Mattie. The one off the parlor. Pull the shades and lay an old blanket on the bed. Ada, go fix a pot of coffee and some sandwiches. There's a ham and some chicken in the icebox. Shift yourselves!"

There are children in the parlor playing hide-and-seek. I chase them out and unlock the door to a small bedroom used by stage drivers or boat captains when the weather's too bad to travel. I realize I've forgotten the blanket and run back to the linen closet for it. I'm back in the room snapping it open over the bare ticking just as Mr. Crabb comes in. I've brought a pillow and a heavy quilt, too. She'll be chilled to the bone, having slept out all night in wet clothing.

Mr. Crabb lays her down on the bed. Cook stretches her legs out and tucks the pillow under her head. The Morrisons come in. Mr. Sperry, the Glenmore's owner, is right behind them. He stares at her, goes pale, and walks out again.

"I'll fetch a hot water bottle and some tea and . . . and brandy," I say, looking at Cook and then Mrs. Morrison and then a painting on the wall. Anywhere and everywhere but at the girl. "Should I do that? Should I get the brandy?"

"Hush, Mattie. It's too late for that," Cook says.

I make myself look at her then. Her eyes are dull and empty. Her skin has gone the yellow of muscatel wine. There is an ugly gash on her forehead and her lips are bruised. Yesterday she'd sat by herself on the porch, fretting the hem of her skirt. I'd brought her a glass of lemonade, because it was hot outside and she looked peaked. I hadn't charged her for it. She looked like she didn't have much money.

Behind me, Cook badgers Mr. Crabb. "What about the man she was with? Carl Grahm?"

"No sign of him," he says. "Not yet, leastways. We got the boat. They'd tipped it, all right. In South Bay."

"I'll have to get hold of the family," Mrs. Morrison says. "They're in Albany."

"No, that was only the man, Grahm," Cook says. "The girl lived in South Otselic. I looked in the register."

Mrs. Morrison nods. "I'll ring the operator. See if she can connect me with a store there, or a hotel. Or someone who can get a message to the family. What on earth will I say? Oh dear! Oh, her poor, poor mother!" She presses a handkerchief to her eyes and hurries from the room.

"She'll be making a second call before the day's out," Cook says. "Ask me, people who can't swim have no business on a lake."

"Too confident, that fellow," Mr. Morrison says. "I asked him could he handle a skiff and he told me yes. Only a darn fool from the city could tip a boat on a calm day . . ." He says more, but I don't hear him. It feels like there are iron bands around my chest. I close my eyes and try to breathe deeply, but it only makes things worse. Behind my eyes I see a packet of letters tied with a pale blue ribbon. Letters that are upstairs under my mattress. Letters that I promised to burn. I can see the address on the top one: *Chester Gillette, 17½ Main Street, Cortland, New York.*

Cook fusses me away from the body. "Mattie, pull the shades like I told you to," she says. She folds Grace Brown's hands over her chest and closes her eyes. "There's coffee in the kitchen. And sandwiches," she tells the men. "Will you eat something?"

"We'll take something with us, Mrs. Hennessey, if that's all right," Mr. Morrison says. "We're going out again. Soon as Sperry gets the sheriff on the phone. He's calling Martin's, too. To tell 'em to keep an eye out. And Higby's and the other camps. Just in case Grahm made it to shore and got lost in the woods."

"His name's not Carl Grahm. It's Chester. Chester Gillette." The words burst out of me before I can stop them.

"How do you know that, Mattie?" Cook asks. They are all looking at me now—Cook, Mr. Morrison, and Mr. Crabb.

"I . . . I heard her call him that, I guess," I stammer, suddenly afraid.

Cook's eyes narrow. "Did you see something, Mattie? Do you know something you should tell us?"

What had I seen? Too much. What did I know? Only that knowledge carries a damned high price. Miss Wilcox, my teacher, had taught me so much. Why had she never taught me that?

frac • tious

My youngest sister, Beth, who is five, will surely grow up to be a riverman—standing upstream on the dam, calling out warnings to the men below that the logs are coming down. She has the lungs for it.

It was a spring morning. End of March. Not quite four months ago, though it seems much longer. We were late for school and there were still chores to do before we left, but Beth didn't care. She just sat there ignoring the cornmeal mush I'd made her, bellowing like some opera singer up from Utica to perform at one of the hotels. Only no opera singer ever sang "Hurry Up, Harry." Least not as far as I know.

> *So it's hurry up, Harry, and Tom or Dick or Joe,*
> *And you may take the pail, boys, and for the water go.*
> *In the middle of the splashing, the cook will dinner cry,*
> *And you'd ought to see them hurry up for fear they'd*
> *   lose their pie . . .*

"Beth, hush now and eat your mush," I scolded, fumbling her hair into a braid. She didn't mind me, though, for she wasn't singing her song to me or to any of us. She was singing to the motionless rocker near the stove and the battered fishing creel hanging by the shed door. She was singing to fill all the empty places in our house, to chase away the silence. Most mornings I didn't mind her noise, but that morning I had to talk to Pa about something, something very important, and I was all nerves. I wanted it peaceful for once. I wanted Pa to find everything in order and everyone behaving when he came in, so he would be peaceable himself and well-disposed to what I had to say.

There's blackstrap molasses, squaw buns as hard as rock,
Tea that's boiled in an old tin pail and smells just like
*   your sock.*
The beans they are sour, and the porridge thick as
*   dough—*
When we have stashed this in our craw, it's to the
*   woods we go ...*

The kitchen door banged open and Lou, all of eleven, passed behind the table with a bucket of milk. She'd forgotten to take off her boots and was tracking manure across the floor.

"A-hitching up our braces and a-binding up our feet."

"Beth, please!" I said, tying her braid with a ribbon. "Lou, your boots! Mind your boots!"

"A-grinding up our axes for our kind is hard to beat..."

"What? I can't hardly hear you, Matt," Lou said. "Cripes' sake, shut up, will you?" she yelled, clapping a hand over Beth's mouth.

Beth squealed and wriggled and threw herself back against the chair. The chair went over and hit Lou's bucket. The milk and Beth went all over the floor. Then Beth was bawling and Lou was shouting and I was wishing for my mother. As I do every day. A hundred times at least.

When Mamma was alive, she could make breakfast for seven people, hear our lessons, patch Pa's trousers, pack our dinner pails, start the milk to clabbering, and roll out a piecrust. All at the same time and without ever raising her voice. I'm lucky if I can keep the mush from burning and Lou and Beth from slaughtering each other.

Abby, fourteen, came in cradling four brown eggs in her apron. She carefully put them in a bowl inside the pie safe, then stared at the scene before her. "Pa's only got the pigs left to do. He'll be in shortly," she said.

"Pa's going to tan your ass, Beth," Lou said.

"He'll tan yours for saying *ass*," Beth replied, still sniffling.

"Now you've said it as well. You'll get a double tanning."

Beth's face crumpled. She started to wail all over again.

"That's enough! Both of you!" I shouted, dreading the thought of Pa getting his strap, and hearing the whack of it against their legs. "No one's getting a tanning. Go get Barney."

Beth and Lou ran to the stove and dragged poor Barney out from behind it. Pa's old hunting dog is lame and blind. He pees his bed. Uncle Vernon says Pa ought to take him out behind the barn and shoot him. Pa says he'd rather shoot Uncle Vernon.

Lou stood Barney by the puddle. He couldn't see the milk, but he could smell it, and he lapped it up greedily. He hadn't tasted milk for ages. Neither had we. The cows are dry over the winter. One had just freshened, though, so there was a little bit of milk for the first time in months. More were due soon. By the end of May, the barn would be full of calves and Pa would be off early every morning making deliveries of milk, cream, and butter to the hotels and camps. But this morning, that one bucket was all we'd had for a long while and he was no doubt expecting to see some of it on his mush.

Barney got most of the milk cleaned up. What little he left, Abby got with a rag. Beth looked a little soggy, and the linoleum under her chair looked cleaner than it did elsewhere, but I just hoped Pa wouldn't notice. There was an inch or two left in the bucket. I added a bit of water to it and poured it into a jug that I set by his bowl. He'd be expecting a nice milk gravy for supper, or maybe a custard, since the hens had given four eggs, but I'd worry about that later.

"Pa'll know, Matt," Lou said.

"How? Is Barney going to tell him?"

"When Barney drinks milk, he farts something wicked."

"Lou, just because you walk like a boy and dress like a boy doesn't mean you have to talk like one. Mamma wouldn't like it," I said.

"Well, Mamma's not here anymore, so I'll talk as I please."

Abby, rinsing her rag at the sink, whirled around.

"Be quiet, Lou!" she shouted, startling us, for Abby never shouts. She didn't even cry at Mamma's funeral, though I found her in Pa's bedroom a few days after, holding a tin likeness of our mother so hard that the edges had cut her hand. Our Abby is a sprigged dress that has been washed and turned wrong side out to dry, with all its color hidden. Our Lou is anything but.

As the two of them continued to snipe, we heard footsteps in the shed off the back of the kitchen. The bickering stopped. We thought it was Pa. But then we heard a knock and a shuffle, and knew it was only Tommy Hubbard, the neighbor boy, hungry again.

"You itching, Tom?" I called.

"No, Matt."

"Come get some breakfast, then. Wash your hands first."

Last time I'd let him in to eat he gave us fleas. Tommy has six brothers and sisters. They live on the Uncas Road, same as us, but farther up, in a shabby plank house. Their land divides ours from the Loomis's land on one side, notching in from the road. They have no pa or they have lots of pas, depending on who you listen to. Emmie, Tommy's mother, does the best she can cleaning rooms at the hotels, and selling the little paintings she makes to the tourists, but it isn't enough. Her kids are always hungry. Her house is cold. She can't pay her taxes.

Tommy came inside. He had one of his sisters by the hand. My eyes darted between them. Pa hadn't eaten yet and there wasn't so much left in the pot. "I just brung Jenny is all," he said quickly. "I ain't hungry myself."

Jenny had on a man's wool shirt over a thin cotton dress. The shirttails touched the floor. The dress barely made it past her knees. Tommy had no overclothes on at all.

"It's all right, Tom. There's plenty," I said.

"She can have mine. I'm sick to death of this damned slop," Lou said, pushing her bowl across the table. Her kindnesses often took a roundabout path.

"I hope Pa hears you," Abby said. "Mouth on you like a teamster."

Lou poked her tongue out, displaying her breakfast. Abby looked as if she'd like to slap her. Luckily, the table was between them.

Everyone was sick of cornmeal mush. Myself included. We'd been eating it with maple sugar for breakfast and dinner for weeks. And for supper, buckwheat pancakes with the last of fall's stewed apples. Or pea soup made with an old ham bone that had been boiled white. We would have loved some corned beef hash or chicken and biscuits, but most everything we'd put in the root cellar in September was gone. We'd eaten the last of the venison in January. The ham and bacon, too. And though we'd put up two barrels of fresh pork, one of them had spoiled. It was my fault. Pa said I hadn't put enough salt in the brine. We'd killed one of our roosters back in the fall, and four hens since. We only had ten birds left, and Pa didn't want to touch them as they provided us with a few eggs now and would make us more eggs—and chickens, too—come summer.

It wasn't like this when Mamma was alive. Somehow

she provided good meals all through the winter and still managed to have meat left in the cellar come spring. I am nowhere near as capable as my mother was, and if I ever forget it, I have Lou to remind me. Or Pa. Not that he says the sorts of things Lou does, but you can tell by the look on his face when he sits down to eat that he isn't fond of mush day in and day out.

Jenny Hubbard didn't mind it, though. She waited patiently, her eyes large and solemn, as I sprinkled maple sugar on Lou's leavings and passed the bowl to her. I gave Tom some from the pot. As much as I could spare while still leaving enough for Pa.

Abby took a swallow of her tea, then looked at me over the top of the cup. "You talk to Pa yet?"

I shook my head. I was standing behind Lou, teasing the rats out of her hair. It was too short for braids; it only just grazed her jaw. She'd cut it off with Mamma's sewing scissors after Christmas. Right after our brother, Lawton, left.

"You going to?" she asked.

"Talk about what?" Beth asked.

"Never mind. Finish your breakfast," I said.

"What, Matt? Talk about what?"

"Beth, if Mattie wanted you to know, she'd tell you," Lou said.

"You don't know, neither."

"Do, too."

"Mattie, why'd you tell Lou and not me?" Beth whined.

"Because you can't never keep quiet," Lou said.

That started another round of bickering. My nerves were grated down bald. "It's *can't ever*, Lou, not *can't never*," I said. "Beth, stop whining."

"Matt, you pick your word of the day yet?" Abby asked. Abby, our peacemaker. Gentle and mild. More like our mother than any of the rest of us.

"Oh, Mattie! Can I pick it? Can I?" Beth begged. She scrambled out of her chair and raced into the parlor. I kept my precious dictionary there, out of harm's way, along with the books I borrowed from Charlie Eckler and Miss Wilcox, and my mother's Waverly Editions of Best Loved American Classics, and some ancient copies of *Peterson's Magazine* that my aunt Josie had given us because, as it said in its "Publisher's Corner," it was "one of the few periodicals fit for families where there are daughters."

"Beth, you carry it but let Lou pick the word," I shouted after her.

"I don't want no part of baby word games," Lou grumbled.

"*Any*, Lou. *Any* part," I snapped. Her carelessness with words made me angrier than her dirty mouth and the filthy state of her coveralls and the manure she'd tracked in, combined.

Beth returned to the kitchen table, carrying the dictionary as if it were made of gold. It might as well have been. It weighed as much. "Pick the word," I told her. "Lou doesn't want to." She carefully flipped a few pages forward, then a few back, then put her index finger on the left-hand page. *"Fff...fraaak...fraktee...frakteeus?"* she said.

"I don't think there's any such word. Spell it," I said.

"F-r-a-c-t-i-o-u-s."

"Frakshus," I said. "Tommy, what's the meaning?"

Tommy peered at the dictionary. "'Apt to break out into a passion ... snappish, peevish, irritable, cross,'" he read. "'P-per-verse. Pettish.'"

"Isn't that just perfect?" I said. *"Fractious,"* I repeated, relishing the bite of the *f,* teeth against lip. A new word. Bright with possibilities. A flawless pearl to turn over and over in my hand, then put away for safekeeping. "Your turn, Jenny. Can you make a sentence from the word?"

Jenny bit her bottom lip. "It means cross?" she asked. I nodded.

She frowned, then said, "Ma was fractious when she chucked the fry pan at me 'cause I knocked her whiskey bottle over."

"She chucked a fry pan at you?" Beth asked, wide-eyed. "Why'd she do that?"

"Because she was out of sorts," Abby said.

"Because she was drinking," Jenny said, licking bits of mush off her spoon.

Jenny Hubbard is only six years old, but the growing season is short in the North Woods, and children, like the corn, have to come up fast if they are to come up at all.

"Your mamma drinks whiskey?" Beth asked. "Mammas shouldn't drink whiskey—"

"Come on, Beth, let's go. We're going to be late," Abby said, hurrying her up from the table.

"Ain't you coming, Matt?" Beth asked.

"In a few minutes."

Books were gathered. Dinner pails, too. Abby bossed Lou and Beth into their coats. Tommy and Jenny ate silently. The shed door slammed. It was quiet. For the first time that morning. And then, "Matt? Come here a minute, will you?"

"What is it, Lou? I've got my hands full."

"Just come!"

I walked into the shed. Lou was standing there, ready to go, with Lawton's fishing pole in her hand.

"Lou, what are you doing?"

"Can't eat no more mush," she said. Then she took hold of my ear, pulled my face to hers, and kissed my cheek. Hard and sharp and quick. I could smell the scent of her—woodsmoke and cows and the spruce gum she was always chewing. The door slammed again and she was gone.

My other sisters, like me, take after our mother. Brown eyes. Brown hair. Lou takes after Pa. Lawton, too. Coal black hair, blue eyes. Lou acts like Pa, too. Angry all the time now. Since Mamma died. And Lawton went away.

When I came back in, Tommy was working his spoon around his bowl so hard I thought he'd take the paint off it. I hadn't had more than a few bites of my mush. "Finish mine, will you, Tom?" I said, sliding my bowl over to him. "I'm not hungry and I don't want it wasted." I plugged the sink, poured hot water into it from the kettle, added a bit of cold from the pump, and started washing. "Where are the rest of you kids?"

"Susie and Billy went to Weaver's. Myrton and Clara went to try at the hotel."

"Where's the baby?" I asked.

"With Susie."

"Your ma's not good today?"

"She won't come out from under the bed. Says she's scared of the wind and can't bear to hear it no more." Tommy looked at his bowl, then at me. "You think she's crazy, Mattie? You think the county'll take her?"

Emmie Hubbard certainly was crazy, and I was pretty sure the county would take her one day. They'd almost done so on two or three occasions. But I couldn't say that to Tommy. He was only twelve years old. As I tried to figure out what I could say—to find words that weren't a lie but weren't quite the truth, either—I thought that madness isn't like they tell it in books. It isn't Miss Havisham sitting in the ruins of her mansion, all vicious and majestic. And it isn't like in *Jane Eyre*, either, with Rochester's wife banging around in the attic, shrieking and carrying on and frightening the help. When your mind goes, it's not castles and cobwebs and silver candelabra. It's dirty sheets and sour milk and dog shit on the floor. It's Emmie cowering under her bed, crying and singing while her kids try to make soup from seed potatoes.

"You know, Tom," I finally said, "there are times I want to hide under the bed myself."

"When? I can't see you crawling under no bed, Matt."

"End of February. We got four feet in two days, remember? On top of the three we had. Blew onto the porch and blocked the front door. Couldn't get the shed door open, either. Pa had to go out the kitchen window. The wind was howling and wailing, and all I wanted to do was crawl under something and never come out. Most of us feel like that from time to time. Your ma, she does what she feels. That's the only difference. I'll go over to her before school. See if I can find a jar of apples to take and a bit of maple sugar. Think she'd like that?"

"She would. I know she would. Thank you, Mattie."

I packed Tommy and Jenny off to school, hoping that by the time I got to the Hubbards', Weaver's mamma would already be there. She was better at getting Emmie out from under the bed than I was. I finished the washing, looking out the window as I did, at the bare trees and the brown fields, searching for spots of yellow among the patches of snow. If you can pick adder's-tongue in April, spring will come early. I was awful tired of the cold and the snow, and now the rain and the mud.

People call that time of year—when the root cellar is nearly empty and the garden not yet planted—the six weeks' want. Years past, we always had money come March to buy meat and flour and potatoes, and anything else we might need. Pa would go off logging at the end of November up at Indian or Raquette Lake. He'd leave as soon as the hay was in and stay there all winter, hauling logs cut the previous summer. He drove teams of horses hitched to jumpers—low flat sledges with big runners. The loads were piled as high as a man standing on another man's shoulders. He took them down off the mountains over icy roads—relying on the weight of the logs and his own skill to keep the jumper from hurtling down the hills and killing the horses and anything else in its way.

Come March, the snow would melt and the roads would soften, and it became impossible to drag the heavy loads over them. As it got toward the end of the month, we would look for Pa every day. We never knew just when he would arrive. Or how. In the back of someone's wagon if he was lucky. On foot if he wasn't. We often heard him before we saw him, singing a new song he'd learned.

We girls would all run to him. Lawton would walk. Mamma would try her best to stay on the porch, to hang back and be proper, but she never could. He would smile at her, and then she was running down the path to him, crying because she was so glad he was home with his hands and feet and arms and legs all still attached. He'd hold her face in his hands, keeping her at arm's length, and wipe her tears away with his dirty thumbs. We'd all want to touch him and hug him, but he wouldn't let us. "Don't come near me. I'm crawling," he'd say. He'd take his clothes off in back of the house, douse them with kerosene, and burn them. He'd douse his head, too, and Lawton would comb the dead lice from his hair.

Mamma would be boiling water while he did all this, and filling our big tin tub. Then Pa would have a bath in the middle of the kitchen, his first one in months. When he was clean, we would have a feast. Ham steaks with gravy. Mashed potatoes with rivers of butter running down them. The last of the corn and the beans. Hot, fleecy rolls. And for dessert, a blueberry buckle made with the last of the put-up berries. Then there were presents for each one of us. There were no stores in the woods, but peddlers knew to make their rounds of the lumber camps just as the men were paid for the season. There might be a penknife for Lawton, and ribbons and boughten candy for us girls. And for Mamma, a dozen glass buttons and a bolt of fabric for a new dress. A cotton sateen the exact shade of a robin's egg, maybe. Or a butterscotch tartan. An emerald velveteen or a crisp yellow pongee. And once he bought her a silk faille the exact color of cranberries. Mamma had held that one to her cheek, looking at my pa as she did, then put it away for months, unable to take the scissors to it. We'd all sit in the parlor that night, in the glow of the cylinder stove, eating the caramels and chocolates Pa had brought, and listen to his tales. He'd show us all the new scars he'd picked up and tell us the antics of the wild lumberjacks, and how wicked the boss was, and how bad the food was, and all the tricks they'd played on the cook and the poor chore boy. It was better than Christmas, those nights that Pa came out of the woods.

He hadn't gone into the woods this year. He didn't want us by ourselves. Without his logging money, things had been hard indeed. He'd done some ice cutting on Fourth Lake over the winter, but the pay wasn't as good as logging money, and the yearly tax bill on our land took it all, anyway. As I stood there drying the dishes, I hoped the fact that we were flat broke and would be for some weeks yet, until Pa could sell his milk and butter again, would make him listen to what I had to say and tell me yes.

I finally heard him come into the shed, and then he was in the kitchen, a small snuffling bundle in his arms. "That devil of a sow et four of her piglets," he said. "Every one except the runt. I'm going to put him in with Barney. Heat'll do him good. Lord, this dog stinks! What's he been eating?"

"Probably got into something in the yard. Here, Pa." I put a bowl of mush on the table and stirred maple sugar into it. Then I poured the watery milk over it and hoped to God he didn't ask for more.

He sat down, looking thunderous, no doubt toting up the money he'd lost on the dead piglets. "Cost your mother a whole dollar secondhand, that book," he said, nodding at the dictionary still open on the table. "Never spent a penny on herself and then throws away a whole dollar on that thing. Put it up before it's covered in grease."

I put it back in the parlor, then poured Pa a cup of hot tea. Black and sweet, just the way he liked it. I sat down across from him and looked around the room. At the red-and-white-checked curtains that needed wash-ing. At the faded pictures cut off calendars from Becker's

Farm and Feed Supply that Mamma had tacked on the walls. At the chipped plates and yellow mixing bowls on the shelf over the sink. At the cracked linoleum, the black stove. At Barney licking the piglet. I looked at everything there was to see and some things twice, practicing my words in my head. I'd just about worked up the nerve to open my mouth when Pa spoke first.

"I'm sugaring tomorrow. Sap's flowing like a river. Got about a hundred gallons already. Wait any longer and it'll all spoil. Weather's unseasonable warm. You're to stay home and help me boil tomorrow. Your sisters, too."

"Pa, I can't. I'll fall behind if I miss a day, and my examinations are coming up."

"Cows can't eat learning, Mattie. I need to buy hay. Used up most everything I cut last fall. Fred Becker don't take credit, so I'll need to sell some syrup to get it."

I started to argue, but Pa looked up from his bowl and I knew to stop. He wiped his mouth on his sleeve. "You're lucky you're going at all this year," he said. "And it's only because the notion of you getting your diploma"—it came out French-sounding, *dee-plo-MA*, as his words do when he's angry—"meant something to your mother. You won't be going next year. I can't run this place by myself."

I looked at the table. I was angry with my father for keeping me home, even for a day, but he was right: He couldn't run a sixty-acre farm alone. I wished then that it was still winter and snowing night and day and there was no plowing or planting, just long evenings of reading and writing in my composition book, and Pa with nothing to say about it. *Fractious*, I thought. *Cross, irritable, peevish.* Fits my father to a T. It was useless to try and soften him up with sweet tea. Might as well try and soften up a boulder. I took a deep breath and plunged ahead.

"Pa, I want to ask you something," I said, hope rising in me like sap in one of our maples, though I tried not to let it.

"Mmm?" He raised an eyebrow and kept on eating.

"Can I work at one of the camps this season? Maybe the Glenmore? Abby's old enough to get the meals and look after everyone. I asked her and she said she'd be fine and I thought that if I—"

"No."

"But Pa—"

"You don't have to go looking for work. There's plenty"—there it was again, his accent, *plain-tee*—"right here."

I knew he'd say no. Why had I even asked? I stared at my hands—red, cracked, old woman's hands—and saw what was in store for me: a whole summer of drudgery and no money for it. Cooking, cleaning, washing, sewing, feeding chickens, slopping pigs, milking cows, churning cream, salting butter, making soap, plowing, planting, hoeing, weeding, harvesting, haying, threshing, canning—doing everything that fell on the eldest in a family of four girls, a dead mother, and a pissant brother who took off to drive boats on the Erie Canal and refused to come back and work the farm like he ought to.

I was yearning, and so I had more courage than was good for me. "Pa, they pay well," I said. "I thought I could keep back some of the money for myself and give the rest to you. I know you need it."

"You can't be up at a hotel by yourself. It's not right."

"But I won't be by myself! Ada Bouchard and Frances Hill and Jane Miley are all going to the Glenmore. And the Morrisons—the ones managing the place—are decent folk. Ralph Simms is going. And Mike Bouchard. And Weaver, too."

"Weaver Smith is no recommendation."

"Please, Pa," I whispered.

"No, Mattie. And that's the end of it. There are all sorts at those tourist hotels."

"All sorts" meant men. Pa was always warning me about the woodsmen, the trappers, the guides, and the surveyors. The sports up from New York or down from Montreal. The men in the theatrical troupes from Utica, the circus men from Albany, and the Holy Rollers that followed in their wake. "Men only want one thing, Mathilda," he was always telling me. The one time I asked, "What thing?" I got a cuff and a warning not to be smart.

It wasn't the idea of strange men that bothered Pa. That was just an excuse. He knew all the hotel people, knew most of them ran respectable places. It was the idea of somebody else leaving him. I wanted to argue, to make him see reason. But his jaw was set firm, and I saw a little muscle jumping in his cheek. Lawton used to make that muscle jump. Last time he did, Pa swung a peavey at him and he ran off, and no one heard from him for months. Until a postcard came from Albany.

I finished the dishes without a word and left for the Hubbards'. My feet were as heavy as two blocks of ice. I wanted to earn money. Desperately. I had a plan. Well, more a dream than a plan, and the Glenmore was only part of it. But I wasn't feeling very hopeful about it just then. If Pa said no to the Glenmore, which was only a few miles up the road, what on earth would he say to New York City?

abe • ce • dar • i • an

If spring has a taste, it tastes like fiddleheads. Green and crisp and new. Mineralish, like the dirt that made them. Bright, like the sun that called them forth. I was supposed to be picking them, me and Weaver both. We were going to fill two buckets—split one for ourselves and sell one to the chef over at the Eagle Bay Hotel—but I was too busy eating them. I couldn't help it. I craved something fresh after months of old potatoes, and beans from a jar.

"Choofe . . . ," I tried to say, but my mouth was full. "Weba . . . choofe a wurb . . ."

"My mamma's pig's got better manners. Why don't you swallow first?" Weaver said.

I did. But not before I'd chewed some more, and licked my lips and rolled my eyes and grinned. Fiddleheads are that good. Pa and Abby like them best fried up with sweet butter, salt, and black pepper, but I like them best right out of the ground.

"Choose a word, Weaver," I finally said. "Winner reads, loser picks."

"Are you two fooling again?" Minnie asked. She was sitting near us on a rock. She was in the family way and was very fat and grumpy.

"We're dueling, not fooling, Mrs. Compeau," Weaver replied. "It's a very serious business, and we would appreciate quiet from the seconds."

"Give me a bucket, then. I'm starving."

"No. You're eating everything we pick," Weaver said.

She turned her hangdog eyes on me. "Please, Mattie?" she wheedled.

I shook my head. "Dr. Wallace said you were to take exercise, Min. He said it would do you good. Get down and pick your own fiddleheads."

"But, Matt, I took my exercise already. I walked all the way up here from the lake. I'm *tired*..."

"Minnie, we're trying to duel here, if you don't mind," Weaver huffed.

Minnie grumbled and sighed. She lumbered off the rock and crouched down amongst the fiddleheads, snapping off one after another. She ate them fast, shoving them into her mouth with the heel of her hand, not even taking time to taste them. Watching her, I had the funniest notion that if I came too near, she would growl at me. She didn't used to like fiddleheads, but that was before she started growing a baby and eating everything in sight. She'd told me she'd licked a lump of coal once when no one was looking. And sucked a nail.

Weaver flipped open the book he was holding. His eyes lit on a word. "*Iniquitous,*" he said, slapping the book closed. We stood back-to-back, cocking the thumbs on our right hands and sticking out our pointer fingers to make guns.

"To the death, Miss Gokey," he said solemnly.

"To the death, Mr. Smith."

"Minnie, you give the orders."

"No. It's silly."

"Come on. Just do it."

"Count off," Minnie sighed.

We walked away from each other, counting off paces. At ten, we turned.

"Draw." She yawned.

"It's supposed to be to the death, you know, Minnie. You could make an effort," Weaver said.

Minnie rolled her eyes. "Draw!" she shouted.

We did.

"Fire!"

"Evil!" Weaver yelled.

"Immoral!" I shouted.

"Sinful!"

"Wrong!"

"Unrighteous!"

"Unjust!"

"Wicked!"

"Corrupt!"

"Nefarious!"

"*Nefarious*? Jeezum, Weaver! Um...um...hold on, I have one..."

"Too late, Matt. You're dead," Minnie said.

Weaver smirked at me and blew on the tip of his finger. "Start picking," he said. He made a cushion out of his jacket and settled himself down with *The Count of Monte Cristo,* folding his long grasshopper legs underneath him. One bucket alone was a lot to fill, never mind two. And Minnie would be no help. She'd already waddled back to her rock. I should have known better than to challenge Weaver to a word duel. He always won.

Picking fiddleheads was only one of our money-making schemes. If it wasn't fiddleheads we were gathering, it was wild strawberries or blueberries or lumps of spruce gum. We'd end up with ten cents here, a quarter there. Twenty-five cents seemed like a fortune to me when all I wanted was a bag of chocolate babies or a licorice rope, but not anymore. I needed money. Quite a bit. New York City, people said, was very expensive. Last November I had five whole dollars, which was only one dollar and ninety cents shy of a train ticket to Grand Central Station. Miss Wilcox entered a poem of mine in a contest sponsored by the *Utica Observer.* I got my name in the paper, and my poem, too, and I won five dollars.

Didn't have it long, though. We needed it to help pay for Mamma's headstone.

"'On the 24th of February, 1810, the lookout at Notre-Dame de la Garde signaled the three-master, the *Pharaon* from Smyrna, Trieste, and Naples. As usual, a pilot put off immediately, and rounding the Château d'If...,'" Weaver began. As he read, I poked around with a stick, searching for the tiny green furls coming up through the wet, rotted leaves, each one curled in on itself like the end of a fiddle. They come up in moist, shady areas, and though they start small, they have a lot of push. I have seen them dislodge heavy rocks in their eagerness to grow. This patch, on a hill of maples and pines a quarter mile west of Weaver's place, is a good one. Nobody besides us knows about it. There are enough fiddleheads for two buckets today and another two tomorrow. We never pick them all. We leave plenty alone to become ferns.

I got my first bucket filled maybe one-third of the way, and then picking started to pale beside the sailors Dantès and Danglars and their goings-on, and I got taken outside myself like I always do by a good story and forgot all about fiddleheads and buckets and money and everything in the world except the words.

"'... We will leave Danglars struggling with the demon of hatred,'" Weaver read, "'and endeavoring to insinuate in the ear of the ship owner some evil suspicions against his comrade and...' Hey! Get picking, Matt! Mattie, did you hear me?"

"Huh?" I stood there in a trance, the bucket at my feet, listening as the words became sentences and the sentences became pages and the pages became feelings and voices and places and people.

"You gotta pick, not stand there looking touched."

"All right," I sighed.

Weaver closed the book. "Forget it. I'll help. We'll never get done otherwise. Give me a hand."

I reached for him and he pulled himself up, nearly pulling me over as he did. I have known Weaver Smith for over ten years now. He is my best friend. Him and

Minnie both. But I still have to smile every time we take hands. My skin is so pale you can nearly see through it, and his is as dark as tobacco. There's more alike than different about Weaver and me, though. His palms are pink like mine. And his eyes are brown like mine. And inside, he's exactly like me. He loves words, too, and there is nothing he would rather do than read a book.

Weaver was the only black boy in Eagle Bay. And Inlet, Big Moose Lake, Big Moose Station, Minnowbrook, Clearwater, Moulin, McKeever, and Old Forge, too. Maybe in all of the North Woods. I had never seen another. Black men came to work on Webb's railroad a few years ago, the new one that runs from Mohawk to Malone and right on up into Montreal. They stayed at Buckley's Hotel in Big Moose Station—a settlement a few miles west of Big Moose Lake—but they left as soon as the last spike was driven in. One told my pa that the Bowery, the roughest stretch of road in New York City, had nothing on Big Moose Station on a Saturday night. He said that the blackflies hadn't managed to kill him, nor had Jerry Buckley's whiskey, nor the brawling lumberjacks, either, but Mrs. Buckley's cooking surely would and he was leaving before it did.

Weaver's mamma moved herself and Weaver up here from Mississippi after Weaver's father was killed right in front of them by three white men for no other reason than not moving off the sidewalk when they passed. She decided the farther north they got, the better. "Heat makes white people mean," she told Weaver and, having heard about a place called the Great North Woods, a place that sounded cold and safe, decided she and her son would move there. They lived about a mile up the Uncas Road, just south of the Hubbards, in an old log house that someone abandoned years ago.

Weaver's mamma took in washing. She got a lot of business from the hotels and lumber camps. She washed table and bed linens in the summer, and in the fall and spring and winter, she washed wool shirts and pants and long johns that had been worn for months at a time. Weaver's mamma boiled them clean in a huge iron pot in her backyard. She boiled the jacks clean, too, making them get in a tin tub and scrub themselves pink before they put their clothes back on. When a whole crew came out at once, it was best not to stand downwind. "Weaver's mamma's cooking underwear soup today," Lawton used to say.

She raised chickens, too. Scores of them. During the warmer months, she fried up four or five every evening, and baked biscuits and pies, too, and took it all down to the Eagle Bay railroad station the next day in her cart to meet the trains. Between the engineer and the conductors and all the hungry tourists, she sold everything she made. She put every penny she earned in an old cigar box that she kept under her bed. Weaver's mamma worked as hard as she did so she could send Weaver away to college. To the Columbia University in New York City. Miss Wilcox, our teacher, encouraged him to apply. He'd been granted a scholarship and planned to study history and politics and then go on to law school one day. He was the first freeborn boy in his family. His grandparents were slaves, and even his parents were born slaves, though Mr. Lincoln freed them when they were tiny children.

Weaver always says freedom is like Sloan's Liniment, always promising more than it delivers. He says all it really means is being able to choose among the worst jobs at the logging camps, the hotels, and the tanneries. Until his people can work anywhere whites work, and speak their minds freely, and write books and get them published, until white men are punished for stringing up black men, no black person will ever really be free.

I was scared for Weaver sometimes. We had hillbillies in the North Woods, same as they had in Mississippi— ignorant folk just itching to blame their no-account lives on someone else—and Weaver never stepped off the sidewalk or doffed his hat. He'd scrap with anyone who called him nigger, and was never scared for himself. "Go round cringing like a dog, Matt," he said, "and folks will treat you like one. Stand up like a man, and they'll treat you like a man." That was fine for Weaver, but I wondered sometimes, How exactly do you stand up like a man when you're a girl?

"*The Count of Monte Cristo*'s a good book already, isn't it, Mattie? And we're only on the second chapter," Weaver said.

"It sure is," I replied, bending down by a big clutch of fiddleheads.

"You writing any more stories yourself?" Minnie asked me.

"I've no time. No paper, either. I used up every page in my composition book. But I'm reading a lot. And learning my word of the day."

"You ought to use your words, not collect them. You ought to write with them. That's what they're for," Weaver said.

"I told you I can't. Don't you listen? And anyway, there's nothing to write about in Eagle Bay. Maybe in Paris, where Mr. Dumas lives—"

"Doo-*mah*."

"What?"

"Doo-*mah*, not Dumb-ass. Aren't you half French?"

". . . where Mr. Doo-*mahhhh* lives, where they have kings and musketeers, but not here," I said, sounding testier than I wanted to. "Here there's just sugaring and milking and cooking and picking fiddleheads, and who'd want to read about any of that?"

"You don't have to snap, you snapping turtle," Minnie said.

"I'm not snapping," I snapped.

"The stories Miss Wilcox sent to New York weren't about kings or musketeers," Weaver said. "That one about the hermit Alvah Dunning and his Christmas all by himself, that was the best story I ever read."

"And old Sam Dunnigan wrapping up his poor dead niece and keeping her in the icehouse all winter till she could be buried," Minnie added.

"And Otis Arnold shooting a man and then drowning himself in Nick's Lake before the sheriff could take him from the woods," Weaver said.

I shrugged, poking in the leaves.

"What about the Glenmore?" Minnie asked.

"I'm not going."

"What about New York? You hear anything?" Weaver asked.

"No."

"Miss Wilcox get anything in the mail?" he pressed.

"No."

Weaver poked around some, too, then said, "That letter will come, Matt. I know it will. And in the meantime you can still write, you know. Nothing can stop you from writing if you really want to."

"It's all right for you, Weaver," I shot back angrily. "Your mamma lets you alone. What if you had three sisters to look after and a father and a big damn farm that's nothing but endless damn work? What about that? You think you'd be writing stories then?" I felt my throat tightening and swallowed a few times to get the lump out. I don't cry much. Pa's got a quick backhand and little patience for sulks or tears.

Weaver's eyes locked on mine. "It's not work that stops you, is it, Matt? Or time? You've always had plenty of one and none of the other. It's that promise. She shouldn't have made you do it. She had no right."

Minnie knows when to quit, but Weaver doesn't. He was like a horsefly buzzing around and around, looking for an opening, a tender spot, then biting so hard it hurt.

"She was dying. You would've done the same for your mother," I said, looking at the ground. I could feel my eyes tearing and I didn't want him to see.

"God took her life and she took yours."

"You shut up, Weaver! You don't know anything about it!" I shouted, the tears spilling.

"You sure have a big mouth, Weaver Smith," Minnie scolded. "Look what you did. You should say you're sorry."

"I'm not sorry. It's true."

"Lots of things are true. Doesn't mean you can go round saying them," Minnie said.

There was a silence between us then, with nothing to break it for quite some time but the *plink plink plink* of fiddleheads dropping in our pails.

A few months back, Weaver did something—something he says he did *for* me, but I say he did *to* me. He took my composition book—which I had tossed across the train tracks and into the woods—and he gave it to Miss Wilcox.

This composition book was where I wrote my stories and poems. I'd only shown them to three people: my mamma, Minnie, and Weaver. Mamma said they made her cry, and Minnie said they were awfully good. Weaver said they were better than good and told me I should show them to Miss Parrish, our teacher before Miss Wilcox came. He said she would know what to do with them. Maybe send them to a magazine.

I didn't want to, but he kept badgering, so I finally

did. I don't know what I was hoping for. Some small praise, I guess. A bit of encouragement. I didn't get it. Miss Parrish took me aside one day after school let out. She said she'd read my stories and found them morbid and dispiriting. She said literature was meant to uplift the heart and that a young woman such as myself ought to turn her mind to topics more cheerful and inspiring than lonely hermits and dead children.

"Look around yourself, Mathilda," she said. "At the trees and the lakes and the mountains. At the magnificence of nature. It should inspire joy and awe. Reverence. Respect. Beautiful thoughts and fine words."

I had looked around. I'd seen all the things she'd spoken of and more besides. I'd seen a bear cub lift its face to the drenching spring rains. And the silver moon of winter, so high and blinding. I'd seen the crimson glory of a stand of sugar maples in autumn and the unspeakable stillness of a mountain lake at dawn. I'd seen them and loved them. But I'd also seen the dark of things. The starved carcasses of winter deer. The driving fury of a blizzard wind. And the gloom that broods under the pines always. Even on the brightest of days.

"I don't mean to discourage you, dear," she'd added. "Why don't you try to find a new subject? Something a little less unsavory. How about spring? There's so much you could write about spring. Like the new green leaves. Or the pretty violets. Or the return of robin redbreast."

I didn't answer her. I just took my composition book and left, tears of shame scalding my eyes. Weaver was waiting for me outside of the schoolhouse. He asked me what Miss Parrish had said, but I wouldn't tell him. I waited until we were a mile out of town, then I pitched my composition book into the woods. He ran right after it. I told him he had no business with it. I wanted it gone. But he said since I'd thrown it away it wasn't mine anymore. It was his and he could do as he liked with it.

Being the malignant weasel that he is, he kept hold of it and he waited. And then Miss Parrish's mother took ill and she left to go to Boonville and nurse her, and the school trustees got Miss Wilcox, who was renting the old Foster camp in Inlet, to take her place. And Weaver gave Miss Wilcox my composition book without even telling me. And she read my stories and told me I had a gift.

"A true gift, Mattie," she'd said. "A rare one."

And ever since, because of the two of them, Weaver and Miss Wilcox both, I am wanting things I have no business wanting, and what they call a gift seems to me more like a burden.

"Mattie . . . ," Weaver said, still dropping fiddleheads into his bucket.

I did not answer him. I did not bother to straighten or look at him. I tried not to think about what he'd said.

"Mattie, what's your word of the day?"

I flapped a hand at him.

"Come on, what is it?"

"Abecedarian," I said quietly.

"What's it mean?"

"Weaver, she don't want to talk to you. Nobody does."

"Be quiet, Minnie."

38

He walked up to me and took my bucket away. I had to look at him then. I saw that his eyes said he was sorry even if his mouth wouldn't.

"What's it mean?"

"As a noun, someone who's learning the alphabet. A beginner. A novice. As an adjective, rudimentary or primary."

"Use it in a sentence."

"Weaver Smith should abandon his abecedarian efforts at eloquence, say uncle, and admit that Mathilda Gokey is the superior word duelist."

Weaver smiled. He put both pails down. "Draw," he said.

$\mathcal{M}$attie, what in blazes are you doing?"

It's Cook. She startles me so I nearly jump out of my shoes. "Nothing, ma'am," I stammer, slamming the cellar door shut. "I . . . I . . . was just—"

"That ice cream done?"

"Very nearly, ma'am."

"Don't *ma'am* me to death. And don't let me see you up out of that chair again until your work's done."

Cook is snappish. More so than usual. We all are. Help and guests alike. Snappish and sad. Except old Mrs. Ellis, who is furious and feels she's entitled to a refund because the dead body in the parlor is interfering with her enjoyment of the day.

I walk back to the ice-cream churn and feel Grace Brown's letters hanging heavy in my skirt pocket. Why did Cook have to come back into the kitchen just then? Two more seconds and I would've been down the cellar stairs and in front of the huge coal furnace. The Glenmore is a modern hotel with gaslights in every room and a gas stove in the kitchen, but the furnace, which heats all the water the hotel uses, burns coal. The letters would have caught immediately. I could have been done with them.

And ever since Grace Brown handed them to me, I have sorely wanted to be done with them. She gave them to me yesterday afternoon on the porch, after I'd brought her a lemonade. I'd felt sorry for her; I could tell she'd been crying. I knew why, too. She'd had a fight with her beau at dinner. It was over a chapel. She wanted to go and find a chapel, but he wanted to go boating.

She'd refused the drink at first, saying she couldn't pay for it, but I said she didn't have to, figuring what Mrs. Morrison didn't know wouldn't hurt her. And then, just as I was turning to go back inside, she asked me to wait. She opened her gentleman friend's suitcase and pulled a bundle of letters from it. She took a few more from her purse, undid the ribbon around them, tied all the letters together, and asked me to burn them.

I was so taken aback by her request, I wasn't able to answer. Guests wanted all sorts of strange things. Omelettes with two and a half eggs. Not two, not three—two and a half. Maple syrup for their baked potatoes. Blueberry muffins without any blueberries in them. Trout for supper as long as it didn't taste like fish. I did all that they asked of me with a smile, but no one had ever asked me to burn letters, and I couldn't imagine explaining it to Cook.

"Miss, I can't—," I'd started to say.

She took hold of my arm. "Burn them. Please," she whispered. "Promise me you will. No one can ever see them. Please!"

And then she pressed them into my hands, and her eyes were so wild that they scared me, and I quickly nodded yes. "Of course I will, miss. I'll do it right away."

And then he—Carl or Chester or whatever he called himself—shouted to her from the lawn, "Billy, you coming? I got a boat!"

I'd put the letters in my pocket and forgot all about them until I went upstairs later in the day to change into a fresh apron. I slipped them under my mattress, figuring I would wait to burn them, just in case Grace Brown changed her mind and asked for them back. Guests could be like that. They'd get cross with you for bringing them the butterscotch pudding they'd ordered, because now they wanted chocolate. And somehow it was your fault if their shirts were too stiff after they'd asked for extra starch. I didn't want Grace Brown complaining to Mrs. Morrison that I'd burned her letters when she hadn't meant me to, but Grace hadn't changed her mind. Or complained. And now she never would.

I'd run upstairs to get the letters right after Grace's body was brought in, and I'd been waiting ever since for Cook to turn her back. It was nearly five now. We'd be serving supper in another hour, and I knew I wouldn't have the time to run down cellar even if I did get the chance.

The door from the dining room swings open and Frannie Hill marches in, an empty tray on her shoulder. "Lord! I don't see how sitting on your backside watching an illustrated lecture about castles in France can make people so hungry," she says. "It's just boring old slides in a lantern and somebody holding forth."

"I must have put six dozen cookies on that tray. They et 'em all?" Cook asks her.

"And drank two pots of coffee, a jug of lemonade, and a pot of tea. And now they're clamoring for more."

"Nerves," Cook says. "People eat too much when they're nervy."

"Watch out for table six, Matt. He's at it again," Fran whispers as she passes by. That's our name for Mr. Maxwell, a guest who always takes table six in the dining room because it's in a dark corner. He has trouble keeping his hands, and other bits, to himself.

The door bangs open again. It's Ada. "Man from the Boonville paper's here. Mrs. Morrison says I should bring him coffee and sandwiches."

Weaver is on her heels. "Mr. Morrison says to tell you he canceled the campfire and sing-along tonight, so you don't need to do the refreshments for it. And he called off the hike to Dart's Lake tomorrow morning, so there's no picnic to pack. But he wants to have an ice-cream social for the children tomorrow afternoon, and he wants sandwiches for the searchers when they come in off the lake tonight."

Cook wipes the sweat off her forehead with the back of her hand. She puts water on to boil and opens a metal canister on the counter next to the stove. "Weaver, I told you to bring up some coffee this morning. Doesn't anyone listen to me?" she grumbles.

43

"I'll get it!" I nearly shout. The large burlap sack of coffee beans is kept in the cellar.

Her eyes narrow. "You are just determined to go down cellar, aren't you? What are you after?"

"Maybe she's got Royal Loomis hidden down there," Fran says, smirking.

"Standing behind the coal bin, waiting for a kiss." Ada giggles.

"Scratching his head wondering who turned out the lights," Weaver adds.

My cheeks burn.

"You stay where you are and finish that ice cream," Cook says to me. "Weaver, go get the coffee."

I pick up the churn's lid and look inside. Not even close. I'd been cranking so long I thought my arm would fall off. Weaver had already cranked a gallon of strawberry, and Fran had done vanilla. The kitchen was busy enough with the hotel and all the cottages full, busier still in the hours since the body was recovered. Mrs. Morrison had informed us that the sheriff was coming all the way from Herkimer tomorrow. And the coroner. And there were bound to be men from the city papers, too. Cook was determined that the Glenmore not be found wanting. She'd baked enough bread and biscuits to feed every man, woman, and child in the county. Plus a dozen pies, six layer cakes, and two pans of rice pudding.

Weaver disappears into the cellar. As he does, I hear gunshots coming from the lake, three in a row.

Ada and Frannie draw near to me. "If he was still

alive, someone would have found him by now," Fran says, voicing what we are all thinking. "Or he would have found his way back. Those gunshots carry."

"I looked in the register," Ada whispers. "Their last names weren't the same. They were traveling together, but I don't think they were married."

"I bet they were eloping," I say. "I served them at dinnertime. I heard them talk about a chapel."

"Did you, Matt?" Ada asks.

"Yes, I did," I say, telling myself that fighting is talking. Sort of. "Maybe Grace Brown's father didn't like Carl Grahm," I add. "Maybe he didn't have any money. Or maybe she was promised to another but loved Carl Grahm. So they ran away to the North Woods to get married..."

"...and decided to take a romantic boat ride together first, to declare their love for each other on the lake...," Ada adds wistfully.

"...and maybe he reached out over the water to pick some pond lilies for her...," Frannie says.

"...and the boat tipped and they fell out and he tried to save her, but he couldn't. She slipped from his grasp...," I say.

"Oh, it's so sad, Mattie! So sad and romantic!" Ada cries.

"...and then he drowned, too. He gave up struggling, because he didn't want to live when he saw that she was gone. And now they'll be together forever. Star-crossed lovers just like Romeo and Juliet," I say.

"Together forever . . . ," Frannie echoes.

". . . at the bottom of Big Moose Lake. Just as dead as two doornails," Cook says. She has ears on her like a jack-rabbit and is always listening when you don't think she is. "You let that be a lesson to you, Frances Hill," she adds. "Girls who sneak off with boys end badly. You hear me?"

Fran blinks. "Why, Mrs. Hennessey, I'm sure I don't know what you mean," she says. She is such a good actress, she should be onstage.

"And I'm sure you do. Where were you two nights ago? Round midnight?"

"Right here, of course. In bed asleep."

"Not sneaking off to the Waldheim to meet Ed Compeau, by any chance?"

Frannie's caught. She turns as red as a cherry. I expect Cook to scold her soundly. Instead, she takes Fran's chin in her hand and says, "A boy wants to go somewhere with you, you tell him to call on you proper or not at all. You hear?"

"Yes, ma'am," Fran mumbles, and from the look on her face, and Ada's, I know they are as unsettled as I am at seeing signs of softness from Cook. I feel even worse when she brushes at her eyes on her way to the cellar stairs. "Weaver!" she bellows down them. "You fetching that coffee or growing it? Hurry up!"

I look at the thin gold ring with a chipped opal and two dull garnets on my left hand. I've never thought it pretty, but I'm suddenly glad, very glad, that Royal gave it to me. Glad, too, that he always calls for me at the Glenmore's kitchen door, where everyone can see him.

I go back to cranking the ice cream and embellishing my romantic and tragic story, writing it all out in my mind. Carl Grahm and Grace Brown were in love. That's why they were here. They were *eloping*, not *sneaking*, no matter what Cook says. I see Carl Grahm smiling as he reaches for the pond lilies, then I see the boat capsize and him struggle valiantly to save the woman he loves. I don't see Grace's tearstained face anymore or the tremble in her hands as she gives me her letters. I don't wonder what's in them or why they're addressed to Chester Gillette, not Carl Grahm. I start to think that maybe I never heard Grace Brown call Carl Grahm *Chester* at all, that I only imagined it.

I end my story with Grace and Carl being buried next to each other in a fancy cemetery in Albany and their parents being so sad they ever stood in the young lovers' way. I decide that I like it. It's a new kind of story for me—the kind that stitches things up nicely and leaves no ends dangling and makes me feel placid instead of all stirred up. The kind that has a happy ending—or at least as happy an ending as is possible with the heroine dead and the hero presumed so. The kind of story I once told Miss Wilcox was a lie. The kind I said I would never ever write.

mis • no • mer

Nothing on our entire farm—not the balky hay wagon, not the stumps in the north field, not even the rocks in the lower meadow—was as unyielding, as immovable, as adamant and uncompromising as Pleasant the mule. I was in our cornfield trying to get him to pull the plow. "Giddyap, Pleasant! Giddyap!" I shouted, snapping the reins against his haunches. He didn't move.

"Come on, Pleasant...come on, mule," Beth wheedled, holding a lump of maple sugar out to him.

"Here boy, here mule," Tommy Hubbard called, waving an old straw hat. Pleasant liked to eat them.

"Move your fat ass, you jackass," Lou swore, tugging on his bridle.

But Pleasant would not be budged. He stood firm, dipping his head occasionally to try and bite Lou.

"Go, Pleasant. Please, Pleasant," I begged.

It was dry and remarkably warm for the start of April, and I was tired and dirty and dripping with sweat. The muscles in my arms ached and my hands were raw from guiding the plow and I was just as mad as a hornet. Pa had kept me home from school again, and I'd wanted to go so badly. I was waiting on a letter, one that was going to come care of Miss Wilcox if it came at all, and it was all I could think about. I told him I had to go. I said my exams were coming up. I said I needed to study my algebra. I told him Miss Wilcox was making us read *Paradise Lost* and that it was hard going and that I would fall behind if I missed a day. Didn't make a bit of difference. He'd been reading the signs—no fog in February, no thunder in March, a south wind on Good Friday—and was convinced the mild weather would hold.

Most people planted corn around Decoration Day, at the end of May, but Pa wanted to plant midmonth, at the latest, and he wanted to start working the soil early, too. There are only about a hundred frost-free days in the North Woods, and corn takes time to ripen. Pa was trying to build our dairy herd. He wanted to keep the calves if he could, rather than sell them, but we couldn't keep them if we couldn't feed them and we couldn't feed them unless we grew enough corn. I was to have two acres turned over that day, and I'd only gotten a third of the way through before Pleasant decided it was quitting time. If I didn't finish, Pa would want to know why. Plowing was Lawton's job, but Lawton wasn't around to do it. Pa would've done it if he could, but he was with Daisy, who was calving. So it fell to me.

I bent down and picked up a stone. I was just winding up to throw it at Pleasant's behind when I heard a voice behind me say, "Peg him with that and you'll scare him. He's like to run. Take himself, that plow, and you across the field and through the fence."

I turned around. A tall blond boy was standing at the edge of the field, watching me. He was taller than I remembered. Broad-shouldered. And handsome. Handsomest one out of all the Loomis boys. He had the rim of a wagon wheel resting on his shoulder. His arm poked through the spokes.

"Hey, Royal," I said, trying to keep my eyes from roosting on any one part of him for too long. Not his wheat-colored hair, or his eyes that Minnie said were hazel but that I thought were the exact color of buckwheat honey, or the small freckle just above his lip.

"Hey."

The Loomis farm bordered ours. It was much bigger. Ninety acres. They had more bog than we did, but Mr. Loomis and his boys had managed to clear forty acres. We'd only got about twenty-five cleared. The best land, where we pulled stumps and rocks, we used for crops. Hay and corn for our animals, plus potatoes—some to keep and some to sell. Places where the stumps were still charred and rotting, or where it was rocky or boggy, Pa used to pasture the cows. The worst patches were planted with buckwheat, as it is not particular and will grow most anywhere. Pa had hoped to clear another five acres over the summer. But he couldn't without Lawton.

Royal looked from me to Pleasant and back again. He let the wagon wheel slide to the ground. "Let me have him," he said, taking the reins. "Giddyap, you!" he shouted, snapping them smartly against Pleasant's rump. Much harder than I had. Pleasant budged. Boy, did he.

Tommy, Beth, and Lou cheered, and I felt as dumb as a bag of hammers.

Royal was the second-eldest boy in his family. There were two younger ones. Daniel, the eldest, had just gotten engaged to Belinda Becker from the Farm and Feed Beckers in Old Forge. *Belinda* is a pretty name. It feels like meringue in your mouth or a curl of sugar on snow. Not like Matt. *Matt* is the sound of knots in a dog's coat or something you wipe your feet on.

Dan and Belinda's engagement was big news. It was a good match, what with Dan so capable and Belinda sure of a nice dowry. My aunt Josephine said there was supposed to have been a second engagement. She said Royal had been sweet on Martha Miller, whose father is the minister in Inlet, but he broke it off. Nobody knew why, but Aunt Josie said it was because Martha's people were Herkimer diamonds—which aren't diamonds at all, only look-alike crystals that aren't worth a darn. Mr. Miller has a nice pair of grays and Martha wears pretty dresses, but they don't pay their bills. I didn't see what that had to do with engagements, but if anyone would know, it was my aunt. She is an invalid and has nothing to entertain herself with other than gossip. She is on every scrap of hearsay like a bear on a brook trout.

Dan and Royal were only a year apart, nineteen and eighteen, and they were forever in competition. Whether it was a baseball game or who could pick the most berries or chop the most wood, one was always trying to outdo the other. I hadn't seen much of them over the last year. I used to visit with them when they came to fetch Lawton for fishing trips, and we all used to walk to school together, but Dan and Royal left school early. Neither one was much for book learning.

I watched him as he plowed a row, turned at the end of the field and came back. "Thanks, Royal," I mumbled. "I'll take him now."

"That's all right. I'll finish it. Whyn't you follow along behind and pull the stones?"

I did as he said, traipsing after him, picking up stones and roots, carrying them in a bucket until I could dump them at the end of a row.

"How are you doing back there?" he called after a few rows, turning to look at me.

"Fine," I said. And then I tripped and dropped my bucket. He stopped, waited for me to right myself, then started off again. He moved fast and it was hard to keep up with him. His furrows were straight and deep. Much better than the ones I'd done. He made me feel clumsy in comparison. And flustered. *Flumsy.*

"Soil's good. Dark and rich."

I looked down at it. It was as black as wet coffee grounds. "Yes, it is," I said.

"Should get a good crop out of it. Why you call your mule Pleasant? He's anything but."

"It's a misnomer," I said, pleased to be able to use my word of the day.

"You call your mule Miss? Miss Pleasant? It's a boy mule!"

"No, not 'Miss Pleasant,' *misnomer*. It means a mis-applied name. Like when you call a fat person Slim. Mis-nomer. It comes from *mesnommer*, which is French—old French—for 'to misname.' It's my word of the day. I pick a word out of the dictionary every morning and memo-rize it and try to use it. It helps build vocabulary. I'm reading *Jane Eyre* right now and I hardly ever have to look up a word. *Misnomer*, though, that's a hard one to use in conversation, but then you asked about Pleasant and there it was! My perfect chance to . . ."

Royal gave me a look over his shoulder—a wincing, withering look—that made me feel like the biggest babbling blabberer in all of Herkimer County. I closed my mouth and wondered what it was girls like Belinda Becker had to say that made boys want to listen to them. I knew a lot of words—a lot more than Belinda, who giggled all the time and said things like "swell" and "chum" and "hopelessly dead broke"—but not the right ones. I kept my eyes on the furrows for a while, but that got to be boring, so I stared at Royal's backside. I had never really noticed a man's backside before. Pa didn't have one. It was as flat as a cracker. Mamma would tease him about it and he'd tell her the lumber bosses worked it off him. I thought Royal's was very nice. Round and proud like two loaves of soda bread. He turned around just then and I blushed. I wondered what Jane Eyre would have done, then realized Jane was English and proper and wouldn't have gone around eyeing Rochester's backside to begin with.

"Where's your pa, anyway?" Royal asked.

"With Daisy. Who's calving. And Abby. Who isn't. Calving, I mean." I wished I could stitch my mouth shut.

There were more questions. What was Pa using for fertilizer. How many acres was he going to clear. Was he planting any potatoes this spring. What about buckwheat. And wasn't it hard for him to run the farm alone.

"He's not alone. He has me," I said.

"But you're still in school, ain't you? Why aren't you out yet, anyway? School's for children and you're what . . . fifteen?"

"Sixteen."

"Where's Lawton? Ain't he coming back?"

"You writing a column for the paper, Royal?" Lou asked.

Royal didn't laugh. I did, though. He was quiet after that. Two hours later, he'd finished the field entirely. We sat down for a rest, and I gave him a piece of the johnnycake I'd brought and poured him switchel from a stone jug. I gave pieces to Tommy and Lou and Beth as well.

Royal watched Tommy eat his piece. "Hubbards is always hungry, ain't they? Can't never seem to fill 'em up," he said. "Why you here, Tom?"

Tommy looked at his johnnycake, crumbly and yellow in his dirty hands. "Like to help Mattie, I guess. Like to help her pa."

"Whyn't you help your own mamma plow her field?"

"We ain't got a plow," Tommy mumbled, a red flush creeping up his neck.

"Guess you don't need one, do you? She's always got someone plowing her field, ain't she, Tom?"

"Cripes, Royal, what's Emmie's field to you?" I said, not liking the hard look in his eyes or the miserable, cornered one in Tommy's. The Loomis boys were always agitating with the Hubbards, like a pack of hounds after possums. Lawton had gotten between the younger ones and Tommy on many occasions.

Royal shrugged, then took a bite of his own cake. "This is good," he said. I was about to tell him that Abby made it, but then his honey-colored eyes were on me, not the johnnycake, and the hardness in them was gone and I didn't.

He looked at me closely, his head on an angle, and for a second I had the funniest feeling that he was going to open my jaws and look at my teeth or pick up my foot and rap the bottom of it. I heard a shout and saw Pa waving from the barn. He walked up to us and sat down. I gave him my glass of switchel. "Daisy had a bull calf," he said wearily, and then he smiled.

My pa was so handsome when he smiled, with his eyes as blue as cornflowers and his beautiful white teeth. He hardly did anymore, and it felt like a hard rain letting up. Like Mamma might come up from hanging wash and join us. Like Lawton might come out of the woods any second, his fishing pole over his shoulder.

Beth, Lou, and Tommy chased off to see the new calf. Pa finished the switchel and I poured him some more. Switchel is easier to drink than plain water when you are hot and thirsty. Mixing a little vinegar, ginger, and maple syrup into the water helps it to digest.

Pa looked at Royal, his shirt soaked with sweat, and my hands, dirty from the stones, and Pleasant un-hitched, and put it all together. "I'm obliged to you," he said. "It's a son's work, planting. Not a daughter's. Thought I had a son to do it."

"Pa," I said quietly.

"Don't understand why he left. Couldn't tear me away from land like this," Royal said.

I bristled at that. I was angry at Lawton for leaving, too. But Royal was not family and therefore had no right to speak against him. Thing of it was, I didn't under-stand why my brother had left, either. I knew they'd had a fight, he and Pa. I saw them going at one another in the barn. First fists and then Pa had gone for his peavey. Then Lawton had run into the house, thrown his things into an old flour sack, and marched out again. I'd run after him. Me and Lou both, but Pa stopped us.

"Let him go," he'd said, blocking our way down the porch steps.

"But, Pa, you can't just let him walk out. It's the dead of winter," I pleaded. "Where's he going to go?"

"I said let him go! Go back in the house, go on!" He pushed us inside, slammed the door, and locked it, as if he were afraid we would leave, too. And afterward, he was so changed, it was as if we'd lost our father as well as our mother and brother. Some days later I asked him what the fight was about. But he wouldn't tell me, and from the anger in his eyes, I knew better than to press.

Royal and Pa talked farming for a bit and milk prices and who was building yet another camp on Fourth Lake or up the hill at Big Moose Lake and how many guests it would hold and how the market for cream and butter ought to go through the roof this season and why would anyone buy the slop that came up on the trains from Remsen when they could now get fresh milk right here.

Then Royal picked up his wagon wheel and said he had to get along to Burnap's. The iron tread was loose and George Burnap was the only one nearby with a forge. After he left, I thought I might get a talking-to for sitting and drinking switchel with him, but I didn't. Pa just gathered Pleasant's traces and walked him back to the barn, asking the mule if he had any idea why Frank Loomis had four good sons and he didn't have one.

som · nif · er · ous

"In the pantheon of great writers, of profound voices, Milton stands second only to Shakespeare," Miss Wilcox said, her boot heels making *pok pok* noises on the bare wood floor as she crossed and recrossed the room. "Now, of course one may argue that Donne deserves..."

"*Pssst*, Mattie! Mattie, look!"

I slid my eyes off the book I was sharing with Weaver, toward the desk to my left. Jim and Will Loomis had a spider on a piece of thread. They were letting it crawl back and forth on its leash, giggling like idiots. Bug taming was a Loomis specialty. First, Jim would pull a piece of thread from his shirt hem and painstakingly fashion it into a tiny noose. Then Will would snatch up a spider or a fly when Miss Wilcox's back was turned. He was quicker than Renfield in Bram Stoker's *Dracula,* though mercifully, he did not eat what he caught. He would hold his victim in cupped hands and shake it until it was stunned. Then as Will held the bug, Jim would slip the noose over its head. When the bug regained its senses, it became the star attraction in the Loomis Brothers Circus, which, depending on the time of year, might also feature a three-legged bullfrog, a half-dead crayfish, an orphaned blue jay, or a crippled squirrel.

I rolled my eyes. At sixteen I was too old to be attending the Inlet Common School. The leaving age is fourteen, and most don't make it that far. But our old teacher, Miss Parrish, told Miss Wilcox about Weaver and myself before she left. She said that we were smart enough to earn high school diplomas and that it was a shame that we couldn't. The only high school in the area, though, was in Old Forge, a proper town ten miles south of Eagle Bay. It was too far to travel every day, especially in winter. We would have had to board with a family there during the week, and neither of us could afford to. Miss Wilcox said she would teach us the course work herself if we wanted to learn it, and she did. She had taught in a fancy girls' academy in New York City, and she knew plenty.

She had come to my house last November to talk with my parents about my getting a diploma. Mamma made us all wash before she came—even Pa—and had Abby make a gingerbread and me do the girls' hair. Mamma couldn't get downstairs that day, and Miss Wilcox had to go see her in her bedroom. I don't know what Miss Wilcox said to her, but after she left, Mamma told me I was to get my diploma even though Pa wanted me to leave school.

Weaver and I had spent most of the year preparing for our exit examinations. We were going to take the hardest ones—the Board of Regents—in English composition, literature, history, science, and mathematics. I was particularly worried about mathematics. Miss Wilcox did her best with algebra, but her heart wasn't in it. Weaver was good with it, though. Sometimes Miss Wilcox would just give him the teacher's guide. He would puzzle through a problem, then explain it to me and Miss Wilcox.

The Columbia University is a serious and fearsome place, and a condition of Weaver's acceptance is that he earn B-pluses or better on all of his exams. He'd been studying hard, and so had I, but that day in the schoolhouse, struggling with Milton, I wasn't sure why I'd bothered. Weaver received his letter back in January, and though it was now the beginning of the second week of April, no letter had come for me.

Jim Loomis leaned over and dangled his spider right in my face. I jumped and swatted at it, which pleased him greatly. "You're going to get it," I mouthed at him, then tried to put my mind back on *Paradise Lost,* but it was hard going. *Somniferous* was my word of the day. It means sleep inducing, and it was a good one to describe that dull and endless poem. Milton meant to give us a glimpse of hell, Miss Wilcox said, and he succeeded. Hell was not the *adamantine chains* he wrote of, though. Nor was it the *ever-burning sulphur,* or the *darkness visible.* Hell was the realization that you are only on line 325 of Book One and there are eleven more books to go. *Torture without end,* all right. There was no place, of course, I would rather have been than in that schoolhouse, and nothing I would rather have done than read, read *anything*...but John Milton was a trial. What on earth did Miss Wilcox see in him? His Satan scared no one and seemed more like the Prince of Fusspots than the Prince of Hell, with all his ranting and carping and endless pontificating.

Fesole, Valdarno, Vallombrosa... *Where in blazes are those places?* I wondered. Why couldn't Satan have decided to visit the North Woods? Old Forge, maybe, or even Eagle Bay. Why didn't he talk like real people did? With a *cripes* or a *jeezum* thrown in now and again. Why did little towns in Herkimer County never get a mention in anybody's book? Why was it always other places and other lives that mattered?

French Louis Seymour of the West Canada Creek, who knew how to survive all alone in a treacherous wilderness, and Mr. Alfred G. Vanderbilt of New York City and Raquette Lake, who was richer than God and traveled in his very own Pullman car, and Emmie Hubbard of the Uncas Road, who painted the most beautiful pictures when she was drunk and burned them in her woodstove when she was sober, were all ten times more interesting to me than Milton's devil or Austen's boy-crazy girls or that twitchy fool of Poe's who couldn't think of any place better to bury a body than under his own damn floor.

"And why do we read Shakespeare and Milton and Donne? Someone other than Miss Gokey, this time. Mr. Bouchard?" Miss Wilcox asked.

Mike Bouchard turned scarlet. "I don't know, ma'am."

"Throw caution to the wind, Mr. Bouchard. Hazard a guess."

"Because we have to, ma'am?"

"No, Mr. Bouchard, because it is a classic. And we must have a good, working acquaintance with the classics if we are to understand the works that follow them and progress in our own literary endeavors. Understanding literature is like building a house, Mr. Bouchard; you don't build the third story first, you start with a foundation..."

Miss Wilcox is from New York City. Up here, you didn't build the third story ever, unless you are rich like the Beckers or own three sawmills like my uncle Vernon.

"...where would Milton have been without Homer, Mr. James Loomis? And where would Mary Shelley have been without Milton, Mr. William Loomis? Why, without Milton, Victor Frankenstein's monster would never have been created..."

At the mere mention of that magic word *Frankenstein,* the Loomis boys straightened up. Jim got so excited, he let go of his new pet spider. It made for the edge of his desk and disappeared, trailing its leash. Miss Wilcox had promised since November that we'd read *Frankenstein* as our last book of the year, as long as everyone—meaning mainly Jim and Will—behaved. She had only to whisper the name *Frankenstein,* and they were suddenly as still and attentive as two altar boys. They loved the idea of stitching dead things together. They talked nonstop of finding frogs and toads to kill, just so they could bring them back to life again.

"...we read the classics to be inspired by the great thoughts of great minds...," Miss Wilcox continued, and then there was a sudden tinkling sound. She had dropped her bracelets again. Abby retrieved them for her. Miss Wilcox often fidgeted as she talked, taking her ring off and putting it back on, snapping chalk in her fingers, or sliding her bracelets off one wrist and onto the other. She was nothing like our old teacher, Miss Parrish. Miss Wilcox had curly auburn hair, and green eyes that I imagined must be the exact shade of an emerald, though I had never seen an emerald. She wore gold jewelry and the most beautiful clothes—tailored waists, fine worsted skirts, and cutaway jackets edged with silk braid. She always looked so odd in our plain schoolroom, with its rusty stove, plank walls, and yellowed map of the world. Like some precious jewel put in a battered old gift box.

After torturing us with a few more pages of *Paradise Lost,* Miss Wilcox finally finished the lesson and dismissed the class. Jim and Will Loomis tore out of the schoolhouse, cuffing Tommy Hubbard on their way, shouting, "Hubbard, Hubbard, nothing in your cupboard!" Mary Higby and I gathered up the half-dozen copies of the book that our class of twelve shared. Abby cleaned the chalkboard, and Lou collected the slates we'd used to do arithmetic earlier in the day.

I stacked the books I'd gathered on her desk and was ready to leave when she said, "Mattie, stay after, will you?" We were all "Mr." and "Miss" during class, but afterward she called us by our first names. I told Weaver and my sisters that I'd catch up. I thought maybe Miss Wilcox had a new book for me to borrow, but she didn't. As soon as the others were gone, she opened her desk, took out an envelope, and held it out to me. It was large and buff colored. It had my name on it. Typed on a label, not handwritten. It had a return address, too, and as soon as I saw what it was, my mouth went as dry as salt.

"Here, Mattie. Take it."

I shook my head.

"Come on, you coward!" Miss Wilcox was smiling, but her voice was quavery.

I took it. Miss Wilcox drew an enameled case from her purse, pulled a cigarette from it, and lit it. My aunt Josie had told me and my sisters that Miss Wilcox was fast. Beth thought she meant the way our teacher drove her automobile, but I knew it had more to do with her smoking and having bobbed hair.

I stared at the letter, trying to find the courage I needed to open it. I heard Miss Wilcox's bracelets tinkle again. She was standing by her desk, cupping an elbow in her palm. "Come *on,* Mattie. Open it, for god's sake!" she said.

I took a deep breath and ripped the envelope open. There was a single sheet of paper inside clipped to my battered old composition book. *"Dear Miss Gokey,"* it read. *"It is with great pleasure that I write to inform you of your acceptance to Barnard College..."*

"Mattie?"

"...furthermore, I am pleased to award you a full Hayes scholarship sufficient to meet the cost of your first year's tuition, contingent upon the successful completion of your high school degree. This scholarship is renewable each year provided grade average and personal conduct remain above reproach..."

"Mattie!"

"...and, although your academic background lacks in certain aspects—notably foreign languages, advanced mathematics, and chemistry—your impressive literary strengths outweigh these deficiencies. Classes begin Monday, September 3. You will be required to report to orientation Saturday, September 1, and may address all questions regarding accommodations to Miss Jane Brownell in care of the college's Housing Office. With all best wishes, Dean Laura Drake Gill."

"Damn it, Mattie! What does it *say?*"

I looked at my teacher, barely able to breathe, much less speak. *It says they want me,* I thought. *Barnard College wants* me*—Mattie Gokey from the Uncas Road in Eagle Bay. It says that the dean herself likes my stories and doesn't think they are morbid and dispiriting, and that professors, real professors with long black gowns and all sorts of fancy degrees, will teach me. It says I* am *smart, even if I can't make Pleasant mind and didn't salt the pork right. It says I can be something if I choose. Something more than a know-nothing farm girl with shit on her shoes.*

"It says I'm accepted," I finally said. "And that I've got a scholarship. A full scholarship. As long as I pass my exams."

Miss Wilcox let out a whoop and hugged me. Good and hard. She took me by my arms and kissed my cheek, and I saw that her eyes were shiny. I didn't know why it meant so much to her that I'd got myself into college, but I was glad that it did.

"I knew you'd do it, Mattie! I knew that Laura Gill would see your talent. Those stories you sent were excellent! Didn't I tell you they were?" She twirled around in a circle, took a deep draw of her cigarette, and blew it all out. "Can you imagine?" she asked, laughing. "You're going to be a college student. You and Weaver both! This fall! In New York City, no less!"

As soon as she said it, as soon as she talked about my dream like that and brought it out in the light and made it real, I saw only the impossibility of it all. I had a pa who would never let me go. I had no money and no prospect of getting any. And I had made a promise— one that would keep me here even if I had all the money in the world.

When he has to, Pa sells some of his calves for veal. The cows cry so when he takes them that I can't be in the barn. I have to run up to the cornfield, my hands over my ears. If you've ever heard a cow cry for her calf, you know how it feels to have something beautiful and new put into your hands, to wonder and smile at it, and then have it snatched away. That's how I felt then, and my feelings must have been on my face, because Miss Wilcox's smile suddenly faded.

"You're working this summer, aren't you?" she said. "At the Glenmore?"

I shook my head. "My pa said no."

"Well, not to worry. My sister Annabelle will give you room and board in exchange for a bit of house-keeping. She has a town house in Murray Hill and she's all alone in it, so there would be plenty of room for you. Between the scholarship and Annabelle, that's tuition, housing, and meals taken care of. For book money and the trolley and clothing and such, you could always get a job. Something part-time. Typing, perhaps. Or ringing up sales in a department store. Plenty of girls manage it."

Girls who know what they're doing, I thought. Brisk, confident girls in white blouses and twill skirts who could make heads or tails of a typewriter or a cash register. Not girls in old wash dresses and cracked shoes.

"I suppose I could," I said weakly.

"What about your father? Can he help you at all?"

"No, ma'am."

"Mattie . . . you've told him, haven't you?"

"No, ma'am, I haven't."

Miss Wilcox nodded, curt and determined. She stubbed out her cigarette on the underside of her desk and put the ashy end in her purse. Miss Wilcox knew how to not get caught doing things she shouldn't. It was an odd quality in a teacher.

"I'll talk to him, Mattie. I'll tell him if you want me to," she said.

I laughed at that—a flat, joyless laugh—then said, "No, ma'am, I don't. Not unless you know how to duck a peavey."

un · man

"Afternoon, Mattie!" Mr. Eckler called from the bow of his boat. "Got a new one. Brand-new. Just come in. By a Mrs. Wharton. *House of Mirth,* it's called. I tucked it in behind the coffee beans, under *W.* You'll see it."

"Thank you, Mr. Eckler!" I said, excited at the prospect of a new book. "Did you read it?"

"Yup. Read it whole."

"What's it about?"

"Can't hardly say. Some flighty city girl who can't decide if she wants to fish or cut bait. Don't know why it's called *House of Mirth.* It ain't funny in the least."

The Fulton Chain Floating Library is only a tiny room, an overeager closet, really, belowdecks in Charlie Eckler's pickle boat. It is nothing like the proper library they have in Old Forge, but it has its own element of surprise. Mr. Eckler uses the room to store his wares, and when he finally gets around to moving a chest of tea or a sack of cornmeal, you never knew what you might find. And once in a while, the main library in Herkimer sends up a new book or two. It's nice to get your hands on a new book before everyone else does. While the pages are still clean and white and the spine hasn't been snapped.

While it still smells like words and not Mrs. Higby's violet water or Weaver's mamma's fried chicken or my aunt Josie's liniment.

The boat is a floating grocery store and serves all the camps and hotels along the Fulton Chain. It is the only store—floating or not—for miles. Mr. Eckler starts out at dawn from Old Forge and makes his way up the chain—through First, Second, and Third Lakes, then all the way around Fourth Lake—stopping at the Eagle Bay Hotel on the north shore and Inlet on its east end—then heads back down to Old Forge again. You can never miss the pickle boat. Nothing on water—or land, for that matter—looks quite like it. There are milk cans on top of it, bins full of fruits and vegetables on the deck, and a huge pickle barrel in the back, from which it takes its name. Inside the cabin are sacks of flour, cornmeal, sugar, oats, and salt; a basket of eggs; jars of candy; bottles of honey and maple syrup; tins of cinnamon, nutmeg, pepper, and saleratus; a box of cigars; a box of venison jerky; and three lead-lined tea chests packed with ice—one for fresh meat, one for fish, and the third for cream and butter. Everything is neat and tidy and fits snugly into place so it won't get tossed about in rough weather. Mr. Eckler sells a few other items as well, like nails and hammers, needles and thread, postcards and pens, hand salve, cough drops, and fly dope.

I stepped onto the boat and went belowdecks. *The House of Mirth* was under *W,* like Mr. Eckler said it would be, only it was wedged in next to *Mrs. Wiggs of the*

Cabbage Patch. Mr. Eckler sometimes gets authors and titles confused. I signed it out in a ledger he kept on top of a molasses barrel, then rooted around behind a crate of eggs, a jar of marbles, and a box of dried dates but found nothing I hadn't already read. I remembered to get the bag of cornmeal we needed. I wished I could buy oatmeal or white flour instead, but cornmeal cost less and went further. I was to get a ten-pound bag. The fifty-pound bag cost more to buy but was cheaper per pound and I'd told Pa so, but he said only rich people can afford to be thrifty.

Just as I was about to climb back upstairs, something caught my eye—a box of composition books. Real pretty ones with hard covers on them, and swirly paint designs, and a ribbon to mark your place. I put the cornmeal down, and Mrs. Wharton, too, and picked one up. Its pages were smooth and white. I thought it would be a fine thing to write on paper that nice. The pages in my old composition book were rough and had blurry blue lines printed on them, and were made with so little care that there were slivers of wood visible in them.

When I got back on deck, I saw that Royal Loomis had come onboard. He was paying for two cinnamon sticks, ten pounds of flour, a tin of tooth powder, and a bag of nails. He frowned at the amount on the till and counted his change twice, chewing on a toothpick all the while.

"Hey, Royal," I said.

"Hey."

I handed Mr. Eckler fifty cents of my father's money

for the cornmeal. "How much is this?" I asked, holding up one of the pretty composition books. I had sixty cents from all the fiddleheads Weaver and I had sold to the Eagle Bay Hotel, plus the spruce gum we'd picked and sold to O'Hara's in Inlet. It was money I knew I should have given to my pa. I'd meant to, I did. I just hadn't gotten around to it.

"Them notebooks? Them are expensive, Mattie. Eye-talians made 'em. Got to get forty-five cents apiece," he said. "I've got some others coming in for fifteen cents in a week or so if you can wait."

Forty-five cents was a good deal of money, but I didn't want the ones for fifteen cents, not after I'd seen the others. I had more ideas. Tons of them. For stories and poems. I chewed the inside of my cheek, deliberating. I knew I would have to write a lot when I went to Barnard—*if* I went to Barnard—and it might be a good idea to get a head start. Weaver had said I should be using my words, not just collecting them, and I knew they would just glide across this beautiful paper, and when I was done writing them, I could close them safely inside the covers. Just like a real book. Guilt gnawed at my insides. I took the money from my pocket and gave it to Mr. Eckler quickly, so the thing was done and I couldn't change my mind. Then I watched breathlessly as he wrapped my purchase in brown paper and tied it with string. I thanked him as he handed me the package, but he didn't hear me because Mr. Pulling, the station-master, was asking him the price of his oranges.

As I stepped onto the dock I heard Mr. Eckler shout, "Hold on, Mattie!"

I turned around. "Yes, sir?"

"Tell your pa I want to buy milk from him. I've only got room for so many cans up top, and I'm running out before I even get up to Fourth Lake. I'd give him my empties and take on four or five full ones. Could sell more on the way back if I had more to sell."

"I'll tell him, Mr. Eckler, but I know he's already promised the Glenmore and Higby's and the Waldheim. Plus the Eagle Bay Hotel. More have asked him, but he doesn't think he'll have enough to go round."

Mr. Eckler spat a mouthful of tobacco juice into the lake. "How big's his herd now?"

"Twenty head."

"Only twenty? But he's got, what? Sixty-odd acres? He could pasture a lot more than twenty on that."

"He only has twenty-five acres cleared, and a lot of it's plowed for crops."

"What's he doing with the rest of it? Thirty-five acres of woodland ain't no use to a farmer. He's paying taxes on the land, ain't he? On land he ain't even using! He ought to clear it for pasture, not let it set idle. He ought to build up his herd."

"He means to clear it. *Meant* to. But then... well, with Lawton gone and all, it's just... hard," I said quietly, conscious that Royal was listening to my every word.

Mr. Eckler nodded. He looked embarrassed. He knew Lawton had left. Everyone did. He'd asked me why, but I couldn't tell him. Or Weaver or Minnie or anyone else who asked. Mamma was gone because she died; I could explain that to people. My brother was gone, too. The brother who once spent all the money he'd made selling bait to sports to buy me a composition book and a pencil when he'd found me crying in the barn because Pa wouldn't buy them. Lawton was gone and I didn't even know why.

"Well, you tell him come see me, Matt. Royal, you tell your pa, too. I just seen men clearing for two new camps on Third Lake. Got Lon Wood building onto his place up here, plus Meeker's and the Fairview doing improvements, too. Got more and more summer people coming every day and it ain't even summer yet. If either of you can get me milk to sell, I can sell it."

"Yes, sir. I'll tell him," I said, then set off for home at a good clip. School had let out an hour before. My sisters would be well up our road. There was milking to do, and manure to shovel, and pigs and chickens to feed, and ourselves to feed, too.

I heard a thump on the dock behind me. "You like a ride, Matt?" said a voice at my elbow. It was Royal.

"Who? Me?"

"Ain't nobody else here named Matt."

"All right," I said, grateful for the offer. The cornmeal was heavy and I'd get home a lot faster if I rode.

I put the cornmeal in the back of the buckboard, climbed up on the hard wooden seat, and settled myself next to Royal. Buckboards are all anyone drives in the

North Woods. Anyone with any sense. Some of the new folks with their just-built camps bring their buggies, but they soon give them up. Buckboards are plain—just a few planks with a pair of axles nailed on under them, a seat or two, and maybe a wagon box on the top. But plain is what works best. The planks have bounce in them, and the bounce keeps the wheels from knocking the teeth out of your head on the bad roads.

"Giddyap!" Royal told the horses. He coaxed them to turn the creaky rig around in the hotel's drive while avoiding a fringe-topped surrey carrying a touring party that had just arrived on the steamer *Clearwater* and was bound for Big Moose Lake. The horses, a pair of bays, were new. Pa said Mr. Loomis had bought them cheap from a man outside of Old Forge who'd lost his farm to the bank. They whickered and blew, shy of the surrey, but Royal kept them calm.

He raised his hand in greeting to Mr. Satterlee, the tax assessor, who passed us on his way to the hotel. Mr. Satterlee waved back but did not smile. "Bet he's just come from the Hubbards'," Royal said. "He's slapping a lien on their land. That good-for-nothing Emmie didn't pay her taxes again."

I wondered at his harshness. And not for the first time. "Royal, what do you have against the Hubbards?" I asked. "They're just poor folks. They don't hurt anyone."

I got a snort for an answer. Royal didn't speak at all as we went up the hotel's long drive, past its freshly manured vegetable garden and its furrowed potato field.

We passed the railroad station and crossed the tracks and then the highway—a narrow dirt road that ran between Old Forge and Inlet. That was Eagle Bay, every bit of it—a bay on Fourth Lake, a hotel sitting on it, a railroad station, a set of railroad tracks, and a dirt road. It wasn't a town. It wasn't even a village. It was at most a destination. Unless you happened to live there. Then it was home.

As Royal steered the team toward the Uncas Road, he suddenly turned to me and said, "You still playing that game?"

"What game?"

"That game of yours. You know, fooling with words and such."

"It's not fooling," I said defensively. He made my word of the day sound childish and silly.

"You really look up a new word every day?"

"Yes."

"What was it today?"

"Unman."

"What's it mean?"

"To break down the manly spirit. To deprive of courage or fortitude."

"Huh. Had that right on the tip of your tongue, didn't you? You sure are a notional girl."

"Notional." Royal talks like all the boys do around here. He says "ramming" when he means *visiting* and "chimley" for *chimney.* Mamma used to swat us for saying "chimley." She said it made us sound like hicks.

Royal also says "don't" when he means *do*. "So don't I," he'd say to Lawton when Lawton said he wanted to go fishing. I tried, more than once, to explain to him that he really was saying "So do not I," which meant he was disagreeing with Lawton and *didn't* want to go fishing, but it never made any impression. At least he didn't say "chiney" for *china* or "popples" for *poplar trees*. That was something.

He nodded at the book in my lap. "What you got there?"

"A novel. *The House of Mirth*."

He shook his head. "Words and stories," he said, turning onto the Uncas Road. "I don't know what you see in them. Waste of time, if you ask me."

"I didn't ask you."

Royal didn't hear me or he didn't care if he did. He just kept right on talking. "A man's got to know how to read and write, of course, to get along in the world and all, but beyond that, words are just words. They're not very exciting. Not like fishing or hunting."

"How would you know, Royal? You don't read. Nothing's more exciting than a book."

The toothpick moved from the left side of his mouth to the right. "That so?" he said.

"Yes, that's so," I said. Finishing it. Or so I thought.

"Huh," he said. And then he snapped the reins. Hard. And barked, "Giddyap!" Loudly. I heard the horses snort as he gave them their head. The buckboard shuddered, then picked up speed.

I looked at the team, new and lively and unpredictable, and then at the Uncas Road, which was nothing but rocks and holes and corduroy. "Are we in a hurry, Royal?" I asked.

He looked at me. His face was serious, but his eyes sparked mischief. "This is the first time I've had them out. Don't really know what they'll do. Sure like to see what they're made of, though . . . Hee-YAW!"

The horses lurched forward in their harnesses; their hooves pounded against the hardpan. Mrs. Wharton's novel slid off my lap and thudded to the floor, along with my new composition book. "Royal, stop!" I shouted, clutching the dash. The buckboard was bouncing and banging over the rutted road so hard I was sure one of us would fly out of it. But Royal didn't stop. Instead, he stood up on the seat, cracked the reins, and spurred the team on. "Slow down! Right now!" I screamed. But he couldn't hear me. He was too busy whooping and laughing.

"Stop, Royal! Please!" I begged. And then we hit a deep hole and I was thrown across the seat. I banged my head on the seat back and only kept myself from falling out by grabbing his leg. I saw colors flash by on the side of the road. The blue of Lou's coveralls, the yellow of Beth's dress. *They can tell Pa,* I thought wildly. *After Royal kills us both, at least they can tell Pa how it happened.*

We took a bend so hard, I felt the wheels on the right side come off the ground, then crash back down. I managed to right myself, one hand still clutching Royal, the other scrabbling at the dashboard. The wind tore my hair free of its knot and made my eyes tear. I looked behind us and saw a cloud of dust rising up from the road. After what seemed like forever, Royal finally slowed the team to a trot and then to a walk. He sat down. The horses pulled at the reins, snorting and shaking their heads, wanting more. He talked to them, shushing and clucking at them, calming them down.

"Hoo-wee!" he said to me. "Thought we was in the ditch for a second there." And then he touched me. He leaned across the seat and pressed his hand to my heart. Palm flat against my ribs. Thumb and fingers jammed up under my breast. In the split second before I slapped it away, I felt my heart beat hard against it.

"Ticker's pounding fit to burst," he said, laughing. "Like to see a book do that."

I picked my things up off the buckboard's floor with shaking hands. There was a smudge on the cover of Mrs. Wharton's novel and the spine was dented. I wanted to answer Royal back with something clever and cutting. I wanted to defend my beloved books, to tell him there's a difference between excitement and terror, but I was too angry to speak. I tried to catch my breath, but every gulp of air brought the smell of him with it—warm skin, tilled earth, horses. I closed my eyes but only saw him standing on the buckboard seat, whooping. Tall and strong against the sky. Heedless. Fearless. Perfect and beautiful.

I thought of my word of the day. *Can a girl be unmanned?* I wondered. *By a boy? Can she be unbrained?*

$\mathcal{H}$amlet is drooling again. Silver strings of slime hang from his lips. He whines, then snorts, then lets out a long, gusty burp. He is my least favorite guest, after table six. I toss him a buttermilk pancake from the plate I'm holding, and he swallows it in one gulp. He eats half a roasted chicken at every meal, a broiled minute steak, and a dozen pancakes. He'd eat ten dozen if he could get them.

Hamlet belongs to Mr. Phillip Preston Palmer, Esquire—a lawyer from Metuchen, New Jersey. I met him two weeks ago, just after he arrived. He bounded into the dining room and backed me into a corner, trying to get at a platter of bacon I was carrying. Hamlet, that is. Not Mr. Palmer.

"He won't hurt you, honey!" Mr. Palmer yelled from the foyer. "His name is Hamlet. You know why I call him that?"

"No, sir, I have no idea," I said, not wanting to spoil his fun. Guests came to the Glenmore to have fun.

"Because he's a Great Dane! Ha! Ha! Ha! Get it?"

I would have liked to tell Mr. Palmer just how old and feeble that joke is, but instead I said, "Oh, of course, sir! How clever of you!" because I had learned a thing or two during my time at the Glenmore. About when to tell the truth and when not to. And for my smiles and admiring words, I earned Mr. Palmer's liking and an extra dollar a week to feed Hamlet and walk him. In the woods. Far away from the hotel. Because the filthy beast shits like a plow horse.

I did not normally look forward to Hamlet's after-supper walk, but tonight I am glad for it. Try as I might, I have not been able to get near the cellar all evening, and Grace Brown's letters are still in my pocket. I figured out a new way to get rid of them, though, and Hamlet is going to help me.

I finish feeding the dog and bring the plate back into the kitchen. Supper ended over an hour ago. It's dusky now. The kitchen is empty except for Bill, the dishwasher, and Henry, the underchef, who is holding a carving knife in one hand and rooting in a drawer with the other.

"Hamlet sends his compliments, Henry," I say. Henry's real name is Heinrich. He is German and started at the Glenmore the same week that I did.

"Cooking pancake for dog," he grumbles. "For this I make journey to America? Mattie, haf you seen my vetstone?"

He means *whetstone.* "No, I'm sorry, Henry, I haven't," I say, heading back out the door. I have told him over and over again that sharpening a knife after dark brings bad luck. He doesn't believe me, though, so now I have hidden it. There has been enough bad luck around here lately without him making any more.

"Come on, boy," I say. Hamlet's black ears prick up. He wags his tail. I unloop his leash from the handle of an empty milk can. We round the back corner of the hotel, and Hamlet lifts his leg on one of the porch columns. "Stop that!" I scold, tugging on the leash, but he doesn't budge until he's hosed it down good. I look around anxiously, hoping Mrs. Morrison hasn't seen us. Or Cook. Luckily, there is no one around. "Let's go, Hamlet. You mind me, now," I warn him. He trots along. We cross the front lawn and head down to the lake. I look back over my shoulder. The Glenmore is all lit up. I can see people on the porch. The men's cigar tips glow like fireflies in the dark. The women look like ghosts, in their white lawn dresses.

We get to the water's edge. "Wait, Hamlet," I say. He stands patiently as I scoop up a handful of stones. "Come on, now," I tell him, leading him onto the dock. He takes a few steps. His nails click against the boards, then dig in. He does not like the way the dock rises and sinks on the lapping water. "Come on, boy. It's all right. Let's see if there are some loons to bark at. You'd like that, wouldn't you? Come on, Hamlet...there's a good dog...," I plead with him, but he won't move, so I play my trump card and pull a cold pancake out of my pocket. He follows me happily.

I feel the letters bumping against my leg as we walk, nagging and badgering. I'll soon be rid of them, though.

The end of the dock is only three yards away. All I have to do is untie the ribbon that's holding the bundle together, slip a few stones into one of the envelopes, tie the bundle back together, and throw it into the water. It's not exactly what Grace Brown asked of me, but it will have to do. The lake is twelve feet deep at the end of the dock—deeper still farther out—and I have a good arm. No one will ever find them.

Finally, I'm there. Right at the dock's edge. I let go of Hamlet's leash and step on it to keep him from running off. I'm just reaching into my pocket for the letters when out of the darkness a voice says, "Going swimming, Matt?"

I'm so startled that I cry out and drop all my stones. I look to my right and there is Weaver, still in his black waiter's jacket, his trousers rolled up to his knees, sitting on the edge of the dock.

"Royal know you're two-timing him?" he asks, nodding at Hamlet.

"Very funny, Weaver! You frightened me to death!"

"Sorry."

"What are you doing out here?" I ask, then realize I know the answer already. He comes here every night now to grieve. I should have remembered that.

"I was looking at the boat," he replies. "The one that couple took out. The *Zilpha* towed it back."

"Where is it?"

"There." He points to the far end of the dock. A skiff is tied there. Its cushions are gone and its oarlocks are empty. "I went into the parlor after supper. To look at her." He is staring out at the lake. He closes his eyes. When he opens them again, his cheeks are wet.

"Oh, Weaver, don't," I whisper, touching his shoulder.

His hand finds mine. "I hate this place, Mattie," he says. "It kills everything."

wan

I used to wonder what would happen if characters in books could change their fates. What if the Dashwood sisters had had money? Maybe Elinor would have gone traveling and left Mr. Ferrars dithering in the drawing room. What if Catherine Earnshaw had just married Heathcliff to begin with and spared everyone a lot of grief? What if Hester Prynne and Dimmesdale had gotten onboard that ship and left Roger Chillingworth far behind? I felt sorry for these characters sometimes, seeing as they couldn't ever break out of their stories, but then again, if they could have talked to me, they'd likely have told me to stuff all my pity and condescension, for neither could I.

At least, that's how it looked to me midway through April. A week had passed since my letter had arrived from Barnard College, but I was no closer to figuring out a way to get myself there. I would have to pick an awful lot of fiddleheads and a wagon load of spruce gum to make enough money for train fare, and books, and maybe a new waist and skirt. *If only I could raise my own chickens and fry them up for the tourists like Weaver's mamma,* I thought. *Or keep the egg money back like Minnie's husband lets her do.*

A blue jay flew overhead, screeching at me, pulling me out of my thoughts. I looked up and realized I had walked past the drive to the Cliff House on Fourth Lake and was nearly at the turnoff that led to my friend Minnie Simms's house. Minnie Compeau, rather. I kept forgetting. I neatened the bunch of violets in my hand. I'd picked them for Minnie. To cheer her up. The baby was only a month off and it was making her tired and weepy. Tired and weepy and *wan*.

Wan, my word of the day, means having a sickly hue or an unnatural pallor. Showing ill health, fatigue, or unhappiness; lacking in forcefulness or competence. It has parents: the Old English *wann,* for "dark" or "gloomy," and the German *wahn,* for "madness." *Wan* shows its breeding; it has elements of *wann* and *wahn* in it, just like the new kittens have elements of Pansy, the barn cat, and Shadow, the wild tom.

Halfway down the turnoff—a dirt road that was corduroyed here and there with logs laid side by side to make it passable—Minnie's house came into view. It was a one-room log house, as low and squat as a hoptoad. Minnie's husband, Jim, had built it from trees he'd felled. She would have liked a clapboard house, painted white with red trim, but that called for money and they didn't have much. Planks laid end to end over the muddy ground served as a walkway. Charred tree stumps stuck up in the front yard, as black and random as an old man's teeth. Jim had cleared a plot for a vegetable garden in back of the house and fenced a field for their sheep and cows. Their land was on the north shore of Fourth

Lake, and they were hoping to take in boarders one day when they had more acreage cleared and a better house built.

Jim liked to say that we were all sitting on a gold mine now and that any man with a strong back and a modicum of ambition could make himself a fortune. My pa said the same, and Mr. Loomis, too. And it was all because Mrs. Collis P. Huntington, whose husband owned Camp Pine Knot at Raquette Lake, was possessed of a delicate constitution and an even more delicate backside.

Used to be that anyone coming up to Fourth Lake had to take a train from Grand Central to Utica, switch to another one to get to Old Forge, then get onboard a steamer and come up the Fulton Chain of Lakes one by one until he got to Fourth. If he wanted to go on from there, he had to take a long buckboard ride to Raquette Lake or hike to Big Moose, but that all changed when Mr. Huntington decided to bring Mrs. Huntington to his new camp. She found the journey so hard that she told her husband he could build a railroad to take her from Eagle Bay to Pine Knot or he could spend his summers by himself.

Mr. Huntington knew a lot about railroads—he'd built one that ran all the way from New Orleans to San Francisco. He had wealthy friends with camps near his, and they put themselves behind his plan. They got the state to approve it by saying the railroad would bring prosperity to a poor, rural area, and the first train had come through six years ago. Pa brought us down in the buckboard to see it. Abby cried when it arrived and Lawton cried when it left. Shortly after, tracks for the Mohawk and Malone line, which heads north out of Old Forge instead of east, were laid. The workmen cut wagon roads through the wilderness so that ties and spikes could be carried through. Those roads allowed men like Mr. Sperry to build hotels in the woods. Tourists came, and suddenly Eagle Bay and Inlet and Big Moose Lake were no longer just places where woodsmen and homesteaders lived. They were fashionable summer destinations for people wanting to escape the heat and noise of the big cities.

Both the Eagle Bay Hotel and the Glenmore had steam heat, sanitary plumbing, telegraph machines, and even telephones. It cost anywhere from twelve dollars to twenty-five dollars a week to stay at them. Their guests ate lobster bisque, drank champagne, and danced to music made by an orchestra, but we didn't even have a schoolhouse in Eagle Bay. Or a post office or a church or a general store. The railroads had brought prosperity, but prosperity didn't seem to want to stay. Come Labor Day she packed up and departed with the rest of the tourists and we were left to our own devices, hoping we had earned enough from May through August selling milk or fried chicken, waiting tables or washing linens, to feed ourselves and our animals during the long winter.

I turned onto Minnie's drive, feeling in my pocket for the letter from Barnard. I'd brought it to show her. I'd already showed it to Weaver, and he'd said I had to go no matter what it took. He said I must move every mountain, brave every hardship, vanquish all obstacles, do that which is impossible. I thought perhaps he had taken *The Count of Monte Cristo* too much to heart.

I wanted to see what Minnie thought about Barnard, for she was clever. She'd made her wedding dress from an aunt's castoff, and I had seen her recut a frumpy woolen overcoat into something stylish and new. If there was some way to fashion myself a ticket to New York out of nothing, she would know it. I wanted to ask her about promises, too, and see if she thought you always had to keep the ones you made just the way you made them, or if it was all right to alter them a bit.

I had so much I wanted to tell Minnie. I thought I might even tell her about my wagon ride with Royal, but I didn't get to tell her anything that day, because as I was halfway up the plank path, I heard a scream. A terrible one, full of fear and pain. It came from inside the house.

"Minnie!" I shouted, dropping my flowers. "Minnie, what is it?"

All I got for an answer was a low, trailing moan. Someone was killing her, I was sure of it. I ran onto the porch, grabbed a log from the woodpile, and dashed inside, ready to bash that someone's head in.

"Put that down, you damn fool," a woman's voice said from behind me.

But before I could even turn around to see who'd spoken, another scream pierced the air. I looked across the room and saw my friend. She was lying in her bed, drenched with sweat, heaving and arching and screaming.

"Minnie! Min, what is it? What's wrong?"

"Nothing's wrong. She's in labor," the voice behind me said.

I whirled around and saw a hefty blond woman stirring rags into a pot of boiling water. Mrs. Crego. The midwife.

Labor. The baby. Minnie was having her baby. "But, she...she's not due," I stammered. "She's only eight months gone. She has another month. Dr. Wallace said she has another month."

"Then Dr. Wallace is a bigger fool than you are."

"You building a fire, Matt?" a weak voice rasped.

I turned again. Minnie was looking at me and laughing, and I realized I was still holding the log aloft. Then quick as it came, her laughter stopped and she groaned, and the fear came back into her face. I saw her twist herself against it, saw her hands clutch at the bedsheets, saw her eyes huge and frightened. "Oh, Mattie, it's going to tear me apart," she whimpered.

I started whimpering right along with her until Mrs. Crego yelled at us, telling us we were witless and useless, the pair of us. She put the pot of rags down near the bed, next to a milking stool, then she took the log out of my hands and pushed me toward Minnie. "Since you're here, you might as well help," she said. "Come on, let's sit her up."

But Minnie didn't want to sit up. She said she wasn't going to. Mrs. Crego got into the bed behind her and pushed, and I pulled, and between the two of us, we got her up and over the edge of the bed. Her shift was all up around her hips, but she didn't care. Minnie, who was so modest she wouldn't undress in front of me when she stayed at our house.

Mrs. Crego crawled out of the bed and knelt down in front of her. She pushed Minnie's knees apart, peered up between them, and shook her head. "Baby won't make up his mind. First he wants to come early, now he don't want to come at all," she said.

I tried not to look at the crimson streaks on Minnie's thighs. I tried not to look at the blood in the bed, either. Mrs. Crego squeezed the water out of a steaming rag and put it on Minnie's back. It seemed to ease her some. She had me hold it there and went to dig in her basket. She pulled out dried herbs, a knob of ginger, and a jar of chicken fat.

"I was on my way up the road to visit Arlene Tanney—she's due in a week—and I thought I'd just stop in to check on your friend here. Even if she ain't my patient," Mrs. Crego said. "Found her on the porch steps, helpless. Said she'd been having pains off and on for two days. Said she told the doctor, but he said she shouldn't worry about it. The jackass. Like to see him have pains for two days and not worry about it. She's lucky I came by. Luckier still you did. It's going to take two of us to get this baby out of her."

"But...but Mrs. Crego," I stammered, "I can't help...I...I don't know what to do."

"You'll have to. There's no one else," Mrs. Crego said matter-of-factly. "You've helped your father bring calves, haven't you? It's the same thing. Pretty much."

Oh no, it isn't, I thought. I loved our cows, but I loved Minnie so much more.

The next six hours were the longest of my life. Mrs. Crego ran me ragged. I built a fire in the hearth to warm up the house. I rubbed Minnie's back and her legs and her feet. Mrs. Crego sat on the milking stool and rubbed Minnie's belly and pressed it and put her ear against it. Minnie's belly was so big it scared me. I wondered how whatever was in it would ever get out. We gave her castor oil to speed the contractions. She threw it up. We got her up and made her walk around and around the room. We sat her down again. We made her kneel, we made her squat, we made her lie. Mrs. Crego had her eat some gingerroot. She threw that up. I stroked her head and sang "Won't You Come Home, Bill Bailey?", her favorite song, only I changed Bill Bailey to Jim Compeau, which made her laugh when she wasn't moaning.

Toward afternoon Mrs. Crego took another herb out of her basket. Pennyroyal. She made a tea out of it and made Minnie drink a big cupful. Minnie kept that down and the pains got worse. She was in agony. She suddenly wanted to push, but Mrs. Crego wouldn't let her. *She* pushed instead—on Minnie's enormous belly—and rubbed and pummeled and kneaded until she was panting and the sweat was streaming down her face. Then she wrenched Minnie's knees apart and peered between them again. "You son of a gun, you...Come on!" she yelled, kicking the stool away. Minnie sank back against me and cried weary, hopeless tears. I put my arms around her and rocked her like she was my baby. She looked up at me, her eyes searching mine, and said, "Mattie, will you tell Jim I love him?"

"I'm not telling him any such mush. Tell him yourself when the baby's out."

"He's not coming out, Matt."

"Hush. He is, too. He's just taking his time, that's all."

I started to sing "Bill Bailey" again, but my heart wasn't in it. I watched Mrs. Crego as I sang. She was heating more water. She dunked her hands in it, then soaped them up, and her wrists and arms, up to her elbows. Then she rubbed her hands with chicken fat. I felt my insides go rubbery. I didn't want Minnie to see what was coming, so I told her to close her eyes and I rubbed her temples gently, singing all the while. I think she slept for a few seconds. Or maybe she passed out.

Mrs. Crego shoved the milking stool back in place with her foot and sat on it. She placed her hands on Minnie's belly, and moved them all around. She was very quiet. It seemed to me that she was listening with her hands. She frowned as she listened, and for the first time I saw fear in her own eyes.

"Is he coming out now?" I asked.

"They."

"What?"

"She's got two babies. One wants to come out feet first. I'm going to try and turn him. Hold her now, Mattie."

I threaded my arms through Minnie's. Her eyes fluttered open. "What's going on, Matt?" she whispered. Her voice sounded so scared.

"It's all right, Min, it's all right..."

But it wasn't.

Mrs. Crego put her left hand on Minnie's belly. Her right hand disappeared under Minnie's shift. Minnie arched her back and screamed. I thought for sure Mrs. Crego would kill her. I held her arms tightly and buried my face in her back and prayed for it to end.

I'd never known it was like this for a woman. Never. We'd always been sent to Aunt Josie's when Mamma's time was near. We would stay there overnight, and when we came back, there was Mamma smiling with a new baby in her arms.

I have read so many books, and not one of them tells the truth about babies. Dickens doesn't. Oliver's mother just dies in childbirth and that's that. Brontë doesn't. Catherine Earnshaw just has her daughter and that's that. There's no blood, no sweat, no pain, no fear, no heat, no stink.

Writers are damned liars. Every single one of them.

"He's turned!" Mrs. Crego suddenly shouted.

I risked a glance at her. Her hands were on Minnie's

knees; her right one was bloodied. Minnie's screams had become short, repeating keens, the kind an animal makes when it's badly hurt.

"Come on, girl, push!" Mrs. Crego yelled.

I let go of Minnie's arms. She took my hands, squeezed them so I thought she would crush them, and pushed for all she was worth. I could feel her against me, arching and gripping, could feel her bones shifting and cracking, and I was astonished. I never knew that Minnie Simms, who couldn't lift the big iron fry pan off the stove when we boiled maple syrup in it for sugar on snow—at least not when Jim Compeau was around to do it—was so strong.

She grunted as she pushed. And snorted. "You sound like a pig, Min," I whispered.

She started laughing then—crazy, helpless laughter—and collapsed against me, but not for long because Mrs. Crego swore at me and told me to keep my mouth shut and told Minnie to keep pushing.

And then, finally, with a noise that was part scream, part groan, part grunt, and sounded like it came from deep inside the earth instead of deep inside Minnie, a baby came.

"Here he is! Go on, Minnie, push! Good girl! Good girl!" Mrs. Crego cheered, guiding the baby out.

He was tiny and blue and covered in blood and what looked like lard, and he struck me as thoroughly unappealing. I started laughing, delighted to see him despite his appearance, and two seconds later, Mrs. Crego handed him to me and I was sobbing, overwhelmed to be holding my oldest friend's brand-new child. The baby was crying, too. He was wailing bloody murder.

The second baby, a girl, came with far less ado. She had a caul over her face. Mrs. Crego pulled it off right away and threw it on the fire. "To keep the devil from getting it," she said. I could not imagine why he would want it. Mrs. Crego tied off the thick gray cords attached to the babies' bellies and cut them, which made me feel woozy. Then she got a needle and thread and began to stitch Minnie up, and I thought I was going to faint for certain, but she wouldn't let me. She bossed me right out of my light-headedness. We got Minnie cleaned up and the babies, too, and found fresh sheets for the bed and set the bloodied ones soaking. Then Mrs. Crego brewed Minnie a pot of tea from fennel seed, thistle, and hops to bring her milk in. She told me to sit down and catch my breath. I did. I closed my eyes meaning to rest for just a minute, but I must have fallen asleep, because when I opened my eyes, I saw Minnie nursing one of the babies and smelled biscuits baking and soup simmering.

Mrs. Crego handed me a cup of plain tea and touched the back of her hand to my forehead. "You look worse than Minnie does," she said, laughing. Minnie laughed, too.

I did not laugh. "I am never going to marry," I said. "Never."

"Oh no?"

"No. Never."

"Well, we'll see about that," Mrs. Crego said. Her face softened. "The pain stops, you know, Mattie. And the memory of it fades. Minnie will forget all about this one day."

"Maybe she will, but I surely won't," I said.

There were footsteps on the porch, and then Jim was inside, bellowing for his supper. He stopped his noise as soon as he saw me and Mrs. Crego, and his wife in bed with two new babies beside her.

"You've got a son," Mrs. Crego said to him. "And a daughter, too."

"Min?" he whispered, looking at his wife, waiting for her to tell him it was true.

Minnie tried to say something but couldn't. She just lifted one of the babies up for him to take. The emotion on his face, and then between him and Minnie, was so strong, so naked, that I had to look away. It wasn't right for me to see it.

I shifted in my chair, feeling awkward and out of place, and heard the letter crinkle in my pocket. I had been so excited to tell Minnie all about Barnard, but it didn't seem like so much now.

I stared into my teacup, wondering what it was like to have what Minnie had. To have somebody love you like Jim loved her. To have two tiny new lives in your care.

I wondered if all those things were the best things to have or if it was better to have words and stories. Miss

Wilcox had books but no family. Minnie had a family now, but those babies would keep her from reading for a good long time. Some people, like my aunt Josie and Alvah Dunning the hermit, had neither love nor books. Nobody I knew had both.

plain · tive

"Is this how you spend the money I give you? Making up Mother Goose rhymes?"

I jerked awake at the sound of the angry voice, uncertain for a few seconds where I was. My eyes grew accustomed to the lamplight and I saw my new composition book under my hand, and my dictionary next to it, open to my word of the day, and realized it was late at night and that I'd fallen asleep at the kitchen table.

"Answer me, Mattie!"

I sat up. "What, Pa? What money?" I mumbled, blinking at him.

There was fury on his face and alcohol on his breath. Through the sleep fog in my head, I remembered that he'd gone to Old Forge earlier that afternoon to sell his syrup. He'd had twelve gallons. We'd boiled nearly five hundred gallons of sap to get it. It was his habit on these trips to go into one of the saloons there and allow himself a glass or two of whiskey from his profits, and some male conversation. He usually didn't get back before midnight. I'd planned to be in bed well before then.

"The housekeeping money! The fifty cents I give you for a bag of cornmeal! Is this where it's gone?"

Before I could answer him, he grabbed my new composition book off the table and ripped out the poem I'd been writing.

"'... a loon repeats her plaintive cry, and in the pine boughs, breezes sigh...,'" he read. Then he crumpled the page, opened the oven door, and threw it on the coals.

"Please, Pa, don't. I didn't spend the housekeeping money on it. I swear it. The cornmeal's in the cellar. I bought it two days ago. You can look," I pleaded, reaching for my composition book.

"Then where did you get the money for this?" he asked, holding it away from me.

I swallowed hard. "From picking fiddleheads. And spruce gum. Me and Weaver. We sold them. I made sixty cents."

The muscle in Pa's cheek jumped. When he finally spoke, his voice was raspy. "You mean to tell me we've been eating mush for days on end and you had sixty cents all this time?"

And then there was a loud, sharp crack and lights were going off in my head and I was on the floor, not at all sure how I'd got there. Until I tasted blood in my mouth and my eyes cleared and I saw Pa standing over me, his hand raised.

He blinked at me and lowered his hand. I got up. Slowly. My legs were shaky and weak. I had landed on my hip and it was throbbing. I steadied myself against the kitchen table and wiped the blood off my mouth. I couldn't look at my pa, so I looked at the table instead. There was a bill of sale on top of it, and money—a dirty, wrinkled bill. Ten dollars. For twelve gallons of maple syrup. I knew he'd been hoping for twenty.

I looked at him then. He looked tired. So tired. And worn and old.

"Mattie... Mattie, I'm sorry... I didn't mean to...," he said, reaching for me.

I shook him off. "Never mind, Pa. Go to bed. We've got the upper field to plow tomorrow."

I am standing in my underthings, getting ready for bed. My camisole is sticking to my skin. It feels like a wet dishrag. It is beastly hot up here in the Glenmore's attic, and so airless I can barely draw a breath. That's no bad thing, though, on a night like tonight when you share a room with seven other girls and all of you have been waiting tables and washing dishes and cleaning rooms in the July heat and none of you has had a bath, or even a swim, for three days running.

Cook comes in. She pokes and scolds, telling this girl to tuck her boots under the bed, that one to pick her skirt up off the floor, threading her way down the middle of the room.

I hang my blouse and skirt on a hook at the side of my bed and pull the hairpins out of the twist Ada did for me this morning—a Gibson-girl style and one that looks better in the drawings in *Ladies' Home Journal* than it does on me. Then I peel off my stockings and lay them on the windowsill to air.

"Frances Hill, you get those boots polished tomorrow, you hear me? Mary Anne Sweeney, put that magazine away . . ."

I lie down on one side of the old iron bed I share with Ada, on top of the faded quilt. Ada is kneeling at the other side, praying. I would like to pray, but I can't. The words won't come.

"Now listen, girls, I want you to go right to sleep tonight. No reading or talking. I'm getting you up early tomorrow. Five-thirty on the dot. Never mind your whining. We've got people coming from all parts—important people—and I want you looking sharp. There's to be no whispering or gossiping or carrying on. Ada?"

"Yes, Cook."

"Lizzie?"

"Yes, Cook."

"Mrs. Morrison needs you all on your very best behavior. Sleep well, girls, and remember that poor thing downstairs in your prayers."

I wonder how I am supposed to remember the dead girl downstairs and sleep well. Seems to me it's got to be one or the other. I hear Ada get up off the floor, then feel the mattress shake and bounce. She plumps her pillow and tussles around. She curls up on her side, then stretches out onto her back. "I can't sleep, Matt," she whispers, turning toward me.

"I can't, either."

"She wasn't much older than us, I don't think. Do you really suppose her young man is still alive?"

"He could be. They haven't found his body," I say, trying to sound hopeful.

"They're still out there, Mr. Sperry and Mr. Morrison

and more besides. I saw them going into the woods after supper. They had lanterns."

We are both silent for a minute or so. I turn on my side and slide one hand under my pillow. My fingers touch the letters.

"Ada?"

"Hmmm?"

"When you make someone a promise, do you always have to keep it?"

"My ma says you do."

"Even if the person you promised to dies?"

"Especially then. On his deathbed, my uncle Ed made my aunt May promise never to take his likeness down off the wall, even if she married again. Well, she did marry and Uncle Lyman, her new husband, didn't care much for Ed watching his every move. But May wouldn't go back on her promise. So Lyman bought a bit of black cloth and glued it across Ed's photograph. Like a blindfold. May reckons that's all right, as Ed never said anything about blindfolds. But you can't break a promise to anyone who's dead. They'll come back and haunt you if you do. Why are you asking?"

Ada blinks at me with her huge, dark eyes, and even though it's boiling hot in our room, I suddenly feel cold. I roll onto my back and stare at the ceiling. "No reason," I say.

Uri · ah the Hit · tite, stink · pot, wart · hog

John the Baptist was looking dustier than a man should. Even a man who spent all his time wandering around in a desert.

"Mattie, be careful with that! You know those figurines mean the world to me."

"Yes, Aunt Josie," I said, gently wiping John's porcelain face.

"Start with the top shelf and work your way down. That way you're—"

"—not dusting the dust that I already dusted."

"A smart tongue does not become a young lady."

"Yes, Aunt Josie," I said obediently. I did not want to anger my aunt. Not today. I wanted her in a good mood today, for I had finally thought up a way to get myself to Barnard—one that didn't involve my father's say-so or a job up at the Glenmore.

My aunt Josephine had money. Quite a bit of it. Her husband, my uncle Vernon, made a good living with his sawmills. Maybe, just maybe, I hoped, she would loan a little bit of it to me.

I was cleaning house for my aunt as I did every Wednesday after school. And she was sitting in a chair by the window, watching me work, as she did every Wednesday after school. My uncle and aunt live in the nicest house in Inlet—a three-story clapboard painted gold with dark green trim. They have no children, but my aunt has nearly two hundred figurines. She says her rheumatism keeps her from doing any real work because it makes her bones ache something wicked. Pa says his bones would ache, too, if they had as much lard hanging off them as hers do. She is a big woman.

Pa does not like my aunt Josie, and he did not want me to clean her house. He said I was not a slave—which was rich, coming from him—but there was not much either of us could do about it. I had started helping my aunt to please Mamma—Josie was unwell and Mamma had worried about her—and it wasn't right to stop just because Mamma died. I knew she wouldn't want me to.

Aunt Josie does not like my pa, either. She never thought he was good enough for my mother. Josie and my mamma grew up in a big house in Old Forge. Josie married a rich man, and she thought my mother ought to have married a rich man, too. She thought Mamma was too fine to live on a farm, and often told her so. They had a falling-out over it once, when Mamma was expecting Beth. They were sitting in Josie's kitchen, drinking tea, and I was in the parlor. I was supposed to be dusting, but I'd been eavesdropping instead.

"That huge farm . . . all the *work*, Ellen," my aunt said. "Seven babies . . . three buried because they weren't strong enough, because *you* weren't strong enough . . .

and now another one coming. What on earth can you be thinking? You're not a field hand, you know. You're going to ruin your health."

"What would you like me to do, Josie?"

"Tell him no, for goodness' sake. He shouldn't make you."

There was a long, cold silence. Then my mamma said, "He doesn't *make* me." And then the parlor door almost hit me in the head as she burst into the room to fetch me home even though I hadn't finished dusting. They didn't speak for weeks after that, and when they finally did make up, there were no more words against my pa.

My aunt could be very trying and she made me angry at times, but mostly I felt sorry for her. She thought that figurines on your shelves and white sugar in your tea and lace trim on your underthings were what mattered, but that was only because she and Uncle Vernon didn't sleep in the same room like my mother and father had, and Uncle Vernon never kissed her on the lips when he thought no one was looking, or sang her songs that made her cry, like the one about Miss Clara Verner and her true love, Monroe, who lost his life clearing a logjam.

I put John the Baptist down and picked up Christ in the Garden of Gethsemane. The quality wasn't so good on that one. Jesus had an odd expression and a greenish cast to his face. He looked more like a man with stomach trouble than one who was about to be crucified. I squeezed him tightly to get his attention, then sent him a quick prayer to make my aunt amenable.

As I polished him, I wondered why on earth someone would collect such junk. Words were so much better to collect. They didn't take up space and you never had to dust them. Although I had to admit I hadn't had much luck with my word of the day that morning. *Uriah the Hittite* was the first word the dictionary had yielded, followed by *stinkpot,* then *warthog.* And then I'd slammed the book shut, disgusted.

After Jesus, there was a bible with THE GOOD BOOK written on it in real fourteen-karat gold. I picked it up and was just going to tell my aunt about Barnard and ask her for the money, when she spoke first.

"Watch you don't polish the gold off that," she cautioned me.

"Yes, Aunt Josie."

"You reading your bible, Mattie?"

"Some."

"You should spend more time reading the Good Book and less reading all those novels. What are you going to tell the Lord on Judgement Day when He asks you why you didn't read your bible? Hmm?"

I will tell Him that His press agents could have done with a writing lesson or two, I said. To myself.

I did not think the Good Book was all that good. There was too much begetting, too much smoting. Not much of a plot, either. Some of the stories were all right— like Moses parting the Red Sea, and Job, and Noah and his ark—but whoever wrote them down could have done a lot more with them. I would like to have known, for example, what Mrs. Job thought about God destroying her entire family over a stupid bet. Or how Mrs. Noah felt to have her children safe on the ark with her while she watched everyone else's children drown. Or how Mary stood it when the Romans drove nails straight through her boy's hands. I know the ones writing were prophets and saints and all, but it wouldn't have helped them any in Miss Wilcox's classroom. She still would have given them a D.

I put the bible back and started in on the Seven Deadly Sins: Pride, Envy, Wrath, Lust, Gluttony, Sloth, Greed. I had to stand on the step stool to reach them. They were on a shelf over one of the parlor's two windows.

"There's Margaret Pruyn," my aunt said, peering out the window and across the street to Dr. Wallace's house. "That's the second time this week she's been to the doctor's. She's not saying what's wrong, but she doesn't have to. I know what it is. She's as thin as a pike pole. Got that waxy look to her, too. Cancer of the breast. I just know it. Same as your mamma, God rest her." There was a sigh, and then a sniffle, and then Aunt Josie was dabbing at her eyes with her handkerchief. "Poor, dear Ellen," she sobbed.

I was used to these displays. My aunt didn't have much to distract her and she tended to dwell. "Look, Aunt Josie," I said, pointing at the doctor's house. "There's Mrs. Howard going in. What's wrong with her?"

My aunt honked and coughed and pulled aside the

curtain again. "Sciatica," she said, brightening considerably. "Pinched nerve in the spine. Told me it pains her something awful." Aunt Josie loves a good illness. She can talk about signs and symptoms for hours on end and is considered to be something of an authority on catarrh, piles, shingles, dropped wombs, ruptures, and impetigo.

"There's Alma on her way home," she said, craning her neck. Alma McIntyre was the postmistress and my aunt's good friend. "Who's she with, Mattie? Who's that talking to her? She handing him something?"

I looked out the window. "It's Mr. Satterlee," I said. "She's giving him an envelope."

"Is she? I wonder what's in it." She knocked on the window, trying to get Mrs. McIntyre's attention, or Mr. Satterlee's, but they didn't hear her. "Arn's been seen up at the Hubbard place twice this week, Mattie. You know anything about it?"

"No, ma'am."

"You find out something, be sure and tell me."

"Yes, ma'am," I replied, trying yet again to find an opening in the conversation so I could make my request, but my aunt didn't give me one.

"There goes Emily Wilcox," she said, watching my teacher walk by. "Thinks quite a lot of herself, that one. She'll never find herself a husband. No one likes a too-smart woman."

Aunt Josie must be reading Milton, too, I thought. *He says the same thing, only in fancier language.*

"You know, Mattie, I'm certain that Emily Wilcox is

from the Iverson Wilcoxes of New York City, but it's odd because Iverson Wilcox has three daughters—two married, one a spinster. That's what Alma said and she would know; after all, her brother used to be a caretaker at the Sagamore, and the Wilcoxes summered there— but Annabelle Wilcox is a Miss and Emily Wilcox is a Miss—Alma says the return address on her letters always say *Miss* Wilcox. And Emily teaches. She would have to be a Miss if she teaches. She gets letters from a Mrs. Edward Mayhew—Alma's sure that's Charlotte, the third sister, and she's obviously married—but if only one is supposed to be a spinster, why are two of them Misses? She also gets letters from an Iverson Jr.—that's her brother, of course. And from a Mr. Theodore Baxter—I don't know who he is. And from a Mr. John Van Eck of Scribner and Sons—a publishing concern. What's a young woman doing corresponding with publishers? They're a very shady bunch. You mark my words, Mattie, there's something fast about that woman."

Aunt Josie said all this with barely a breath. Pa says Uncle Vernon should rent her out to the forge; they could use her for a bellows. As soon as my teacher had turned a corner and Aunt Josie couldn't see her anymore, she stopped disparaging Miss Wilcox and changed the topic. To me.

"I heard you were out gallivanting with Royal Loomis the other day," she said.

I groaned, wondering if the entire county knew. I still hadn't heard the end of it, espccially from Weaver, who'd said, "Gee, Matt, I always knew you liked dumb animals, but Royal Loomis?"

Lou teased me, then told everyone she knew, and they teased me, too. I tried hard to be good-natured about it, but I couldn't. Anyone with eyes could see that Royal was handsome and I was plain. And them going on and on about me being sweet on him was mean. Like asking a lame girl what she's wearing to the dance.

"I wasn't 'gallivanting,'" I told my aunt. "Royal and I happened to be at the pickle boat at the same time and he gave me a ride home, that's all."

But a simple ride home was not good gossip and Aunt Josie was having none of it.

"Now, Mattie, I know when a girl's sweet on a boy..."

I didn't say a word, just kept on dusting.

"I have a present for you, dear," she wheedled. "Did you see that nice tablecloth I left on the kitchen table? That's for you."

I'd seen it. It was old and yellowed and frayed. I thought she'd meant for me to wash it, or mend it, or throw it out. I knew I'd better thank her lavishly, though, because that's what she expected. And what Mamma would have wanted me to do. So I did.

"You're welcome, Mathilda. Perhaps I can help you out with your trousseau. After you're engaged, that is. Perhaps your uncle Vernon and I could help you with your china and cutlery..."

I turned around to face her, determined to nip her engagement talk in the bud before it got to Alma McIntyre and all over Inlet and back to Eagle Bay and Royal Loomis himself. "Don't you think you're rushing things a bit, Aunt Josie? It was just a ride home."

"Now, Mattie, I understand your reluctance to make too much of this, honestly I do. You're very levelheaded and you're probably thinking that attention from a boy like Royal Loomis is a bit more than a plain girl like you should expect. But it doesn't do to be too shy. If he's showing interest, you'd do well to pursue it. You might not get another chance with a boy like Royal."

I felt my face turn red. I know I have too many freckles and lank brown hair. Mamma used to call it chestnut, but it's not; it's just plain brown like my eyes. I know that my hands are rough and knobby and my body is small and sturdy. I know I do not look like Belinda Becker or Martha Miller—all blond and pale and airy, with ribbons in their hair. I know all this and I do not need my aunt to remind me.

"Oh, Mattie, dear, I didn't mean to make you blush! This has been bothering you, hasn't it? I could tell something was. You needn't be so modest! I know this must all be very new to you, and I know it must be hard—having lost your dear mother. But please don't fret, dear. I understand a mother's duty toward her daughter, and since your own mamma is gone, I will fulfill it for her. Is there anything you want to know, dear? Anything you need to ask me?"

I clutched the figurine I was polishing. "Yes, Aunt Josie, there is."

"Go ahead, dear."

I meant to be slow and sensible in my speech, but my words came out of me in a big, desperate gush. "Aunt Josie, can you...would you...I want to go to college, Aunt Josie. If you were going to give me money for china and silver, would you give it to me for books and train fare instead? I've been accepted. To Barnard College. In New York City. I applied over the winter and I got in. I want to study literature, but I haven't the money to go and Pa won't let me work at the Glenmore like I want to, and I thought that maybe if you...if Uncle Vernon..."

Everything changed as I spoke. Aunt Josie's smile slid off her face like ice off a tin roof.

"...you wouldn't have to give it to me if you didn't... if you didn't want to. You could loan it to me. I'd pay it all back...every penny of it. Please, Aunt Josie?" I spoke those last words in a whisper.

My aunt didn't reply right away; she just looked at me in such a way that I suddenly knew just how Hester Prynne felt when she had to stand on that scaffold.

"You are just as bad as your no-account brother," she finally said. "Selfish and thoughtless. It must come from the Gokey side, because it doesn't come from the Robertsons. What on earth can you be thinking? Leaving your sisters when they need you? And for a terrible place like New York!" She nodded at the figurine I was clutching. "Pride. That's very fitting. Pride goeth before a fall. You're on a very high horse, Mathilda. I don't know who put you there, but you'd best get down off it. And fast."

The lecture would have gone on, but there was a

sudden smell of smoke. It had my aunt up and out of her chair in no time, waddling off to the kitchen to check on the pie she had baking. For an invalid, she moves faster than a water snake when she has a mind to.

I remained on the ladder, looking at the figurine in my hand. *You're wrong, Aunt Josie,* I thought. *It's not pride I'm feeling. It's another sin.* Worse than all the other ones, which are immediate, violent, and hot. This one sits inside you quietly and eats you from the inside out like the trichina worms the pigs get. It's the Eighth Deadly Sin. The one God left out.

Hope.

xe • roph • i • lous

Mrs. Loomis's kitchen was so orderly and clean that it scared me. Kind of like Mrs. Loomis herself did. Her apron was always bright white and she darned her dishrags. I was standing in her kitchen, along with Lou and Beth, apologizing for Daisy, our cow. She and her calf had smashed through the fence that divides our land from Frank Loomis's. I could see them out of the kitchen window, wallowing in the cow pond.

"I'm sorry about the fence, Mrs. Loomis," I said. "Pa's fixing it. Ought to have it done in an hour or two."

Her pale blue eyes darted up from the potato she was peeling. "That's the second time this month, Mattie."

"I know it, ma'am. I don't know why she does it. We have a perfectly good cow pond ourselves," I said, twisting the rope noose I'd brought with me to fetch Daisy back.

"Your pa feeding alfalfa?"

"No, ma'am."

"Must be she's headstrong, then. Tie her in her stall for a few days and cut her feed. That'll fix her."

"Yes, ma'am," I said, knowing I would do no such

thing to Daisy. "Well, I guess I'll go and get her now. Come on, Lou, Beth."

Mrs. Loomis had taken a tray of molasses cookies out of the oven just as we'd arrived. They were cooling on the counter, scenting the air with ginger and clove. My sisters couldn't take their eyes off them. Mrs. Loomis saw them looking. Her thin lips got even thinner. She gave the girls one to split. She didn't give one to me. I saw Mr. Loomis take some eggs to Emmie Hubbard yesterday. I thought it was very kind of him and wondered how he put up with such a mean and stingy wife.

Xerophilous, my word of the day, means able to withstand drought, or adapted to a dry region. Standing in Mrs. Loomis's spotless kitchen, where there were no incontinent dogs or flea-bitten Hubbards or yellowed pictures from old calendars curling up on the walls, I wondered if only plants could be xerophilous or if people could be, too.

"Let me see if one of the boys is around to help you," Mrs. Loomis said. "Will! Jim! Royal!" she shouted out of the window.

"It's all right, we can manage," I said, heading for the back door.

I walked past the barn to the cow pond. Lou and Beth trailed behind me, taking tiny nibbles out of their cookie halves, seeing who could make hers last the longest. Daisy was at the farthest end of the pond, near to where the Loomis's pasture started. She was making a terrible noise, bellowing like someone had cut off all four of her legs. Baldwin the calf—named by Beth because he had a long, somber face like Mr. Baldwin the undertaker—was hollering, too.

"Here, boss! Come on, Daisy! Come on, boss," I shouted, rubbing my fingers together like I had a treat for her. "Come on, girl!"

Lou and Beth finished their cookie and started calling to the cow, too. Between the three of us shouting and Daisy and Baldwin bawling, we were making quite a racket.

"Sounds like the Old Forge town band. Just about as loud and just about as bad."

I turned around. It was Royal. His shirtsleeves were rolled up, showing his muscled arms, already brown from the sun. His color was high from working, his cheeks were streaked with dust. He stood with his hands in his pockets and his sturdy legs rooted to the ground, belonging to this place. As much as the silvery streams belonged, and the great, scudding clouds, and the deer in the woods. He was as beautiful as these things, too. He took my breath away. His eyes were the color of amber. Not hazel, not buckwheat honey like I'd thought, but warm, dark amber. His hair, golden and too long, was curling over his ears and down his neck. His shirt collar was open, and I couldn't take my eyes off the patch of smooth skin showing through it. He saw me looking and I blushed. Furiously.

"Don't none of them books of yours tell you how to get a cow out of a pond?" he asked.

"I don't need a book to tell me how to get a cow out of a pond," I replied, and called to Daisy in a louder voice. When that didn't work, I shook the noose at her and succeeded only in scaring Baldwin. He ran deeper into the pond and his mother followed.

Royal stooped down and picked up a few stones. Then he walked around behind Daisy and aimed at her backside. The first one surprised her and the second one got her moving. She ran right toward us. Lou was able to grab her, and I slipped the noose over her head, scolding her soundly. We didn't need to tie Baldwin. He would follow his mother.

I thanked Royal, though it killed me. "I don't know why she comes here," I said. "She has a fine pond of her own."

Royal laughed. "She don't come 'cause she wants a swim. It's him she's after," he said, pointing past the pond to the pasture behind it. I couldn't see what he was talking about at first, but then I spotted him—standing at the very edge of the field in the shadows of some pines. The bull. He was huge and fearsome and as black as midnight, and he was watching us. I saw his dark eyes blink and his velvet nostrils twitch, and I hoped greatly that the fence around him was stronger than the one Daisy had plowed through.

"Well, thanks again, Royal. We'd best be going," I said, starting off toward the dirt drive that led back home.

"I'll walk you," he said.

"You don't have to."

He shrugged. "'T'ain't nothing."

"I want to lead her, Matt," Beth said. I let her. She started singing another one of Pa's lumberjack songs. Lou walked next to her, her cropped hair swinging free, the cuffs of Lawton's coveralls dragging on the ground.

Royal talked about farming as we walked. About the corn he and Dan were going to plant and how his father was thinking about buying some sheep. He talked steadily, never giving me a chance to speak. After a while, though, he took a breath, and just to say something, I told him I was going to college. I told him that I had been accepted to Barnard and that if I could only come up with some money, I would go.

He stopped dead in his tracks. "What on earth you want to do that for?" he asked, frowning.

"To learn, Royal. To read books and see if maybe I can write one myself someday."

"Don't know why you'd want to do that."

"Because I do," I said, annoyed by his reaction. "And anyways, what do you care?"

He shrugged again. "Guess I don't. Don't understand it, that's all. Don't see why your brother left. Don't see why you would. Your pa know you're planning this?"

"No, and don't you tell him, either," I said.

We had fallen behind my sisters and the cows, and it was no surprise when, halfway to the Uncas Road, they disappeared over a hill.

What was a surprise, though, was when Royal stopped suddenly and kissed me. On my mouth. Quick and hard. I didn't protest, I couldn't—I was speechless. All I could think was that kisses from boys like Royal Loomis were for girls like Martha Miller, not me. He took a step back and looked at me. He had an odd expression on his face, the kind of look Lou gets when she's tasted something I've cooked and is trying to decide if she can stomach it.

And then he did it again, pulling me to him, pressing his body against mine. The feel of him, and smell of him, and taste of him, made me warm and dizzy. His hands were on my back, pressing me tighter against him. And then on my waist. And then one moved higher and before I knew what was happening, he was kneading my breast, pushing and pulling on it like he might a cow's teat.

"Stop it, Royal," I said, breaking away, my face flaming.

"What's wrong?" he asked. "You saving them?"

I couldn't look at him.

"For who, Matt?"

And then he laughed and started back home.

mono · chro · mat · ic

"No, no, no, Mattie! *X* is the *unknown* quantity. If it were known, you wouldn't need the *X*, would you? Jeezum, but you're making this hard," Weaver said.

I was standing in the middle of the highway, on the verge of despair, staring at the equation he'd drawn in the dirt.

"Figuring polynomials is just a matter of simplifying a bunch of values to a few. Just like boiling down a lot of sap to a little bit of syrup. It's easy, so stop being such a mule."

"Hee-haw! Hee-haw! Hee-haw!" Jim Loomis shouted, running by us.

"I'm not being a mule. I don't get this, I just don't!" I cried, scraping my foot through the equation. We'd spent all week on polynomials, I still didn't understand them, and we had a test coming at the end of the week, a practice for our Regents exam. "I'm going to fail, Weaver, I know I am!"

"No, you're not. Just calm down."

"But I can't see how—"

"Hold on a minute, will you?" He chewed his lip and stared off down the road, tapping his stick on the ground.

"What are you doing?" I asked, shifting the books I was carrying from one arm to the other.

"Trying to think like a mule. If you want to explain something to a mule, you have to put it so the mule can understand."

"Thank you. Thank you very much."

"Look out, Mattie! Ben's coming!" Will Loomis shouted, running toward us.

"What? Ben who?"

"Ben Dover!" he yelled, knocking my books out of my arms.

"For cripes' sake!" I snapped, swatting at him, but he was already past me, hooting and laughing as he watched me stoop down and brush dust off my books.

"Here, Matt, listen," Weaver said. "Let's try a written problem. Maybe putting it in practical terms will help." He opened his copy of Milne's *High School Algebra* and pointed. "This one."

I read it: "A man earned daily for 5 days 3 times as much as he paid for his board, after which he was obliged to be idle 4 days," it said. "Upon counting his money after paying for his board he found that he had 2 ten-dollar bills and 4 dollars. How much did he pay for his board, and what were his wages?"

"All right. Think now," Weaver said. "How would you begin to solve it? What's your X?"

I thought. Very hard. For quite some time. About the man and his meager wages and shabby boardinghouse and lonely life. "Where did he work?" I finally asked.

"*What?* It doesn't matter, Matt. Just assign an X to—"

"A mill, I bet," I said, picturing the man's threadbare clothing, his worn shoes. "A woolen mill. Why do you think he was obliged to be idle?"

"I don't know why. Look, just—"

"I bet he got sick," I said, clutching Weaver's arm. "Or maybe business wasn't good, and his boss had no work for him. I wonder if he had a family in the country? It would be a terrible thing, wouldn't it, if he had children to feed and no work? Maybe his wife was poorly, too. And I bet he had..."

"Damn it, Mattie, this is *algebra*, not composition!" Weaver said, glaring at me.

"Sorry," I said, feeling like a hopeless case.

Weaver looked up at the sky. He sighed and shook his head. Then, all of a sudden, he snapped his fingers and smiled. "Remember your word of the day?" he asked me, writing *monochromatic* in the dirt.

"Yes," I said. "It means of one color. Or it can describe a person who's color-blind. But what does that have to do with algebra?"

"Say you didn't have a dictionary, but you knew prefixes, suffixes, and roots. Same way you know the value of numbers. How would you get at the meaning of a word?"

"Well, you'd look at the pieces. *Mono,* a prefix for 'single' from the Greek word *monos*. And *chroma,* for 'color,' also from the Greek. The *ic* at the end would tell you it's an adjective. Then you'd blend all the pieces into one to get the meaning."

"Exactly! Algebra's the same, Matt. You blend all the

pieces into one to get the meaning, which in this case is a number, not a word. You combine your knowns with your unknowns, your numbers with your *X*s and *Y*s, one by one, until you have all your values. Then you add them or subtract them or whatever the equation tells you to do, and then you have your final value, the *meaning.*"

He wrote out another equation, and I began to see what he was talking about. "Solve it," he said, handing me the stick. I stumbled a bit with the first one and he had to help me, but by the time he'd written out three more, I'd gotten the idea well enough so that I wouldn't be completely lost when I sat down to do my lessons that night.

"Just keep at it. You'll get it," he told me. "I know you will."

I shook my head, thinking about Barnard and how badly I wanted to go there. "I don't know why I should," I said. "There's no point."

"Don't say that, Matt. Did you ask your aunt? She give you anything?"

"A lecture."

"Did you tell your pa yet?"

"No."

"Why don't you tell him? Maybe he'd let you go. Maybe he'd even help you."

"Not a chance, Weaver," I said.

"Maybe you can earn the money picking berries over the summer."

I thought of all the buckets of berries I would need to pick and sighed.

We started walking again. We were halfway to Eagle Bay on our way home from school. My sisters were a good ways ahead of us, walking with the Higby girls. The Loomises were a little farther up, playing kick the can with Ralph Simms and Mike Bouchard. The Hubbard kids were behind us. Miss Wilcox kept them after sometimes. "For remedial work," she always said. But Weaver and I often stayed after to study with her, and we knew that she gave them sandwiches. Jim and Will didn't know it, though, since they never stayed after, so that was one less thing they could torment them over.

As we rounded the last bend in the road before Eagle Bay, we saw the afternoon train pull into the station. It was bound for Raquette Lake, but it wouldn't depart for another thirty minutes or so. It was still only April, but some tourists and camp owners were already coming and it took a little while to unload them and their belongings—as well as the mail, any stray lumberjacks on their way back into the woods, and groceries and coal for the hotels.

"There's Lincoln and my mamma," Weaver said, before the massive locomotive pulled in, blocking out most of the station and the people near it. "Let's see if she's finished up, Matt. Maybe we can get a ride."

We crossed the tracks and walked to the station, a plain plank affair. It was nowhere near as grand as the ones in Raquette Lake or Old Forge, which have restaurants in them, but it had its own stationmaster and a stove for the colder months and benches and a proper window with bars, where travelers bought their tickets. We threaded our way among the tourists and the conductors and Mr. Pulling, the stationmaster, and some workmen bound for one of the hotels.

Weaver's mamma was next to the station, selling chicken and biscuits and pie. Lincoln, her hinny, was hitched to the Smiths' cart, facing away from the train, so that Weaver's mamma could more easily get at her wares. Lincoln was a patient animal. Pleasant would never have stood so quietly. But hinnies, which are bred from a female donkey and a male horse, are more tractable than mules, which are bred from a male donkey and a female horse.

"Need some help, Mamma?" Weaver asked.

"Oh yes, honey!" she said. Her face lit up like a lamp at the sight of her son. It always did, even if she'd just seen him ten minutes ago. Weaver's mamma has a first name, of course. It is Aleeta. And strangers call her Mrs. Smith. But everyone around Eagle Bay calls her Weaver's mamma, for that's what she is. More than anything else.

"Hello, Mattie, darlin'," she said to me in her soft drawl.

I greeted her and she handed me a biscuit. She wore a blue calico dress and an apron she'd made from a flour sack. A bit of calico, the same as her dress, was wrapped around her braids and knotted at the back of her head. She was handsome like her son. Her face was strong and her skin was smooth, with hardly a line in it. Her eyes were kind, but they didn't match her young face. They had an ancient look to them, as if she'd seen most everything there was to see in this world and would be surprised by nothing.

"See that lady waving from the window, Weaver? Take this to her," she said, handing him a bundle wrapped in a sheet of newspaper. She made another bundle. "That's for the engineer, Mattie. Hand it up to him, honey." I shoved the rest of my biscuit into my mouth, put my books down in her cart, and took the bundle. I walked to the front of the train, not liking the *chumpf chumpf* noises it made or its sharp coal smell or the big whuffs of steam that came billowing out from under it.

"That you, Mattie Gokey?" a big voice boomed down at me.

"Yes, it is, Mr. Myers. I brought your supper."

Hank Myers, his face red and sweaty, leaned down and scooped up his bundle. He lived in Inlet. Everyone knew him. He threw candy out of the window for the children on the stretches between towns. Sour balls and bull's-eyes and pieces of chewing gum.

"Here's the money, Mattie. Tell Weaver's mamma thank you for me." He tossed me some coins and a bull's-eye. The candy went in my pocket for Beth. I would put the coins in Weaver's mamma's change can. I knew that when she got home, she would empty it into the cigar box she kept under her bed—Weaver's college fund.

As I walked back to the Smiths' cart, I passed a couple from the city standing by their luggage. "Gee whiz, Trudy, hold on, will you?" I heard the man say impatiently. "I don't see a porter anywhere. Ah! There's a darky. You, boy! I need some help over here!"

Weaver was farther down the platform, but he heard the man. He turned around and I saw a bad look in his eyes. One I knew too well. It was the kind of look horses will get when they are young and saddle shy and would rather dash themselves to pieces than be broken by a rider.

I skirted around the man, caught up with Weaver, and took his sleeve. "Don't pay him any mind," I said, pulling him along. "Let him stand there and bellow, the ignorant fool—"

"You! Sam! I said I need help over here!"

Weaver shook me off. He turned around and smiled. A huge, horrible smile. "Why, sure, Mistuh Boss, suh!" he hollered. "I be right along, suh, right along! On de double!"

"Weaver!" his mother called. Her voice sounded frightened.

"Weaver, don't!" I hissed, not knowing what he was going to do but knowing from experience that it wouldn't be smart or good.

"Here I is, suh!" he said, bowing to the couple.

"Take my bags to that wagon," the man said, pointing at a waiting buckboard.

"Right away, boss!"

Weaver picked up the largest one, a sleek leather suitcase with shiny brass clasps, lifted it over his head, and threw it on the ground.

"Hey!" the man yelled.

"Lan' sakes! I sure is sorry, suh! I'se one clumsy darky, all right. Don't worry, Mistuh Suh, I'll fix it. Yessuh!" Weaver said. And then he hauled off and kicked the suitcase. So hard that it whizzed across the platform, hit the front of the station, and sprang open. Clothes flew everywhere. He kicked it again. "Yes, suh! Right away, suh! I'se coming, suh! Sho nuff!" he shouted.

The man shouted, too. So did his wife. And Weaver's mamma. Everyone else cleared out of the way. And still Weaver kicked the bag. Over and over again. Across the platform and back. And then the conductors were hurrying out of the station, where they'd gone for a cup of coffee, and Mr. Pulling, too, and Mr. Myers was jumping down from the train, yelling and waving, and in my panic I thought about Weaver's father. And I imagined what Weaver must have seen. White hands on black skin. So many white hands. And I knew that the men running toward us would only make things worse. So I jumped between Weaver and the suitcase just as he was winding up another kick.

"Please, Weaver," I said, flinching. "Stop."

And he did. He turned away at the last possible second and kicked a mailbag instead of me. I swallowed. Hard. Weaver is slender but he is strong, and that kick might have shattered my ankle. I took him by his wrists very gently and pushed him backward, one step at a time. His arms were stiff and trembly. The breath was rasping from his throat. I could smell anger coming off him. And grief. I pushed him over to his mamma's cart, then I gathered the man's clothing and tried my best to shake the dirt out of it. I folded it all neatly and put it back in the suitcase. The case was badly dented, but the clasps still worked. I closed it and placed it with the rest of the man's luggage.

"Now, see here! This won't do at all! He damaged my things!" the man sputtered.

"He's sorry, sir. He didn't mean to."

"He certainly did mean to! He ought to at least pay to have my clothing laundered. And for a new suitcase, too. Do you have a cop in this place? A sheriff or something? I don't want to make trouble, but he really ought to—"

"No, please!" It was Weaver's mamma. Her eyes were frantic. She was clutching her chicken money. "I'll pay you—"

But she didn't get to finish her sentence, because another voice cut in. "No, mister, you surely don't want to make trouble. Best be on your way before his pa shows up. Or his brothers. He's got five. And each one of 'em's meaner than the next."

It was Royal. He was standing on the platform, arms crossed over his chest. He stood tall. His shoulders were broad under his shirt, his arms were thick and powerful. Jim and Will were right behind him. I didn't know where he'd come from. I looked past him and saw his father's buckboard with milk cans in it. He must have been delivering.

The man looked Royal up and down. He looked at Mr. Pulling and Mr. Myers, whose faces betrayed nothing, and then he looked up the tracks as if expecting to see Weaver's father and his five ornery brothers bearing down on him. He shot his cuffs. "Well!" he said. "Well." Then he picked up his suitcase, took his wife by the elbow, and stalked off to the waiting buckboard. I saw him put coins into the driver's hand and point at his remaining bags.

"That boy's going to bring a world of trouble on his head one day," Mr. Pulling said. "Everything all right now?"

"Sure is," Royal said. Then, after Mr. Pulling left, he said, "You like a ride home, Matt?"

"Thank you, Royal, but I'd better see to Weaver."

He shrugged.

I ran back over to the Smiths' cart. Weaver's mamma had Weaver off to one side and was giving him the tongue-lashing of the century. She was furious. Was she ever! Her eyes were blazing and she was shaking her finger at him and slapping her palm against his chest. I couldn't hear it all, but I did hear that "damn fools who get themselves locked up in jail can't go to college." Weaver's eyes were on the ground, his head was hanging. He raised it for a few seconds, long enough to say something to her, and then in an instant all the rage left her and she went limp like a popped tire and started crying and Weaver put his arms around her.

I didn't think I should intrude, so I dropped the money from Mr. Myers's supper into the change can, took my schoolbooks out of the cart, and ran to catch up with Royal. He was just crossing the tracks in the buckboard. Jim and Will were in the back, sitting on milk cans. I figured I was safe. Royal wouldn't try to kiss me or touch what he wasn't supposed to with the two of them there. I felt relieved. And disappointed.

"Can I still have that ride?" I called to him.

"Sure."

"You won't go too fast?"

"Get in, will you, Matt? Train's ready to pull out and I'm right in the way."

I ran around to the other side of the buckboard and climbed in. I was glad to sit down next to him. Glad to have his company on the way home. I was upset by what had happened and in need of someone to talk it over with. "Thank you, Royal," I said.

"For what? I'm on my way home anyway."

"For getting Weaver out of trouble."

"Looks like he's still got plenty," he said, glancing back at Weaver and his mother.

"I think his mamma's upset because of what happened to his pa," I said. Royal knew what had happened to Weaver's father; everyone did.

"Might well be," Royal said, urging his team across the tracks.

"Maybe that started off just like this suitcase thing did," I said, my emotions still churning.

"Maybe."

"With just a few words. And then a few more. And then the words turned into insults and threats and worse, and then a man was dead. Just because of words."

Royal was silent, chewing on all I'd said, I imagined.

"I know you told me words are just words, Royal, but words are powerful things—"

I felt a poke in my back. "Hey, Mattie . . ."

I turned around. "What, Jim? What do you want?" I asked, irritated.

"There goes Seymour! Ain't you going to wave?"

"Who?"

"Seymour, Mattie! Seymour Butts!"

Jim and Will howled with laughter. Royal didn't actually laugh, but he grinned. And I was silent the rest of the way home.

*D*ead. That's what I'll be if Cook catches me. In Ada's threadbare robe, my hair loose, walking down the hotel's main staircase as if I were a paying guest. We are only supposed to use the back stairs, but I'd have to walk right by Cook's bedroom to get to them and she's a light sleeper.

It's midnight. I hear the huge grandfather clock in the entry strike the hour. It's dark, but I don't dare light a lamp. There's a big summer moon, though, and the Glenmore has lots of windows, so I can see well enough to not fall down the stairs and break my neck.

The main house has four stories plus an attic. Forty rooms in all. When the hotel is fully booked, as it is this week, there are over a hundred people in the building. All strangers to one another, coming and going. Eating and laughing and breathing and sleeping and dreaming under the same roof.

They leave things behind sometimes, the guests. A bottle of scent. A crumpled handkerchief. A pearl button that fell off a dress and rolled under a bed. And sometimes they leave other sorts of things. Things you can't see. A sigh trapped in a corner. Memories tangled in the curtains. A sob fluttering against the windowpane like a bird that flew in and can't get back out. I can feel these things. They dart and crouch and whisper.

I get to the bottom of the staircase and listen. The only sound is the ticking of the clock. To my right is the dining room. It's dark and empty. Straight ahead, through the porch windows, I can see the boathouse and the lake, calm and still, its black surface silvered by the moon. I pray I don't run into anyone. Not Mrs. Morrison waiting up for her husband. Or Mr. Sperry doing the accounts as he does when he can't sleep. Or, God forbid, table six lurking in a corner like some horrible spider.

I walk under the antler chandelier in the foyer, and by the coat tree made of branches and deer hooves. I pass the hallway that leads to the parlor and get a fright when I see light spilling out of the room onto the hall carpet, but then I remember: That's where Grace Brown is laid out. Mrs. Morrison left a lamp burning because it's unkind to leave the dead all alone in the dark. They have darkness enough ahead of them.

I creep through the dining room toward the kitchen doors. The kitchen does not have many windows, and it takes my eyes a few seconds to adjust to the heavier darkness inside it. Slowly, Cook's worktable and her big, looming range come into focus. The cellar door is just to the left of them. I'm almost there when my foot catches on something and there's an earsplitting crash and then I'm under the worktable, quivering like one of Cook's aspics.

I wait for lights to come on and the sound of feet and angry voices, quickly rehearsing a story in my head, but no one comes. Cook is all the way upstairs and Mrs. Morrison's room is on the other side of the hotel and Mr. Morrison and Henry and Mr. Sperry must still be out searching in the woods and I am very lucky.

I crawl out from under the table and see that it is the rotten ice-cream churn that tripped me. I run the rest of the way to the cellar door, twist the knob, and . . . it's locked.

Now what? Grace Brown is gone and her letters should be, too. They're her love letters, they must be. They're private and no one should ever see them. I think about lighting the big gas range and holding them over a burner. I know if Cook caught me doing it, she would fire me on the spot, for the range is temperamental and the Glenmore is built of wood. There's always the lake, and for a moment I consider sneaking out to it and pitching the letters off the dock as I'd planned to do earlier, but it's not decent to run around outside in your nightclothes, and the search party could come back at any time. I'll have to wait until tomorrow when it will be busy and Cook will be distracted.

I leave the kitchen and head back to the attic. I tell my feet to keep going, to take me directly upstairs, but they have their own ideas. They take me into the parlor instead, and then to the little bedroom off of it. The bruises on Grace Brown's lips look darker in the lamplight, and the cut on her forehead looks meaner.

She probably hit her head on the gunwale as the boat

136

tipped, I tell myself. Or maybe she came up under the boat after she fell into the water and banged her head against it. Yes, that would explain it. That *does* explain it. I do not want to ponder this question any longer, for it brings too many others with it. I neaten Grace's skirt instead.

Her clothes are still damp. Her hair is, too. She had left a small valise in the foyer. Someone has placed it on the floor next to the bed. Along with a black silk jacket that Mr. Morrison found floating near the overturned boat. Carl Grahm's things are not here. He took them with him. I'd wondered, as I saw him and Grace walk across the lawn to the boathouse, *What kind of fool takes a suitcase and a tennis racket rowing?*

I am very sorry for Grace Brown, here amongst strangers. She should be in her mother's house, with her own things around and her family to sit up through the night with her. I decide it's only proper that I keep her company for a spell. I sit down in a wicker chair, wincing as it creaks, and stare at the picture on the wall and try to think of good things about the deceased, like you do at a wake. Grace Brown had a sweet face, that's a start. Sweet and gentle. She was a brunette. Small boned, with a pretty figure. I remember her eyes. They were gentle, too. And kind . . . and . . . and it's no good. All I can think about, though I am trying so hard not to, is that cut, livid and ugly, on her forehead.

I look at it—I can't help myself—and the questions I've kept penned up all day rush at me thumping and squealing like my pa's pigs at feeding time.

Why did Grace Brown give me her letters to burn? Why had she looked so sad? And Carl Grahm—was he Carl or was he Chester? Why did he write "Carl Grahm, Albany" in the register if Grace called him Chester and addressed her letters to "Chester Gillette, 17½ Main Street, Cortland, New York"?

I pull the letters from my pocket. I shouldn't do this; I know it's wrong, but so is that wound on Grace Brown's forehead. I slide the top letter out from under the ribbon, open it, and start to read. My eyes winnow out lines about friends and neighbors, travel plans and dresses, searching for my answers.

> *South Otselic, N.Y.*
> *June 19, 1906*
> *My Dear —*
>   *I have often heard the saying, 'it never rains but it pours,' but I never knew what it meant until to-day . . . When I got in Cincinnatus and just as we are starting for home I heard my sister was very ill. When I reached her home I sent my trunks and the carriage home and here I am. The house was full of friends and relatives crying and talking in little groups. I have a new niece, but the doctor has given up all hopes of my sister being up and strong for a year at least . . .*

I lean back in the chair and feel relief flooding through me. Grace Brown was sad because her sister was ill. And she and Chester had had a spat about the chapel and maybe she was still miffed at him and she wanted to burn the letters out of spite. And I don't know why he put a fake name in the register, but I don't care because none of this is any of my business. And then a line a bit lower down catches my eye and I'm reading again, when all I meant to do was fold the letter up and be done with it.

> *. . . Chester, I have done nothing but cry since I got here. If you were only here I would not feel so badly . . . I can't help thinking you will never come for me . . . Everything worries me and I am so frightened, dear . . . I will have my dresses made if I can and I will try and be very brave, dear . . . Chester, do you miss me and have you thought about everything to-day? . . . I get so lonesome, dear. You won't miss me as much on account of your work, but, oh dear— please write and tell me you will come for me . . . Please write often, dear, and tell me you will come for me before papa makes me tell the whole affair, or they will find it out for themselves. I can't just rest one single minute until I hear from you . . .*

I look out the open window. I can smell the pines and the roses and the lake on the night air, but even these sweet, familiar smells can't comfort me. Why did Grace want him to come for her? And why was she so frightened that he wouldn't? He had, hadn't he? He'd brought her to the Glenmore. And why do I care? Why?

Once, when I was eight years old and it was early December, I went out on the ice of Fourth Lake, though Pa had told me not to. "It's not solid yet," he'd said. "It won't be for some weeks. Stay off'n it." But it had looked solid to me and I wanted so much to play on it. So I did. I went running and sliding across it, going farther and farther out with each slide. When I was about thirty feet from the shore, I heard a long, shivering crack, and I knew that the ice was breaking under me and that I might well drown. There was no one to help me. I had sneaked off by myself, knowing that if Lawton or Abby found out where I was going, they would tell. I could see the Eagle Bay Hotel and several other camps from where I stood, but they were boarded up for the winter. I was all alone, and what I'd thought was firm beneath my feet was not. I turned around slowly ... very, very slowly ... and slid one foot toward the shore. For several long seconds nothing happened, and then there was another crack. I gasped and stood perfectly still. Then I slid my other foot forward. Nothing, then two more cracks, as sharp and sudden as gunshots. I sobbed out loud and peed down my leg, but I kept going, one small, sliding step at a time. When I was about six feet from the shore, the ice gave way and I fell into the frigid water up to my knees. I crashed through the remaining few feet of ice and ran home as fast as I could, dreading my pa's strap, but dreading frostbite more.

I feel like that now. Like there is nothing solid beneath my feet, like the ice is breaking all around me.

re · cou · ri · um · phor · a · tion

"Pa! Pa, come quick! There's a monster in the manure pile!"

"Stop shouting, Beth."

"But, Pa, there's a monster! I thought he was dead, but he's not! I poked him with a stick and he growled at me!"

"Elizabeth Gokey, what did I say about telling fibs?"

"I'm not, Pa. I swear! You've got to come and kill him. Quick! So we can get his sack of gold. He's got a sack of gold with him!"

I heard all this from the milk house, a room off the cow barn. I was pouring buckets of warm, foamy milk through a length of cheesecloth to strain out flies and bits of hay. I wiped my hands, clapped Pansy and her kittens out from under my feet, and went into the barn itself to see what the commotion was all about. Pa was walking toward the door. Abby was already outside. Lou was up in the hayloft, tossing down bales.

"What's going on?" I asked her.

"Beth's telling tales again," she said. "I hope she gets a licking."

I followed my family outside and around the back of the barn and saw, to my shock, that Beth was not telling tales at all. There was a man, a very dirty man with long, wild black hair, lying facedown in our manure pile. He was wearing dungarees, suspenders, and a plaid wool shirt. There was a large sack near him and a pair of Croghan boots with their laces knotted together.

Beth still had her stick. She prodded him with it. "Mr. Monster?" she whispered. "Mr. Monster, are you dead?"

The monster groaned. He turned over on his back, opened his bloodshot eyes, and winced at the light. "Ba da holy jeez, yes. Yes, I tink so," he said.

"Uncle Fifty?" Abby whispered.

"Uncle Fifty!" Beth shouted.

"Damn it, Francis!" my father barked. "Get up out of there!"

"B'jour, mon frère, b'jour. Tais-toi, eh? Ma tête, elle est très tendre..."

"C'est pas assez que tous que tu dis c'est de la merde, François? Tu veux coucher dans la merde, aussi?"

Only my uncle Fifty, my father's younger brother, can make him angry enough to speak French.

"Mathilde, allez à ma chambre—," Pa said to me, before he caught himself. "Go to my bedroom and get him some clothes. Don't let him in the house until he washes. Make him some coffee, too. Abby, go back in and finish straining the milk." He looked at his brother one more time, spat, then returned to the cows.

"Come on, Uncle Fifty, let's get you cleaned up," I said impatiently. By the time I got water boiled for a

142

bath and got the nits and tangles out of my uncle's hair, I'd be good and late for school. And Miss Wilcox was giving the last of the Regents exams.

Lou came running out. "Uncle Fifty!" she shouted. She looked at him and her smile changed to a frown. "Uncle Fifty, why are you sitting in the manure?"

"Because da manure, she warm," he said, getting to his feet. "I come last night, very late, Louisa. I don't wake up da whole house, no? So I sleep out here."

"You smell terrible!" Lou said, pinching her nose.

He did, too. Manure and whiskey fumes made an unholy combination.

"What? I smell sweet as da rose! You give your uncle François a beeg keese!" He put out his arms and staggered toward her, and she ran away squealing and laughing.

"Uncle Fifty . . . what's in that bag?" Beth asked, eyeing his satchel hopefully.

"In dere? Oh, noting. Just dirty clothes," he said. Beth's face fell.

"Uncle Fifty, you come on," I said. "I haven't got time for this. I've got important tests to take today."

"Test? What kine of test?"

"For my high school diploma. The last exams are today. I've been studying for months."

"Ba da holy jeez, Mathilde Gauthier! You wan smart girl for to take dese test. You go on to school. Your mamma will help me wid da bath."

"Oh, Uncle Fifty, where have you been? You haven't heard, have you?"

"Heard what? I been on da Saint Lawrence for wan year and den da Ausable and da Saint Regis, too."

I sighed. "Come on. Let's get the kerosene. There's lots to tell you. And none of it good."

I had Lou to help me, so I was able to get my uncle seen to quicker than I'd thought. I had to sit with him and hold his hand for a while, though, after I told him about my mother and brother. Uncle Fifty doesn't hold much back. When he's happy he laughs, and when he is heartbroken—as he was to hear my mamma had died—he cries like a child. Pa says that's because he is one.

I got to school two hours late. Classes were over for the rest of the students; it was just Weaver and myself going then. Miss Wilcox was standing outside the schoolhouse looking for me when I arrived. "I thought you weren't coming, Mattie! What happened?" she asked. "Weaver's on his second exam already."

I explained everything, settled myself, and started my tests. Each one was two hours long. We'd taken two yesterday and were taking three more today. When we finished, I felt pretty confident that I'd passed them. They were my best subjects, though—composition, literature, and history. Yesterday's—mathematics and science—had been harder. On the walk home Weaver told me he thought he'd done quite well on mathematics and history and fairly well on literature and science, but he was worried about composition. It would be another week until we found out our grades. I wondered again, as we walked, why I even bothered. I still had no way of getting myself to New York.

By the time I got home, it was nearly six o'clock. I had been so wrapped up in my exams, and in rehashing them with Weaver, that I'd forgotten all about my uncle. Until I smelled cooking. And heard music from a harmonica, and laughter. And saw lights blazing in the kitchen. It didn't smell, nor sound, nor even look like my house. Not at all.

"Ba cripes!" my uncle bellowed when I came in the door. He was clean, his hair was shorter, and his beard had been trimmed. He was wearing a fresh shirt and trousers and my mother's apron. "Where you been? Da supper, she ready since two weeks!"

"I'm sorry, Uncle Fifty," I said. "I had a lot of exams."

"You pass all your test?"

"I don't know. I hope so. I think so."

"Good! We make a drink to you den ..." He poured a short glass of whiskey, handed it to me, then lifted his glass. My pa was sitting by the fire with his own glass of whiskey. I looked at him uncertainly, but he nodded at me. "To Mademoiselle Mathilde Gauthier ... da first wan of all les Gauthiers to get a deeploma!" my uncle said, then knocked back the contents of his glass in one go. My pa did, too. I took one swallow and coughed myself breathless. It burned like the dickens. Poor man's vacation, Pa calls it. I'd never had a vacation, but if that's what one was like, I'd just as soon stay home. My sisters laughed at me and cheered. Beth blew on Uncle Fifty's harmonica. Uncle Fifty whooped. I felt my cheeks burn with whiskey and pride.

"Come on, Mattie, wash up, would you? We're starving!" Beth said. Only then did I notice the mess—the pots and pans on the stove, the sink full of bowls and dishes, the flour all over the floor, and Barney in his bed, gnawing on a big greasy bone.

Uncle Fifty had cooked a feast for us—a real lumberjack supper. He made us all sit down at the table, then he started pulling dishes out of the warming oven one after another. We could barely believe our eyes. There was fried pork and milk gravy speckled with bits of crackling, potatoes hashed with onions, baked beans flavored with smoky bacon, maple syrup, and mustard, hot biscuits, and a towering stack of pancakes stuck together with butter and maple sugar. There was not one green vegetable. Lumberjacks are not fond of them.

"Uncle Fifty, I didn't know you could cook," Abby said.

"I learn dis past weentair. Da cook on da Saint Regis job, he drop dead. Bad heart. All da lombairjock have to take turn cooking. I learn."

"You learned good, Uncle Fifty," Lou said, shoveling beans onto her plate. "You get an A-plus. Will you teach Mattie how to cook? She can only make mush and pancakes. And a pea soup that's so bad, it's more pee than soup."

Uncle Fifty roared. My sisters laughed. Especially Lou. Pa raised an eyebrow at her, but that didn't quiet her. She knew she was safe because our uncle was laughing.

"Don't mind them, Mattie," Abby said, petting me.

"You like my pea soup, don't you, Ab?" I asked, hurt.

She looked at me with her kind eyes. "No, Mattie, I don't. It's awful."

My family laughed harder then, even Pa cracked a smile, and I laughed, too, and then I ate until I thought I would burst out of my dress. And when we were all so stuffed that we were groaning, Uncle Fifty took a huge rhubarb pie out of the oven and we ate that, too, doused with fresh cream.

When dinner was over, my father and uncle went to sit in the parlor. Uncle Fifty took his whiskey bottle, his satchel, his Croghan boots, and a tin of mink oil with him.

Beth's eyes never left his satchel as he walked out of the room. "Do you really think he's got dirty clothes in there?" she whispered.

"I think the dishes need scraping," I said. "Get started."

We washed the dishes, wiped the table, and mopped the floor just as fast as we could so that we could go sit with our uncle. His visits were rare. He mostly lived in Three Rivers, Quebec, where he and my father were born, and only showed up every two or three years, when logging jobs brought him near.

By the time we settled ourselves in the parlor, Pa had made a fire in the cylinder stove. He was mending Pleasant's bellyband—he was always mending something Pleasant had broken—and Uncle Fifty was oiling his boots. My uncle is a riverman and a riverman's boots are his most prized possession. The soles, studded with calks—metal points—help him keep his footing as he walks on floating logs. The best ones are made in Croghan, New York. Pa used to tell Lawton never, ever fight with a riverman in the winter. If a man gets kicked by a frozen Croghan, he is a goner for sure.

Uncle Fifty drank his whiskey while he worked, and he told us stories—which is what we'd all been waiting for. He told us how a bear got into his bunkhouse a month before and all the jacks ran out except a man named Murphy, who was sleeping off a drunk. As the rest of the jacks watched through the window, the bear sniffed him, then licked his face. And Murphy, still sleeping, smiled and put his arms around the bear's neck and called him sweetheart. He told us about the raging glory of the river drives, when the ice went out and a dam was opened and thousands upon thousands of logs were sent through the sluice and downriver, churning and rolling, crashing against rocks, plunging down falls. He said the noise alone would take your breath away. He told us about the jams and the danger of breaking them up and how he'd been on a jam when it suddenly gave way and then had to ride a log half a mile down the Saint Lawrence before he could leap to safety. And how two other men didn't make it and how their bodies looked when they were finally pulled out, all twisted and smashed. He told us that he was the number one champion birler on the Saint Lawrence, and that he could knock any jack off any log, any jack at all. Except for one—my pa.

It had been years since Pa worked a drive, but I could tell from the look on his face as my uncle talked that he missed it. He flapped a hand at the stories and tried to seem all disapproving, but I saw the pride in his eyes as Uncle Fifty told us that there was no one more skillful with a bateau, no one faster or more fearless. He said my pa was the most surefooted riverman he'd ever seen, that he stuck to logs like bark. He said he'd seen him dance a hornpipe on a log once, and do a cartwheel and a handspring, too.

They were whoppers, my uncle's stories, every one. We knew it and we didn't care. We just loved the telling. My uncle has a beautiful North Woods voice. You can hear the dry bite of a January morning in it and the rasp of wood smoke. His laughter is the sound of a creek under ice, low and rushing. His full name is François Pierre, but Pa told us his initials really stand for Fifty Percent, because you can only believe half of anything he says.

Pa and Fifty are four years apart in age. Pa is forty and my uncle thirty-six. They have the same rugged faces, the same blue eyes and black hair, but that is where the resemblance ends. Uncle Fifty is always smiling and my father is always grim. Fifty drinks more than he should. Pa only drinks on occasion. Fifty sounds like the Frenchman he is. My father sounds like he was born and bred in New York and has no more French in him than Barney the dog does.

I once asked my mother why Pa never spoke French, and she said, "Because the scars run too deep." I thought she must have meant the ones on his back. Pa's stepfather put them there with a belt. Pa's real father died when he was six. His mother had seven other children and married the first man who asked her, because she had to feed them. Pa never talked about his mother or his stepfather, but Uncle Fifty did. He told us that the man beat them and their mother for nothing. Because the supper was too cold or too hot. Because the dog was in when he was supposed to be out, or out when he was supposed to be in. He did not speak French and wouldn't allow it to be spoken in the house, because he thought his stepchildren would use it to talk behind his back. My father forgot once and that's how he got the scars. Uncle Fifty said their stepfather used the wrong end of his belt and the buckle took the skin clean off. I try my best to remember those scars whenever Pa is harsh. I try to remember that hard knocks leave dents.

Pa ran away from home when he was only twelve and found work as a chore boy in a lumber camp. He worked his way south, into New York, and never went back to Quebec. His mother died some years back, and his brothers and sisters scattered. Uncle Fifty was the only one he ever saw.

Our uncle kept us entertained with his stories for hours. But around eleven o'clock, Beth got sleepy-eyed and Lou started yawning and Pa told us it was time for bed. As we were all standing up to say good night, Beth cast one last, hopeful glance at our uncle's satchel. Uncle Fifty saw her do it and smiled. He opened the bag and said, "Well, I plaintee tired myself. I tink I get out my nightshirt now and... ba gosh! Wat is in here? Where you tink all dese present come from? I don't reemembair to buy no present!"

Beth jumped up and down. Lou squealed. Even Abby was excited. I was, too. Uncle Fifty always gave the nicest presents. Pa said he drove the peddlers crazy, making them unpack everything, choosing this and that, then changing his mind and starting all over again. He never gave horrible gifts, like handkerchiefs or mints. He always picked out something special. That night he started with Beth and worked his way up, always pretending he'd forgotten to get something for the next one in line. It was agony waiting for your turn and agony when it came. We didn't get many presents and weren't used to the drama and anticipation. Beth received her very own harmonica with an instruction book and loved it so much, she burst into tears. For Lou, there was a carved wooden box containing a dozen hand-tied fishing flies. Abby was given a gold-plated locket, which made her flush pink with pleasure. And then it was my turn.

"Oh no! I forget someting for Mathilde!" my uncle cried, looking at me. He dug in his bag. "No, no, wait! I have someting..." He pulled out a dirty wool sock, which made everyone laugh. "Or dis..." Out came his red long johns. "Or maybe she like dis..."

He placed a narrow ivorine box in my hands, and when I opened it, I gasped. It was a pen. A real honest-to-God fountain pen, with a metal nib and a silver-plated case and cap. It was as shiny as a minnow in its bed of black felt. I had never had a pen in my life—only pencils—and I couldn't even imagine what it would feel like to put words onto paper in rich blue ink instead of smudgy lead. I could feel my eyes welling up as I looked at the pen, and I had to blink once or twice before I could thank my uncle.

Pa was next—he got a new wool shirt—then Uncle Fifty pulled out a fearsome hunting knife and a pretty beaded bag. "For Lawton. And your mamma," he said. "Maybe you geev heem da knife when he come home, eh?"

"But Uncle Fifty, he ain't never . . . ," Beth started to say. A look from Abby silenced her.

"And maybe you girls can share da purse."

We all nodded and said we would, but no one took the purse and no one touched the knife. We thanked our uncle again, and hugged him and kissed him, and then it really was time for bed. I picked up all the brown wrapping paper, smoothing it out for another use, as my sisters made their trips to the outhouse.

While I waited for my turn, I noticed the fire in the cylinder stove was low and went to fetch more wood for it. On my way back, just as I was about to push the parlor door open, I heard my uncle say, "Why you stay here squeezing cow teets all day long, Michel? Wat kine life dat be for a reevairman? Why you not come back and drive da logs?"

Pa laughed. "And let four girls raise themselves? All that whiskey's addled your brain."

"Your Ellen, she make you come off da reevair. Don't tink I don't know. But she gone now, and I tink da reevair be a better ting for you. You like dis farming?"

"I do."

I heard my uncle snort. "Now who tell da tales, eh?"

About ten years ago, my mother and father had had a terrible, terrible fight. We were living in Big Moose Station then. Pa had just come home from a spring drive. He had Ed LaFountain, another woodsman, with him. They got to drinking after supper and Mr. LaFountain got to telling stories and he told one about my pa working a bateau and how close he and his crew had come to getting swallowed up by a loosening jam.

Mamma went crazy when she heard it. Before Pa had left for the woods that year, she'd made him promise he wouldn't work the jams, that he'd stay on the shore. It was too dangerous, she said. Men were killed all the time. Jams tended to give way with no warning, and unless the oarsman could get his crew back into the boat and row clear in time, the boat would be pulled under. Pa apologized to her. He said he'd only done it for the money. Most woodsmen made less than a dollar a day, but a good oarsman got three and a half, sometimes four, and Pa was one of the best.

Mamma didn't want to hear any apologies, though. She was furious. She told him she wanted him to come out of the woods for good and work for her father in his sawmill. They could live in Inlet, she said, right in the village, near Josie. He'd make good money. The children would be closer to a school. Things would be easier for everyone.

"Never, Ellen," he'd said. "You know better than to ask me."

"Papa said he would forgive everything, Michael. He said he'd help us."

"*He* would forgive? Forgive what? Forgive me for falling in love with you?"

"For us running away. For not..."

"*He's* the one needs forgiving, not me. He's the one called me no-account French trash. The one who said he'd rather see you dead than married to me."

"What are you trying to do, Michael, make me a widow? I won't have you on a bateau!"

"I ain't working for your father, and I ain't—" Pa didn't get to finish his sentence, because Mamma slapped him. Good and hard. My mamma, who never even raised her voice to him. She slapped him and put on her coat and made us put on our coats, and she put us in a buckboard at the train station and paid the man to take us to Aunt Josie's.

We stayed with my aunt for three weeks, and she refused to let my father in for two of them. But then one day, Pa came to the door and pushed her aside and got my mamma to go for a walk with him. Lawton cried something fierce; he didn't want her to go. When they came back, Mamma gave Pa all her jewelry—all the pretty things her parents had given her before she married. Pa went to Tuttle's, a secondhand store in Old Forge, the following day and traded it all for cash money. And the next thing we knew, he was clearing trees on sixty acres of land he'd bought in Eagle Bay. He built us a house from the trees he felled—a real house, not some pokey log cabin with hemlock bark for a roof. He had the trees milled into planks at Hess's sawmill in Inlet, not at my grandfather's mill or my uncle's. He built a barn and a smokehouse and an icehouse, too. And though he did haul lumber out of the woods in the winter to make extra money, he never worked a river drive again.

"And someting else," my uncle continued, "why you don't teach your girls to speak French?"

"They have no use for it," Pa said gruffly. "And neither do I."

"Dey be French girls, Michel. Dey be Gauthiers"— he pronounced it Go-*chay*—"not Gokey. Gokey! Ba jeez, what da hell is Gokey?"

Pa sighed. "It's the way they say it here. The way they wrote it on the tax rolls. It's easier, Francis. I've told you all this before. Lord, but you're a pain in the ass. You never let anything go."

"Me? You a pot who tell da kettle he's black! She gone, Michel. Your Ellen, she dead."

"I know that, Francis."

"But you not let her go! You bleed for her in your heart. You make beeg sorrow. I see it in your face, in your eyes. How you walk. How you talk. She gone, but you still here, Michel, and your girls, dey still here. Don't you see dis?"

"Anything else you want to bust my nuts about, Fran?"

"Yes, der is. Why your son leave, eh?"

There was no answer.

"I tink I know. I tink because you wan miserable son-bitch, dat's why. I see dat you are. You never a barrel of monkey, Michel, but you better den dis. What da hell wrong wid you? Dose girls, dey lose someone, too. Dey lose der mamma, den der brothair. But dey not turn into miserable stinking ghost like you."

"You've had too much whiskey, Francis. As usual."

"Not so much dat I don't know what I see."

"There's plenty you don't see."

Pa came out then, on his way to the outhouse, and I pretended only to be bringing the wood and not eavesdropping.

"I am proud of you, Mathilde, for all dese test you take. Very proud," Fifty said, as I opened the door to the cylinder stove.

"Thank you, Uncle Fifty." I was pleased that he said it, but his words made me sad, too. I wished my father could have told me he was proud of me.

"What you do now wid all dese test? You be teechair?"

I shook my head, put two logs in the stove, and closed the door. "No, Uncle Fifty. You need more schooling for that."

He thought about that, then said, "Why you don't go for dis schooling? You plaintee smart girl. I bet you da smartest girl in da whole nord contree. Dis schooling, it cost money?"

"The school doesn't. But the train ticket and clothes and books do."

"How much? Twentee dollair? Thirtee? I give you da money."

I smiled at him. His offer was so kind, but I knew he'd spent most of his stake, if not all of it, on the supper and our extravagant presents. He probably only had five or ten dollars left to his name, all of which he'd need to get himself back into the woods to his next job. "Good night, Uncle Fifty," I said, getting up to kiss his cheek. "I'm glad you've come to see us. We missed you."

"You tink I don't have it, but you see," he said, winking at me. "I don't just tell de tale. Not always."

I was back in the kitchen when Barney started whining, so I opened the back door and let him out. "You stay out of the garden, you hear?" I told him. I waited till Pa came back in, then I made a trip to the outhouse myself. Barney was waiting for me by the shed steps when I'd finished. I got him settled, then made my way upstairs to my own bed.

Lawton was the one who discovered that voices in the parlor carry right through the wall into the stairwell. The knowledge came in handy around Christmas, when we wanted to find out if there would be any presents. I could hear my father and uncle still talking as I walked up the steps.

"Francis, you spent your entire stake, didn't you? On the supper and the presents and this bottle here, and God knows how much whiskey wherever you were last night."

Pa's voice was disapproving. *Why, oh why is he always*

so sour? I wondered. A wonderful supper and presents, and he still can't say anything nice.

"No, I deed not."

"I don't believe you."

"Well den, look here, Meester Poleeseman..." I couldn't hear anything for a few seconds, then, "...a bankair's draft for wan hondred dollair. What you say now, eh?"

"A banker's draft?" Pa said.

"A banker's draft?" I whispered. *My goodness, he really does have the money,* I thought. He has a hundred dollars and he's going to give me some of it and I am going to college after all. I'm going to Barnard. I'm going to New York City.

"Dat's right. Da boss, he give us our money one-half in cash, one-half in dis paper."

"I'd say he's looking out for you, Fran. You going to hold on to it for a change? Put it in a bank instead of pissing it all away in some Utica whorehouse?"

"I have someting in mind for it. You be very surprise."

Silence. Then, "Francis, you didn't go making any woman promises, did you? That gal up to Beaver River, the one you proposed to on your last spree, she still thinks you're going to marry her. Asks me when you're coming back every time I see her."

"You wait and see what I do. Dat's all I say. In five, six day, I go to Old Forge and cash dis paper. Den you be surprise, indeed. Now, Michel...where is dat whiskey? Where da hell she go?"

I nearly flew the rest of the way up the staircase. I hadn't told anyone in my family about Barnard. I hadn't seen the point, since I didn't think I would ever get to go, but right then, I wanted to tell Abby powerfully bad. I couldn't, though. We all slept in the same room. Lou and Beth would hear and they both have big mouths. One of them would tell Pa for sure, and I didn't want him to know until I was ready to go. Until I was sure of a room in Miss Annabelle Wilcox's home and I had my things packed and thirty dollars in my pocket. Pa had knocked me out of my chair for buying a composition book. He'd swung a peavey at Lawton. I wasn't going to give him the chance to swing one at me. I pictured the look on his face as I told him I was leaving, and I was glad at the imagining. I was. He'd be furious, but only because he was losing a pair of hands. He wouldn't miss me one bit, but that was all right. I wouldn't miss him, either.

As I burrowed down under the covers in the bed I shared with Lou, I realized it had been such a long, eventful day that I had completely forgotten to look up a word in my dictionary. It was too late now; I'd have to go all the way back downstairs to the parlor to do it and I was too tired. So I made up my own word. *Recouri-umphoration*. *Re* for "again," and *cour* for "courage" and a bit of *triumph* tacked on, too, for good measure. *Maybe it will get into the dictionary one day,* I thought. *And if it does, everyone will know its meaning: to have one's hope restored.*

fur · tive

"How about wintergreen hearts, Mattie? Should I get those as well as lemon drops? Abby likes them, too. Lou likes the horehound candy. There's bull's-eyes, too; what about bull's-eyes?"

"Why don't you get a few of each?" I said. "Just stand out of the way, Beth, so folks can get around you."

The two of us were on the pickle boat with a dozen other people, tourists mainly. We'd just dropped off four cans of milk and three pounds of butter. We'd received no money for them. Pa had bartered with Mr. Eckler for a side of bacon earlier in the week, and the delivery was payment against it. As I waited for Beth to make her choice, I watched the other people on the boat. A man was buying fishing line. Two girls were picking out postcards. Others were buying groceries for their camps.

When I had bought my composition book from Mr. Eckler a few weeks before, I'd only spent forty-five cents of the sixty cents I'd made picking fiddleheads. I still had fifteen cents that I hadn't given to Pa, and I was using it that afternoon to buy candy for my sisters. Abby had her monthlies and was feeling awfully blue. She'd had the cramp something wicked that morning and had to lie down until it passed, and Pa asked me why she wasn't in the barn milking with the rest of us like he always does because he forgets, and then I had to explain and he got mad at me because it made him embarrassed. Cripes, it wasn't my fault. What did he go and have four girls for?

I thought some lemon drops would be just the thing to cheer Abby up. It would be a *furtive* purchase, as I really should have given the money to Pa, but after he'd hit me, I'd decided I wouldn't. *Furtive*, my word of the day, means doing something in a stealthy way, being sly or surreptitious. *Sneaky* would be another way of putting it. I did not wish to become a sneak, but sometimes one had no choice. Especially when one was a girl and craved something sweet but couldn't say why, and had to wait till no one was looking to wash a bucket of bloody rags, and had to say she was "under the weather" when really she had cramps that could knock a moose over, and had to listen to herself be called "moody" and "weepy" and "difficult" when really she was just fed up with sore bosoms and stained drawers and the fact that she couldn't just live life in the open, swaggering and spitting and pissing up trees like a boy.

That fifteen cents was all the money I had in the world right then, but I felt I could afford to be generous with it. Uncle Fifty had left for Old Forge that morning. He planned to stay there overnight and return on the morning train. I'd have my thirty dollars by dinnertime the next day. He'd only been gone half a day, but we missed him already. It had been wonderful having him with us all week. He pulled stumps and rocks with Pa and helped us with the milking, too. The evening milking, not the morning one. He wasn't very lively most mornings. His head usually hurt him. He perked up as the day went on, though, and at night he made us special desserts—*tarte au sucre,* which is a pie made out of maple sugar; or dried apple fritters with cinnamon; or doughy raisin dumplings boiled in maple syrup. After supper he'd sit down with his whiskey and pour himself glass after glass. The liquid leaped and sparkled as it left the bottles, and once it got into my uncle, it made him sparkle, too. He laughed loudly, and played his harmonica, and told us stories every night, like Scheherezade come to life in our parlor. We couldn't get enough of him. I would watch him as he chased Beth around the kitchen—mimicking the snarls of an angry wolverine, or as he staggered back and forth, knees buckling under the weight of a phantom buck—and find it almost impossible to believe that he was related to my quiet, frowning father.

"I think I'm going to get some coconut drops, too, Mattie," Beth said, still deliberating. "Or maybe some King Leo sticks. Or Necco's."

"All right, just don't be all day," I told her.

I saw the Loomises' buckboard pull up to the dock. Royal was driving. I wondered how he managed to be so handsome no matter what he was doing—plowing, walking, driving, whatever. He looked better dirty and sweaty in a pair of worn trousers and a frayed cotton shirt than most men did when they'd bathed, shaved, and put on a three-piece suit. I thought about the kiss he'd given me, and the thinking alone made me feel warm and swoony. Just like all those silly, fluttery girls in the stories in *Peterson's Magazine*.

Royal's mother was with him. They didn't see me. Beth and I were on the far side of the boat. Mrs. Loomis got out, and he handed her down a basket of eggs and a large crock of butter. She boarded the pickle boat and gave them to Mr. Eckler. He gave her a dollar bill in return. She thanked him and returned to the dock.

"All right, I'm ready," Beth said. She'd put her candies in a small brown bag.

"Go pay, then," I said, giving her my money.

She trotted to the back of the boat and handed Charlie Eckler the bag. "I'm going to the circus next week. The one in Boonville," I heard her tell him.

"Are you, dolly?"

"Yes, sir. My uncle promised to take me. He went to Old Forge this morning, but he's coming back tomorrow and then he's going to take me. Me and Lou both."

"Well, you'll have a fine time, I'm sure. That'll be ten cents."

Mr. Eckler asked her if she was going to see the two-headed man and the snake boy. She said she was going to see everything there was to see, her uncle Fifty said she could. I barely heard them. I was watching Royal. He was talking to John Denio, a teamster for the Glenmore. They were nodding and laughing. His smile was as warm as fresh biscuits on a winter morning. I couldn't take my eyes off him. Had someone that handsome really kissed me? I wondered. Or had I dreamed it? I found myself wishing that I was pretty like Martha Miller, so that he would kiss me again someday. And then I wondered if he'd miss me at all when I went away to college. And if maybe he'd want to write me and then I could write him back.

As I continued to moon, his mother climbed back into the buckboard and settled herself. Mr. Denio made small talk with them for a few more minutes, then headed toward the dock to pick up some guests. As soon as he left them, Mrs. Loomis fished in her pocket for the money Mr. Eckler had given her, then handed it to Royal. She said something to him, and he nodded and put the dollar bill in his pocket. And then she turned her head and looked all around herself and caught me watching. Her eyes narrowed, and if eyes could talk, hers would have said, "Mind your own damn business, Mattie Gokey." I thought it was very strange, as I did not care one hoot what Mrs. Loomis did with her egg money.

I watched them head up the drive and across the railroad tracks, and then Beth handed me a nickel change and we jumped down off the boat onto the dock.

"Tell your pa I should have his bacon by tomorrow, Mattie."

"I will, Mr. Eckler. Thanks."

We climbed into our buckboard and I told Pleasant to giddyap, and of course he didn't budge until I told him five more times and finally snapped him a good one with the reins. The ride home was uneventful, but when I turned the buckboard into our drive, I got quite a surprise. There was an automobile in it. A Ford. I knew who it belonged to. I maneuvered Pleasant around it, got the buckboard into the barn and Pleasant into the pasture, then went inside. When I opened the kitchen door, I saw Lou and Abby sitting on the staircase, leaning toward the wall.

"What's going on?" I asked.

"Miss Wilcox is in the parlor with Pa," Abby whispered. "She brought your exam results. You got an A-plus on your English literature and composition tests, an A in history, a B in science, and a B-minus in mathematics. Her and Pa are talking about you. She says you have genius in you and that you got into college and that Pa should let you go."

"Jeezum, Matt, I didn't know you had a genius in you," Lou said, wide-eyed. "You kept him hid real good."

Lou's backhanded compliment didn't even register. My heart had sunk to someplace down around my ankles. Miss Wilcox meant well, I knew she did, but I also knew Pa. She'd never get him to say yes; she'd only rile him. Why, oh why, had she come today? Right before my uncle was due to give me the money? Tomorrow I wouldn't need Pa's say-so, because I'd have thirty dollars in my pocket and that was all the say-so anybody needed, but I didn't need him furious at me in the meantime.

I sat down next to Lou on the step below Abby. Beth sat below us and passed out candy as if we were all spectators at some theater show. I had no appetite for sweets just then. I was busy straining my ears, trying to hear what was being said.

"...she's gifted, Mr. Gokey. She has a unique voice. An artist's voice. And she could make something more of herself, much more, if she were allowed—"

"She don't need to make something more. She's fine as she is. There ain't a thing wrong with her."

"She could be a writer, sir. A real one. A good one."

"She's already a writer. She writes stories and poems in them notebooks of hers all the time."

"But she needs the challenge of a real college curriculum, and the guidance of talented teachers, to improve. She needs exposure to emerging voices, to criticism and theory. She needs to be around people who can nurture her talent and develop it."

There was a silence. As I sat there on the stairs, I could picture my father's face. There would be anger on it as there so often is, but underneath it, there would be uncertainty and the painful shyness he has around educated people and their big words. My heart suddenly turned traitor on me, and I wanted to take Miss Wilcox by the arm and drag her out of the parlor and tell her to leave my pa alone.

"She wants to go, Mr. Gokey. Very badly," Miss Wilcox said.

"Well, I blame you for that, ma'am. You went and put ideas in her head. I haven't got the money to send her. And even if I did, why would I send my girl where she don't know anyone? Away from her home and her family, with nobody to look after her?"

"She's a sensible young woman. She would get along fine in New York. I know she would."

"She's got a flighty streak in her. Got it from her mamma. She was flighty, too."

"Mrs. Gokey never gave me that impression."

"Well, she was. When she was younger. Round Mattie's age. It's what got her married to me. It's what got her sixty acres of stumps and rocks, and a headstone at thirty-seven."

"Surely not, Mr. Gokey. I only visited with your wife on two or three occasions, but my reading of her was a woman who loved—"

"Your *reading* of her?"

Oh, Lord, I thought. I nearly got to my feet, then realized he couldn't possibly have his peavey with him. Not in the parlor.

"People ain't books, Miss Wilcox. What's inside 'em ain't all typewrit on the page for you to read. Now, if you're about through, ma'am, I've got plowing to do."

There was a silence again, then: "I am. Good-bye, Mr. Gokey. Thank you for your time."

I heard Miss Wilcox's brisk step in the hallway, and then she was gone. She was the kind of woman who came and went through the front door, not the back.

"Oh, Mattie, don't go! You won't, will you? I'd miss you so," Beth fretted. She put her arms around my neck and kissed me with her sticky candy lips.

"Hush, Beth. Don't be so selfish," Abby scolded.

Next thing I knew, Pa was in the kitchen. We all scrambled to our feet. "I guess the four of you just happened to be coming down the stairs all at once," he said. "Wouldn't be you were listening in on conversations you had no business listening in on?" No one said a word. "Abby, you salt the butter yet? Lou, you muck out the cow stalls? Beth, have the chickens been fed?"

My sisters scattered. Pa looked at me. "You couldn't tell me yourself?" he asked.

His eyes were hard and his voice was, too, and all the soft feelings I'd had for him only moments before swirled away like slop water down a drain.

"What for, Pa? So you could say no?"

He blinked at me and his eyes looked hurt, and I thought, just for a second, that he was going to say something tender to me, but no. "Go, then, Mattie. I won't stop you. But don't come back if you do," he said. Then he walked out of the kitchen, slamming the door behind him.

ses · qui · pe · da · lian

"*Sesquipedalian* is a funny word, Daisy," I whispered to the cow. "It means one and a half feet in length, but it also means given to using long words. It's such a long word itself, though, that it is what it accuses others of being. It is a hypocrite, Daisy, well and truly, but I still like it. And I plan on dropping it into a conversation or two when I'm in New York City."

Daisy chewed her cud. If she had an opinion about my word of the day, she kept it to herself. My cheek was pressed into her warm belly, my hands were busy squeezing milk from her udder, and my lips were whispering all my secrets to her. I had told her all about Uncle Fifty and how he was coming back from Old Forge any minute now and bringing me the money I needed to go to Barnard.

It was near the end of April and twelve of our twenty cows had calved and we were drowning in milk. Morning and night, the milk was poured into wide, deep pans and allowed to set. When left long enough, the cream separated from the milk and rose to the top of the pan. Then it was skimmed off. The leftover milk went into large, two-handled cans for delivery. We sold some of the cream just as it was, the rest we churned into butter. The buttermilk—which is what was left after the butter came—was fed to our pigs and chickens. Nothing was ever wasted.

"Mattie?"

I turned my head. "Beth, don't stand right behind a cow. You know better than that."

"Daisy wouldn't kick me. She never would."

"But Pa will if he sees you that close to a cow's hind end. Now step over."

"But Mattie..."

"What, Beth? What's wrong?"

"Why isn't Uncle Fifty back? He said he'd be back from Old Forge by dinnertime today and it's already gone five. He told me he was going to take me to see the circus in Boonville. He said he was."

"He'll be back. He probably just got talking with someone and took a later train. You know what he's like. I bet he came across an old friend, that's all. He'll be back soon."

"Are you sure, Matt?"

"I'm sure," I said. I wasn't. I didn't want to admit it, not even to myself, but I was just as worried as Beth was. Our uncle should have been back hours before.

"Hallooo!" a man's voice shouted from the barn door.

"There he is, Beth! See? I told you!"

"It's not Uncle Fifty, Matt. It's Mr. Eckler," she said, skipping off to see him.

"Well, hello there, my girl! Your pa around?"

"I'm right here, Charlie," Pa called out. "You're up this end of the lake awful late, aren't you?"

"I am at that. It's so busy these days, I'm not getting back to Old Forge before six, seven o'clock at night. I brought you the bacon we traded for. It's a nice piece of meat. And I wanted to ask if I can get five cans from you tomorrow instead of four, and any extra butter you've got."

"I've got the milk. Cows are giving about fifteen pounds of milk a day each. Got plenty. Should have the butter, too."

"Glad to hear it. Well, I've gotta get back, but say . . . I saw your brother this morning."

"What was he doing? Taking the slow train home?"

"No, not quite. He was on a fast train, if you take my meaning. Bound for Utica."

"Poleaxed?"

"Yup."

I felt all the breath go out of me. I leaned my forehead against Daisy and squeezed my eyes closed.

My father spat a mouthful of tobacco juice. "Bet he don't even make it to Utica. Bet he don't get past Remsen," he said.

"Pa?" Beth's voice was quavery.

"In a minute, Beth."

"All right then, Michael. I'll see you tomorrow."

"Night, Charlie."

"Pa!"

"What, Beth?"

"What's *poleaxed* mean? Where's Uncle Fifty? He said he'd take me to the circus, Pa. Ain't he coming back? He said he'd take me, Pa."

"You can't believe everything your uncle says."

"But he said he'd take me!"

"Beth, he ain't going to and that's that, so hush."

"But he promised! I hate him, Pa!" she sobbed. "I hate him!"

I was sure Beth was going to get cracked for that, but Pa only said, "No more than he's going to hate himself in a day or two." Then he told her to stop her noise and take the bacon in to Abby.

I sat slumped on my milking stool, knowing that the last chance I had to go to Barnard was on its way into the till of some bartender. Knowing that my uncle was off on a three-day spree. Or four. Or five. Or however many days it took to spend a hundred dollars. It was a hard and hopeless thing.

Recouriumphoration. What a stupid, stupid word. I'd do better thinking up a word to describe how it felt to have your hopes dashed over and over again, rather than restored. *Dolipeatalous* or *vicipucious* or *nullapressive* or ... *bitter*. Yes, *bitter* did the job just fine.

"What is it?" a brusque voice suddenly said. It was Pa. He was standing next to Daisy, frowning down at me.

"Nothing," I said, wiping my eyes. I grabbed my bucket, brushed past him, and went to work in the milk house. I heard his footsteps behind me as I poured the milk into a separating pan.

"Mattie, I don't know what Francis might've said to you, but when he promises things, it's the whiskey promising, not him. You know that, don't you? He don't mean bad; he can't help it." I felt his eyes on my back, heard him take a step toward me.

"I'm fine, Pa," I said sharply. "I'll be along."

He stood where he was for a few seconds, then left. I was glad for once that straining the milk was my job. Glad of the time it took to pour it into the pans. Glad no one could see me sitting on a bench and bawling. Served me right, my uncle breaking his promise to me, seeing as I'd been only too eager to break the promise I'd made.

When I'd cried myself dry, I wiped my face, covered the milk pans with cheesecloth, and left the barn for the kitchen. Abby had started the supper. There would be no apple fritters or *tarte au sucre* tonight. No songs. No music. No stories.

But there would be fresh spinach, the first crop. And potatoes fried with the bacon Pa had traded for. There would be a big jug of milk, a loaf of bread, and a dish of butter to spread on it.

My father had put these things on the table.

I looked at him standing by the sink. He was washing his hands, splashing water on his face. My mamma left us. My brother, too. And now my feckless, reckless uncle had as well. My pa stayed, though. My pa always stayed.

I looked at him. And saw the sweat stains on his shirt. And his big, scarred hands. And his dirty, weary face. I remembered how, lying in my bed a few nights before, I had looked forward to showing him my uncle's money. To telling him I was leaving.

And I was so ashamed.

*Y*ou can't argue with the dead. No matter what you say, they get the last word.

I try to have it out with Grace as I sit with her. I tell her that she was wrong to have given me her letters and that sneaking around on her behalf will cost me my job if I'm not careful and that I need my wages because I am to be married and they'll help pay for a stove and pots and pans. I tell her it is entirely possible that Carl Grahm is really Carl Grahm and that Chester Gillette is someone else entirely and the fact that Grace called Carl "Chester" and wrote "Chester, I have done nothing but cry" and "Chester, do you miss me"—while certainly a big fat coincidence—proves nothing. I tell her I have taken plenty of risks for her already and that I won't take another. I say I'm not going to read any more of her letters, either, and if it was her intention all along to get me to, then she is very selfish and underhanded.

Was. She *was* very selfish and underhanded.

I look at her arm as I argue with her, because I don't want to look at her face anymore. I notice that the fabric of her sleeve is puckered from dampness. I see tiny hand stitches where some lace was added at the cuffs, and I wonder if she'd made those stitches herself or if maybe her mother had. Or if she had a sister who was good at sewing, like my sister Abby is. I wonder how she got her nickname, Billy. It was what Chester—no, *Carl,* his name is *Carl*—had called her. Did her pa give it to her? Maybe she had a brother who called her that. It sounded like a nickname a brother would give. Lawton was the one who'd first called me Mattie. Tillie would've been so much prettier. Or Millie. Or Tilda. Or even Hilda.

I open another letter.

South Otselic
June 20, 1906
My Dear Chester —

I am writing to tell you that I am coming back to Cortland. I simply can't stay here any longer. Mamma worries and wonders why I cry so much and I am just about sick. Please come and take me away to some place, dear . . . My headache is dreadful to-night. I am afraid you won't come and I am so frightened, dear . . . You have said you would come and sometimes I just know you will, but then I think about other things and I am just as certain you won't come . . . Chester, there isn't a girl in the whole world as miserable as I am to-night, and you have made me feel so. Chester I don't mean that, dear. You have always been awfully good to me and I know you will always be. You just won't be a coward, I know . . .

I was hoping for good news in that letter. I try another one.

South Otselic
June 21, 1906
My Dear Chester —
    I am just ready for bed, and am so ill I could not help writing to you. I never came down this morning until nearly 8 o'clock and I fainted about 10 o'clock, and stayed in bed until nearly noon. This p.m. my brother brought me a letter from one of the girls, and after I read the letter I fainted again. Chester, I came home because I thought I could trust you. I do not think now I will be here after next Friday. This girl wrote me that you seemed to be having an awfully good time and she guessed my coming home had done you good, as you had not seemed so cheerful in weeks... I should have known, Chester, that you didn't care for me, but somehow I have trusted you more than anyone else...

Voices drift past the window. Men's voices. I freeze.
"...thinks his name is Gillette." That's Mr. Morrison.
"Who?" That's Mr. Sperry.
"Mattie Gokey."
"She say so?"
"She did. Said she heard the girl call him Gillette. Chester Gillette."
"Well, hell, Andy, I called the police department in

176

Albany and told them that a Carl Grahm had likely drowned and asked them to notify the family. That's what it said in the register, 'Carl Grahm, Albany,' not Chester Gillette..."

The voices fade. I can tell that the men are walking across the west lawn, from the direction of the boathouse. They are headed for the porch, and I know that it's their habit to have a drink together at night and that the whiskey is kept in the parlor.

I bolt out of the parlor, race down the hallway, through the foyer, and up the main staircase. I make it to the first landing just as the front door opens, and duck down behind the railing, not daring to move, not daring to breathe, lest a floorboard creak or the banister rattle.

"...and there's Gillettes down Cortland way, too," Mr. Sperry says, closing the door behind him. "Well-heeled bunch. One of them owns a big skirt factory."

"South Otselic, where the girl's from...that's near Cortland, isn't it?" Mr. Morrison says.

"Thirty-odd miles outside it. Mrs. Morrison ever get hold of her folks?"

"Yes, she did. Farm family."

Mr. Sperry takes a deep breath and blows it out again.

"It's a strange thing. You'd think one would be near the other."

"What would? The towns?"

"The bodies. In the water. You'd have thought we'd find one near the other. There's no current to speak of in the bay. Nothing strong enough to move a body, least-ways." He is silent for a few seconds, then says, "You fancy a nightcap, Andy?"

"I do."

"I'll get the bottle. Let's have it on the porch, though. Wouldn't be right to drink in the parlor. Not tonight."

Mr. Sperry disappears down the hall and Mr. Morrison busies himself at the reception desk, opening his mail and sorting telephone messages and checking the telegraph machine. I stay put on the landing.

A few minutes go by, then Mr. Sperry reemerges with a bottle in one hand and two glasses in the other. "Andy," he says quietly. "She was so young. Just a girl."

Mr. Morrison doesn't seem to hear him. "Dwight, look at this," he says, coming out from behind the desk.

"What is it?"

"A wire from Albany. From the chief of police. About Carl Grahm."

"What's it say?"

"It says there's no such person by that name living in the city."

The two men look at each other, then they go out on the porch. And I run back to the attic and shove Grace Brown's letters back under my mattress and climb into bed and squeeze my eyes shut and press my hands over my ears and pray and pray and pray for sleep to come.

tott • lish, frowy, blat, meaching

"Mattie, honey, you fixed all right for dust rags?"

"Yes, Aunt Josie."

My aunt never worried over how I was fixed for anything, and she never called me *honey*.

"I'm having the Reverend Miller for tea tomorrow; you'll make sure those figurines are sparkling, won't you?"

"Yes, Aunt Josie."

She wasn't concerned about her figurines. She just wanted to keep me up on my step stool dusting, and away from the parlor door, so I couldn't hear what she was saying or see what she was doing. The door wouldn't close all the way. It had rained for two days straight and the dampness had swollen the wood. If I bent my knees and craned my neck just so, I could see my aunt and Alma McIntyre through the gap. They were sitting at the kitchen table. My aunt was holding an envelope up to the light.

"This is *stealing*, Josie," I heard Mrs. McIntyre say. "We're stealing Emmie Hubbard's mail."

"It's not 'stealing,' Alma. It's *helping*. We're trying to help a neighbor, that's all," my aunt said.

"Arn Satterlee gave it to me right before I closed for

lunch. I've got to put it into the outgoing mailbag by two o'clock or it won't get to Emmie today."

"You will, Alma, you will; it'll only take a minute…"

My aunt said more, but her voice dropped and I couldn't hear it. I got down off the step stool and moved it closer to the door.

"You all right in there, Mattie?" she hollered.

"Yes, Aunt Josie. I'm just moving the step stool."

"Don't come too close to the door with it. The floor's uneven right around there and the stool's tottlish. I wouldn't want you to fall, dear."

"I won't, Aunt Josie."

Tottlish means tippy, and is used mostly to describe boats. Miss Parrish never let us use words like *tottlish* in our essays, but Miss Wilcox did. She said words like those are *vernacular*. She said Mark Twain had a pitch-perfect ear for the vernacular of the Mississippi River and that this talent of his changed writing forever by allowing a wild, truant boy to sound like a wild, truant boy, and an ignorant drunk to sound like an ignorant drunk. I decided *tottlish* would be my word of the day even though *rectitude* was what the dictionary had given me. I wasn't sure I'd find *tottlish* in the dictionary. Or *frowy* either, which describes butter that has gone rancid. Or *blat*, which means to cry—the loud, whiny kind of crying Beth gives out with when she doesn't get her way. Or *meaching*. Which means skulking or slinking, and can describe a certain kind of expression, too. Like the one that must've been on my aunt's face right then, when Mrs. McIntyre suddenly yelped, "Josie, don't you dare!"

"Hush, Alma!"

"Josephine Aber, I would ask you to remember that I am a bona fide government employee, duly sworn to uphold the laws of this land, and tampering with government property is in direct violation of those laws!"

"Alma McIntyre, I would ask *you* to remember that our great government was made for the people and by the people, was it not?"

"What's that got to do with anything?"

"I am the people, Alma, therefore I am the government, too. It's my tax money that pays your wages and don't you forget it."

"Well, I just don't know."

"Land's sake, Alma, I never took you for an unfeeling woman. Don't you care what happens to a poor, helpless widow with six children and a baby? Don't you care at all?"

I rolled my eyes. My aunt didn't give a hoot what happened to Emmie Hubbard; she just wanted to know her business.

"Of course I care what happens to her!"

"Well, then."

"All right, here. But hurry."

I heard the sound of water running and the kettle being filled, and I knew that the two of them weren't making a pot of tea. From their conversation I had figured out that Arn Satterlee was sending Emmie Hubbard a letter, and since it was Arn sending it, and Emmie getting it, it had to be about her taxes.

"Alma, look! Oh, my goodness! Arn Satterlee is auctioning Emmie Hubbard's land!"

I stopped polishing.

"He isn't!

"He is! It says so right here! He's auctioning it to recover the back taxes. She owes twelve dollars and seventy cents and hasn't paid a penny of it."

"But why, Josie? Why now? Emmie never pays her taxes on time."

"Because she's 'habitually derelict'... It says so right here, see?"

"Oh, nonsense! This year's no different from any other. Arn gives her a warning or puts a lien on the property if the county makes him, but he never goes so far as to put the land up for sale."

"Look, Alma, look right here," my aunt said, "it says there's an interested party."

"Who?"

"It doesn't say. It only says something about 'confidential inquiries made by an interested party.'"

"But who'd be interested? You think it's one of her neighbors?"

"Don't see how it could be. She's only got the three. There's Aleeta Smith, and she wouldn't do a thing like that to Emmie. Michael Gokey wouldn't, either. And even if they would, they couldn't afford to. Neither of 'em has a pot to piss in. That only leaves Frank Loomis, and I doubt he has the money, either. Not after paying for those new horses, and poor Iva going around in that same tired linsey dress every day of the week."

There was a pause, then Mrs. McIntyre said, "He wouldn't want Emmie gone, anyway."

Their voices dropped way down low then. I stretched my neck as long as a giraffe's, but I couldn't hear a thing. Only "... disgraceful, Josie..." and "... I wouldn't tolerate it..." and "... fills her belly, all right..." I couldn't sense their meaning but thought they must be talking bad of Emmie like most everyone does.

They were silent for a minute or so, then my aunt clucked her tongue and said, "Alma, I'm sure as I'm sitting here that no local person would do a thing like this. It's a city person, I just know it. Some low-down, no-good, sneaky wheeler-dealer from New York, I'd bet, looking to buy himself cheap land for a summer camp."

"Oh, Josie, this is terrible! What will happen to those children?"

"I imagine the county will take them."

"Poor little things!"

"I mean to find out who's behind this, Alma."

"How?"

"I'll ask Arn Satterlee."

"You can't. He'll know we opened the letter if you do."

"I'll wait a few days, then. Give Emmie time enough to open the letter and start carrying on to the whole county about it. But I'm going to find out, Alma. You mark my words."

I had heard enough. I got down off the step stool again and dragged it all the way across the room to the fireplace. The mantel was covered with figurines. An ormolu clock sat in the middle of them. I polished it viciously, for I was upset.

Where would Emmie get that kind of money? I wondered.

I knew the answer: She wouldn't. Any one of her neighbors would've loaned it to her if they'd had it, but no one did. Aunt Josie did, though. She had twelve dollars and seventy cents, and plenty more besides. And if she really cared about Emmie Hubbard and her children, she could have given it to her. And if she'd really cared about me, she could have helped me get to New York City. But all she cared about was her damn figurines.

Emmie would lose her house and land, and the county would take her kids. I couldn't bear the thought of her children being taken and separated and farmed out to strangers. Especially Lucius, the baby, who was so small.

It was one more hard and hopeless thing, and I was tired of hard and hopeless things.

I finished polishing the clock and picked up one of the figurines next to it. It was in the shape of an angel and on the angel's gown were printed the words: ALMIGHTY GOD, GIVE US SERENITY TO ACCEPT WHAT CANNOT BE CHANGED, COURAGE TO CHANGE WHAT SHOULD BE CHANGED, AND WISDOM TO KNOW THE ONE FROM THE OTHER.

What if you couldn't do that? Couldn't change things and couldn't accept them, either?

I took hold of the angel's head and snapped it off. And then I snapped one wing off, and then the other. I broke his arms off, too, and then I asked him how serene he was feeling now. I put the pieces in my pocket.

That got rid of most of my anger. I had to swallow what was left.

"We could walk to Inlet and look in the window of O'Hara's," Ada Bouchard said. "They've got some pretty summer fabric just come in."

"Or hike up to Moss Lake," Abby said.

"Or Dart's Lake," Jane Miley said.

"We could go visit Minnie Compeau and see the babies," Frances Hill said.

"Or sit under the pines and read," I said.

"*Read?* On a day like today? You need your head checked, Mattie," Fran said. "Let's draw straws. Short one decides what we do."

We were all outside, clustered at the bottom of the Uncas Road. We were off on a jaunt, we just had to decide where. It was a warm and glorious spring afternoon, a Saturday. We'd all managed to escape chores and parents and little brothers and sisters, and we wanted to talk and laugh and be outside for a few hours.

Fran broke off some twigs from a bush, and made one shorter than the rest. We were about to start drawing them when my choice was suddenly made for me. A buckboard pulled up, one drawn by two bay horses.

"Well, Royal Loomis! What brings you this way?" Fran asked. She and Royal are cousins but look nothing alike. She has curly carrot-red hair and eyes the color of molasses. She is tiny. In the same way that a stick of dynamite is tiny.

I saw Ada tuck a wisp of hair behind her ear and Jane press her lips together to redden them.

Royal shrugged. "Went out for a ride and ended up here," he said.

"Come to gaze at the lake?" Fran teased.

"Something like that."

"How romantic."

"Ain't you got any work to do, Fran? Any children to scare or kittens to drown?"

"Well! I guess I know when I'm not wanted."

"Hardly. Hey, Matt, you feel like taking a ride?"

I almost fell over. "Me?" I said, shading my eyes to look up at him.

"Get in, will you?"

I looked at my friends, not quite sure what to do. Fran winked. "Go on!" she whispered. Jane looked at me like she'd never seen me before.

"Well . . . yes, all right," I said, climbing up.

Royal snapped the reins as soon as I was settled. Jane leaned over to Ada and whispered something in her ear. I realized I would be a topic of conversation amongst my friends for the rest of the day if not the rest of the week. It was a strange feeling—worrisome and exciting all at once. *Wexanxilicious?*

Royal didn't say much as we rode west toward the entrance of the Big Moose Road. Nor did I. I was too busy trying to figure out what this sudden appearance of his was all about.

"Want to go to Higby's?" he eventually asked me. "Man who works at the boathouse is a friend. They're getting the boats ready for the season. He'll let us take a skiff for free."

"All right," I said, thinking that this was all very odd. If it were some other girl, I'd have said Royal was sweet on her, but it was only me and I knew better. Then I had another thought. "Royal, don't you think you can kiss me again, or . . . or anything else. I won't have it," I said.

He looked at me sideways. "All right, Matt, I won't. Not unless you want me to."

"I don't want you to. I mean it," I said. *I'm not your batting practice,* I thought. *Someone to get it right with before you go see Martha Miller.*

"Hey, Matt? How about we just go boating, huh?"

"All right, then."

"Good."

When we arrived at Higby's, Royal unhitched his team and put them in the corral. His friend let us have our pick of boats, and Royal rowed us out onto Big Moose and didn't do anything stupid or show-offy, like trying to stand up in the boat, and I sat facing him and let the perfection of a spring day in the North Woods take my breath away. When Royal got tired of rowing, we drifted awhile under some shaggy hemlocks leaning out from the shore. He didn't talk much, but he did point out a family of mallards, a pair of mergansers, and a blue heron. I watched him as he watched the heron take flight, his eyes never leaving it, and wondered if maybe I'd been wrong about him. I'd always thought him inarticulate, but maybe he had a different sort of eloquence. Maybe he appreciated things other than words—the dark beauty of the lake, for example, or the awesome majesty of the forest. Maybe his quietness masked a great and boiling soul.

It was a quaint notion and one he soon dispelled.

"Skunk et all my chicks last night," he said. "Guts and feathers all over the yard. They were mine, those chicks. Planned to raise 'em and sell 'em come fall."

"I'm sorry to hear that, Royal."

He sighed. "At least I've still got the hen. She oughta breed again, and if she don't, at least she'll fatten up nice. Make good eating."

"I'm sure she will."

"I'll miss that money, though. I'm saving up, trying to put some money aside for when I'm out on my own."

"Are you? What do you want to do?"

"Farm. Land's getting dear up here. A man's got to have a few dollars behind him nowadays. I'd like to have a going dairy concern. Maybe even my own cheese factory someday. A man could make a living out of cheese. It keeps."

He was silent for a few seconds, then he said, "You couldn't give me enough land, Matt. I'd want fifty acres just for my dairy herd. Fifty more for sheep. Twenty for corn, twenty for potatoes, and twenty for fruit. Why, you could keep every camp on the lake swimming in berries all summer long."

"Yes, you could," I said, trailing my hand in the lake. I shook the water off and shaded my eyes so I could see him better. He was leaning forward with his arms crossed over his knees. His face was in profile, but then he turned and smiled at me, and my breath caught and I wondered if this was how it felt to be pretty.

"You ever go berrying, Matt? I like to go in the evening, when it cools down and the crickets start singing. You ever notice how good everything smells then? I've been watching for the wild strawberries. Won't be too much longer now. Cultivated ones from the plants I put in a couple years back won't be ready till the end of June. Got tons from those plants last year. My pa took 'em with him on his milk rounds. Cook at Dart's said they were the sweetest she ever had. I'm going to use the money I make on 'em this year to buy more chickens. It's free money, the berry money. It's not even a chore to pick when you can be out in the fields at dusk..."

I realized that Royal Loomis was talking a blue streak. In fact, I'd never heard him talk so much in all the years I'd known him. I guess I never had him on the right topic. Start him off on farming and he waxed downright poetical. For the first time, I saw what was in his heart. And I wondered if he might ever want to look deep enough to see what was in mine.

When he finished talking about chickens and cheese and berries, I took a turn talking. I talked about my exams and the grades I'd gotten, but I could tell he was bored. I talked about the book I was reading, but that bored him, too. So then I talked about Barnard. And how even though my aunt wouldn't loan me the money and my uncle had broken his promise to me and I knew I couldn't go, I still wished I could.

"You going to?" he asked me.

"I want to..."

"But why? Why would you want to do that? Go all the way to New York City just to read books?"

"So maybe I can learn how to write them someday, Royal. I told you this already," I said, suddenly wanting him to understand. Wanting it desperately. But he didn't even hear me; he was too busy talking.

"Why can't you read books right here? School's a waste of money and New York City's a dangerous place."

"Oh, never mind," I said crossly. "I wish I'd never told you. You don't even listen."

He moved forward in the boat until his knees touched mine. "I heard what you said, it just don't make sense. Why do you always want to read about other people's lives, Matt? Ain't your own good enough for you?"

I didn't reply to that because I knew my voice would quaver if I did. Turned out I didn't need to, because he kissed me. Even though I'd told him earlier that I didn't want him to. He kissed me and I kissed him back and that was reply enough.

Plain old kisses at first and then a real deep one. And then he put his arms around me and held me to him as best he could in a rowboat, and it felt so good. No one had so much as hugged me since my mamma died. I wished I had the words to describe how I felt. My word of the day, *augur,* which means to foretell things from omens, had nothing to do with it as far as I could see. I felt warm in his arms. Warm and hungry and blind.

He moved his hands to my breasts. He was more gentle this time than the time before, and his palms against me made me feel breathless, but I still pushed him away because it is so hard to always, always want the things you cannot have.

"Stop it, Royal. I'll jump out of the boat if you don't, I swear I will."

"Let me, Mattie," he whispered. "It's all right for a boy and girl to do that . . . as long as they're sparking."

I pulled away from him. "Sparking?" I said, shocked. "That is news to me, Royal."

"Why else would I have taken you boating? And why did I kiss you in the woods when your cow got out? Why did I plow your field for you? For someone who reads so many books, you're awfully damned stupid."

"But, Royal . . . I thought . . . People said that you and Martha Miller were an item."

"People talk too much and so do you," he said. And then he kissed me again, and I tried to tell myself that none of this made any sense. He'd never shown a bit of interest in me unless I counted that one kiss he'd given me when Daisy got out, and now we were sparking. But his lips were sweeter than anything I'd ever tasted and his hands felt like comfort and danger all mixed up and I knew I should stop them, stop him, find my voice and tell him no. But then the warmth of him under my own hands, and the smell of him all soap and sweat, and the taste of him, overwhelmed me.

And so I closed my eyes and all I knew was his nearness. And all I wanted was my own story and no one else's.

And so I said nothing. Nothing at all.

glean

"Lou, stop."

"'. . . then comes Junior in a baby carriage . . .'"

"I said stop."

"'. . . sucking his thumb, wetting his pants, doin' the hula-hula dance . . .'"

"Lou!"

"You're blushing, Matt! You're sweet on Royal Loomis! I know you are!"

"Nobody's sweet on anybody. And stop saying so."

Lou started singing her stupid song again, but then something appeared up ahead of us on the road that interested her far more than tormenting me did. An automobile. It could only be some well-heeled tourist driving it, or Mr. Sperry, or Miss Wilcox. No one else could afford one. The driver saw us and leaned on the horn. The car veered across the road, directly toward us. I grabbed the back of Lou's coveralls and pulled her into the grass.

"Let go, Matt," she whined. "I want to see it."

The driver pulled up and cut the engine. It was our teacher. She tossed the cigarette she'd been smoking and removed her goggles. "Hello, Mattie! Lou!" she bellowed, her cheeks pink. She wore a tan duster, gloves, and a flowered silk scarf over her hair.

"Hello, Miss Wilcox," we said together.

"Where are you two off to?"

"We're on our way home from Burnap's. Pleasant, our mule, cracked his bit. We had to get it repaired," I explained.

"I see. I, myself, have been for a drive. Up to Beaver River and back. First one since the fall. The roads are finally dry enough to allow it. It's beautiful up there! Such freedom! I'm famished now, though. Driving always gives me an appetite. Why don't you two hop in? We'll go back to my house and have some lunch."

I was frightened of Miss Wilcox's automobile. "I think we'd best get home, ma'am," I said. "Our pa will be looking for us. He needs the bit."

"Oh, come on, Matt! Pa won't mind," Lou pleaded.

"I'll tell you what...come for lunch and then I'll drive you home. It'll save some time."

"Pleeeeeease, Matt?" Lou begged.

"I guess it's all right," I said, more for Miss Wilcox's sake than Lou's. For all her giddy, breathless excitement, she seemed a little bit lonely. And I was curious, too. I had never seen the inside of my teacher's house. She had such nice clothes and jewelry, and a real automobile, so there was no telling what she might have at home.

Miss Wilcox got out, crank in hand, and started the engine again. It coughed and sputtered, finally caught, then fired off what sounded like cannon shot. I jumped out of my skin. Miss Wilcox laughed at me. Miss Wilcox laughed a lot. I knew she was wealthy, and wondered if money made everything funny.

"Hear that, Matt?" Lou whispered, giggling. "Just like Pa in the outhouse!"

"Shut up, Lou!" I hissed, hoping Miss Wilcox hadn't heard. "Go get in the back." She did, but not before she'd stooped down, quick as a weasel, and picked up the remains of Miss Wilcox's cigarette. I put my hand out for it, but she shoved it in her pocket and stuck her chin out at me.

When we were seated, Miss Wilcox engaged the gears and we were off. "It's a nice car, isn't it?" she shouted, turning toward me. "Brand-new. I had a Packard before. When I lived in New York. But a Ford's better for the country."

I nodded and kept my eyes straight ahead. One of us had to.

"It's wonderful here in the woods," Miss Wilcox said, swerving to avoid a squirrel. "Such freedom! You can do whatever you like and no one minds."

No, but how they talk! I thought.

Glean, my word of the day that day, is a good word. It is old and small, not showy. It has a simple meaning— to gather after the reapers—and then meanings inside the meanings, like images in a prism. It is a farming word, but it fits people other than farmers. Aunt Josie never bent her back in a field one day in her life, but she is a gleaner. She combs other people's leavings—hints, hearsay, dropped words—looking for nuggets of information, trying to gather enough bits together to make a whole story.

Miss Wilcox drove us out of Eagle Bay and a mile and a half up the road to Inlet. The old Foster camp on Fourth Lake is a two-story log house with a stone foundation. Dr. Foster was a retired bachelor doctor from Watertown who loved the North Woods and built himself a large camp here. The word *camp* means different things to different people. To Pa and Lawton, it means a lean-to. To city people, it means a real house with all the comforts but tricked out like a cabin. Aunt Josie once told me that Mr. John Pierpont Morgan has crystal champagne glasses in his camp on Lake Mohegan, and a Steinway piano and telephones in every room and a dozen servants, too. And Mr. Alfred G. Vanderbilt has solid-gold taps on his bathroom sink at the Sagamore. Dr. Foster is dead now. His sister inherited the house and rents it out. Usually only in the summer and to big families with enough children and grandparents and aunts and uncles to fill up all the rooms and crowd the porch, but my teacher had been living in it all year and had it entirely to herself.

Miss Wilcox pulled into the driveway, which curves around in back of the house in a horseshoe shape, and then we went inside. The camp has a real doorbell and Lou asked if she could ring it, then kept doing it until I pulled her away. It was cool and dark inside and smelled like oil soap. There were carpets everywhere and wainscoting halfway up the walls and velvet curtains thick and heavy enough to shut out the whole world. There were pictures of deer and trout on the walls, and mirrors in frames, and pretty blue-and-white plates. It was very beautiful, but most of all, it was quiet. So quiet you could hear a clock ticking from two rooms away, and boards creaking under your feet, and your own thoughts inside your head. It was never that quiet in our house.

Miss Wilcox led us out of the entry past rooms that looked as if no one ever stepped into them, filled with furniture that looked as if no one ever sat on it, to an enormous, spotless white kitchen that looked like no one ever cooked in it. There, she set about fixing us dainty little sandwiches with the crusts cut off, and tiny iced cakes from a box, and tea. I tried to help, but she wouldn't let me.

"Don't no one else live here, Miss Wilcox?" Lou asked looking all around at the spotless stove and the shining floor and the painted cabinets with no finger-prints on them, or broken knobs.

"Lou...," I said, cautioning her.

"No, Lou. Just me. And it's *doesn't*. Doesn't anyone else live here."

Lou digested this, then said, "Were you bad, Miss Wilcox?"

Miss Wilcox's knife clattered to the counter. She turned to look at my sister. "'Bad'?" she said. "Lou, how...why do you ask that?"

"When I was bad, my mamma used to make me sit

in the parlor by myself. For an hour. With the door closed. It was awful. Are you being punished? Is that why you have to live here all alone?"

Miss Wilcox's hand fluttered to her throat. Her fingers twined themselves in the circlet of amber beads there. "I like living alone, Lou," she said. "I like the quiet and the solitude. I have a lot of reading to do, you see. And lessons to prepare during the school year."

Lou nodded, but she didn't look convinced. "If you ever get lonely, we could bring Barney by. Our dog. He could keep you company. He has gas, but he's still a nice dog. He wouldn't pee on the settee or anything. He don't see well enough to find it—"

"Lou!" I hissed.

"What? Oh, jeezum...*doesn't.* Doesn't. Doesn't. Doesn't. He doesn't see well enough."

I could see Miss Wilcox was trying not to laugh, but I didn't find it funny. Not one bit. Lou knows better than to ask personal questions or talk about Barney's gas. She knows what good manners are. Mamma taught her same as she taught all of us. Lou is hungry for attention, though. Any kind. She and Pa used to be inseparable, but now he looks right through her. Through all of us. I know it hurts her, so I try not to be cross, but sometimes she goes too far.

"Shall we take our lunch into the library?" Miss Wilcox asked, her eyes moving from me to Lou and back again.

"Where? On the pickle boat?" Lou asked, looking confused.

I didn't scold her for that because I was wondering the same thing.

This time Miss Wilcox did laugh. "No, right here in the house. Come on."

She put the lunch on a tray, along with some plates and napkins, then led us out of the kitchen, down a different hallway, and through a set of tall pocket doors.

What I saw next stopped me dead in my tracks. Books. Not just one or two dozen, but hundreds of them. In crates. In piles on the floor. In bookcases that stretched from floor to ceiling and lined the entire room. I turned around and around in a slow circle, feeling as if I'd just stumbled into Ali Baba's cave. I was breathless, close to tears, and positively dizzy with greed.

"Won't you sit down and have your lunch, Mattie?" Miss Wilcox asked.

But eating was the last thing on my mind. And I didn't see how Miss Wilcox could eat, or teach, or sleep, or ever find any reason to leave this room. Not with all these books in it, just begging to be read.

"Are these all Dr. Foster's books?" I whispered.

"No, they're mine. I had them sent up from the city. They're in a bit of a shambles. I never seem to get around to arranging them properly."

"There are so many, Miss Wilcox."

She laughed. "Not really. I think you and Weaver have read half of them already."

But I hadn't. There were dozens of names I didn't know. Eliot. Zola. Whitman. Wilde. Yeats. Sand. Dickinson. Goethe. And all those were in just one stack! There were lives in those books, and deaths. Families and friends and lovers and enemies. Joy and despair, jealousy, envy, madness, and rage. All there. I reached out and touched the cover of one called *The Earth*. I could almost hear the characters inside, murmuring and jostling, impatient for me to open the cover and let them out.

"You can borrow anything you like, Mattie," I heard Miss Wilcox say. "Mattie?"

I realized I was being rude, so I made myself stop staring at the books and looked at the rest of the room. There was a large fireplace with two settees in front of it, facing each other across a low table. Lou sat on one of them, stuffing herself with sandwiches and slurping her tea. There was a writing table under a window, with pens and pencils and a stack of good paper. I touched the top sheet. It felt like satin. A few more sheets, covered with handwriting all in lines like a poem, were spread haphazardly across the tabletop. Miss Wilcox came over and shuffled them into a pile.

"I'm sorry," I said, suddenly remembering myself. "I didn't mean to pry."

"That's all right. It's just a lot of scribbling. Won't you eat something?"

I sat down and took a sandwich, and to make conversation, Miss Wilcox said she saw me riding the other day with a tall and handsome boy.

"That's Royal Loomis. Mattie's sweet on him," Lou said.

"No, I'm not," I said quickly. I was, of course. I was

as dopey as a calf for him, but I didn't want my teacher to know. I wasn't sure she understood about amber eyes or strong arms or kisses in a boat, and I thought she might be disappointed in me for being swayed by those sorts of things.

Miss Wilcox raised an eyebrow.

"I'm not. I don't like any of the boys around here."

"Why not?"

"I suppose it's hard to like anyone real after Captain Wentworth and Colonel Brandon," I said, trying my best to sound worldly wise. "Jane Austen ruins you for farm boys and loggers."

Miss Wilcox laughed. "Jane Austen ruins you for everything else, too," she said. "Do you like her books?"

"I like them some."

"Just 'some'? Why not a lot?"

"Well, ma'am, I think she lies."

Miss Wilcox put her teacup down. "Does she?"

"Yes, ma'am, she does."

"Why do you think that, Mattie?"

I was not used to my elders asking me what I think—not even Miss Wilcox—and it made me nervous. I had to collect myself before I answered her. "Well, it seems to me that there are books that tell stories, and then there are books that tell truths...," I began.

"Go on," she said.

"The first kind, they show you life like you want it to be. With villains getting what they deserve and the hero seeing what a fool he's been and marrying the heroine and happy endings and all that. Like *Sense and Sensibility* or *Persuasion*. But the second kind, they show you life more like it is. Like in *Huckleberry Finn* where Huck's pa is a no-good drunk and Jim suffers so. The first kind makes you cheerful and contented, but the second kind shakes you up."

"People like happy endings, Mattie. They don't want to be shaken up."

"I guess not, ma'am. It's just that there are no Captain Wentworths, are there? But there are plenty of Pap Finns. And things go well for Anne Elliott in the end, but they don't go well for most people." My voice trembled as I spoke, as it did whenever I was angry. "I feel let down sometimes. The people in books—the heroes—they're always so ... heroic. And I try to be, but ..."

"... you're not," Lou said, licking deviled ham off her fingers.

"... no, I'm not. People in books are good and noble and unselfish, and people aren't that way ... and I feel, well ... hornswoggled sometimes. By Jane Austen and Charles Dickens and Louisa May Alcott. Why do writers make things sugary when life isn't that way?" I asked too loudly. "Why don't they tell the truth? Why don't they tell how a pigpen looks after the sow's eaten her children? Or how it is for a girl when her baby won't come out? Or that cancer has a smell to it? All those books, Miss Wilcox," I said, pointing at a pile of them, "and I bet not one of them will tell you what cancer smells like. I can, though. It stinks. Like meat gone bad and dirty clothes and bog water all mixed together. Why doesn't anyone tell you that?"

No one spoke for a few seconds. I could hear the clock ticking and the sound of my own breathing. Then Lou quietly said, "Cripes, Mattie. You oughtn't to talk like that."

I realized then that Miss Wilcox had stopped smiling. Her eyes were fixed on me, and I was certain she'd decided I was morbid and dispiriting like Miss Parrish said and that I should leave then and there.

"I'm sorry, Miss Wilcox," I said, looking at the floor. "I don't mean to be coarse. I just . . . I don't know why I should care what happens to people in a drawing room in London or Paris or anywhere else when no one in those places cares what happens to people in Eagle Bay."

Miss Wilcox's eyes were still fixed on me, only now they were shiny. Like they were the day I got my letter from Barnard. "Make them care, Mattie," she said softly. "And don't you ever be sorry."

She glanced at Lou, set the whole plate of cakes before her, then rose and beckoned me to her writing table. She picked up a glass paperweight shaped like an apple and took two books from under it. "*Thérèse Raquin*," she said solemnly, "and *Tess of the D'Urbervilles*. Best not tell anyone you have them." Then she took her writing paper out of its box, put the books in the box, covered them with a few sheets of paper, and handed the box to me.

I smiled, thinking that my teacher sure was dramatic. "Cripes, Miss Wilcox, they're not guns," I said.

"No, they're not, Mattie, they're books. And a hundred times more dangerous." She stole another glance at Lou, then asked me, "Has there been any progress?"

"No, ma'am. And there's not likely to be."

"Would you consider working for me, then? I need help with my library, as you can see. I'd like you to come and arrange my books. Sort them into nonfiction and fiction, and then sort fiction into novels, plays, short stories, and poetry, and shelve them alphabetically. I'll pay you. A dollar each time."

It was only the first week of May. If I worked for Miss Wilcox one day a week throughout the summer, I'd have sixteen dollars or so by the time September came. Enough for a train ticket and then some. I wanted to say yes so badly, but then I heard Royal asking me why I was always reading about other people's lives, and felt his lips on mine. I heard my aunt telling me to get down off my high horse and Pa saying I didn't need to go to Miss Wilcox's to find work, there was plenty for me at my own house. And I heard my mamma, asking me to make a promise.

"I can't, Miss Wilcox," I said. "I can't get away."

"Surely you can, Mattie. Just for an hour or two. I'll drive you home. Come this Saturday."

I shook my head. "I've got the chickens to do. The coop needs whitewashing and Pa said he wants it done by Sunday."

"I'll do it, Matt," Lou said. "Me and Abby and Beth. Pa won't know. He'll be out plowing. He won't raise Cain, long as the work gets done."

I looked at my sister, who wasn't supposed to be listening. I saw the crumbs around her mouth, the lank hair hanging in her face, the dirty cuffs of Lawton's coveralls slopping down over her boots. I saw her blue eyes big and hopeful, and I loved her so much I had to look away.

"If you come, you can borrow anything you like, Mattie. Anything at all," Miss Wilcox said.

I imagined myself here on a Saturday afternoon, in this calm, quiet room, digging among all these books, gleaning my own treasures.

And then I smiled and said yes.

de • his • cence

It was seven o'clock on a May evening. It was after the supper was cooked and served, the dishes washed, the pots scrubbed, dried, and put away, the stove wiped down, the coals banked, the floor mopped, the dishrags put to soaking, and Barney fed. Lou and Beth were polishing their boots. Abby was sitting in front of the fire with a heap of darning. Pa was sitting across from her, mending Pleasant's bridle. And me? I was standing in the middle of the kitchen, looking at my family, each one of them close enough to touch, my heart pounding so hard I thought it would burst.

There were more chores to do. The wood box next to the stove was nearly empty. There were ashes to dump down the outhouse and Abby could have used my help with the darning, but I felt as if the very walls themselves were pressing in upon me. As if I would go crazy if I stayed in this prison of a kitchen for one second longer. I leaned against the sink and closed my eyes. I must have sighed or groaned or something, because Abby suddenly said, "What's wrong, Mattie?"

I opened my eyes again and saw her looking up at me. Lou and Beth looked up, too. Even Pa did. *Dehiscence* was my word of the day. It is a fine word, a five-dollar word. It means when pods or fruits burst open so that their seeds can come out. How was it that I could learn a new word every day, yet never know the right ones to tell my family how I felt?

"Nothing's wrong. I'm fine. Just tired, that's all. I . . . I think I forgot to latch the barn door," I lied, then ran to the shed, grabbed my shawl, and kept going. Out into the yard, past the garden and the outhouse, past the black earth of the cornfields.

I kept going until I got to the eastern edge of Pa's land, where the fields give way to woods and there's a stream, and just past it, a small clearing ringed with tamaracks. To the place where my mother is buried.

I could hardly breathe by the time I got there. I walked around and around her grave, trying to get hold of myself. My head felt giddy and light, like the time Minnie and I filched brandy from her father's cupboard. Only this time it wasn't alcohol I'd had too much of. It was books. I should have stopped after Zola and Hardy, but I hadn't. I'd gone right on like a greedy pig to *Leaves of Grass* by Walt Whitman, *Songs of Innocence* by William Blake, and *A Distant Music* by Emily Baxter.

I'd borrowed the volumes of poetry on Saturday, when I'd gone back to Miss Wilcox's house to start organizing her books. "You can keep this one, Mattie," she'd said about the Baxter, "but keep it to yourself." I didn't need telling. I'd heard all about *A Distant Music*. I'd read articles about it in Aunt Josie's cast-off newspapers. They said that Emily Baxter was "an affront to common decency," "a blight on American womanhood," and "an insult to all proper feminine sensibilities." It had been banned by the Catholic Church and publicly burned in Boston.

I thought there would be curse words in it for sure, or dirty pictures or something just god-awfully terrible, but there weren't—only poems. One was about a young woman who gets an apartment in a city by herself and eats her first supper in it all alone. But it wasn't sad, not one bit. Another was about a mother with six children, who finds out she's got a seventh coming and gets so low spirited, she hangs herself. One was about Penelope, the wife of Ulysses, setting fire to her loom and heading off to do some traveling herself. And one was about God being a woman instead of a man. That must've been the one that made the pope boiling mad.

Jeezum... What if God *was* a woman? Would the pope be out of a job? Would the president be a woman, too? And the governor? And the sheriff? And when people got married, would the man have to honor and obey? Would only women be allowed to vote?

Emily Baxter's poems made my head hurt. They made me think of so many questions and possibilities. Reading one was like pulling a stump. You got hold of a root and tugged, hoping it would come right up, but sometimes it went so deep and so far, you were halfway to the Loomis farm and still pulling.

I took a deep breath. I smelled wet earth and evergreens and the dusk coming down, and they calmed me some. I was agitated something fierce. There was a whole other world beyond Eagle Bay, with people like Emily Baxter in it, thinking all the things you thought but weren't supposed to. Writing them, too. And when I read what they'd wrote, I wanted to be in that world. Even if it meant I had to leave this one. And my sisters. And my friends. And Royal.

I stopped pacing and hugged myself for warmth. My eyes fell on my mamma's headstone. ELLEN GOKEY. BE-LOVED WIFE AND MOTHER. BORN SEPTEMBER 14, 1868. DIED NOVEMBER 11, 1905. Her maiden name was Robert-son, but Pa wouldn't allow it on the headstone. Her father had disowned her for marrying my pa. He'd forbidden the match, but my mamma went against him. She loved to tell the story of her courtship with Pa. Pa didn't like the stories; he'd always leave the room when she started. We liked them, though. Especially the one about how she'd seen him for the first time showing off at her father's sawmill on the Raquette River. He was birling a log with another lumberjack, trying to knock him off. Whoever lost had to give the other man his bandanna. My pa saw my mother watching, dumped the other man in the water, and gave her his bandanna. She was buried with it in her hand.

Mamma also liked to tell us how Pa had asked her to marry him in the woods, in the dead of winter, under a bough of snowy pine branches. And how—on the night they'd eloped—he'd told her to take just a carpetbag with her. "Pack your most important things," he'd said, thinking she would know he meant dresses and boots and underthings and such, but she was so young and giddy, she'd packed her favorite books, a box of caramels, and her jewelry. He'd had to sell a gold bracelet right off to get her some clothes. He'd wanted to sell the books, not the bracelet, but she wouldn't let him.

I hardly recognized the man in those stories as my pa, but I recognized my mother in them. I missed her all the time, my mamma, and I missed her dreadfully just then. I wondered what she would make of Emily Baxter. I wondered if she'd scold me for reading such a book, or touch a finger to her lips and smile and say, "Don't tell Pa," like she did when she spent money he'd given her for nails or paint on ribbons and candy.

I traced the letters of my mother's name on the cold gray stone and conjured my favorite memories of her. I saw her reading to us at night from *Little Women* or *The Last of the Mohicans,* or reading us stories from *Peterson's Magazine* like "Aunt Betsey's Best Bonnet" or "Flirting on Skates." I saw her reading the poems I wrote her for Valentine's Day and her birthday. She used to tell me that I wrote real nice, as nice as the poems on the fancy cards at Cohen's in Old Forge. As nice as Louisa May Alcott, even.

I remembered her singing as she cooked. And standing downstairs in the root cellar in November, smiling at all the food she'd put up. I remember how she made us fancy braided hairdos and how she trudged through the winter fields on snowshoes to bring Emmie Hubbard's kids a pot of stew.

I tried very hard to remember only the good things about my mamma. To remember her the way she was before she got sick. I wished I could cut the rest out of me the way the doctor tried to cut the cancer out of her, but I couldn't. No matter how hard I struggled to keep my last images of her at bay, they came anyway.

I saw her as she looked right before she died, her body wasted, her face hollowed out.

I saw her as she wept and moaned with pain. And as she screamed and threw things at us, her sunken eyes suddenly bright with rage.

I saw her as she pleaded with the doctor and Pa and Aunt Josie and the Reverend Miller not to let her die. As she kissed Lawton and me and my sisters over and over again, pressing our faces between her hands. As she cried and cried, frantically telling me that Pa didn't know how to braid hair or mend a dress or put up beans.

I saw her as she begged me never to go away, as she made me promise to stay and take care of her babies.

And I saw myself, tears in my eyes, promising her I would.

The memories faded. I opened my eyes. The peepers had started up. It was getting late. Pa would be wondering where I was. As I turned to go, I nearly trod on the body of a young robin half hidden in the grass. Its wings were twisted and bent. Its body stiff and bloodied.

A hawk's work, I thought, wondering if the robin had seen the brilliant blue of the sky and felt the sun on its back before its wings were broken.

*M*attie, shut the light! What are you doing up?" a voice hisses in the darkness.

"Nothing, Ada," I say, quickly tucking Grace Brown's letter back in its envelope. "Just reading."

"At this hour? Go to sleep, for cripes' sake! Cook'll have us up soon enough!"

"Stop your damn noise, you two!"

"You don't want to let Cook hear you curse, Fran," Ada warns. "She'll box your ears."

"I'll box yours if you don't shut up, I swear I will—"

"Box *my* ears? I'm not the one who lit the lamp and woke the whole room! And after the day we've had... after everything that's happened..." Ada's voice catches and turns to tears.

"I'm sorry, Ada. I'll shut the light, all right? There, it's out. Go back to sleep now."

There's a gulp, a sniffle, and then, "She's right downstairs, Matt. All cold and dead."

"Then she won't be bothering you, will she? Go to sleep."

I mean to go to sleep, too. I try to, but I can't. Every time I shut my eyes, I see Grace's battered face. I hear

Mr. Morrison tell Mr. Sperry that there's no Carl Grahm in Albany.

I wait for a bit. Until I hear no bedsprings creaking, no sighs or groans as some girl tries to make herself comfortable in the heat. And then quietly, carefully, I unfold the letter again. I only get the pages open partway, when they crinkle. I stop and hold my breath, waiting for Ada or Fran to scold again, but neither of them stirs. It's dark in the room now, but there's a window next to my bed and I can make out Grace's words if I hold her pages in the moonlight.

South Otselic
June 23, 1906
My Dear Chester —

I am just wild because I don't get a letter from you. If you wrote me Tues. night and posted it Wed. morning there isn't any reason why I shouldn't get it. Are you sure you addressed the letter right? I have been home nearly a week and have not had one line from you... When I didn't hear from you Thurs. morning I cried and as a result had a nervous headache and stayed in bed all day. You can't blame me, dear, for of course I thought of everything under the sun. That night when my brother came up he said that if I would get up early he would take me driving... I was so tired and went to bed for an hour after getting home; then I went downstairs and got some dinner all alone. Now, dear, I know you are laughing—in fact, I can hear you, almost—but honestly I had splendid luck. My brother, who seldom says a word in praise of anything, said, "It's not half bad, Billy." That is a whole lot for him to say ... I miss you, oh dear, you don't know how much I miss you ... I am coming back next week unless you can come for me right away. I am so lonesome I can't stand it. Week ago to-night we were together. Don't you remember how I cried, dear? I have cried like that nearly all the time since I have left Cortland ...

There is no Carl Grahm, only a Chester, a "Dear Chester." He lived in Cortland, not Albany, because the letters are addressed to him there. And Grace lived there, too, at some point, even though the return address on her letters says South Otselic, because she mentions she left the place, and says she will come back if he doesn't come for her.

... I am awfully blue ... I was telling Mamma yesterday how you wrote and I never got it and she said, "Why Billy, if he wrote you would have received it." She didn't mean anything but I was mad and said, "Mamma, Chester never lies to me and I know he wrote." If you were only here dear, how glad I would be ... they are calling me to dinner and I will stop. Please write me or I shall be crazy ...

"Frannie says someone struck her," Ada whispers, making me jump. "She went to look at her after supper.

She said there was a huge bloody cut on her face. And bruises."

"Frannie embroiders. You know that. Why are you up again?"

"Can't stay asleep. You saw her, Matt. What did she look like?"

"Like someone who drowned."

"Cook says the undersheriff's on his way. And the coroner. And the strict attorney."

"The district attorney."

"And the men from the Utica paper. Do you think they'll put us in the paper?"

"Go to sleep, Ada. You heard Cook. We'll be busier than ever tomorrow."

"Are those letters from Royal?"

"Um . . . yes. Yes, they are."

"There are so many. It'll take you all night to read them. You must love him."

I don't say anything in reply.

Ada rolls over and I open another letter. It has no greeting.

S. Otselic
Sunday Night
   I was glad to hear from you and surprised as well. I thought you would rather have my letters affectionate, but yours was so businesslike that I have come to the conclusion that you wish mine to be that way . . . I think —pardon me—that I understand

my position and that it is rather unnecessary for you to be so frightfully frank in making me see it. I can see my position as keenly as any one I think . . . You tell me not to worry and think less about how I feel and have a good time. Don't you think if you were me you would worry? . . . I understand how you feel about the affair. You consider it as something troublesome that you are bothered with. You think if it wasn't for me you could do as you liked all summer and not be obliged to give up your position there. I know how you feel, but once in a while you make me see these things a great deal more plainly than ever. I don't suppose you have ever considered how it puts me out of all the good times for the summer and how I had to give up my position there . . .

Was Grace sick? I wonder. Is that why she had to give up her position? Did they work at the same place? Maybe at that place Mr. Sperry was talking about—the skirt factory that the well-heeled Cortland Gillettes owned. But why would they both have to give up their positions? It didn't make any sense.

> *. . . Chester, I don't suppose you will ever know how I regret being all this trouble to you. I know you hate me and I can't blame you one bit. My whole life is ruined and in a measure yours is, too. Of course it's worse for me than for you, but the world and you, too, may think I am the one to blame, but somehow I can't—just simply can't think I am, Chester. I said*

no so many times, dear. Of course the world will not know that but it's true all the same. My little sister came up just a minute ago with her hands full of daisies and asked me if I didn't want my fortune told. I told her I guessed it was pretty well told...

My eyes latch on to one line again: "I said no so many times, dear"...and then I gasp out loud, because I have said no a few times myself, dear, and I finally understand why Grace was so upset: She was carrying a baby—Chester Gillette's baby. *That's* why she had to give up her position and go home. That's why she was so desperate for him to come and take her away. Before her belly got big and the whole world found out.

And then I think of something else...that I am the only person, the only person in the entire world, who knows this.

I fold the letter, slide it back into its envelope, and look out the window. It's so dark outside and there is no sign of the dawn.

Break a promise to the dead and they'll haunt you, Ada says.

Keep the promise and they'll haunt you just the same.

mal • e • dic • tion

It was a Saturday, my very favorite day of the week, for on Saturdays I got to work in Miss Wilcox's library. I had just trotted up the back steps to her house and was standing on the porch, about to knock on her door, when I heard voices inside. Loud, angry voices.

"And what about your father? And Charlotte? And Iverson Junior? The shame of it all! They can't even go out in public! Have you never once thought of them, Emily?" That was a man's voice.

"They're not children. They'll manage. Annabelle does." That was Miss Wilcox.

I raised my hand to knock, then lowered it again. Miss Wilcox was expecting me and I had plenty of work to do, but this was surely a private discussion and I thought maybe she'd prefer for me to come back later. I didn't know what to do, so I stood there dithering.

"How did you find me? Whom did you pay to inform on me? And how much?"

"Emily, just come home."

"Under what conditions, Teddy? Knowing you, there will be conditions."

"There's to be no more scribbling, no more foolishness. You're to come home and take up your duties and responsibilities. If you do, I promise I will do my best to forget any of this ever happened."

"I can't. You know I can't."

There were a few seconds of silence and then the man spoke again. He wasn't shouting anymore. His voice was calm and steady and all the more frightening for it.

"What you've done is not only embarrassing and distressing, Emily, it is immoral. *Threnody* should never have been written, never mind published. Anthony Comstock has involved himself. Do you know who he is?"

"The applesauce king?"

I did not know Miss Wilcox could be so flippant. I didn't think she should be. Not around an angry man.

"He's the secretary for the Society for the Suppression of Vice. He's ruined people, driven some to suicide. Never in all my born days did I think I would see your name alongside the names of deviants and pornographers."

"I am neither a deviant nor a pornographer, Teddy. You know this. And the odious Mr. Comstock does as well."

"He says you are obscene. And when Comstock says something, the entire country listens. You are doing grievous injury to the names of Wilcox and Baxter, Emily. I will seek help for you if you refuse to seek it yourself."

"Meaning what, Teddy?"

"My meaning is perfectly clear."

"No, it damn well isn't! Have some guts for once in your life! Say what you mean!"

"You leave me no choice, Emily. If you do not come

home—on my conditions—I will sign you over to a doctor's care."

There was a terrible crash and the sound of glass breaking, and then I heard Miss Wilcox scream, "Get out! Get out!"

"Miss Wilcox! Miss Wilcox, are you all right?" I shouted, banging on the door.

The door was wrenched open and a man stormed by me. I think he would have knocked me right on my backside if I hadn't stepped out of his way. He was tall and pale, with fine dark hair and a mustache, and he barely gave me a glance.

I ran inside, frightened for my teacher. "Miss Wilcox!" I shouted. "Miss Wilcox, where are you?"

"In here, Mattie."

I hurried into the library. The writing table had been upended. Papers were all over the floor. The beautiful red apple paperweight had been smashed to bits. My teacher was standing in the middle of the room, smoking.

"Miss Wilcox, are you all right?"

She nodded, but her eyes were red and she was trembling. "I'm fine, Mattie," she said, "but I think I'm going to lie down for a bit. Just leave the mess. I'll see to it. Help yourself to whatever's in the kitchen. Your money's on the table."

I heard her speaking, but my eyes were on the broken glass and the scattered pages. He'd done this. *Malediction* was my word of the day. It means bad speaking, like a curse. I felt a shiver run up my spine and left the library to lock the front and back doors. When I returned, Miss Wilcox was on the staircase.

"Will that man be back?" I asked her.

She turned around. "Not today."

"I think you should call for the sheriff, Miss Wilcox."

Miss Wilcox smiled sourly at that and said, "He wouldn't come. It's not illegal, not yet at least, for a man to destroy his wife's home."

I didn't say anything, but my eyes must have been as big and as round as two fried eggs.

"Yes, Mattie, that was my husband. Theodore Baxter."

"Baxter? *Baxter!* Then you're not . . . then that . . . that makes you . . ."

"Emily Baxter, poet."

ab · scis · sion

According to the article I'd read in *Peterson's Magazine*, if you wish to attract a man, you need to be "attentive and receptive to his every word, put his own interests before yours, and use the eloquent, unspoken language of the female body to let him know that he is the very center of your universe, the primary reason for your existence." The first two bits of advice were clear to me. I had trouble with the third one, though.

I thought it meant I should bat my lashes, but when I tried it, Royal looked at me with a puzzled expression, and asked if I'd gotten some grit in my eye.

We were halfway down the Loomises' drive. Daisy had gone and smashed through their fence again. Pa was furious. Mrs. Loomis was, too. I pretended to be, but really I was glad, for it meant I got to see Royal without looking like I wanted to. He'd been in the barnyard, just as I'd hoped. He'd helped me get Daisy and Baldwin out of the pond again and then he walked me home.

We met Will and Jim coming the other way. They had their fishing rods over their shoulders and a creel full of trout.

"Oh, Mattie, dear, be mine until Niagara Falls!" Jim cooed.

"I will, Royal, darling, until the kitchen sinks!" Will gushed.

They were blowing kisses at each other when Royal slipped Daisy's noose off and cracked Jim on the ass with it. He took off howling, with Will right behind him. Then Royal picked up where he'd left off, telling me what turkeys ate and how they'd be good to raise alongside chickens and geese. As I nodded and smiled and *umm-hmm*'d and *oh, my*'d my way down the drive, I wondered if boys had any sort of magazine that told them how to attract women and, if so, did it ever tell them to put the girls' interests first?

I was just bursting to tell someone that we had the country's most scandalous lady poet right in our midst. I could've told Weaver, but I hadn't seen him for days. He was up at the Glenmore already, helping get the boats ready and the porch painted. I could've told Abby, but I was worried she might tell Jane Miley, her best friend, and Jane might spread it around, and I thought it might be dangerous to Miss Wilcox if people knew who she really was, seeing as everyone was so up in arms over *A Distant Music*. I wanted to tell Royal most of all. I wanted to share it with him and have it be our secret, just ours, but he never gave me the chance.

"Look at that stretch of land right there, Matt," he said, sweeping his hand out in front of him. "Nice and flat, well drained, and a good stream besides. Make good growing land. I'd farm it for corn in a second."

The stretch of land he was talking about included Emmie Hubbard's property and a bit of my father's, as well as Loomis land. "Well, I think Emmie might have something to say about that. And my pa, too."

He shrugged. "A man can dream, can't he?"

And before I could say anything in reply, he asked me if I'd like to go riding with him to Inlet and back that very night. I said I would. And as soon as I told him yes, he let go of Daisy's rope, pulled me in under some maple trees, and kissed me. I guess the unspoken language of my body must've been pretty eloquent after all, because that was just what I'd wanted him to do. He pressed himself into me and kissed my neck, and it was as if everything strong and solid inside me, heart and bones and muscle and gut, softened and melted from the heat of him. For the first time, I dared to touch him. It must have been the beautiful May day that made me so bold. Springtime in the woods can make you half mad. I ran my hands over his arms and laid them upon his chest. His heart was beating slow and steady unlike my own, which was thumping like a thresher. I guessed it must be different for a boy than it was for a girl. I felt his hands circling my waist, and then one slipped down lower. To a place Mamma told me no one should ever touch, only a husband.

"Royal, no."

"Aw, Mattie, it's all right."

He pulled away from me and frowned and his face darkened and I felt I had done something wrong. My word of the day was *abscission*. It means an act of cutting off or a sudden termination. I felt its meaning as I looked at Royal's face, all clouded. I felt frightened and bereft, as if I had somehow cut myself off from the sun. He looked at the ground, then back at me. "I ain't playing, Matt, if that's what you think. I seen a ring in Tuttle's."

I blinked for a reply, because I didn't understand what he meant.

He sighed and shook his head. "If I was to buy it, would you want it?"

Good Lord, *that* kind of ring. I thought he meant a ring for a harness or a pulley, but he meant a real ring. Like the one his brother Dan had given Belinda Becker.

"Oh yes! Yes, I would," I whispered. And then I threw my arms around his neck and kissed him and nearly sobbed with relief when I felt him kiss me back. I didn't think what it meant, saying yes. All I wanted was Royal right then, and I didn't think how saying yes to him would mean saying no to all the other things I wanted.

"All right, then," he said, breaking away from me. "I'll call for you after supper tonight."

"All right."

He picked up Daisy's rope and handed it to me, and I walked the rest of the way home by myself. And it was only much later, after he'd called at our place and asked

Pa if I could go riding, and we'd been up to Inlet and back and I was upstairs in my bed remembering every one of his kisses, that I wondered if he was supposed to have said he loved me when he told me about the ring. Or if maybe that came later.

his · pid · u · lous

"Bill Mitchell you know he kept our shanty. As mean a damn man as you ever did see..."

"Beth, don't curse."

"I didn't, Matt, it was the song. 'He'd lay round the shanty from morning till night. If a man said a word, he was ready to fight...'"

"Can't you sing a nicer song? How about the one Reverend Miller taught you? 'Onward, Christian Soldiers'?"

She wrinkled her nose. "I like 'Township Nineteen' better. The lumberjacks are more fun than Jesus. I never seen him work a jam and he can't birl, neither. Not in that nightshirt he's always wearing."

The nearest church was in Inlet and we hadn't been to it since Mamma died. She was the one who made us go; Pa wasn't one for religion. I wondered if maybe I should take my sisters on the coming Sunday.

"One morn before daylight, Jim Lou he got mad. Knocked hell out of Mitchell and the boys was all glad..."

I sighed and let Beth sing. The two of us were on our way to Emmie Hubbard's. We were walking close together under our mother's old black umbrella. A soft, pattering rain was coming down, the gentle kind that

227

made the color and smell of everything around us—the grass, the dirt road, the balsams and violets and wild lilies of the valley—come up strong.

Beth finished her song. "Is Emmie going away, Matt?" she asked me. "And her kids? That's what Tommy said."

"I don't know. Maybe she'll tell us."

Tommy and Jenny had come for breakfast again that morning, and Tommy had been very upset. He'd told us about a letter that had come from Arn Satterlee. It was the second one Emmie had received from Arn. The first one—the one I knew about thanks to my aunt Josie but had to pretend I didn't when Emmie showed up on our doorstep to ask Pa what it meant—said that her land would be auctioned. Tommy said the second one had set August 20 as the date of the auction. He said the letter had his mother broken down and crying, and Weaver's mamma wasn't at home, because she was down to the railroad station selling her chicken, and would I please come.

I hadn't been able to go right away. There was too much work in the mornings then, with the cows giving so much milk. Plus, it was planting time and I had the cabbage seed to get in. The moon had been full the night before, and things that grow in a head have to be planted when the moon's full, so they'll take a similar notion and come up big and round. Right after dinner, though, I'd wrapped up the leftover biscuits and set off up the road. I'd made extra with the Hubbard kids in mind. We could afford to be more generous with food since we had milk money coming in.

Beth chattered as we walked. She talked about Miss Wilcox's automobile and how the entire Burnap family was down with the grippe and that J. P. Morgan's Pullman car had gone through Eagle Bay yesterday, and that Jim Loomis had been playing tricks on tourist kids who wanted to go boating on Fourth Lake, telling them to go inside the Eagle Bay Hotel and ask the manager for Warneck Brown, he'd take them. And they actually did it and how dumb could city kids be when everyone knew Warneck Brown was chewing tobacco, not a person. Beth tended to flit from one topic to another faster than a hummingbird. "Mattie, what's your word of the day today?" she finally asked me.

"*Hispidulous.*"

"What's it mean?"

"Covered in short hairs. Bristly."

"You got a sentence for it?"

"It's *have*, Beth, not *got,* and no, I don't. I can't think of anything that's hispidulous."

She thought for a few seconds, then said, "Pa's face is with his beard. So's the piglet."

I laughed. "You're right," I said.

She smiled at me and took my hand. "I'm glad you're not going to college, Matt. I'm glad you're staying here. You won't go, will you? You'll stay and marry Royal Loomis, won't you? Abby says he's sweet on you."

"I'm not going anywhere, Beth," I said, forcing a smile. More and more, I was seeing my dreams of going to college as just that—dreams. I couldn't leave. I knew that. Deep inside, I'd always known it. Even if I wasn't sparking with Royal. Even if I earned enough money working for Miss Wilcox to buy my train ticket and Pa personally escorted me to the railroad station. I had promised my mamma I would stay.

I tried to think about the future now. A real future, not a dream one. I thought about what Royal and I might do for Decoration Day—hear the town band in Old Forge or go to a picnic in Inlet. And if I should spend a little of the three dollars I'd earned from Miss Wilcox on fabric for a new skirt or save it all to go toward household things.

When we got to Emmie's, I was surprised to see that her kids were all outside. Tommy and Susie were standing under a pine tree with Lucius, the baby. Jenny, Billy, Myrton, and Clara were standing out in the muddy yard with their clothing soaked and their hair plastered to their heads. I looked at the chimney pipe sticking out of Emmie's bleak gray house. There was no smoke coming out of it. The poor things would be chilled to the bone and there would be no fire burning in the stove to warm them when they went in. They'd be sick in no time. Anger flared up inside of me. Mostly I felt sorry for Emmie, but she made me mad sometimes, too. She was a mamma seven times over, but she still needed a mamma herself.

As soon as the children saw Beth and me, they swarmed us like kittens around a milk pail. There always seemed to be more of them than I remembered.

"Why are you kids out in the rain?" I asked them.

"Ma sent us out. She's busy," Myrton said, wiping his nose on his sleeve.

"Busy with what?" I asked.

"Mr. Loomis is here. He's helping her fix the stove. She said it's dangerous and she doesn't want us back in the house till he's finished," Tommy said.

"That's silly. I'm sure it's fine to go in," I said. I couldn't see how fixing a woodstove would be dangerous.

"Mattie, you can't go in. Don't." There was a lick of anger in Tom's voice. "They've got the whole stove apart; there's pieces all over the floor."

"Cripes, Tom, it's just a stove. I'll be careful of it," I said, irritated. "I've come all this way in the rain because you asked me to, and I'm not going back again without seeing your ma."

I trotted up the broken steps onto the porch. The house's one front window was right next to the door. I glanced in before I knocked, just to make sure there weren't any stove parts in front of the door, and what I saw stopped me dead in my tracks.

Emmie was bent over the stove with her skirts up around her waist. Mr. Loomis was behind her with his pants down around his ankles. And neither of them was fixing anything.

I turned around, grabbed Beth's arm, and yanked her off the porch. "Ow, Mattie, jeezum! Let go, will you?" she howled.

"Tommy... tell your ma... tell her I'll call on her a bit later, all right? All right, Tom? Here... here are some biscuits. Take them in to her when . . . when you can."

Tommy didn't answer me. His thin shoulders sagged from the weight of knowing. I could feel the heaviness, too, and it made me angry. I didn't want it. Didn't want to carry it. Tommy took the food, but he wouldn't look at me. I was glad of it, for I couldn't have met his eyes.

"Ain't we going inside, Matt? I thought you wanted to see Emmie."

"Later, Beth. Emmie's busy. She's fixing the stove. It's dangerous."

"But you said—"

"Never mind what I said! Just come on!"

Beth whined and rubbed her arm all the way home. And I tried to tell myself that I had not just seen what I had seen, for it had looked so ugly and rude and seemed more like barnyard animals than a man and woman. It didn't look like *making love;* it looked like all the filthy words I'd ever heard it called. I wondered if that was how Minnie got her babies. If it was how my mamma got us. I wondered if that's how it would be between Royal and myself when we were married. If it was, I'd tell him to keep himself to himself, for I wanted no part of it.

Poor Tommy. His brothers and sisters hadn't seemed to know what was happening, but he did. I hoped Mrs. Loomis would never find out. Or Royal or his brothers. It would hurt them terribly. Beth hadn't seen anything and surely Tommy was much too ashamed to tell. It would stay a secret. No one else would ever know.

As we finally turned in to our own drive, our shoes sodden and our skirts muddied, I realized I had figured out a way to use my word of the day after all. Mr. Loomis's shirttails had not quite covered his bare behind, and I had seen, though I truly wished I hadn't, that it was pale, flabby, and horribly hispidulous.

Put the letters away, Mattie, I say to myself.
No, myself answers.
You're no better than your aunt Josie. Reading other people's letters is something she would do. You're a snoop.
I don't care.
Stop this. Go to sleep. You know all you need to know.
But I don't. I know that Grace was pregnant. And I know she got that way because of Chester Gillette. And I think that they came to the Glenmore to elope. There's just one thing I don't know, and if I can find it out, I will put the letters away and go to sleep: I don't know why Chester Gillette wrote *Carl Grahm* in the guest book, and until I find that out, I'm going to keep reading.

South Otselic
June 25, '06
Dear Chester,

I am much too tired to write a decent letter or even follow the lines, but I have been uneasy all day and can't go to sleep because I am sorry I sent you such a hateful letter this morning. So I am going to write and ask your forgiveness, dear. I was cross and wrote things I ought not to have written. I am very sorry, dear. I shall never feel quite right until you write and say you forgive me...I am very tired tonight, dear, I have been helping mamma sew today... I never liked to have dresses fitted and now it is ten times worse. Oh Chester, you have no idea how glad I shall be when this worry is all over...I am afraid the time will seem awfully long until I see you, Chester... Oh! dear, I do get so blue. Chester, please don't wait until the last of the week before you come. Can't you come the first of the week? Chester, I need you more than you think I do...

I keep reading, but there's nothing in the letter about Carl Grahm. Maybe I'm looking in the wrong place. I put Grace's letter down and shuffle through the bundle until I find what I'm after—a few letters written by Chester. I open the first one.

June 21
Dear Grace,

Please excuse paper and pencil, as I am not writing this at home and have nothing else here. I received your letter last night and was just a little surprised although I thought you would be discouraged. Don't worry so much and think less about how you feel and have a good time...

There is more in the letter about a trip some of his friends are taking and that he cannot leave Cortland before the seventh of July, but nothing about Carl Grahm. I open the next one.

July 2, 1906
Dear Kid—
I certainly felt good when I got your letter although I also felt mean as I hadn't written all week. Wednesday and Thursday I had to work on the payroll and Friday a friend came and stayed all night. Saturday I went up to the lake and am so burned tonight I cannot wear a collar or coat. We went out in the canoe and to two other lakes, and, although the canoe was heavy to carry, we had a good time ... As for my plans for the Fourth I have made none as the only two girls I could get to go with me have made other arrangements because I didn't ask them until Saturday ...

Now I see why Grace sounded so worried in all her letters. There were other girls. She wasn't the only one. There were girls that maybe he wanted to be with more than he wanted to be with her. Lord, what a mess of trouble she was in. Chester had put her in the family way and she needed him to marry her, but he didn't seem to want to. Not if she had to plead with him to come for her, not if he barely wrote to her, and when he did, told her about other girls he was taking around.

Not if he fought with her at dinner about trying to find a chapel.

I can't imagine how frightened Grace must have been, alone with her terrible secret, waiting and waiting for Chester to come. I remember all Pa's warnings about men and the one thing they want, and I shudder to think what would happen to me if I ever found myself a baby before I found myself a husband. But then I comfort myself with the knowledge that Chester *did* do right by her in the end. He came and got her and brought her to the North Woods to elope, didn't he? Even if they did fight about the chapel. Why else would he have brought her here if it wasn't to elope?

I am so confused. I don't know what to think. I feel like the little feather shuttlecock in the badminton games the guests play, batted about from one side to the other.

There is one more Chester letter. It is out of order in the stack, dated earlier than the previous one. Maybe it will tell me what I want to know.

June 25, 1906
Dear Grace —
  . . . Three of us fellows went up to the lake and camped in a small house that one of the boys owns. We had a dandy time even though there were no girls. We went in swimming in the afternoon, and the water was great. I went out in the canoe in the evening and wished you had been there . . .

I stop reading. All of Chester's good and dandy times, I realize, took place on a lake. In a canoe.

Earlier that day, when the men had brought Grace's body in, we all thought that her companion, Carl Grahm, had drowned, too, and that it would only be a matter of time until his body was found.

But there was no Carl Grahm. I couldn't find him anywhere. There was only Chester Gillette. And Chester Gillette could handle a boat. Chester Gillette could swim.

You have your answer now, don't you? I say to myself. *That's what you get for prying.*

But myself is not listening. She refuses to listen. She's picking up another letter and another and another, frantically looking for a different answer.

She feels sick, so sick she could vomit.

Because she thinks she knows why Chester brought Grace here.

And it wasn't to elope.

ico · sa · he · dron

"And don't you ever go in a room by yourself with a strange man . . ."

"Yes, Pa."

". . . no matter what the reason. Even if he says you're just to bring him a towel. Or a cup of tea."

"I won't, Pa."

"And you watch yourself around the help, too. Work-men and barkeeps and such."

"I'll be all right, Pa. The Morrisons run a respectable place."

"That may be, but any low-down jack with a few dollars in his pocket can take a room at a fancy hotel. Things ain't always what they seem, Mattie. You remember that. Just because a cat has her kittens in the oven, it don't make 'em biscuits."

Things are never *what they seem, Pa,* I thought. I used to think they were, but I was wrong or stupid or blind or something. Old folks are forever complaining about their failing eyesight, but I think your vision gets better as you get older. Mine surely was.

I'd seen Miss Wilcox as a spinster teacher with a fondness for the mountains. She wasn't. She was Emily

Baxter, a lady poet who'd run away from her husband. I'd seen Mr. Loomis as someone who was just being kind whenever he brought Emmie Hubbard eggs or milk. He wasn't. He was most likely the reason her three younger kids all had blond hair. I'd seen Royal Loomis as too fine to ever notice the likes of me, but now we were out driving together every night and he was going to buy me a ring. I'd seen my chances of working at one of the hotels as zero, but there I was, just two weeks before Decoration Day and the official start of the summer season, sitting next to my father in the buckboard on my way to the Glenmore. My mamma's old carpetbag—packed with my dictionary, a few other books from Miss Wilcox, my nightclothes, and two of Mamma's better skirts and waists that Abby had taken in for me—was on the floor between us, heavy as a hod of bricks.

Two days before, I'd gone into the barn to fetch Pleasant out and found him stiff and cold in his stall. No one knew why. He wasn't ailing. Pa said it was old age. He was upset when I told him. He couldn't be without a mule. He needed one to harrow the crops and deliver milk and pull stumps, but a good one cost about twenty dollars and he didn't have it. He was far too stubborn to borrow it, but old Ezra Rombaugh in Inlet, whose son and new daughter-in-law were working his land with their oxen, said he'd sell Pa his six-year-old for fourteen dollars and let him pay off the cost so much every week. That's when he decided I would go to the Glenmore. He didn't like the idea any more in May than he had in March, but he had no choice.

I should have been excited. I should have been beside myself. I'd wanted to go to the Glenmore for months, ever since Weaver and I first cooked up the idea over the winter. And I was finally going. But it felt bittersweet. I wasn't working to get myself to Barnard. I was working because Pa needed help to pay for the new mule.

My mamma once had a beautiful glass basket that my aunt Josie gave her. It was a deep indigo blue, with a braided handle and ruffled edges, and it had SOUVENIR OF CAPE MAY written on it. Mamma loved it. She'd kept it on a shelf in the parlor, but Lou took it down one day to play with it and dropped it on the floor. It smashed into a million pieces. Lawton thought maybe he could glue it back together. He tried, but it was too badly damaged. Mamma didn't throw the shards out, though. She put them into an old cigar box and kept them in the bureau in her bedroom. She would look at them every once in a while. She would hold a piece up to the window and watch the light come through it, then put the box away again. When I was younger, I never understood why she kept the broken pieces around, why she didn't just throw them out. Riding up the Big Moose Road with my pa that day, waiting for the Glenmore to come into view, I finally did.

After talking to Ezra Rombaugh, Pa had inquired at the hotel to see if they still had any positions vacant, and they did. I was sorry I couldn't work for Miss Wilcox anymore, but the Glenmore paid more and she was happy for me to go. She said my wages would more than cover the price of a train ticket to New York City. I hadn't the heart to tell her that I'd written Dean Gill to say I wasn't coming.

I was to receive four dollars a week. Pa said I could keep back a dollar for myself. I told him I would keep back two or I would not go. "You know I'm keeping company with Royal Loomis," I said. "I'll have need of a few dollars myself soon." I had three dollars from Miss Wilcox, plus the nickel left over from my fiddlehead money, but I'd need more. Setting up house was an expensive proposition. Pa blinked at me, but I didn't blink back. I'd counted on him still feeling bad enough about hitting me to let me have my way on this, and I was right. There is an advantage to be found in most everything that happens to you, even if it is not immediately apparent.

Pa went right to Inlet after I found Pleasant, and left word at O'Hara's for Bert Brown to come get him. It was only the end of May, but the days could get warm. Bert collected dead livestock and rendered them down. He didn't pay anything for them, but he saved you digging a hole. I was sure that any soap made from Pleasant would be harsh enough to take the skin off your hands, and any glue made from him would be stronger than nails. *Icosahedron,* my word of the day, means twenty-sided. It is an almost entirely useless word, unless, of course, you want to describe something with twenty sides. Then it is perfect. It was a fitting word for Pleasant, who mostly dug his heels in and bit and kicked, but who got me to the Glenmore when I couldn't get myself there.

Pa turned right off the Big Moose Road, and then right again, into the Glenmore's drive. I could see the hotel now, looming tall. A trio of beautifully dressed women strolled toward the dock, parasols over their slender shoulders. A family alighted from a surrey at the front of the hotel and walked leisurely across the lawn. Their maid stayed behind, counting the pieces of luggage as they were unloaded. Suddenly I wanted to tell my father to turn around. I didn't know the first thing about fine people, or how to behave around them. What if I dropped soup in someone's lap? Or spoke before I was spoken to? Or poured wine into the water glasses? Pa needed that new mule badly, though—I knew he did—so I didn't say a word.

"Abby know how to deal with that stove?" he asked me as Licorice, the new mule, pulled the buckboard up to the Glenmore's back entrance.

"Yes, Pa. Better than I do." Abby was going to be in charge of everyone, and she would get the meals, too.

"I talked with Mr. Sperry. You're to serve in the dining room and help in the kitchen and clean the rooms, but I don't want you nowhere near the bar, you hear? You stay away from the dancing pavilion, too."

"Yes, Pa." What did he think I was going to do? Knock back a few shots every now and again and show off my fancy quickstep?

"Anything happens and you want to come home, you just send word. Don't walk all the way by yourself with that bag. I'll come and get you. Or Royal. One of us will."

"I'll be fine, Pa. Really I will."

I got out. My father did, too. He lifted my bag down, walked me to the kitchen door, and peered inside. I waited for him to hand me the carpetbag, but he didn't. He held it hard against him. "Well, you going in or not?" he asked me.

"I need my bag, Pa."

As he handed it to me, I saw he'd gripped it so tightly his knuckles had turned white. We were not the kissing kind, me and Pa, but I wished that maybe he would at least hug me good-bye. He just toed the ground and spat, though, told me to mind myself, and took off in the buckboard without once looking back.

ob · strep · er · ous

I was cleaning the table when I saw it. A dime. Lying next to the sugar bowl. I picked it up and ran after the woman who'd left it.

"Ma'am? Pardon me, ma'am!" I called.

She stopped in the doorway.

"You left this, ma'am," I said, holding the coin out to her.

She smiled and shook her head. "Yes, I did. For you." And then she turned and walked out of the dining room and I did not know what to do. Cook warned us nine ways to Sunday to turn in anything that we find— money, jewelry, buttons, anything. But how could I turn it in if its owner didn't want it back?

"Put it in your pocket, you fool," a voice behind me said. It was Weaver. He was busing a huge tray of dirty dishes. "It's called a tip. They leave it for good service. You get to keep it."

"For real?"

"Yup. But if you don't get your table cleared and your rear end back in the kitchen, it'll be the only one you ever get." He started walking away, then turned and said, "Boisterous."

"Unruly," I replied, hurrying back to clear my table.

On the way into the kitchen, I had to pause outside the doors for a second, trying to remember which was in and which was out. I'd already been yelled at for going out the in one. As I pushed open the right door, struggling to balance the heavy tray on my shoulder, Cook bawled at me for being slower than a snail on crutches. "Table ten needs water, butter, and rolls! Look alive, Mattie!" she yelled.

"I'm sorry," I said.

I rushed past the other girls, past the smoke and steam pouring from the massive black stove, and slammed my tray down by the sink. "Don't slam it!" Bill the dishwasher yelled. "Aw, look at that, will you? You're supposed to scrape the dishes, then stack them. Just look at that mess!"

"I'm sorry," I mumbled.

I ran to the warming oven, skidded on a slice of tomato, and just managed to right myself before I smashed into Henry, the new underchef, who had arrived at the Glenmore the day before, same as me, and was carrying a basket of lobsters. Henry, Mrs. Morrison had informed us, had apprenticed in the finest kitchens of Europe, and the Glenmore was fortunate to have him.

"*Mein Gott!* Vatch out!" he yelled.

"I'm sorry," I whispered.

"You sure are," Weaver said, whizzing past me.

"Weaver, Ada, Fran, pick up! Pick up!" Cook hollered.

I grabbed a clean tray, a dish of butter from the cold station, and a jug of water.

"Uncontrollable," Weaver shot at me, on his way back to the dining room.

"Clamorous," I shot back. We had a word duel going for my word of the day—*obstreperous*. I saw that it was going to be tough to play my word games here. I'd barely had time to wash my face and braid my hair that morning, never mind look in my dictionary.

I had challenged Weaver to a duel out of spite after I learned that he was making a whole dollar more a week than I was. I'd asked him how he did it, and he'd said, "Never take what's offered, Matt. Always ask for more." And then he took off his cap and held it in his hands. "Please, sir, I want some more," he said, mimicking Oliver Twist.

"Just look where that got Oliver," I'd grumbled, put out at how Weaver always seemed to be able to bend the world, just a little, to his will. Just because he dared to.

I rushed to the warming oven, got a basket down off the top of it, and lined it with a clean napkin. I burned my fingers getting the hot rolls. My eyes teared, but I didn't dare let on.

"Henry! Heat these up, will you?" Cook shouted. And then three metal cans went sailing over my head, one after another.

"Vas is?" Henry yelled.

"Sweet milk. For a caramel sauce," she shouted back.

"Obnoxious," Weaver said, suddenly beside me and scooping rolls into a basket. He stuffed a corn dodger into his mouth, then yowled, as Cook, passing us on a return trip to the oven from the icebox, cuffed his head.

"Bumptious," I said, giggling.

Weaver had a reply, but he couldn't get it out because his mouth was full. "To the death, Mr. Smith," I said. I blew on my finger like it was a pistol stock, hoisted my tray, and headed for the dining room.

It was my first full day at the Glenmore, and though it was only about six miles from my house, it was a whole different country to me, a whole new world—the world of tourists. Tourists are a race of people who have money enough to go on vacation for a week or two, sometimes a month or even the whole summer. I couldn't imagine it—not working for a whole summer. Some of them were quite nice, some were not. Mrs. Morrison was bossy and Cook was a bear, but I didn't mind any of it. It all seemed like a grand adventure to me. I wasn't quite as nervous as I'd thought I'd be. Fran, who was head waitress, had explained things to me.

I placed the rolls and butter down on table ten. A family was dining there. A father, mother, and three young children. They talked and laughed. The father rubbed noses with his little girl. I stared at them until the mother noticed me and I had to look away.

Table nine was a party of four burly sporting gentlemen up from New York City. They'd gone fishing with a guide in the morning and planned to go back out at dusk. I thought they would empty the entire kitchen. I brought them cream of green pea soup. Three baskets of rolls. A plate of sweet gherkins, radishes, olives, and chowchow. The trout they'd caught, fried and served with Sarah Bernhardt potatoes. Chicken livers sautéed with bacon. Entrecôtes of beef. Dishes of spinach, stewed tomatoes, beets, and creamed cauliflower. And for dessert, coconut layer cake sandwiched together with custard and covered with pillows of boiled icing.

Table eight was a single woman. She was sitting quietly, sipping lemonade and reading. I couldn't take my eyes off her. "I'd kill for a dress like that," Fran said as she passed by me. But it wasn't her dress I wanted, it was her freedom. She could sit by a window and read, with nobody to say, "Are the chickens fed? What's for supper? Have the pigs been slopped? The garden hoed? The cows milked? The stove blacked?" I thought she was the luckiest woman on the face of the earth. She had a small appetite and ordered no starters, only the trout. But she wanted it poached, not fried.

Cook grumbled, but she poached the fish. When I brought it out, the woman wrinkled her nose. "It smells off," she said. "Would you please tell your cook that I like my fish fresh?"

I returned to the kitchen and went up to Cook with the plate in my hands, thinking that my life would surely end right then and there, but she just grumbled, took the lettuce and tomato garnish off, flipped the fish over, put on a new garnish of spinach leaves and carrot coins, then told me to wait five minutes and take it back out again. I did. The woman pronounced it perfect.

Table seven was two young married couples. They had maps with them and were planning a buckboard tour of the area. The men wore light wool suits and had smooth, clean hands and all their fingers. The women wore cycling skirts and striped waists with silk bow ties at the collar.

"Say, Maude, maybe our little waitress here will know!" one of the gentlemen said as I prepared to take their orders.

"Do you know where I can find Indians?" the woman named Maude asked me. "I'm here in the Ho De Ron Dah and I want to see Indians."

"Beg your pardon, ma'am," I said uncertainly, "but this is the Glenmore."

The entire table burst into laughter. I felt stupid and I didn't even know why.

"*Ho De Ron Dah* is an Indian word, dear. It's Iroquois. It means 'bark eaters.' It's what the Iroquois called their enemies, the Montagnais. The Montagnais hunted here in the mountains, but if they couldn't catch anything, they ate roots and twigs. The Iroquois found that terribly gauche. White people, however, pronounce the word Ad-i-ron-dack. You know, the Adirondacks? Where you live!"

I live in the North Woods, I said silently. *The Adirondacks* was a name the travel brochures used to lure summer people. It was pretty and clever, like the tricked-out fishing flies Charlie Eckler sold to the tourists. The ones no guide would be caught dead using.

"So, tell me," the woman said, "where can I find some Indians?"

I cleared my throat nervously. I didn't want to say

something else stupid and have them laugh at me again. "Well, ma'am, there's the Traversys. And the Dennises. They're Abenakis, I'm told. They weave sweet-grass baskets and sell them in Eagle Bay. At the railroad station..."

The woman wrinkled her nose. "Those are faux Indians. I want the real thing. The noble savage in the wilderness. Primitive man in all his glory."

"I'm sorry, ma'am, I don't know...," I started to say, miserably awkward.

Weaver was suddenly at the table refilling the water glasses. I had no idea how he got there, and I wished he hadn't. He had that look in his eyes. The one I knew too well.

"You want to see Mose LaVoie, ma'am," he said. "He's a full-blooded Saint Regis. Lives up past Big Moose Station. In a tepee in the woods."

My mouth dropped open.

"There you go, Maudsy!" the gentleman said.

"How exciting!" the woman said. "How will we know him?"

"He's hard to miss, ma'am. He wears buckskins. Though that's only when it's cold. This time of year, he just wears a loincloth. And a bear-claw necklace. And feathers in his hair. Just go up to the Summit Hotel and ask for Injun Mose."

I nearly choked. Mose LaVoie was an Indian, but he certainly did not live in a tepee. He lived in a log house and he wore a shirt, trousers, and suspenders like every other man. He was nice enough if he knew you, but he had a temper and it came out when he drank. He'd take a swing at a locomotive if he thought it was looking at him the wrong way. He'd put out the windows in the Summit on more than one occasion, and he was certain to knock the head off any fool tourist who called him Injun Mose instead of Mr. LaVoie.

"A genuine redskin! Imagine that! He'll be the perfect guide to the real Ho De Ron Dah!"

Weaver grinned from ear to ear. "Yes, ma'am, he sure will," he said.

I caught up with him at the coffee station. "You're going to have four murders on your conscience, Weaver Smith. I hope you're all right with that."

"They shouldn't laugh at you," he said. "And they shouldn't call me colored."

"Oh, Weaver, they didn't." He hates being called that word, *colored.* He says he is a person, not an Easter egg.

"They did. Last night when they arrived and again at breakfast. Ever seen Mose LaVoie when he's mad?"

"Only from a distance."

"Me, too. And I reckon this ought to make us just about even."

Table seven was bad, but table six was the worst of all. The very worst. It was a single man. A Mr. Maxwell. He was small and slight. Balding. And sweating, too, even though it wasn't terribly warm. One must always steer clear of men who sweat when it isn't warm. He held the menu on the table and bent his head toward it, squinting and mopping his brow with his handkerchief as he studied it.

"I'm afraid I've left my glasses in my room," he finally said. "Would you mind reading the entrées for me?" I thought his eyes must be very bad indeed, because he looked at my bosom as he spoke, not my face.

"I'd be happy to," I said, just as green as a frog. I leaned over him and started reciting. "Baked ham, broiled spring chicken, boiled tongue..."

Just as I got to the veal in aspic, he pulled his napkin off his lap. Under it was something that looked rather like a frankfurter. Only no frankfurter I'd ever seen stood at attention.

"I'll have the veal in aspic," he said, covering himself again.

My face was flaming as I went back into the kitchen. It was so red that Cook noticed it immediately. "What have you done?" she barked. "Did you drop something?"

"No ma'am, I...I just stumbled, that's all," I lied. I couldn't bear to say what really happened. Not to anyone.

Fran, picking up an order, heard us. She came up to me. "Table six?" she whispered.

I nodded, looking at the floor.

"The dirty dog! He did it to me yesterday. You should drop something, all right. A jug of ice water. Right in his lap! Don't go back there, Matt. I'll get Weaver to take the table."

"Fran! Where are you?" Cook bellowed. "Pick up, pick—"

She didn't get to finish her sentence, because just then, the kitchen fell under attack.

There was an explosion. Louder than the Old Forge town cannon on the Fourth of July. Worse than anything I'd ever heard. Ada screamed. I did, too. *"Oh, mein Gott!"* Henry yelled. Shrapnel went whizzing through the air and hit one of the gas lamps. Glass came raining down. Ada and I ducked behind the cold station, clutching each other. There was another explosion, and another. There was more screaming and more glass. I chanced a look up; the ceiling was dented in half a dozen places. More lamps had been smashed. A window was broken.

I felt a wetness on my face. It was hot. "Ada!" I said frantically. "Ada, I think I'm bleeding." Ada raised her head and looked at me. She touched my cheek. I looked at her fingers, expecting to see crimson, but instead I saw white. Ada sniffed it. "Smells like milk," she said. We stood up cautiously, still holding on to each other.

Fran and Weaver were peering out from behind the icebox. Bill was crouched under the sink. Two more waitresses and another busboy had hidden in the cellar way. I saw the door open a crack and their eyes blinking from the gloom. The kitchen was a complete disaster. The mess was breathtaking. The same sticky goo that was on my face was dripping from the ceiling. There was glass on every surface—on the plates, in the cutlery trays, on the serving platters, all over the floor. A cake batter, three pies, a bowl of biscuit dough, a pan of gelatin, a pot of soup, four trays of cookies, and a crab mousse were ruined.

I heard a moan coming from under the big plank worktable in front of the stove. It was Cook. She was lying facedown on the floor. Ada and I ran to help her up. She looked all around, shaking her head at the devastation.

"Where's Henry?" she gasped. "Where the devil is he?"

Henry came out from the pantry. He was ashen and trembling.

"You put those cans right on the stove, didn't you?" she yelled at him.

"You...you try to kill me!" Henry shouted at her. "You tell me heat milk, then *Blam! Blam! Blam!*"

"In a pot, you jackass! In a pot! You can't heat cans; they explode. Don't you know that? What kind of god-forsaken ass-backward caveman country do you come from?" she roared.

"You try to kill me," Henry insisted. Obstreperously.

"Not hard enough," Cook said. She picked up a carving knife. Henry bolted out through the screen door. She was right on his heels.

Half an hour later, she was back at her stove, wiping it clean, and Henry was nowhere to be seen. The rest of us were busy washing and mopping. I was at the sink, rinsing out my rag, convinced I'd come to work at a lunatic asylum. Only here, the lunatics were allowed to roam free, blowing things up or threatening to kill one another. I remembered what Pa had told me: He'd come after me, or get Royal to, if I wanted to go home. I remembered what he'd said about low-down jacks taking rooms in fancy hotels, too, and wished I could tell him what table six had done. Pa would settle that man's hash for him, but then I'd be on my way home whether I wanted to go or not, hearing "I told you so" the whole way. And then Weaver came up to me and pressed something crinkly into my hand. A whole dollar bill.

"What's this?" I asked him.

"Your tip. From table six."

I shook my head. "I don't want it," I said, trying to hand it back. "Not from him."

"Don't be stupid. It's the easiest money you'll make all summer. Hell, the old duffer can flash *me* for a dollar."

Fran appeared with a bucket of dirty water. "I'd give it another look for a quarter," she said, giggling.

Both Fran and Weaver jollied me until we were all three laughing, until I took the dollar and put it in my pocket along with the dimes and nickels I'd collected from my other tables, until Cook—seeing us idle—picked up her knife, pointed it at us, and said, "Stop loafing and start working before I tell Mr. Morrison to dig three more graves right next to the one he's digging for Henry."

So we did.

li · mic · o · lous

Everyone in Big Moose and Eagle Bay and Inlet and the whole North Woods knew that it was bad luck to sharpen a tool after dusk. Everyone, it seemed, but Henry.

It was evening, about eight or so, and Cook had sent me down to the boathouse, where the guides were giving a fly-casting demonstration, with a tray of sugar cookies and a pitcher of lemonade. When I came back, there was Henry—sitting on the kitchen steps, sharpening a filleting knife. Cook had got it out of him that his so-called apprenticeship in the finest kitchens of Europe had consisted of mopping floors and emptying garbage pails. He was in disgrace and had to do all the menial jobs, like cleaning fish, and making stock from bones and peelings, and sharpening knives. She would have liked to send him packing, but she couldn't. The season was under way and help—good or bad—was hard to find.

"Henry, don't do that!" I scolded. "It's bad luck!"

I could do that now—scold Henry and tease Bill and joke with Charlie, the bartender, and the guides—for I'd been at the Glenmore a whole week and had received my first wages, and I belonged now, too. Just as much as they did.

"Vat luck? No luck but luck vat you make," Henry said stubbornly, keeping on with his task.

Well, he made some luck all right. Bad luck. And not for himself, either.

I thought of that knife, and of the sharpening stone, the second I saw Weaver's face. It was maybe half an hour later and Cook and I were hanging out dishrags on a line near the back steps when John Denio brought him to the kitchen door. We gasped at the sight of him, then hustled him inside as fast as we could, hoping the Morrisons and Mr. Sperry wouldn't find out. But they did.

"Weaver, why can't you ever stay out of trouble?" Mr. Sperry shouted, storming in from the dining room. "I send you to Big Moose Station on a simple errand—to help John pick up new arrivals—and look what happens. One of the guests said there was a fight. Were you in it?"

Weaver lifted his chin. "Yes, sir, I was."

"Damn it, Weaver, you know my policy on fighting..."

"It wasn't his fault, Mr. Sperry," I quickly said, dabbing witch hazel on the cut below Weaver's eye. "He didn't start it."

"But he could have stopped it," Cook said, wiping blood from Weaver's nose. "Could have stepped aside and let the trash blow down the sidewalk, but no, he has to run his mouth."

"What happened?" Mr. Sperry asked.

John Denio answered. All three of us—Cook, Mr. Denio, and myself—knew better than to let Weaver do the talking.

"He was attacked," John said. "In front of the station.

The train was late. I went to talk to the stationmaster and left Weaver in the wagon. Three men came out of the Summit Hotel. Trappers. They were drunk. They said some things. Weaver answered back. One of them hauled him out of the seat and all three of them beat him. I heard the noise, ran out, and broke it up."

"Three to one, Weaver? For God's sake, why didn't you just keep quiet?"

"They called me nigger."

Mr. Sperry took Weaver's chin in his hand and grimaced at the damage. A cut eye that was already blackening. A nose that might well be broken. A lip as fat and shiny as a garden slug. "It's just a word, son. I've been called worse," he said.

"Beg your pardon, Mr. Sperry, but you haven't," Weaver said. "I'm going to the justice of the peace tomorrow," he added. "I'm telling him what happened. I'm pressing charges."

Mr. Sperry sighed. "You're just bent on kicking skunks, aren't you? From tomorrow on, you're to stay in the kitchen. You can wash dishes and mop floors and do whatever else Cook can find for you until your face heals."

"But why, Mr. Sperry?" Weaver asked, upset. He wouldn't earn tips working in the kitchen.

"Because you look like you fell into a meat grinder! I can't have you serving guests with a face like that."

"But it's not right, sir. I shouldn't be called names. Shouldn't catch a beating. Shouldn't have to stay in the kitchen, either."

"How old are you, Weaver? Seventeen or seven? Don't you know that what should be and what is are two different things? You should be dead. Luckily, you aren't. You think on that the next time you decide to take on three grown men." He stormed back out. Cook went after him to ask about a delivery, John returned to his horses, and the two of us were left alone.

Limicolous, my word of the day, means something that lives in the mud. I thought it was a very good word to describe the men who beat Weaver, and told him so. Weaver had other words to describe them, though, and it was a good thing Cook didn't hear them.

"Hush, Weaver, just let it go," I said, wrapping up a chunk of ice in a towel. "A few days in the kitchen won't kill you. It's better than losing your job. Here, hold this against your lip."

"Don't have much of a choice, do I?" he grumbled. He pressed the ice to his lip, winced, then said, "Three more months, Matt. Just three more months and I'm gone from here. Once I get through Columbia, once I'm a lawyer, ain't no one ever going to hand me a suitcase. Or call me boy or nigger or Sam. Or hit me. And if they do, I'll make sure they go to jail."

"I know you will," I said.

"I'll find myself a new place. A better place than this one, that's for sure. We both will, won't we, Matt?" he said, his eyes searching mine.

"Yes, we will," I said, busying myself with the witch hazel, for I could not meet his gaze.

I'd already found myself a new place, one I'd never in-tended to find, but I was in it now all the same. It was a place for myself alone and one I couldn't tell Weaver about, no more than I could tell Miss Wilcox. It was in Royal Loomis's arms, this place, and I liked it there. Weaver would never understand that. Sometimes I barely did myself.

$\mathcal{I}$ hear a loon calling from the lake. The tourists all say it's a beautiful sound. I think it's the loneliest sound I know. I am still reading. Still looking for a different answer. Another outcome. A happier ending. But I already know I'm not going to find it.

South Otselic
June 28, '06
My Dear Chester,
...I think I shall die of joy when I see you, dear. I will tell you I am going to try and do a whole lot better, dear, I will try not to worry so much and I won't believe horrid things the girls write. I presume they do stretch things, dear. I am about crazy or I could reason better than I do. I am awfully pleased you had such a jolly time at the lake, dear, and I wish I had been there, too. I am very fond of water, although I can't swim. I am crying and can't half write. Guess it's because my sister is playing her mandolin and singing "Love's Young Dream." I am a little blue...

It is a long letter and there are many more lines to read, but my eyes keep straying back to one line: *I am very fond of water, although I can't swim.* A chill grips me. I throw it off and keep reading.

> *... Chester, my silk dress is the prettiest dress I ever had, or at least that is what everyone says. Mamma don't think I have taken much interest in it. I am frightened every time it is fitted. Mamma says she don't see why I should cry every time they look at me... Chester dear, I hope you will have an awfully nice time the 4th. Really, dear, I don't care where you go or who you go with if you only come for the 7th. You are so fond of boating and the water why don't you go on a trip that will take you to some lake?...*

I can't read any more. I try to stuff the letter back into its envelope, but my hands are shaking so hard, it takes me three tries.

He knew she couldn't swim. He knew it.

I begin to weep then. I hold my hands over my face so that no noise gets out, and cry as though my heart is breaking. I think it is.

There are a few more letters, but I can't read them. I should never have read the first one, never mind nearly all of them. I stare into the darkness and I can see Grace's face as she handed me the letters. I hear her saying, "Burn them. Please. Promise me you will. No one can ever see them."

I burrow down into my pillow and close my eyes. I feel so old and so tired. I desperately want to sleep. But the darkness swirls behind my eyelids, and all I can think about is the black water of the lake closing around me, filling my eyes and ears and mouth, pulling me down as I struggle against it.

I am very fond of water, although I can't swim...

grav · id

The last time I saw her, Miss Wilcox said that "A Country Burial" by Emily Dickinson was perfection in eight lines.

Ample make this bed.
Make this bed with awe;
In it wait till judgment break
Excellent and fair.

Be its mattress straight,
Be its pillow round;
Let no sunrise' yellow noise
Interrupt this ground.

These lines astounded me. They were as beautiful, as pure, as a prayer. I repeated the poem silently to myself as Royal told me about the new hybrid corn they had at Becker's Farm and Feed.

It was a Wednesday afternoon, and I had a half day off from the Glenmore. Royal was driving me to Minnie's house on his way into Inlet. He'd come to fetch me at the hotel and Fran and Ada giggled and Weaver rolled his eyes and Cook smiled, but I ignored them all.

Royal talked a mile a minute as we rode. I nodded and did my best to listen, but I was thinking how much better *Ample make this bed* is than *Make this bed amply*, which is what I would have written. And I was thinking that Emily Dickinson was a dreadful woman. She flitted and hid prettily amongst her words like a butterfly in a garden. She lulled you into thinking she was only talking about a burial, or a bed, or roses, or sewing. She got your trust. Then she sneaked up behind you and whacked you over the head with a plank. In "Charlotte Brontë's Grave." In "The Chariot." In "The Wife." And "Apocalypse."

"... and Tom L'Esperance says the new seed gives ears that are twice as big as the seed we've been using and that..."

Even after having had the book in my possession for several weeks, I would start a poem feeling that I was up to the task—girded—and then, before I even knew it, I was wiping tears off the pages lest the water pucker them. Sometimes I took her meaning in my head, and that was bad enough. Other times she was more veiled and I could only understand it with my heart, and that was even worse. She provoked so much feeling with her small, careful words. She did so much with so little. Like Emmie Hubbard, with the paints she made from berries and roots. And Minnie making filling dinners for Jim and the hired hands out of nothing. And Weaver's mamma getting Weaver all the way from Eagle Bay to the Columbia University with her wash pot and chickens.

"...which means you get more silage out of the same acreage. I can't hardly believe it! It's like planting twenty acres, but getting the sort of yield you'd expect from thirty..."

Emily Dickinson riled me, but I never managed to be cross with her for long, because I knew she'd been fragile. Miss Wilcox said she had a hard time of it. Her pa was overbearing and hadn't let her read any books that he didn't like. She became a recluse, and toward the end of her life, she never ventured farther than the grounds of her father's house. She had no husband, no children, no one to give her heart to. And that was sad. Anyone could see from her poems that she had a large and generous heart to give. I was glad that I had someone to give my heart to. Even if he didn't know a poem from a potato and tended to go on and on about seed corn.

"...the seed costs more, being that it's brand-new and a hybrid and all, but Tom says you'll make the money back a hundred times over. And you'll spend less on fertilizer, too..."

Why didn't Emily Dickinson leave her father's house? Why didn't she marry? I wondered. Miss Wilcox had given me another book of poems to take with me to the Glenmore—*April Twilight,* by a *Miss* Willa Cather. And a novel—*The Country of the Pointed Firs,* by a *Miss* Sarah Orne Jewett. Why hadn't Jane Austen married? Or Emily Brontë? Or Louisa May Alcott? Was it because no one wanted bookish girls, like my aunt Josie said? Mary Shelley married and Edith Wharton, too, but Miss Wilcox said both marriages were disasters. And then, of course, there was Miss Wilcox herself, with her thin-lipped bully of a husband.

"...it's really too late to plant, but Pa said to buy half a pound anyway, plant it and see what we get. Whoa! Whoa, there!" Royal said, stopping the horses at the bottom of the road that leads to Minnie's. "Matt, I'm going to let you out right here. Jim's drive is a bit narrow for this old wagon. I'll be back for you in a couple of hours. I thought we could ride up and see Dan and Belinda's land. Forty acres they've got. Just bought it from Clyde Wells with the money Belinda's father give 'em."

Gave them, Royal, gave *them,* I thought. "All right," I said, jumping down, careful not to hurt the posy I'd picked for Minnie.

He turned the horses around, talking as he did. "Wells charged them good for it, but still, forty acres."

"Royal!" I suddenly said. Too loudly.

"What?"

"Just...don't forget. Don't forget to come back for me."

He frowned at me. "I said I'd be back in two hours. Didn't you hear me?"

I nodded. *I did hear you, Royal,* I thought, *but I don't believe you. I still don't believe any of this.* Not the boat ride on Big Moose Lake. Not the walks and buckboard rides since then. Not your promise of a ring. You'll forget all about me and I'll have to walk home from Minnie's and I'll see you on the way, riding with Martha Miller, and you'll look right through me and I'll wake up and realize that it was all a dream. *Please come back for me*, I said silently, watching him go. *Please take me riding. Because I like how everyone looks at us when we pass by. And I like sitting next to you in the wagon with your leg pressed against mine. And I don't even mind listening to all the characteristics of hybrid corn, because I want you to touch me and kiss me even if I am plain and bookish. Especially because I am those things.*

The buckboard disappeared around the bend, and I turned and headed up the road toward Minnie's house. As I walked, I waved to the hired hands. They were building split-rail fences from the trees they'd felled to enclose Jim's land. I saw Thistle, one of the cows, grazing nearby. She was huge and would calve any day now. *Gravid* was my word of the day. It means pregnant. When I read it that morning, I thought it was the strangest-sounding word for pregnant. Until I'd read on and learned that it also means burdened or loaded down. Looking at Thistle, with her heavy belly and her tired eyes, it made perfect sense.

I smelled the flowers I'd picked for Minnie. I hoped she would like them. It had been so long since I'd seen her—weeks—and I had so much to tell her. Last time I went to visit, I'd just received the letter from Barnard, but I never got the chance to show it to her, because she'd been laboring with her twins. And then I was busy with the farm and Miss Wilcox's library, and then I'd gone to the Glenmore, and it seemed like ages since I'd really been able to talk to her. I still wanted to tell her about the letter, even if I wasn't going. I wanted to tell her about Royal, too, and the ring he was going to give me. I wanted to see if maybe she could help me figure a way to both be married to Royal and still be a writer, to be two things at once—like one of those fancy coats they have in the Sears and Roebuck catalog that you can change into a whole different coat just by turning it inside out.

When I got to her porch, the front door banged open. Jim greeted me sullenly, stuffed the remains of a sandwich in his mouth, and trotted down the steps to join the hired hands.

"Minnie?" I called, stepping inside. A nasty smell hit me. A sour reek of old food and dirty diapers.

"Matt, is that you?" a tired voice asked. Minnie was sitting on her bed, nursing her twins. She looked so thin and drawn that I barely recognized her. Her blond hair was greasy. Her clothing was stained. The babies were sucking at her hungrily, making greedy grunting noises. Her eyes darted around the room. She looked anxious and embarrassed.

"Yes, it's me. I brought you these," I said, holding out the flowers.

"They're so pretty, Mattie. Thank you. Will you put them in something?"

I went to find a glass or a jar, and it was then I noticed how filthy the place was. Plates and glasses crusted with food littered the table and counters, cutlery filled the sink. Dirty pots covered the stove top. The floor looked like it hadn't been swept in ages.

"I apologize for the state of things," Minnie said. "Jim's had four men helping him all week. Seems I just get one meal cooked and it's time for the next one. The babies are always hungry, too. Here, take them for a minute, will you? I'll make us a cup of tea."

She handed one of the babies to me, wincing as she pulled him off her swollen, blue-veined breast. Her skin, where the baby's mouth had been, was livid. Tiny droplets of blood seeped from a crack in it. She saw me staring and covered herself. She handed me the other baby, and in no time flat, they were both screaming. They twisted and kicked. They screwed up their tiny faces and opened their little pink mouths like two screeching baby birds. Their diapers were soggy. Their cheeks were rashy. Their scalps were crusty. They stank of milk and piss. I was trying to settle them, so they'd stop screaming, so the wet from the diapers wouldn't soak into my skirt, when the next thing I knew, Minnie was standing over me, her arms at her side, her hands clenched.

"Give them to me! Give them back! Don't look at them like that! Don't look at me! Just get out! Go! Get out of here!" she shouted.

"Min . . . I . . . I'm sorry! I wasn't . . . I didn't mean . . ."

But it was too late. Minnie was hysterical. She crushed the babies to her and started to cry. "You hate them, don't you, Mattie? Don't you?"

"Minnie! What are you saying?"

"I know you do. I hate them, too. Sometimes. I do." Her voice had dropped to a whisper. Her eyes were tormented.

"You hush right now! You don't mean that!"

"I do mean it. I wish I'd never had them. I wish I'd never gotten married." The babies struggled and howled against her. She sat down on the bed, opened her blouse, and grimaced as they latched on to her. She leaned back against the pillows and closed her eyes. Tears leaked out from under her pale lashes and I was suddenly reminded of a story Lawton once told me, after he'd come home from walking a trapline with French Louis Seymour. Louis had caught a bear in one of his steel traps. A mother bear that had two cubs. The trap had broken her front leg. By the time Louis and Lawton got to her, she was mad with fear and pain. She lay on her side, keening. Her other side was gone. There was no fur there, no meat, only a livid mass of gore and bones. Her frantic, starving cubs had eaten her flesh away.

"You're just weary, Min," I said, stroking her hand. "That's all."

She opened her eyes. "I don't know, Matt. It all seemed so exciting when we were sparking, and then just married, but it isn't now. Jim's always at me..."

"He's probably just worn down, too. It's hard work clearing—"

"Oh, don't be dense, Mattie! I mean *at me*. But I can't. I'm so sore down there. And I just can't have another baby. Not right after the twins. I can't go through it again. Mrs. Crego said that nursing will keep me from quickening, but it hurts so, I think I'll go crazy with the pain. I'm sorry, Matt... I'm sorry I shouted at you. I'm glad you came...I didn't want to tell you all these things...I'm just so tired..."

"I know you are. You lie there for a minute and rest. Let me make the tea."

Within minutes Minnie had fallen asleep and the babies with her. I got busy. I boiled water and washed all the pots and pans and dishes. I boiled some more and set the dirty dishrags and aprons to soaking. I filled the big black washing kettle with water, threw in a pailful of dirty diapers I'd found in the kitchen, and started a fire under it in the backyard. It wouldn't reach a boil for some time, but at least she wouldn't have to haul the water. Then I scrubbed the table and swept the floor. I set the table, too, thinking the men would be back in for supper before long, and put my flowers in the middle of it. When I'd finished, the house looked and smelled much better, and I looked and smelled much worse. Then I heard wagon wheels at the bottom of the drive. I looked out the window and saw Royal. Already. He and Jim were talking, but he'd expect me momentarily. I'd never even had the chance to tell Minnie about him.

As I quickly patted my hair back into place, it hit me: Emily Dickinson was a damned sneaky genius.

Holing up in her father's house, never marrying, becoming a recluse—that had sounded like giving up to me, but the more I thought about it, the more it seemed she fought by not fighting. And knowing her poems as I do, I would not put such underhanded behavior past her. Oh, maybe she was lonely at times, and cowed by her pa, but I bet at midnight, when the lights were out and her father was asleep, she went sliding down the banister and swinging from the chandelier. I bet she was just dizzy with freedom.

I have read almost a hundred of Emily's poems and memorized ten. Miss Wilcox says she wrote nearly eighteen hundred. I looked at my friend Minnie, sleeping still. A year ago she was a girl, like me, and we were in my mamma's kitchen giggling and fooling and throwing apple peels over our shoulders to see if they'd make the initial of our true loves. I couldn't even see that girl anymore. She was gone. And I knew in my bones that Emily Dickinson wouldn't have written even one poem if she'd had two howling babies, a husband bent on jamming another one into her, a house to run, a garden to tend, three cows to milk, twenty chickens to feed, and four hired hands to cook for.

I knew then why they didn't marry. Emily and Jane and Louisa. I knew and it scared me. I also knew what being lonely was and I didn't want to be lonely my whole life. I didn't want to give up my words. I didn't want to choose one over the other. Mark Twain didn't have to. Charles Dickens didn't. And John Milton didn't, either, though he might have made life easier for untold generations of schoolkids if he had.

Then Royal hollered for me and I had to wake Minnie to tell her good-bye. When I got outside, the afternoon was bright and sunny, and Royal took my hand as we rode to his brother's land, and he told me we would have land, too, and a house and cows and chickens and an old oak bureau his grandmother had promised him, and a pine bed, too. He said he had some money saved up, and I proudly told him I had ten dollars and sixty cents saved up between money I'd had before I went to the Glenmore and two weeks' wages (minus the four dollars I'd given Pa), and tips. He said that was almost enough to pay for a good stove. Or maybe a calf instead. He pleased himself so much just talking about these things that he smiled and put his arm around me. It was the nicest feeling. Lucky and safe. Like getting all your animals inside the barn just before a bad storm hits. I nestled against him and imagined what it would feel like to lie next to him in a pine bed in the dark, and suddenly nothing else seemed to matter.

sal • tant

"Not another one, Weaver, damn it!" Cook shouted, slapping her spatula against the worktable.

"Sorry," Weaver said, bending down to pick up the pieces of the plate he'd just broken. The second one that morning. He'd also smashed a drinking glass.

"No, you're not. Not in the least," Cook said. "But you will be. Next thing you break is coming out of your wages. I've had it with you. Go down cellar and bring up some new plates. And don't you dare drop them."

It was Bill the dishwasher's day off and we all missed him terribly. We hadn't appreciated him enough. We never realized how quietly and graciously he went about his work. We did that morning, though, because Cook put Weaver—whose face was still as bruised and mottled as a piece of old fruit—on dishwashing duty and Weaver wasn't the least bit quiet or gracious about it. He muttered and grumbled, swore and complained.

Four whole days had elapsed since Mr. Sperry had put him on kitchen duty, long enough for most people to get their noses back in joint, but Weaver was still furious about it. Fran had tried to jolly him on several occasions and I'd tried to interest him in a few word duels, but neither of us had had any success.

I'd made an extra special effort that morning. I told him all about *saltant,* my word of the day. "It means dancing, leaping, or jumping, Weaver," I'd said. "Its root comes from the Latin *sal,* for salt. Isn't that interesting? You can see the connection, can't you? A bit of salt sprinkled over pork chops or eggs can make them dance, too." I thought my observation was fascinating, but Weaver did not. He continued to sulk, and fight with Cook, and generally make the kitchen a thoroughly miserable place to be.

No one was pleased with the arrangement. Fran and Ada and I hated it almost as much as Weaver did, for we all had to take turns waiting on table six. That horrible man grew bolder by the day. Ada had a bruise the size of a silver dollar on her bottom from his pinching fingers.

Cook was the unhappiest one of all. She didn't want Weaver in her kitchen any more than he wanted to be there. On the first day, she told him to season a huge pot of chicken soup and he'd oversalted it. On the second, she gave him a quart of heavy cream to whip and he'd turned it to butter. On the third, she'd told him to change the sticky fly tapes that hung down from the gaslamps and he'd dropped one into a pan of béarnaise sauce.

That's when she blew up at him. She yelled at him for being careless and clumsy, and then she told him he had his head straight up his ass and that he had a lot of nerve moping and carrying on when it was nobody's fault but his own what had happened. And that if he wanted to work in the dining room instead of the kitchen, he'd have to learn to stay out of fights.

"You brought it on yourself, Weaver, and now you have to deal with the consequences," she'd scolded.

"I did not bring it on myself."

"Yes, you did."

"How? Did I call myself names? Haul myself down out of the wagon? Beat myself up?"

Cook's answer to that was to banish him to the back steps with a paring knife and four bushels of potatoes. It did not pay to fight with Cook.

I think Weaver would have kept up his surly behavior all week, and possibly have gotten himself killed by Cook or Bill or the rest of us, if Mr. Higby hadn't come by.

Mr. Higby owned Higby's camp on the south shore of Big Moose Lake and was the local justice of the peace. He was also Mr. Sperry's brother-in-law, and when he suddenly appeared in the kitchen toward the end of the breakfast service, we all thought that's who he was after.

"Hello, Jim, you eat yet?" Cook asked him. "Mattie, go get Mr. Sperry."

"No need, Mrs. Hennessey," Mr. Higby said. "I'll find him. I've got to see Weaver first, anyway."

"Lord God, what did he do now?" Cook sighed, walking to the cellar door. "Weaver!" she shouted. "Get those plates and get back up here! Mr. Higby wants a word with you!"

Weaver came up and put the new plates down on the drain board, clinking them together loudly. Cook gritted her teeth. "Make my day, Weaver," she said. "Tell me you robbed a bank or held up the train and that Jim's going to take you out of my kitchen right now and put you in jail for the next twenty years."

Weaver did not deign to reply. He simply lifted his chin, crossed his arms over his chest, and waited for Mr. Higby to speak.

"Just thought you'd like to know that I found the men who gave you that licking, Weaver. They were raising Cain up at the Summit just as I happened to be picking up some guests from the train station. Broke a stool and a window. I fined them five dollars on the spot for the damages, and when the bartender told me they were the same men who attacked you, I arrested them. They spent the night locked up in the Summit's basement. John Denio's had a look at them and says I've got the right ones. Now I need you to do the same, and then I'm going to give them a short vacation in Herkimer, as guests of the State of New York. They'll get a cozy little room and some new clothes,too. The kind with stripes on 'em."

For the first time in days, Weaver smiled. "Thank you, Mr. Higby. I appreciate you taking the time over it."

"Just doing my job. I've got to find Dwight and talk business for a bit. I'll call for you on my way out."

Mr. Higby went to find Mr. Sperry and Weaver went back to the sink. His head was high. His back was straight. His eyes, so dark with anger for the last four days, were filled with a clear and righteous light.

Sometimes, when you catch someone unaware at just

the right time and in just the right light, you can catch sight of what they will be. Once I saw Beth lift her head at the sound of a coyote's cry at twilight. Her eyes widened—half in wonder, half in fear—and I saw that she would be beautiful some day. Not just pretty, truly beautiful. I saw the restlessness in Lawton long before he left. I saw it when he was only a boy and would toss sticks and leaves into the rushing waters of the Moose River and watch them go where he could not. I have seen Royal stop working to wipe his brow in the bright noon sun and have glimpsed the farmer he will be. Better than his pa, better than mine. The sort who can scent rain coming on a dry day and know the ripeness of his corn by the rustle of its leaves alone.

Just then, I saw what Weaver would be, too. I saw him in a courtroom, thundering at the jury, commanding their eyes and ears, their hearts and souls and minds—on fire with the strength of his convictions, the passion of his words.

Weaver wasn't that man yet, he was only a boy, tall and lanky, scrubbing a greasy roasting pan. But he would be. Scrubbing was only for today for Weaver Smith, not for ever.

Cook watched him as he worked, her eyes all squinty, her lips pursed up tighter than a cat's hind end. She couldn't stand to be wrong. He must have felt her eyes on him, because he glanced up at her from the sink.

"It doesn't change anything. You know that," she said.

"It changes everything," he replied. "That's three

men who might think twice before they go around calling people names and beating them up."

"Three out of a million."

"Then I've only got 999,997 left to go, haven't I?"

That was Weaver. Determined to change the world.
Three dirty, drunken, no-good trappers at a time. I
smiled at him, my heart swelling up like bread dough,
knowing full well that the remaining 999,997 didn't have
a prayer.

aby

When Tommy Hubbard appeared at the Glenmore's kitchen door at seven o'clock in the morning, I felt in my bones that something was badly wrong. I was busy shaping butter pats for the breakfast tables when I heard him.

"Hello! Is Mattie here? Is she here?" he yelled.

"Who is that? Stop shouting!" Cook shouted.

"It's me, Tommy Hubbard. I need to see Mattie."

"Don't you set foot in my kitchen, Tom!"

"I'm not itching, I swear, I—"

"You stay out there! I'll find her for you."

"I'm right here," I said, opening the screen door. Tears had washed tracks through the dirt on Tom's face. He was panting like a horse played out.

"I ran fast as I could, Mattie . . . fast as I could . . . ," he sobbed.

"From where? From *home*?" It was a mile through the woods from Tommy's house to the Big Moose Road, and five more up to the Glenmore.

"You've got to come home," he said, tugging on my hand. "You've got to come *now*—"

"I'm working, Tommy, I can't! Calm down and tell me what's wrong."

"It's your pa and your sisters, Matt. They're powerful sick..."

I dropped the knife I was holding.

"I went over early to see if Lou wanted to go fishing, and I knocked and knocked but no one came. The cows were bellowing, so I went in the barn. Daisy's real bad. She ain't been milked. Ain't none of them have. I didn't know what to do, Matt. I went inside the house... They're all real bad. I found Lou in the grass by the outhouse, I got her inside, but—"

I didn't hear anything else for I was already running. Down the back steps to the Glenmore's drive and out to the Big Moose Road. Tommy was right behind me. I didn't get more than a hundred yards down the road when I saw a buckboard coming toward me.

I ran to it, shouting and waving my arms. The driver stopped. It was John Denio coming to work from his home in Big Moose Station.

"Please, Mr. Denio, my pa's sick. My whole family... I've got to get home—"

"Get in," he said, reaching down for my hand and lifting me clear across him. Tommy scrambled into the back. Mr. Denio turned his horses around in the road, then cracked the reins. "Woman at the Lakeview took sick the other day," he said. "Fever and chills. Your pa was delivering his milk there, and the manager asked him if he'd take her down to Dr. Wallace's. She said she'd give him two dollars for the ride. Looks like she give him more besides."

Mr. Denio drove fast, but a coach and four couldn't have gotten me home fast enough. I was more scared than I have ever been in my life. Tommy said the cows were bellowing, that no one had milked them. Pa would never let them go unmilked. Never. My mouth went dry. My blood, my bones, everything inside me turned to sand. Not my pa, I prayed. Please, please, not my pa.

As we turned into my drive, I heard the sound of a second buckboard turn in behind us. It was Royal. "I was delivering to the Waldheim," he shouted. "Saw Mrs. Hennessey on my way back. She told me what happened. Go on inside. I'll see to the cows."

I was out of Mr. Denio's buckboard before it stopped. I could hear Royal yelling at Tommy to tie the horses. I could hear the cows bellowing in pain and the calves answering in fear. They were in the barn, in their stalls, which meant Pa had done a milking...but when? Yesterday? Two days ago? It only takes a day, sometimes less, before the milk collects and swells the udder and infection sets in.

We're going to lose them, I thought wildly. Every damn one.

"Pa!" I shouted, running into the shed. "Abby!" There was no answer. I burst through the kitchen door and ran straight into the thick, low stench of sickness. Barney lifted his head when he heard me and thumped his tail weakly. There were dirty pots in the sink, plates of half-eaten food on the table. Flies crawled over them, feasting on the crusted remains.

"Pa!" I yelled. I ran through the kitchen toward the stairs and found a figure crumpled at the bottom of them. "Lou! Oh, Jesus God . . . Lou!" I screamed.

She picked her head up and blinked at me. Her eyes were glassy and her lips were cracked. Her coverall bib was crusted with vomit. "Mattie . . . ," she rasped. ". . . thirsty, Mattie . . ."

"It's all right, Lou, I'm here; hold on." I lifted her up, draped her arm around my neck, and dragged her up the stairs to our bedroom, the air growing fouler with every step. I opened the door to our room and gagged on the stink. The room was dark, the shades were drawn.

"Beth? Abby?" I whispered. There was no answer. I laid Lou down on our bed, then crossed the room and pulled on the shade. I saw Beth then. She was lying in her and Abby's bed, still and pale. There were flies crawling on her. On her face and hands and feet.

"Beth!" I cried, rushing to her. Her eyes fluttered open and I sobbed with relief. She closed them again and began to weep, and I realized her bowels had let go. I touched her cheeks and forehead. She was on fire.

"Ssshh, Beth, it's all right. I'll get you fixed up, I promise . . . ," I said. But she didn't hear me. I went back to Lou. "Where's Abby?" I asked her.

She licked her lips. "With Pa."

I ran out of our room and down the short hallway to Pa's bedroom. My father was lying rigid in his bed, mumbling and shivering. My sister was slumped over him.

"Abby!" I called to her. "Abby, wake up!"

She raised her head. Her eyes were dark hollows. Her cheekbones were sharp beneath her skin. "He's real bad, Mattie," she said.

"Since how long?"

"Since two days. Fever got worse this morning."

"Go to bed, Ab. I'll look after him now."

"I'll help you, Matt—"

"Get in your bed!" I snapped.

She raised herself up and walked toward the door, her steps as slow and shuffling as an old woman's. I touched my father's face. His skin was dry and hot. "Pa," I called softly. "Pa."

He opened his eyes and looked right through me. His hands scrabbled at the bedding. "Pa, can you hear me?" I said.

"...killed her, I killed her...," he jabbered, "...my fault..."

I put my hands over my eyes then and whimpered with fear. I didn't know what to do. They were all so sick. I was all they had and I couldn't think of the first thing to do.

"Yarrow, Mattie," Abby rasped from the doorway. "Get him to take some yarrow tea. He's got fever and chills and a deep cough. Try onions..."

"...and goose grease and turpentine...," I said, suddenly remembering how Mamma had treated coughs. Abby's voice, gentle even now, calmed me and helped me to think. "And baths. I'll try a cool sponge bath," I said.

"Beth and Lou have the scours. I tried blackberry syrup, but it didn't do any good. Get some roots."

"Roots? What roots?" I almost shouted.

"Blackberry, Matt. Chop up a handful and simmer them until the water's brown. Make them drink it."

Abby's legs shook then and she had to grab the door-jamb to keep from collapsing. I helped her into bed next to Lou. She squeezed my hand and her eyes closed, and I was alone. Utterly alone.

I raced downstairs and ran outside, thinking to get a spade in the barn to dig up some blackberry roots. I stopped halfway. The bushes were way up past the corn-fields, a good fifteen minutes' walk. And Lou needed water. And there was the yarrow tea for Pa. And there was Beth, lying in her own filth . . . I ran back inside and put the kettle back on the stove to boil. Then I pumped water into a large enameled basin, ran back upstairs, and stripped Beth's clothes off. I pulled her out of the bed onto the bare floor and washed her.

She shivered under my hands and moaned for me to stop. "It's cold, Mattie, it hurts," she whimpered, trying to pull away from me, her thin limbs shuddering.

"Hush, Beth, I know," I soothed. "Hold still, hold still." I tried to think of my word of the day, *aby,* to take the fear from my mind. I recalled that it meant to en-dure, to atone, and found I didn't care.

When Beth was clean, I put a fresh nightgown on her and tucked her in with Abby and Lou. Her own bed was rank, but it would have to wait. Then I took Lou's dirty coveralls off her and drew the quilt up over all three of them. Abby was sweating now. Her underthings were damp and her hair was plastered to her head. I would give her a sponge bath. Just as soon as I started some soup. I remembered that Mamma always made chicken soup when someone was poorly. I dreaded killing one of our hens, but there was no way round it.

I ran downstairs, pumped clean water into a jug, snatched a glass, and ran back up again. I gave everyone a good, tall drink, holding their heads up so they could swallow. It was a struggle getting Beth to take any water, but Lou, Abby, and Pa drank greedily. The dirty things stank powerfully and I knew that breathing tainted air wasn't good, so I bundled all the clothing, Beth's soiled bedding and her straw tick, and took it all outside. While I was in the yard, I looked up toward the barn. Three calves had been put in the pasture. Another was heading for the drive. Two more were in the cornfield, trampling the fragile plants. My heart lurched. We needed every ear, every stalk, for winter feed. A movement caught my eye. It was Tommy. He was near the beehives, trying to push another calf—Baldwin—toward the pasture, but Baldwin didn't want to go. He stopped dead, lifted his head, and bawled piteously. Manure gushed from his backside and splashed all over Tommy. Tommy cursed and punched the calf in the face. Again and again and again. The animal's bawling turned into shrill, terrified bleats. His front legs crumpled.

"Stop it, Tommy!" I screamed, running to them.

Tommy looked at me and shrank back, shame flushing his cheeks. His eyes were red and watery. A livid welt bloomed under one. "I was afraid," he sobbed. "I didn't mean for them to all get out . . . they ran at me—".

"Tommy, who hit you . . ." I started to say, reaching for him. But he ducked me and took off after the calf in the drive. Baldwin's bleats were soft little moans now. He was bleeding under his eye. "Come on, Baldwin. Come on, now," I said to him, gently lifting him back onto his feet. I gave him my fingers to suck, which soothed him, then managed to lead him to the pasture one step at a time. Once he was in, I went after the two calves in the corn. They were standing together, their heads above the young stalks. "Come on, Bertie. Come on, Allie," I called. They were twins and I knew if I could get one to come to me, the other would follow. But as soon as they heard me, they split apart and trotted off, cutting more channels through the precious corn.

"Bertie, Bertie, come on, Bertie," I sang, my voice breaking. "Please, Bertie . . ." He stopped, looked at me, then took off again. Beth had named them Albert Edward and Alexandra for the king and queen of England after seeing a picture of them in *Harper's Magazine*. Noisy, boisterous Beth, whose voice was only a whimper now. Whose small, busy hands had fluttered like doves against me as I'd washed her. Tears filled my eyes. I quickly wiped them away.

When I wanted to coax one of the cows, I would pick a fat handful of grass and wave it before her, but the twins weren't eating grass yet. Pa was still feeding them milk mixed with linseed and oatmeal. I suddenly knew what to do. I ran into the milk house, grabbed the metal pails that Pa mixed their feed in, and clattered them together. Bertie pricked his ears. He trotted toward me. Allie followed and I was able to lead them to the pasture.

They bawled when they realized I didn't really have any food for them. They were bound to be hungry. God only knew the last time they'd been fed. Or would be fed. If garget had set into the cows' udders, their milk would be streaked with pus and blood. Where would I get fresh milk for the calves? How would I treat the infection? I didn't know how to doctor a cow; only Pa did.

One thing at a time, Mattie, one thing at a time, I told myself, fighting down the panic frothing up inside me.

I ran back into the kitchen. The kettle was boiling furiously. I grabbed a handful of yarrow from the tin where Mamma kept it, put it in a teapot, and poured hot water over it. The tea would be ready when the color came out of the petals. Mamma had learned about yarrow from Mrs. Traversy, an Abenaki woman, when she'd had childbed fever after Beth was born and Mrs. Traversy cured her. She stayed with us while Mamma got her strength back, and told us many things about doctoring. I wished to God I'd listened.

When the tea was dark, I put the pot, several cups, and a jug of cold water on a tray. *Just get it down them,* I told myself, walking up the stairs. Then they'd sleep and I could see to feeding the pigs and chickens and starting a fire under the wash kettle and finding out from Royal and Mr. Denio how bad the cows were. Having a plan gave me some confidence.

Every scrap of it disappeared, however, as soon as I got upstairs. Pa was shivering so hard, his bed rattled. Cords stood out in his neck, and he was babbling worse than before about killing someone. It was the fever. It was roasting him alive.

I put the tray down on his dresser and poured a cup of tea. "Pa?" I whispered, touching his cheek. "Pa, you need to drink this." He didn't hear me, didn't even know I was there. "Pa?" I said, louder now. "Pa!"

He opened his eyes. His hands shot up at me; his fingers closed on my blouse. I screamed as he jerked me to him. I felt hot tea burn my legs, heard the cup smash on the floor.

"Robertson, you bastard!" he yelled. "*Qu'est-ce que tu dis?* That I'm no good? You tell her this? You son of a bitch... *Écoute-moi, vieux, écoute-moi...*"

I shook free of him, stumbled to the dresser, and poured another cup of tea. "You drink this, Pa!" I shouted at him. "Right now! You stop your nonsense and drink this tea!"

He blinked at me, his eyes suddenly mild. "Where's Lawton, Mattie?" he asked me. "Is he back yet? I hear the cows..."

"He's back, Pa. He's... he's in the barn, milking," I lied.

"That's good. I'm glad he's back," he said. And then I saw that tears were rolling down his cheeks, and I was terrified. My father never cried. "He ran away, Mattie. Ran away because I killed her."

"Hush, Pa, don't talk so. You didn't kill anyone." He was only babbling, but the more he talked, the more upset he became. I was afraid he'd get wild again.

"I didn't kill her, Mattie," he said, his voice rising. "I didn't!"

I thought it best to humor him. "Of course you didn't, Pa. No one says you did."

"Lawton does. Said it was my fault. That I killed her with hard work. Said I should have moved us all to Inlet and worked in the sawmill. Said I killed your mother and I wasn't going to kill him." And then his face crumpled and he sobbed like a child. "I didn't kill her; I loved her . . ."

I had to steady myself against the dresser. I felt like someone had taken my legs out from under me. *That's why they'd fought,* I thought. That's why Pa had swung the peavey at Lawton and why Lawton had run away. That's why Pa never smiled anymore. Why he was so angry. Why he looked at us but never saw us. *Oh, Lawton,* I thought, *some things should never, ever be said.* Words are just words, Royal would say. But words are more powerful than anything.

"Lawton didn't mean it, Pa. The cancer killed Mamma, not you."

He nodded, but his eyes were elsewhere and I knew he believed my brother's words, not mine. He was exhausted from his agitation, though, and I took advantage of it to make him swallow some tea. As I lifted his head, I felt that his skin was blazing. I undressed him, laying the dresser scarf over all the things I wasn't supposed to see. I bathed him with cold water, holding the cloth to his wrists and the insides of his elbows and behind his knees to cool the blood.

I had never seen my pa naked. We were not allowed in the kitchen when he bathed. The skin on his chest was soft and lightly furred with black hair. There were scars on his back, from his shoulders to his waist—thick, livid welts from his stepfather's belt buckle. I pressed my hand to his ribs and felt his heart fluttering. There were scars there, too. I knew it now, even though I couldn't see them. He shivered terribly as I sponged him, and he clenched his teeth, but he didn't try to throttle me. That was something. When I was done, I pulled the bedding back over him, piled two quilts on top, and made him drink another cup of hot tea. I didn't know much about fevers, but I knew he needed to sweat. Sweating would bring the sickness out of him.

"I'll miss you, Mattie," he suddenly said.

"I'm only going across the hall, Pa," I told him.

He shook his head. "Cow goes with a bull. Cow don't go with a sheep. Don't go with a goat. Goats don't read, Mattie, they don't read books..."

He was talking gibberish again. "Hush now, Pa," I told him. "Try to sleep."

When he had closed his eyes, I picked up the tea tray to take it in to my sisters. I put what Lawton had said out of my mind. I didn't want to think about it. I had gotten to be so good at not thinking about things.

Then I went in our bedroom and saw that Lou had sicked up the water I'd given her and that Abby was out of bed and lurching about trying to clean Beth, who'd messed herself again. It was my fault. I'd given them too much water.

"Mattie! Matt, where are you?" a voice called from downstairs.

"Up here!"

Feet pounded up the stairs and then Royal was in the doorway. He winced at the smell.

"What is it?" I asked, coming out into the hallway.

"One of the cows is real bad. The one with the star on her head—"

"That's Daisy. It's not a star; it's a flower," I said stupidly.

"She's suffering, Matt. Real bad. John wants... he wants to know where your pa keeps his gun."

"No, Mattie, no! Don't let him!" Lou yelled from her bed.

I shook my head.

He took me by the shoulders. "Matt, she's bad off... it ain't kind."

"In the shed. Above the door."

He went back downstairs, and I thought of Daisy's large, dark eyes and her whiskered, mumbly lips. And how she never kicked when I milked her but always let me rest my cheek against her soft belly. I thought of poor

Baldwin. And of the bull, fierce and black, up in the Loomises' meadow. And how he frightened Daisy and Baldwin, but they still bashed through the fence every chance they got, just to be near him.

I heard the crack of a rifle, heard Lou shout my name, then curse. I heard the chamber pot go over in my father's room, heard him tell someone named Armand to shoot the damn bear already.

Then I heard the sound of choked, quiet tears, as I sat down on the top step and wept.

fu · ga · cious

"You still taking the cod-liver oil I left at your place?" Mrs. Loomis asked me. She was sitting on her front porch, shelling peas into a blue enameled basin. I was sitting across from her, on an old wicker settee. Royal was next to me, his legs stretched out in front of him.

"Yes, ma'am," I lied. I was pouring it down the sink, a little bit every day. I'd rather have the grippe, well and truly, than swallow any more cod-liver oil. Mrs. Loomis had dosed me good. She'd come to our house a week ago, as soon as Royal had gotten home and told her how it was with us. She'd brought all sorts of things with her—blackberry root and barley water to bind loose bowels. Onion syrup, whiskey, and gingerroot to bring a fever down. Lard mixed with camphor and turpentine for a rattling chest. She said it was one of the worst cases of grippe she'd ever seen. She doctored us and cooked for us and pulled us all through it. Weaver's mamma helped her. I don't know what we would have done without them. Pa had the remains of a cough and Beth was still too weak to get out of bed, but they were out of danger.

"Still feeding Beth plenty of ginger tea?"

"Yes, ma'am. She's a lot better. My pa said to tell you

he's much obliged. And that he'll be over to pay a call in a day or two."

"I don't want his thanks, Mattie. Seeing a neighbor through is thanks enough for me. And besides, it ain't all my doing, anyway. Weaver's mamma did as much as I did."

"Yes, ma'am."

"She told me what happened to Weaver, by the way. It's a terrible thing. Heard Jim Higby put those men in the county jail. Guess it's right what they say about the squeaky wheel."

"Yes, ma'am."

"You'll be getting back to the Glenmore soon, I expect?"

"Pa's taking me tomorrow morning. That's why I brought your basket and jars. I wanted to make sure you got them back before I left."

She raised her head, fixing me with her faded blue eyes. "You learning a lot up there? Cooking and ironing and such?" she asked.

"A bit."

"That's good. Eileen Hennessey makes a nice pie-crust. A good Baltimore cake, too. She's a methody cook, as I recall. Writes everything down. You should see if she'll give you some of her recipes." She straightened her back. I heard it crack. "Well, I reckon that's that," she said, picking up her basin. "Royal, take the pods out to the pigs before you come in."

"Yup."

The screen door slammed and we were alone.

"You're going back up tomorrow?" he asked me.

"Yes. First thing."

"You got a day off anytime soon?"

"I don't think so. Don't dare ask for one. Not after being home for a whole week."

"Huh."

There was a minute or two of silence. I stared at Mrs. Loomis's peony bushes. Some of the flowers were already losing their petals. I hadn't the time or the inclination to look up a word while my family was so sick, and even if I'd had, I'd left my dictionary up at the Glenmore. *Fugacious* was one of the last words I'd found, though. It means falling or fading early, fleeting. The dying peonies reminded me of it.

"Well, here then," Royal suddenly said.

He held out a small square of tissue paper. It was folded over several times. There was something inside of it. I opened it and saw a dull gold ring. It was set with three stones—a chipped opal flanked by two tiny garnets. It must've been pretty once.

I looked at him. "Royal, do you . . . do you love me?" I asked.

"Aw, Matt. I bought you a ring, didn't I?"

I looked at the ring again and thought how we'd lost two cows and would've lost more if it hadn't been for Royal. The surviving animals had been very sick. They'd only just started to give good milk again. Royal had fed them and cared for them for a whole week.

He'd looked after the calves, too. He'd driven three of his father's milkers over to keep them from starving. They'd latched right on, every one except for Baldwin. He wouldn't take milk from the Loomises' cows, only from a pail. And he wouldn't pick his head up. He no longer frisked with the other calves, he just stood by himself in the pasture, day after day. As soon as she was able, Lou went into the pasture after him. She offered him little lumps of maple sugar, but he wouldn't take them. She scratched behind his ears and rubbed his neck, but he pulled away. She wasn't what he wanted; he wanted Daisy. But he couldn't have Daisy, so he finally took what was offered.

Like we all do.

"I've got ten dollars of my own saved up, Mattie. And my ma, she's got some put aside, too. She'll help us. And you'll have some savings, too, won't you, by the end of the summer? It'll be enough to make a start, all of it together."

I stared at the ring hard.

"Will you, Mattie?"

I slipped the ring on my finger. It fit.

"I will, Royal," I said. "You'd best come home with me now so we can tell my pa."

South Otselic
July 2, '06
Monday Night
My Dear Chester:

I hope you will excuse me if I don't follow the lines for I am half lying down. Have worked awfully hard today... This morning I helped mamma with the washing and then helped with the dinner. This p.m. I have been after strawberries. It was fun, only I got so awfully tired. The fields here are red with berries. Tonight mamma is canning them and making bread and cookies. We have had berries nearly every day since I came. Mamma says I am getting to be a splendid cook. What do you think of that? I got supper alone tonight and had potato dice and French toast and a whole lot of good things...

I stop reading Grace's letter and stare off into the darkness. I miss my own mamma so much right now that it hurts. She used to can strawberries, too, and she made the most delicious pink strawberry cake. It was as sweet as her kiss on my cheek. Sometimes she would pick a basketful of berries in the afternoon and set them, sun-warmed and fragrant, on the kitchen table, along with a dish of fresh cream and one of maple sugar. We would dip them first into the cream, then in the sugar, then bite into them greedily. Somehow, they always tasted of more than themselves. They tasted like my pa whistling as he came in from the fields at night, or like a new calf getting to its feet for the first time, or like Lawton telling us ghost stories around the fire. I think that what they tasted of was happiness.

Once, Mamma made this treat just for me and her. It was after I'd started my monthlies. She'd sat me down at the kitchen table and covered my hand with her own, and told me that I was a grown woman now, not a girl anymore, and that a woman's virtue was the greatest treasure she possessed and that I must never, ever give mine to any man but the one I married.

"Do you understand me, Mattie?" she'd said.

I thought I did, but I wasn't sure. I knew what *virtue* means—goodness, purity, and excellence—because it had once been my word of the day. But I didn't think men wanted to get ahold of those things because Fran told me all they want to get ahold of is your bosoms.

"Where is it, my virtue?" I finally asked her.

"Up under your skirts," she said, coloring a bit.

I colored, too, for I knew what she meant then. Sort of. At least, I knew where a cow's virtue was, and a chicken's, too, and what they were for.

Then I asked, "How do you know if a man loves you, Mamma?"

"You just do."

"How did you know? Did Pa say 'I love you' and give you a nice card or something and then you knew?"

Mamma laughed. "Does that sound like your pa?"

"Then how did you *know*, Mamma?"

"I just did."

"How will I know?"

"You just will."

"But *how*, Mamma, *how*?"

She never answered me. She just shook her head and said, "Oh, Mattie, you ask too many questions!"

Grace must have loved Chester very much to give him her virtue before they were married. I can see why she would have. He was very handsome. He had dark hair and full lips and the kind of slow, easy smile that makes your stomach flutter. He dressed nicely and walked with a sauntering, almost lazy, gait, hands in his pockets. I try to remember what his eyes looked like, but I can't. He never looked me full in the face.

I wonder how Grace convinced herself that Chester loved her. And if she kept pretending it right to the end. Men rarely come right out and tell you. Minnie says you have to look for signs from them. Do they wash before they come to call on you? Do they let you climb up in the buckboard yourself, or get out to help you? Do they buy you sweets without your hinting for them?

Royal washes. And he puts on a clean shirt, too. And if he says he will call for me at seven o'clock, he is there at seven o'clock. He does other things, too. I lie back against my pillow and spend a long time silently repeating them to myself, over and over and over again like a litany, but it's no use. Mamma said I would know. And I do. I guess I have all along.

"Poor, sad, stupid Grace," I whisper to the darkness. "Poor, sad, stupid Matt."

thren · o · dy

"Mattie, you get the package that came for you?"
Mrs. Morrison asked me. She was standing behind the
front desk, sorting through the mail. It was three o'clock.
Dinner was over and the dining room was closed until
supper, which began at six. We were never idle, though,
and I was just on my way upstairs to restock the second-
floor linen closet with a pile of freshly ironed sheets.

"No, ma'am. What package?"

"A package from the teacher. She left it about an hour
ago. I looked for you, but I couldn't find you. I had Ada
bring it upstairs."

I thanked her and ran to the attic as fast as I could,
dumping off the sheets on my way. I was powerfully curious. No one had ever sent me a package before. When I
got upstairs, I saw that it was a heavy parcel, wrapped in
brown paper and tied with twine. There was an envelope
tucked under the twine, too; it was Glenmore stationery.
I opened the package first, eager to see what was inside of
it. There were three books: *Sister Carrie,* by Theodore
Dreiser; *The Jungle,* by Upton Sinclair; and *Threnody,* a
volume of poetry by Emily Baxter. Miss Wilcox had written another book even though her husband told her not

to! I was so excited, I hugged the little volume to me. I didn't know the meaning of *threnody*, so I pulled my dictionary out from under my bed and looked it up. It was defined as a song of lamentation, a funeral dirge. I smiled at that, pleased to know that I was not the only one in these parts given to things morbid and dispiriting. Next I opened the envelope, unfolded the sheet of paper inside, and caught my breath as a five-dollar bill fluttered out. I picked it up. There was a letter, too.

> *Dear Mattie,*
>
> *I thought you might like these books. (Do take care to hide the Dreiser.) I hope, particularly, that you enjoy the volume of poetry, as I wish to leave you something by which to remember me. I am departing Eagle Bay tomorrow. I won't be teaching next year. I had hoped to tell you this in person, but Mrs. Morrison was unable to locate you. I am including Annabelle's, my sister's, address in this note. I've told her all about you and she's very eager to have you as a boarder. The enclosed will help get you to her house ...*

There was more, but I didn't read it. "You can't go!" I said aloud. "You can't!" I ran out of the room and was downstairs in the kitchen in no time flat. Weaver was sitting at the table, eating ice cream. The trappers' handiwork was still visible on his face. His eye hadn't healed completely and his mouth was still tender. Cook and Mr. Sperry had the top of the stove off and were frowning down into it.

"Can I please take the trap, Mr. Sperry?" I asked, panting. "I've got to go to Inlet. I've got to."

"Have you lost your mind? Supper's only a few hours away. And besides, you can't handle Demon by yourself," Cook said.

"I'll be back in time, I swear it," I said. "And I can manage Demon. I know I can. Please, ma'am . . ."

"No. And that's the end of it," Cook said.

"I'll walk, then."

"You'll do no such thing."

"Mattie, what's this about?" Mr. Sperry asked.

"It's a friend of mine. She's . . . she's in trouble and I've got to go to her."

"You can't go alone. Mrs. Hennessey's right, Demon's a handful. I'd take you if I could, but I've got to get this stove working before supper."

"But I've got to," I sobbed. "I've got to."

Mr. Sperry, Cook, and Weaver all looked at me. The other girls are always crying for some reason or another—homesickness, moods, a spat—but I have never cried here. Not once.

Weaver put his spoon down. "I'll go with her," he said.

Mr. Sperry looked from me to Weaver and back again. He shook his head. "Go on, then. But be back here ready to serve supper by six sharp. Or else."

I hitched up Demon, Mr. Sperry's own horse, and drove hell-for-leather all the way down Big Moose Road to the highway and on into Inlet. I told Weaver about the package on the way and who Miss Wilcox really was.

When we arrived at Dr. Foster's camp, Weaver took the reins and told me to go in. "I'll wait outside," he said. "I can't stand a lot of female drama."

I knew that was just his way of giving me time alone with Miss Wilcox, and I appreciated it. I ran up the back steps, past the boxes and crates piled up on the porch, and banged on the door.

"Mattie, is that you?" Miss Wilcox said, opening the door. "How did you get here?"

"Miss Wilcox, why are you leaving? Please, please don't go!" I said.

"Oh, Mattie!" she said, hugging me. "Come in. Come in and sit down."

She led me into the library. I sat down next to her on the settee and looked around. The books were gone. Every last one of them. The desk was bare. The fine paper, pens, and pencils were all packed away.

I heard a match flare, smelled the sulfur. Miss Wilcox was smoking. "Would you like a cup of tea?" she asked me.

"Why are you leaving, Miss Wilcox?" I asked, fighting back my tears. "You can't go. You're all I have."

I heard her bracelets tinkle, felt her hand on my arm. "Oh, Mattie, that's not true. You have your family and Weaver and all your other friends."

"They aren't what you are!" I shouted angrily. "All these weeks, Miss Wilcox, when I tried to get the money to go to Barnard from my aunt Josie and my uncle Fifty, and you came to speak to Pa and he said no, just knowing you were here in this room reading your books and writing your poems made me feel good and brave. Why are you leaving? *Why?*"

"My husband made good on his threat. He's furious about the new book. He's cut off my funds. And he's made sure I can't earn my own living. At least not here. He's written the school trustees and told them who I am. I've had to step down."

"But you're a good teacher! The best one we ever had!"

"Unfortunately, Mattie, the trustees don't agree with you. They say I am a pernicious influence on young minds."

"But they wanted to keep you on. They wrote you a letter in May. You told me they did."

"They wanted Emily Wilcox, not Emily Baxter."

"Can't you stay, anyway? You could give readings at the Glenmore. They have literary evenings. Or you could—"

"My husband is on his way, Mattie. My sister wired that he's a day away at most. If I'm still here when he arrives, the next stop for me is a doctor's office. And then a sanatorium and so many drugs pushed down my throat, I won't be able to remember my own name, much less write."

"He can't do that."

"He can. He's a powerful man with powerful friends."

"Where will you go?" I asked, afraid for her.

She sat back against the settee and blew out a long plume of smoke. "My grandmother left me a little bit of money. It's in a trust and my husband can't touch it. It's not much, but it's something. Plus I have my car and a few pieces of jewelry. I'm going to hock them and go to Paris. I won't miss the jewelry so much, but I'll sure miss that car." She took another drag on her cigarette, then stubbed it out in a plate on the table.

"I'm driving it back to the city tomorrow. I'll go as far as McKeever on the main road and then take the Moose River Road to Port Leyden. I can take back roads from there to Rome, then head straight for New York. I don't want to risk running into Teddy. The car's big enough to hold my clothes and a few boxes of books. That's all I need for now. I'm having the rest of my things sent to my sister's. I'm going to hide out at her house while I sell the car. And once I'm in France, I'm going to do my best to get a divorce. Teddy's dead set against it, but I'm hoping I can make him so angry that he'll change his mind. A few more volumes of poetry should do the trick." Miss Wilcox smiled as she said that, but I saw the cigarette tremble between her fingers.

"I'm sorry," I said.

"For what?"

"For shouting at you. I was selfish."

She squeezed my hand and said, "You are many, many things, Mathilda Gokey, but selfish isn't one of them."

We sat together in silence for a few minutes, Miss Wilcox smoking and holding my hand. I didn't ever want to leave this room. Or my teacher. But I knew the

309

longer I stayed, the longer I kept her from packing. And come morning, she had to be gone.

"I have to go," I finally said. "Weaver's waiting for me outside. We have to be back by six or we're going to be in trouble."

"Well, we can't have that, Mattie. You need your wages. Maybe you can visit me in Paris someday. Or maybe, if all goes well, I can come home sooner rather than later. And then we can have lunch on the Barnard campus."

"I don't think so, Miss Wilcox," I said, my eyes on the floor.

"But why not?"

"I'm not going to Barnard. I'm staying here."

"My god, Mattie, why?" she asked, releasing my hand.

I couldn't answer her for a few seconds. "Royal Loomis asked me to marry him," I finally said. "And I told him yes."

Miss Wilcox looked like someone had drained all the sap from her. "I see," she said. She was about to say more, but I cut her off.

"Here's your five dollars back," I said, pulling the bill out of my skirt pocket. "Thank you, Miss Wilcox, it was very generous, but I won't be needing it."

"No, Mattie, you keep that," she said. "Money can be tight when you're first married. You keep that for yourself. Use it for paper and pens."

"Thank you," I said, knowing that was what she wanted me to say. Knowing, too, that it would likely be spent on seed corn or chickens, never on paper or pens.

"You take care of yourself, Mattie," my teacher said, walking me to the door.

"You, too, Miss Wilcox."

She said good-bye to Weaver as I climbed into the trap. She gave him a hug and told him to study hard at Columbia. She told him she was going to spend some time in Paris and that he should come visit her there. I looked back as we drove off and saw her silhouetted in the doorway. She looked small to me. Small and fragile and defenseless. She had not looked that way when I'd arrived.

"Giddyap!" I told Demon, snapping the reins. He broke into a trot.

"You all right?" Weaver asked.

"I'm fine," I said, driving down the middle of the street. Past the saloon. Past O'Hara's and Payne's stores, past the barber's and the post office and the school.

As soon as I made it out of the village, I pulled up on the reins until Demon stopped, then leaned my head into my hands.

"Aw, Matt," Weaver said, thumping my back. "She didn't die; you'll see her again."

"She may as well have. I won't see her again. I know I won't."

"You will so. She won't stay in France forever. She'll be back in New York one day."

"But I won't be," I said quietly.

"What?"

I didn't want to tell him, but I had to. I'd kept it from him for weeks, but I couldn't keep it from him forever.

"Weaver ... I'm not going. I'm not going to New York City," I said.

"Not going? *Why?*"

"Royal and I ... we're sparking. I'm going to ... he's ... I'm staying here. We're going to be married."

"To *Royal*? Royal Loomis?"

"You know another Royal?"

"Jeezum, Mattie! I don't believe this! I've seen him call for you, seen you out riding together, but I didn't think it was serious. Why don't you marry Demon? Or Barney? Or that big rock over there?"

"Weaver, stop it."

"But he's nowhere near good enough for you! Does he write? Can he write a story like you can? Does he read? Does he even know how?"

I wouldn't answer.

"You ever show him your composition book? He ever read your stories? Just tell me that. Just answer that one thing."

I didn't answer. There wasn't much point. I couldn't explain to him that I wanted books and words, but I wanted someone to hold me, too, and to look at me the way Jim looked at Minnie after she'd given him a new son and daughter. Or that leaving my family—that breaking the promise I'd made to my mamma—would be like tearing my own heart out.

Weaver railed on and on as we drove. I let him. There was nothing else I could do.

If you harness two horses together and one is stronger, the weaker horse gets buffeted and bruised.

That's what being friends with Weaver was like. A farmer can put an evener on his team's yoke to compensate for the weaker horse by shifting some of the load to the stronger one. But you can't put an evener on two people's hearts or their souls. I wished I could just up and go to New York City. I wished I was as strong as Weaver was. I wished I was as fearless.

But I was not.

con • fab • u • late

"Ada! Weaver! Mattie! Frances! Get those pies out-side! And that ice cream, too!" Cook bellowed from the doorway.

"Yes, ma'am!" we hollered in unison.

"And don't forget the lemonade!"

"Yes, ma'am!"

"And stop shouting! This is a resort, for pete's sake, not a lumber camp!"

"Yes, ma'am!" we shouted, laughing as we clambered out of the kitchen, through the dining room, out the front door, across the porch, and down the steps to the Glenmore's front lawn.

"Chat," Weaver said, passing me.

"Converse," I shot back.

It was the Fourth of July, the biggest night of the summer season, and no hotel on Big Moose Lake, or Fourth Lake, or any other lake in the whole state of New York threw a better party than the Glenmore. We had about a hundred of our own guests, plus some guests from the other hotels who'd rowed across the lake espe-cially, plus just about every family from Big Moose Sta-tion, Eagle Bay, and Inlet, too. Anyone could come, and most did. The hotel charged a dollar for grown-ups and fifty cents for children, and people saved all year to bring their entire families. For your money you got to eat as much barbecued chicken and pork spareribs and corn on the cob and potato salad and three-bean salad and macaroni salad and biscuits and strawberry shortcake and pie and ice cream and beer and lemonade as you could hold. You got to listen to a brass band from Utica, and you could dance, too, if you wanted. You could walk in the woods or take a boat out. And when it got good and dark, around nine-thirty or so, you got to see real fireworks shot off from the dock.

The hotel itself looked as pretty as a painting. Red, white, and blue bunting had been ruched all around the porch and the balconies. The red roses were in full bloom, and the blue hydrangeas, too. Every window was lit, even the dock was aglow with lanterns. Tables, made out of boards and sawhorses, covered with stars-and-stripes cloths, sagged under the weight of all the food and drink. All you could hear was laughter and music.

The lawn itself was teeming. There were people everywhere. Scores of tourists in linen suits and fancy dresses, and local people in their faded and mended Sunday best. Even Hamlet was turned out for the occasion, with a red-white-and-blue ribbon tied around his neck. My pa was there. He stood talking with Frank Loomis and George Burnap and a few other men. He nodded when he saw me. Weaver's mamma was talking to Alma McIntyre. My aunt Josie was interrogating poor Arn Satterlee about Emmie Hubbard's land and who was after buying it. I did my best to avoid her. She had told the whole county how selfish and uncaring I was to have gone to the Glenmore. She was only mad because Pa wouldn't allow Abby to clean her house and she now had to pay a girl from the village to do it. Uncle Vernon was talking to the Reverend Miller and his wife, and Mr. and Mrs. Becker. Mrs. Loomis was filling her plate with macaroni salad. Emmie Hubbard, looking thin and anxious, was swatting her kids away from the pie table. She didn't have the money to bring them, but Mr. Sperry always let them in for free. No one was supposed to know, for Mr. Sperry didn't like people thinking he was soft. Mrs. Hill, Fran's mother, had taken Fran aside and was scolding her for something. Probably for sneaking off to the Waldheim after Ed Compeau. Fran was making her eyes all big and serious, trying to look as innocent as the day.

Weaver zoomed by again, an empty pitcher in each hand. "Discuss," he said.

"Confer," I replied.

Confabulate was my word of the day and Weaver and I were dueling with it. It means to chat or talk familiarly. I like it a lot because it is a word that winks at you. It has shades of the word *fable* in it, as if it wants you to know that that's what most conversation is—people telling each other tales.

"Matt? Where should I put these? Mrs. Hennessey handed them to me on my way in."

It was Royal. He had a pie in each hand. I was aware of people's eyes on us. It made me feel special and proud. I took them from him and placed them on the dessert table.

"I'm going to talk to Tom L'Esperance," he said, squeezing my arm. "I'll see you later," and then he was gone.

I passed Belinda Becker on my way back to the kitchen. She was wearing a very pretty dress of dotted swiss tied with a pale blue sash and was leaning on Dan Loomis's arm like she couldn't stand up without him. Martha Miller was with them. She stared at me long and hard with a face sour enough to shame a lemon.

I saw Minnie and Jim. They were standing down by the lake. Minnie's face was turned up to her husband's. She still looked tired to me, but she was smiling. He was, too, and before they headed back up to the lawn, he bent his head to hers and kissed her. Right on the mouth. I knew it was sweet, what they had. Despite their troubles. And I hoped I would have something like it.

"I thought you hated him," I said, as Minnie waved and ran up to me.

"You'll understand when you're married," she said, kissing my cheek.

"Smug little witch."

"Who's smug? Why didn't you tell me about Royal Loomis? It's all anyone's talking about!"

"I tried! You had a crying fit and passed out on me. I have lots to tell you, Min. So much—"

"Minnie! What kind of pie do you want?"

"Coming, Jim!" Minnie yelled. She kissed me again and ran to her husband.

I watched her go, watched her fall in with the endless and needless fussing women make over unimportant things like pie and lemonade, and remembered with a twinge of jealousy how we had once belonged only to each other. Now she belonged to her children. And Jim. And their home, their life. Not me.

I felt a thump on my head. Weaver trotted by with a tray in his hand. "Speak."

"Talk," I said, swatting at him.

"That's weak," he said.

"So's *speak*!"

"Mattie! More chicken, please, ja?" It was Henry. He was manning the barbecue grill.

"Right away, Henry," I said, gathering my skirts in my hands to run back inside. He was also sharpening a carving knife. Even though it was dusky, I saw it and wished I hadn't. I knew it was only a silly superstition, but it made me nervous.

Before I could run back inside, Ada came up to me, grabbed my hand, and said, "Royal and Martha Miller just had a fight!"

I blinked at her. "Royal? That can't be. He was just here. Did you see them fighting?"

"No."

"Then how—"

"My nosy brother Mike. He was pissing out back of the boathouse. They didn't know he was there. He said he couldn't see anything and couldn't hear everything, but he did hear Martha tell Royal that it looked like his broken heart had healed up mighty quick."

My own heart felt like lead. "He told me he was going to talk to Tom L'Esperance."

"Tom L'Esperance? He's not even here. I'm going to find Mike and see if he knows more. Maybe I can find Royal, too."

"Ada, don't...," I started to say. Then I heard my name shouted and felt arms around my waist. It was my littlest sister. "For heaven's sake, Beth, what's all round your mouth?"

"Strawberry pie, Matt! It's so good!" And then she ran off, screeching and giggling with two other little girls. I was glad to see her recovered and lively again.

I saw somebody waving to me. It was Abby. She was standing with Minnie's two younger sisters, each of whom had one of Minnie's babies in her arms.

"Ask Mattie," I heard her say as I joined them, "she'll know."

"Know what?" I asked, half distracted, looking around for Royal. And Martha.

"Know why Miss Wilcox suddenly disappeared," Clara Simms said in hushed, dramatic tones. She was a girl who liked to stir the pot.

"She wanted to go to Paris," I said. I didn't want to talk about Miss Wilcox. I missed her too much.

Clara's eyes narrowed. "That's not what I heard. I heard she wrote dirty poems under another name and when the school trustees found out it was her writing them, they sent her packing."

"She wrote beautiful poems, Clara," I said, bristling. "Have you ever read one?"

"I wouldn't. Not ever. My mother says her books aren't decent. She says they're dangerous."

Miss Wilcox once said that books are dangerous things, too. Maybe in the right hands. A book could only be dangerous in Clara Simms's hands if she hit someone over the head with it.

"Mattie, my chicken, ja?" Henry shouted.

"I'll be back," I said, running inside. I got the chicken and made another trip for corn and biscuits and bean salad—dodging table six on the front stairs as I did. He was pulling one of his tricks—bending over to brush some nonexistent dirt from his shoes. When a girl lifted her skirts, so as to not trip over them on the steps, he was perfectly positioned to ogle her ankles.

As soon as I'd made sure Henry had everything he needed, I rejoined Abby and the Simms girls. "Where's Lou?" I asked them, looking around for her.

"You haven't seen her yet?" Abby said.

"No, why?"

Abby pointed toward a large brown keg. There was a wiry boy with a bad haircut standing next to it, sneaking a glass of beer.

"What's he got to do with Lou?" I said.

"Mattie, that *is* Lou."

"Lord, Abby! What's she done to her hair?"

"Cut it off. All of it. Keeps threatening to run away. I wish she would."

I came up behind her. "What are you doing?" I hissed, snatching the glass away.

"Drinking beer." She snatched it back, guzzled its contents in one go, then let out a burp so long and so loud it made her lips flap.

I grabbed her by the wrist. "Louisa Anne Gokey, I'm ashamed of you!"

"I don't care."

"Look at your hair! You're half bald! What did Pa do when he saw you?"

"Nothing. He didn't even notice. He never does. Let go, Matt, let go!" And then she yanked her skinny arm free and flew off, sparrowlike, to join the younger Loomis boys in some fresh mischief.

"What's wrong with her? She got the mange?" It was Royal. He offered me a biscuit from his plate. I took it.

"She cut her hair. Again."

"Why?"

"Because she's angry." So angry that she made me afraid. She was growing wild. Why didn't Pa see that? Why didn't he do something?

"She don't like the color or something?"

"No, Royal, it's nothing to do with the color," I said impatiently. "It's to do with losing our mother and then Lawton . . ." I saw that he was looking at his bean salad, not me, and gave up. "Where were you?" I asked.

"Getting something to eat. Talking to Tom."

"Is he here?"

"Tom? He's right over there," he said, pointing to the porch. And he was. He was leaning against a column, having a parley with Charlie Eckler.

Ada must've been wrong, I thought. Her brother hadn't *seen* the fight, after all; he'd only heard it. Maybe he'd made a mistake. Maybe Martha had fought with someone else, not Royal.

"Your pa oughtn't to clear those northern acres of his," Royal said, swallowing a bite of pie. "He told me he was thinking of it."

"No? Why not?" I asked absently, still looking for Martha despite myself.

"I was up there berrying the other day. Where our land touches yours and the Hubbards'. He's got good blueberry bushes up there. Should keep 'em. Camps want 'em for pies and pancakes and such."

Minnie, who'd managed to sneak away from Jim, joined us. So did Ada and Fran. They started talking about who was here with whom, and Royal, uncomfortable around so much female chatter, went to talk to his brother.

"Oh, he's so handsome, Mattie!" Ada sighed as soon as he was out of earshot. "How did you get him?"

Ada didn't mean anything by the question, but hearing it made me uneasy nonetheless. I often wondered the same thing myself.

"She let him kiss her in a boat out on Big Moose Lake, that's how," Fran teased.

"How do you know? You certainly weren't there," I said.

Fran grinned. "Never make love in the country, Matt. 'Cuz the potatoes have eyes . . ."

"...and the corn has ears," Ada finished, giggling.

"She'll be Mattie Loomis before long," Minnie said. "Did you set a date yet? I bet it'll be before the new year. I bet you're married before the hay's in. I'm sure of it."

"I wouldn't be."

I turned around, startled by the new voice. It was Martha Miller. She and Belinda Becker had joined our group. Belinda looked like she'd smelled something bad. Martha's face was pale and pinched.

"I hope you have a dowry, Mattie Gokey. A good one," Martha said.

"Unlike some around here, Mattie doesn't *need* a dowry," Minnie retorted.

"Not when she has such nice big bosoms," Fran said, giggling.

I turned crimson and they all giggled. Even Belinda. Not Martha, though. She just looked at me with eyes that were hard and mean. I saw that they were puffy, too. She'd been crying.

"Royal's the second-eldest," she said. "Dan will get the bulk of the Loomis farm one day. But the Loomis land borders your father's, doesn't it, Mattie?"

"Martha, come on. Let's go," Belinda said.

Martha paid her no mind. "If Royal marries you, he might be able to get his father to give him a few acres, and your father, too. Maybe ten or fifteen altogether. Why, he might even get your father's whole farm one day. After all, Lawton left and he's not coming back, is he?"

"Martha!" Belinda chided, tugging on her arm. Martha shrugged her off.

"And then there's Emmie Hubbard's land," she said. "Twelve acres. Nice the way it nestles in between the Loomises' land and your father's, isn't it? Funny, too, how it just happens to be up for auction next month."

"Oh, who cares, Martha? Whyn't you go poison the punch or something?" Fran said.

My blood froze up inside me. "What are you saying, Martha?"

"Emmie doesn't pay her taxes on time for four or five years running and nobody cares. Now, all of a sudden Arn's auctioning her land. You don't wonder about that?"

"Only because there's an interested party," I said, remembering Aunt Josie and Alma McIntyre steaming Emmie's letter open. "Someone inquired. Someone from the city looking for cheap land."

Martha smiled. "Oh, there's an interested party all right, but he's not from the city. He lives right in Eagle Bay and his name is Royal Loomis."

Fran burst into laughter. "You sure are a horse's ass, Martha. Royal doesn't have that kind of money."

"No, but his mother does. Iva's been saving for two years. Skimming a quarter here, fifty cents there off the egg money or the butter money. She stitched up two quilts over the winter and sold them to Cohen's. She took in sewing for the summer people, too. She's the one who pushed Arn to slap a lien on Emmie. She wrote his boss down in Herkimer. Said it wasn't fair that Emmie got to slide all the time when everyone else paid their taxes."

"Why'd she do a thing like that?" Ada asked.

Martha shrugged. "She's got her reasons. She's also got herself a nice little bundle and she's giving it to Royal so he can buy the Hubbard land and farm it. And like I said, a few acres as a wedding gift from your pa, Mattie, and Royal's pa, too, would round it out nicely, wouldn't it?"

I couldn't answer her. The words stuck in my throat like burrs.

"Thought you were so smart, didn't you, Mattie? You, with your head always shoved in a book. Royal says you know a lot of words, but you don't even know how to please..."

"Martha, you say one more word and I'll slap your mouth right off your face," Fran said. "I swear to God I will."

"Come on, Martha, let's go. Dan's waving for me," Belinda said. She pulled on her friend's arm again and they left.

"Don't you mind her nonsense, Matt. She made it all up. She's so jealous over Royal, she's pissing vinegar," Minnie said.

"Discourse!" It was Weaver. He'd come up behind me.

I looked at him, dazed. "Gossip," I said dully. "Embroider. Fabricate. Tell lies. To others. Or yourself. Especially yourself."

"*What?* That's way off, Mattie. I'll give you another shot. You miss it again, you're dead as a—"

"Oh, go away, Weaver!" Minnie snapped. "This is girls only!"

"Jeez, Minnie, bite my head off, why don't you?"

"Go on! Get lost!"

All the pride I had felt earlier, over Royal carrying the pies to me and people seeing him do it, vanished like a spooked doe. I felt sick. My friends could stick up for me and say all the nice things they wanted; it didn't matter. All I could hear was Royal's voice telling me, "Your pa oughtn't to clear those northern acres of his . . . he's got good blueberry bushes up there . . ." I felt such a fool for thinking that he might try to see past plain brown hair and plain brown eyes to what was inside of me. Or value what he saw.

"Come on, let's get some dessert. Cook won't know. Fireworks are going to start soon and I'm dying for a bite of that shortcake," Ada said, trying to jolly me.

"I'm not very hungry—," I began to say, but Minnie cut me off.

"Oh, Mattie, don't fret so. You'll have the last laugh when you're married with ten children and your own house and farm and she's still a sour old maid picking up the hymnbooks after her father's service."

I forced a smile.

"Hey, Matt, is Cook going to let you watch the fireworks?" It was Royal.

We all looked at him—myself, Minnie, Ada, and Fran. Not one of us said a word.

"Jim'll wonder where on earth I've got to," Minnie said, rushing off.

"Cook wants us, Ada. Come on," Fran said, following her.

"Guess I must've stepped in manure," Royal said, watching them all go.

I looked at the ground but didn't see it. I saw something that had happened the day I'd rushed home to nurse my sick family. Something I'd forgotten about until now. I saw Tommy Hubbard. He was struggling with Baldwin. He was crying and hitting the calf. Someone had hit him, too. He had an ugly red welt under his eye. Royal hated Tommy. And Emmie. And all the Hubbards.

"Royal..."

"What?"

"Martha Miller just...she just told me some things."

He snorted. "You believe what she says?"

I looked up at him. "Royal, are you the one fixing to buy Emmie Hubbard's land?"

He looked away and spat and then he looked right back at me with his beautiful amber eyes. "Yes, Matt," he said. "Yes, I am."

ide · al

"Jeezum, Mattie, you're in for it now!" Fran said. "Why'd you leave the broom out in the middle of the kitchen?"

"I didn't! I swept the floor and put it away!" I was folding napkins in the dining room, readying the tables for tomorrow's breakfast.

"Cook just tripped over it and dropped a whole pot of consommé. She said for you to get in there right away."

"But I didn't..."

"Go *on*, before she comes out here after you!"

Fran disappeared back into the kitchen. I just stood where I was, a lump growing in my throat, thinking how an earful from Cook would make a perfectly awful end to a perfectly awful day. *Ideal* was my word of the day. A standard of perfection, or something existing only in the imagination, was its meaning. The dictionary must have been playing a joke on me. There had been nothing perfect or excellent about this day. It was the fifth of July, my birthday. I'd turned seventeen and no one had remembered. Fran and Ada knew the date very well. So did Weaver. And not one of them had so much as mentioned it. I'd been blue about it all day. I'd been blue about other things, too. About the rotten things Martha Miller had said to me at the party the night before. And the fight I'd had with Royal. Right after I'd asked if he was the one buying Emmie's land.

"I don't want to talk about that," he'd said.

"Well, I do," I said. "Why are you doing it? It's not right."

He took my arm and led me away from the tables and the people and the noisy brass band playing "I'm a Yankee Doodle Dandy." We walked a little ways into the woods.

"Why do you want to buy Emmie's land, Royal?" I said as soon as we were alone.

"Because it's good land. It'll make good growing land, good pasture, too."

I said nothing for a minute, trying to work up my courage, then I asked him, "Is that the only reason?" I was afraid of the answer.

"No, Mattie, there's another..."

I looked at the ground. Martha was right. It was Pa's land Royal wanted, not me.

"...I want Emmie Hubbard gone."

I saw Frank Loomis's hairy behind in my mind's eye and Emmie bent over the stove. "Royal, you...you know?"

"For god's sake, Mattie. Everyone in the whole damn county knows."

"I didn't know."

"That ain't hardly a surprise. You're too interested in what Blueberry Finn and Oliver Dickens and all the rest of them made-up people are doing to see what's going on right around you."

"That's not true!"

He rolled his eyes.

"Royal, are you buying that land for us? To live on?"

"Yes."

"I don't want it, Royal. How can we start a life there knowing we took it away from a widow and seven children? It's all they've got. If you buy it and kick the Hubbards off, where will they go?"

"To hell, I hope."

"But Lucius..." I didn't know how to say it, so I stopped. Then I started again, for it had to be said. "That baby... he's your half brother, isn't he?"

"None of Emmie's brats is any kin to me."

"He can't help how he got here; he's only a baby," I said softly.

He looked at me like I was Judas himself. Then he said, "What if it was your pa, Mattie? Taking the first milk of the year over to Emmie's when you and your sisters hadn't yet tasted any? Lying to your ma, leaving her standing in the barn crying? You think you'd give a damn what happened to the Hubbards then?" His voice had turned husky. I saw that it cost him to say these things. "My ma... she can't leave the house some days, she's that ashamed. Them books of yours tell you how that feels? You keep reading, maybe you'll find out." And then he walked off and left me standing by myself.

I was upset the rest of the night. I didn't even hear the fireworks going off, and when the party was over and everything cleaned up and it was finally time for bed, I couldn't sleep. I'd stayed awake, turning it all over and over in my mind like a puzzle box, but I couldn't find an answer to any of it. I didn't want to see Emmie kicked off her land. She was a trial, but I liked her and I liked her kids. I loved Tommy. He was around so much he was almost like our brother. I felt for him and his family. We only had one parent, too. It could've been us in their shoes if Pa didn't provide as well as he did. But I could also understand Royal's feelings. If I were him and it were my father paying visits where he shouldn't and my mother crying, I'd want Emmie gone, too.

The kitchen door banged open again, startling me. "For pete's sake, Mattie, Cook wants you! Come on!" Fran ordered.

I put down the napkin I was holding. The lump in my throat got bigger. It was unfair that I was in trouble for something I hadn't even done. And on my birthday, too. I opened the kitchen door expecting the rough edge of Cook's tongue, and instead I got the shock of my life when twenty people yelled "Surprise!" at the top of their lungs.

Then there was singing and Cook emerged from the pantry bearing a white sheet cake with a candle stuck into it and HAPPY BIRTHDAY, MATTIE written on it. I grinned ear to ear and thanked everyone and made a wish, and then there was ice cream and lemonade to go along with the cake, and a bouquet of wildflowers that the girls had picked.

Cook called for a toast and Mike Bouchard said he'd do it. "Dear Mattie," he began, holding up his lemonade, "I love you much, I love you mighty, I wish my pajamas were next to your nightie. Now don't get mad at what I said, I meant on the clothesline and not in the bed." I turned beet red. Everyone hooted and laughed except Cook. She slapped the side of Mike's head and made him go sit on the back steps. Ada and Fran teased me and told me what a hangdog face I'd had all day, then said how clever they were for keeping the surprise a secret.

After the little party, Cook bawled at everyone to get back to work and Mrs. Morrison handed me a sugar sack. "Your father left it with the milk this morning," she said.

Inside the sack was a tiny painting of my house with the yard around it and the pines and maples and the garden and cornfields at the back. It was beautiful and made me feel yearny for home. The note inside it read: "My ma made this for you. Happy Birthday. Tommy Hubbard." There was a homemade card in the sack, too, decorated with pressed flowers and hand-drawn hearts. My sisters had all written nice messages on the card except Lou, who told me I lived in the zoo, smelled like a monkey, and looked like one, too. There was a small tin of butterscotch candies from my aunt Josie and uncle Vernon. And under all that, wrapped up in the same sort of brown paper I recognized from Mr. Eckler's boat, was a thin, flat package. I opened it. It was a brand-new composition book. There was no inscription, but I knew it was from my pa. It was a nice thing for him to do and it should've made me happy, but instead it made me want to cry.

"Oh, Mattie, you've got a visitor," Fran said in a sing-song.

I looked up and saw Royal in the doorway, looking as awkward as a hog on stilts. I was partly glad to see him, partly worried. I wondered if he was still angry about our falling-out and had come to get his ring back.

"Why, Royal Loomis!" Cook said. "You here to bring me more of those nice strawberries?"

"Uh, no...no, ma'am. I...uh, brought this"—he held up a package—"for Matt."

"Well, I'll want some tomorrow morning, then. And mind you come here first, not Burdick's. I don't want anyone's leavings."

"Yes, ma'am."

"Like some cake? There's a few slices left over from Mattie's party. Mattie, get your guest some cake. Get him some ice cream and a glass of lemonade. Sit down for a spell, Royal."

Cook was a dreadful shameless flirt. I fixed some re-freshments for Royal and sat down next to him. He pushed his package across the tabletop. "For you. It's a book," he said.

I couldn't believe it. He might as well have said it was a diamond necklace.

"Is it really?" I whispered.

He shrugged, pleased by my reaction but trying not to show it. "I know you like books."

My heart lifted. It soared! Martha was wrong about Royal. I was wrong about Royal. He did care enough to look down inside of me. He didn't like me for my pa's land; he liked me for me. He did! To think that Royal had gone to a store—maybe to O'Hara's in Inlet or Cohen's in Old Forge—and picked this out. Just for me. My fingers trembled as I undid the string. What had he chosen for me? What could it be? An Austen or a Brontë? Maybe a Zola or a Hardy?

I opened the paper and saw that it was a Farmer. Fannie Farmer. A cookbook.

Royal leaned forward. "Thought you might be needing that soon."

I opened it. Someone else's name was written on the title page. I flipped through the pages. A few were stained.

"It ain't new, only secondhand. Got it at Tuttle's. It's got different sections, see? Meats and poultry...baked things..."

I could see in his eyes he wanted me to like it. I could see that he'd tried and it only made it worse.

"Why, Mattie, isn't that a nice gift?" Cook said, poking me in the back. "So thoughtful. And practical, too. Girls nowadays do not know how to cook. I hope you told him thank you . . ."

"Thank you, Royal," I said, smiling so hard my face hurt. "Thank you so very much."

a · busion

"I heard Royal came by last night," Weaver said.

It was ten o'clock. Breakfast was over. We were shelling peas on the back steps.

"Yes, he did."

"Heard he got you a book for your birthday."

"Yes, he did."

"Novel?"

I didn't answer.

"Huh."

"Huh what, Weaver? What's the *huh* for?"

"I was just wondering..."

"Wondering what?"

"Wondering if there's a word in your dictionary for when people know the truth but pretend they don't."

$\mathcal{M}$attie."

"Mmmm."

It's very late. Or very early. I'm not sure which. Either way, I'm asleep. Finally asleep. And I want to stay that way. But I hear the sound of boot heels on the floorboards. They're coming toward my bed. It's Ada or Fran, must be, come to get me up. I don't want to get up. I want to sleep.

"Mattie."

"Go away," I murmur.

I hear something strange then. Water. I hear the sound of water dripping.

"Mattie."

I open my eyes. Grace Brown is standing by my bed. She's holding my dictionary in her hands. Her eyes are as black and bottomless as the lake.

"Tell me, Mattie," she says. "Why does *gravid* sound like *grave*?"

non · pa · reil

"Did Hamlet go?" Fran asked me.

"He sure did."

"Big one?"

"Big as an elephant's."

"How do I look?"

"Sweller than Lillian Russell," I said, tucking a rose behind her ear.

"Hold on," Ada said, pinching her cheeks. "Now bite your lips." She did.

"All right, then," Fran said. "You two know what to do. Hide in the trees and wait. If it all goes off, I'll see you in the lake. If not, for god's sake, come and rescue me."

"Go get him, Frannie," I said.

Fran straightened the skirt on her swimming costume, pulled the fabric taut over her bosoms, gave us a wink, and trotted off toward the guest cottages. Ada and I, also in our costumes, waited until she was out of sight, then headed into the woods.

Table six had gone too far.

Poor little Ada had walked down to the boathouse the evening before to collect the plates and glasses after

338

the weekly fly-casting demonstration. She'd thought the place was empty. The guides had already left. The guests, too. That is, all but one—table six. She'd managed to get away from him before he could show her what she didn't want to see, but not before he'd told her to crank his handle, and various other dirty things that don't bear repeating.

Fran wanted to tell Cook or Mr. Sperry. She said he'd cornered Jane Miley when she was cleaning his room the other day, and that enough was enough. Ada wouldn't let her, though. She said if it ever got back to her pa, he'd be angry with her. Fathers had a way of making that sort of thing your fault. Ada said her pa would make her give up her position and come home and she didn't want to.

We were all burning mad about table six and his shenanigans, but we didn't know what to do about him. By the time we got Ada's story out of her, I had to give Hamlet his nightly walk. Ada and Fran came with me. Ada was hiccuping and Fran thought a bit of air would do her good. They followed me across the lawn and through the woods to Hamlet's very favorite spot—a huge patch of ferns in an out-of-the-way place, about fifty or so yards from the lake.

The smell was so bad it stopped Ada's hiccups. She pinched her nose and made a face. I did, too. Fran didn't. Instead, she parted the ferns, looked at what was on the ground beneath them, and smiled. "We're going to fix table six," she said. "And how."

"Us?" Ada asked.

"And him," Fran said, pointing at Hamlet. "Here's what we'll do. Now, listen . . ."

Fran told us her plan. It was clever but risky, too. Things could easily go wrong. But if they went right, we'd never be troubled by table six again.

That night we assembled our weapons. Fran asked Cook for permission for the three of us to take a swim the next morning after the breakfast service. She said we could. None of us owned a swimming costume, but there were a few old ones kicking about that Mrs. Morrison let the help use. Fran borrowed three and stashed them under our pillows. Ada returned to the boathouse on the pretense of having left a tray there, and came back with a length of rope stuffed in her drawers. I ran upstairs, pulled my fountain pen and composition book out from under my bed, and composed a note. "Flirty, but demure," Fran had instructed. "You know . . . a come-hither note." I didn't know. But I gave it my best.

Before we went to bed, Fran gave us our final orders. "Ada, get that rope out to the woods first thing tomorrow before anyone's around to see you do it. Mattie, make sure you feed that dog well," she said.

I told her I would, and I did. I stuffed him to the gills. I gave him his usual breakfast, plus two biscuits, four slices of bacon, and a fried egg left over from the help's meal. Afterward, he nearly pulled my arm off trying to get to his fern patch, and once there he did himself proud.

When breakfast was over, the three of us raced upstairs and changed. The woolen swimming costumes were awful things. They were baggy and scratchy, with sleeves that went down past our elbows and leggings that covered our ankles and skirts that came down past our knees. As soon as we got them fastened, we tied our hair up in scarves, then ran down the back stairs and out the kitchen door before Mike Bouchard or Weaver could see us and laugh.

"Do you think he'll come?" Ada asked me breathlessly as we ran through the woods.

"He's bound to. Fran made eyes at him at breakfast and she left him that note."

"If you show, I won't tell," it said. "Meet me at the far cottage after breakfast."

We arrived at the fern patch sweating and panting. It was only ten o'clock or so, but it was already hot and muggy.

"Where'd you put the rope?" I asked, looking at the ground around us.

"Right here," Ada said, pulling it out from under a stand of spruce trees.

"Where can we tie it?"

"Around that pine?"

"Its trunk is too bare. He'll see it."

Ada bit her lip, looking all around.

"How about that balsam over there? Its branches go down nearly to the ground."

We tied the rope around the tree, but then discovered it was too short. It needed to snake along the ground from the balsam tree past the front of the fern patch and into the bushy stand of spruce trees where we planned to hide ourselves, but it didn't quite reach.

"What are we going to do, Mattie? They're going to be here soon," Ada fretted, looking back toward the hotel.

"We'll have to tie it to the pine after all and just hope he doesn't see it," I said. "Come on, we've got to hurry."

I quickly unknotted the rope and retied it tightly around the trunk of the pine tree, about six inches up from the ground. Then I walked back to the stand of spruces, letting the rope play out along the ground. Ada followed me, carefully covering it with pine needles, leaves, and dirt.

"Cripes, but it stinks. Won't he know?"

"He'll be too intent on other things. Here...look, Ada, we made it. With plenty left to spare."

Ada glanced at me and I showed her that we had about an extra yard of rope to hold on to in the spruces.

"Good," she said. "Help me with the covering, will you?"

We buried the rope completely, then stepped back to survey our work. It wasn't perfect, but we decided that if you weren't looking for it—and table six wouldn't be— you'd never see it. The only problem was the pine tree. The loop and knot at the end of the rope showed too starkly against its bark.

"Here I am! This way!" a voice trilled from the distance.

It was Fran.

"Jeezum, Matt, they're coming!" Ada squeaked. "What are we going to do?"

I looked around wildly. My eyes lighted on the fern patch. I ran to it and broke off a few fronds. I scratched a small hole in the dirt in front of the pine tree with my fingers, stuck the stems in, then tamped the dirt back around them. They looked like a young fern plant and covered the rope completely.

We heard Fran giggle. She was much closer.

"Come on! Quick!" Ada hissed. She grabbed my hand and pulled me into the spruce trees. The branches bobbed and shook. We frantically tried to still them.

"This way! Over here! Aren't you coming?" Fran sang.

Ada crouched and peered through the branches. I knelt down on the ground and wound the end of the rope around my hand.

"He's coming. Get ready, Matt." It was Ada's job to say when and my job to pull. "He's about ten yards away now."

I peered through the branches, wincing as a needle poked me in the eye. I had a good view of the fern patch to my right but could see nothing to my left.

"I can't find you!" a man's voice shouted. It was table six. My insides shriveled like bacon in a pan. Our plan had seemed so simple, but now I didn't see how it could work and wished to god we hadn't allowed our anger to make us so bold. Fran had to be in just the right place, and table six did, too, and the rope . . . had we buried it too close to the ferns? Or not close enough?

"I'm right here! Come on!" Fran called. She giggled fetchingly, I saw a blur of black fabric and white skin as she skirted around the fern patch and then she was behind it.

"Where?" he called out.

"Right over here!"

"Five yards," Ada said, in a whisper so small, I barely heard it.

Fran broke off a feathery frond and held it in front of her face, then she flicked it away and blew a kiss. She waved her pretty hand and toyed with buttons on her swimming costume. She was a revelation. *Nonpareil* was my word of the day. It means peerless, and that's what she was. Neither Lillie Langtry, nor the great Sarah Bernhardt herself, could have done as well. Her gestures were bold and coy all at once, and they had the same effect on table six that a red rag has on a bull. I still couldn't see him, but I could hear him. He took a running start and came barreling straight at the fern patch.

"Now, Mattie!" Ada hissed.

I pulled on the rope just as hard as I could, but nothing happened. *We've put it in the wrong place,* I thought. *We've messed the whole thing up. Oh Lord. Oh no. He'll get hold of Fran and then . . .*

. . . And then there was a hard twang on the rope that I both felt and heard, and the force of it jerked me forward, just as if I'd caught a big fish, and I gasped out loud as the coils bit into my hand and then there was another sound . . . the sound of table six hollering at the top of his lungs in surprise, and then shock, and then horror, as he tripped and tumbled headfirst through the air, and landed with a thick, wet thud in a heaping pile of dog shit.

A cloud of black flies swarmed up over the ferns, upset at being disturbed. Fran stood stock-still. Her mouth was hanging open. Mine was, too. I stumbled out from my hiding place and quickly uncoiled the rope from my hand. Ada came out after me. None of us made a sound. All we could hear was the angry buzzing of the flies and the high-pitched "Oh! Oh!" of a man in great distress.

Table six's head popped out of the ferns. His eye glasses were hanging from his left ear. Fran looked at him and burst into laughter. Ada and I did, too. He got to his knees, stood up, and looked with disbelief at his brown palms. Hamlet's handiwork was smeared across them. It was everywhere else, too—on his tie, and all down the front of his white suit jacket.

Fran's laughter turned into helpless, rolling peals. "Now you look just as dirty as you are!" she hooted at him.

His eyes widened. "Why, you . . . you little bitch!" he sputtered. "You did this on purpose! I'll have your job! I'll have all your jobs!"

Fran wasn't cowed. "You'll keep your mouth shut and your pizzle in your pants, mister, or I'll tell my pa what you've been up to and you'll get even worse!" she said. She wouldn't do any such thing, but table six didn't know it.

She turned and ran off toward the lake and Ada and I ran after her, laughing and crowing the whole way. I glanced back over my shoulder once and saw table six stumbling back to camp. I wished I could see his arrival. Mrs. Morrison would never let him inside the Glenmore like that. She'd tell him to go jump in the lake first. Literally.

When she got to the shore, Fran whipped her head scarf off and tossed it on the sand. She shook out her blazing red curls, then dove into the lake and came up a few seconds later, still laughing. She sucked in a mouthful of water and spouted it out like a fountain. Ada and I did the same, and then we all swam out as far as we dared and treaded water in a circle, reliving our victory. Ada and I kept saying how brave Fran was, and Fran kept saying how she never would have dared to do any of it if it wasn't for us and that we were clever as foxes for hiding the rope so well and pulling on it at just the right time.

We swam some more, and splashed each other, and played like otters. I lifted my face to the sun. I knew I shouldn't—Mamma had told me a million times that sunning myself would only make my freckles worse—but I didn't care. I felt happy and more than happy. I felt triumphant. We'd fixed table six.

We floated on our backs for a bit, letting the lake cool us, before we got out to dry off. The water weighed our swimming costumes down and made them baggier than ever. The crotch on Fran's was hanging so low when she got out of the water that she looked like a penguin. We told her so and she started waddling around with her feet jutting out, which made us laugh some more. We finally collapsed in a heap in the sand, shook our hair out and spread it over our shoulders to dry. We were all quiet for a while, listening to the locusts singing in the trees. The scent of the balsams was so strong in the heat, it made us drowsy. We watched as a family of ducks came to see whether we had something for them to eat—but still, no one spoke.

I was the one who finally broke the silence. "We better think about heading back," I said. "Cook will skin us if we're late to supper."

"Oh, Matt, I don't want to go back," Ada said. "It's so nice and peaceful here. So calm."

"It's the calm before the storm," Fran said. "Cook told me we've got a hundred and five coming for dinner. And ninety for supper."

Ada and I groaned.

Fran gave us a wicked smile. "Who's going to wait on table six today?" she asked.

"Me!" I said.

"No, I want to!" Ada said.

"Let's race for it," Fran said. "First one to the back steps!"

Ada won the race, but she didn't get to serve table six. After we'd changed and come back downstairs, Cook told us that one of the guests, a Mr. Maxwell, had had some sort of mishap in the woods and was so upset by it that he'd retired to his room for the evening with a hot-water bottle and a rum toddy. She said Mrs. Morrison would be seating a family of four at his table—table six.

It was all I could do to hold the giggles in as she told us. Ada, too. I glanced at her and saw that she was biting her lip.

Not Fran, though. She was as cool as a cucumber. "He must've been quite upset, Mrs. Hennessey," she said.

"Yes, he was," Cook said. "I asked him would he at least come down for dinner—I thought he should eat something—but he wouldn't hear of it. I just don't understand it. I've got fried chicken on the menu and he's very partial to it. Why, I even fixed his favorite dessert, but when I told him I had, he went all green around the gills."

"Really? What is it?" Fran asked.

"Chocolate pudding. I made it with extra eggs and nice fresh milk and...and...Fran? Frances Hill, you stop that right now! What the devil's got into you? Ada, you should be ashamed! Braying like a mule, you are! And you, Mattie Gokey...would you like to tell me what could *possibly* be so funny?"

do · lor

Our happy state of mind persisted for two whole days, then disappeared instantly, as birds will right before it rains, when my father came into the Glenmore at the end of the dinner service on a beautiful afternoon to tell us that Weaver's mamma's house had burned down.

Weaver raced out of the hotel right then and there. Cook made the rest of us—myself, Ada, Fran, and Mike—wait until dinner was over and the dining room readied for supper, and then John Denio drove us down in his buckboard.

During the ride, I thought about my words and their meanings, as I do when I'm anxious or scared, as a way of taking my mind off things. My word of the day was *doughnut*, a silly word at the best of times. I decided *dolor*, a word I'd seen as I'd paged back from *doughnut*, would be a better choice, given what had happened. It means grief, distress, or anguish. There was a piece of it in *doleful* and *condolence*, too.

We'd talked amongst ourselves on the way down the hill, never doubting that the fire was an accident. We figured an oil lamp had tipped over. Or maybe sparks from the wash-pot fire had flown up and landed on the roof, though Weaver's mamma is always careful to build her fire a good ways from the house. But as soon as we saw Lincoln, the hinny, lying in the road with blood soaked into the dust all around him, and dead chickens everywhere, and the pigsty smashed apart, we knew different.

My father was standing by the smoking ruins with Mr. Loomis and Mr. Pulling. Mr. Sperry, Mr. Higby, and a handful of neighbors from Fourth Lake were there, too. I ran up to them. "Pa, what happened?" I asked.

"Mattie, what are you doing here? This ain't for you to see."

"I had to come, Pa. I had to see Weaver's mamma. Is she all right?"

"She's across the road at the Hubbards'."

I started to run toward Emmie's.

"Mattie, wait . . ."

"What, Pa?"

"You know anything about those men who beat Weaver?"

"Only that they were trappers. And that Mr. Higby put them in jail. Why?"

"They must've just got out. Weaver's mamma says they're the ones did this. Killed the hinny and most every chicken she owned. Pig got away, at least. Ran off across the field into the woods. Got the Loomis boys out after her."

I couldn't believe what he was telling me. "Pa, no," I said.

"She says they were mad as blazes about the jail time. She says they set fire to the house, then took off into the woods, heading north. At least that's what I think she said. She ain't making much sense right now. She's bad off, Mattie. She fought with them. One broke her arm."

I pressed my palms to my cheeks and shook my head.

"You listen to me now, Matt. No one knows for sure where those men got to. I don't want you outside the hotel after dark. Not till they're found. You keep Weaver in, too. You hear?"

I nodded, then bolted off to Emmie's.

Cook was already inside, trying to find some coffee or tea and muttering about the state of the place. Mrs. Burnap and Mrs. Crego were there. Dr. Wallace, too. And Weaver. Most of the Hubbard kids were huddled wide-eyed on a worn settee or sitting on the floor in front of it. Lucius was playing in a pile of dirty clothing.

"Come on, Mamma, you've got to let the doctor see to your arm," Weaver said.

Weaver's mamma shook her head no. She was sitting on Emmie's bed, cradling her right arm with her left and rocking back and forth. Emmie was sitting next to her, her arm around her, crooning to her, shushing her, telling her everything would be all right. Weaver's mamma didn't seem to hear her, though. She didn't hear anyone. Her head was bowed. She kept saying, "It's gone, it's all gone! Oh, Jesus, help me—it's gone!"

Weaver knelt down in front of her. "Mamma, please," he said.

"Mrs. Smith, I need to take a look at that arm," Dr. Wallace said.

Emmie shooed him away. "Leave her set and rock for a bit, she'll come round. I always do," she said.

"She's got a bad fracture. I can tell by the angle of it."

"Oh, it ain't goin' nowhere. You can see to it in a minute. Whyn't you set yourself down for a spell and stop worryin' everyone?"

Dr. Wallace gritted his teeth, but he sat. Weaver stood up and paced the small room.

"Sip of my bitter hops syrup will put her to rights," Mrs. Crego said, reaching into her basket.

"There's no need," Dr. Wallace said briskly. "It'll only interfere with the laudanum I'm going to give her."

Mrs. Crego glowered at him. He glowered back. Cook found some chicory in a tin. Lucius gurgled in the dirty clothes. Mrs. Burnap picked him up and made a face when she discovered his diaper was full. And all the while, Weaver's mamma kept rocking and keening.

I walked over to Weaver and took his hand. "What is it? Why is she doing that? Is it the house?"

"I don't know," he said. "Maybe it's the animals . . . or her things. She had photographs and such. Or maybe it is the house—"

"The devil take the house!" Mrs. Smith suddenly

cried. "You think I give a damn about an old shack?" She lifted her face. Her ancient eyes were bloodshot from tears and smoke. "They found your college money, Weaver," she said. "They took it all. Every last nickel. It's gone, it's gone. Lord Jesus, it's all gone."

lep · o · rine

"Where's Weaver? Where is he?" Cook asked me. "He's always trying to wheedle a slice of coconut cream pie out of me. Now I've got one for him and he's disappeared. Mattie, go find him, will you?"

It wasn't like Cook to save slices of pie for anyone, but she was concerned about Weaver. We all were. I had an idea where he might be and I soon found him. He was sitting on the dock. He had his trouser legs rolled up and his feet in the water.

"Why isn't real life like book life?" I asked, sitting down next to him. "Why aren't people plain and uncomplicated? Why don't they do what you expect them to do, like characters in a novel?" I took my shoes and stockings off and dangled my feet in the water, too.

"What do you mean?"

"Well, Bill Sikes is bad. So's Fagin. Just plain bad. Oliver and Mr. Brownlow are good. So's Pip. And Dorrit."

Weaver thought about this, then said, "Heathcliff is both. He's more than both. So's Rochester. You never know what they're going to do." He looked at me. "This is about Emmie, isn't it? You don't know what to make of her now."

"No, I don't."

Emmie Hubbard had us all puzzled. She had taken Weaver's mamma in and refused to even hear of her going to Mrs. Loomis's or Mrs. Burnap's or anywhere else. She'd tucked her up in her own bed and tended to her. She'd even had the presence of mind, on the day the Smiths' house burned, to make her kids pluck and clean all the chickens the trappers had killed, right away. She made stew out of a few, fried a few more, and sold the rest to the Eagle Bay Hotel before they went bad. She used the money she got from them to pay Dr. Wallace for setting Weaver's mamma's arm.

"I can't figure it out, Weaver," I said. "I saw my pa this morning when he was delivering. He said the Hubbard kids haven't been over for breakfast since the fire."

"Cook says she saw Emmie at the train station the other day. Selling pies and biscuits. She told Cook my mamma told her what to do, and she did it."

"I don't know. Maybe she likes being the strong one for a change. Maybe she never had a chance to be that," I said, kicking at the water. "Or maybe she just got tired of being the town fruitcake. Probably wears a body out after a while."

Weaver laughed, but it wasn't a real laugh. I could tell.

His mamma had lost her house. And some had said it was his fault for going to the justice. They said none of it would have ever happened if he'd just stepped aside for those trappers in the first place and kept his big mouth shut.

Mr. Austin Klock, the undersheriff, came up from

Herkimer to investigate the fire. By the time he left, those three men had a whole new list of charges against them in addition to the ones Weaver originally filed. No one really thought they'd ever be made to answer them. They hadn't been seen since the day Weaver's house burned. Mr. Klock himself said that it would be next to impossible to catch three trappers who knew every tree, rock, and hidey-hole in the North Woods. He said they were probably halfway to Canada already, fixing to have themselves a time with Weaver's college money.

Weaver had hardly eaten since the fire. Or spoken. Or smiled.

"Cook's got a piece of pie for you. Coconut cream. Your favorite," I told him.

He didn't say anything.

"Did I tell you my word of the day? It's *leporine*. It means like a rabbit."

He toed the water.

"You could use it to describe someone with buck-teeth, maybe. Or a twitchy nose. It's an interesting word, *leporine*."

No reply.

"I guess it's not so interesting."

"I'm staying on here, Matt," he finally said. "After Labor Day. I just talked to Mr. Morrison. He said he'd have work for me."

"How can you do that?" I asked. "You have to be in New York well before Labor Day. Don't your classes start the first week of September?"

"I'm not going."

"*What?*" I wondered if I'd heard him right.

"I'm not going to Columbia. Not until my mamma's well. I can't leave her now. Not all by herself."

"She's not all by herself. She has Emmie looking after her."

"For how long? It's only another month or so before Emmie's land is auctioned. And besides, I don't have the money now for my room or train fare or books or any of it."

"What about your wages? Haven't you been saving them?"

"I'll need them to pay for a room for Mamma and me. My house burned down, remember?"

"But Weaver, what about your scholarship? Won't you lose it?"

"There's always next fall. I'm sure I could get them to hold it over for a year," he said, but I could hear in his voice that even he didn't believe it.

I did not cry when Miss Wilcox left. Or when Martha Miller said such mean things to me. I did not cry when Pa knocked me out of my chair, and I don't cry in my bed at night when I think about Barnard. But I cried then. Like a baby. I cried as if someone died.

Someone had.

I could see him in my mind's eye—a tall, proud black man in a suit and tie. He was dignified and fearsome. He was a man who could cut down a roomful of other men with only the brilliance of his words. I saw him walking down a city street, brisk and solemn, a briefcase under his arm. He glanced at me, walked up a flight of stone steps, and disappeared.

"Oh!" I sobbed. "Oh, Weaver, no!"

"Matt, what is it? What's wrong?" he asked.

I scrambled to my feet. I couldn't bear it. To think of him stuck here. Working in a dining room or a tannery or up at a lumber camp. Day after day. Year after year. Until he was old and used up and all his dreams were dead.

"Go, Weaver, just go!" I cried. "I'll look out for your mamma. Me and Royal and Minnie and Jim and Pa and Mrs. Loomis. All of us. We will. Just go! Before you're stuck here forever. Like an ant in pitch."

Like me.

It must be after four o'clock now. I haven't been able to go back to sleep. Not since Grace came to visit me. The sky outside my window is still dark, but I can hear the rustlings of night creatures seeking their beds and the first, questing chirrups of the birds.

I have read all of Grace's letters, all but the last one.

South Otselic
July 5, 1906
My Dear Chester,
I am curled up by the kitchen fire and you would shout if you could see me. Every one else is in bed. The girls came up and we shot the last fire-crackers. Our lawn looks about as green as the Cortland House corner. I will tell all about my Fourth when I see you. I hope you had a nice time. This is the last letter I can write, dear. I feel as though you were not coming. Perhaps this is not right, I can't help feeling that I am never going to see you again. How I wish this was Monday. I am going down to stay with Maude next Sunday night, dear, and then go to DeRuyter the next morning and will get there

about 10 o'clock. If you take the 9:45 train from the Lehigh there you will get there about 11. I am sorry I could not go to Hamilton, dear. Papa and mamma did not want me to go and there are so many things I have had to work hard for in the last two weeks. They think I am just going out there to De Ruyter for a visit.

Now, dear, when I get there I will go at once to the hotel and I don't think I will see any of the people. If I do and they ask me to come to the house, I will say something so they won't mistrust anything. Tell them I have a friend coming from Cortland; that we are to meet there to go to a funeral or a wedding in some town further along... Maybe that won't be just what I will say but don't worry about anything for I shall manage somehow...

I have been bidding good-by to some places to-day. There are so many nooks, dear, and all of them so dear to me. I have lived here nearly all my life. First I said good-by to the spring house with its great masses of green moss, then the apple tree where we had our playhouse; then the "beehive," a cute little house in the orchard, and of course all of the neighbors that have mended my dresses from a little tot up, to save me a threshing I really deserved.

Oh, dear, you don't realize what all of this is to me. I know I shall never see any of them again, and mamma! great heavens how I love mamma! I don't know what I shall do without her. She is never cross and she always helps me so much. Sometimes I think if I could tell mamma, but I can't. She has trouble enough as it is, and I couldn't break her heart like that. If I come back dead, perhaps if she does know, she won't be angry with me. I will never be happy again, dear. I wish I could die. You will never know what you have made me suffer, dear. I miss you and I want to see you but I wish I could die. I am going to bed now, dear, please come and don't let me wait there. It is for both of us to be there . . .

She knew. Somehow Grace Brown knew that she wasn't ever coming back. She hoped that Chester would take her away and do the right thing by her, but deep down inside, a part of her knew. It's why she wrote about never seeing the things and places and people she loved again. And why she imagined coming back dead. And why she wanted her letters burned.

I slide the letter back into its envelope. I gather all the letters together, slip the ribbon around them, and carefully retie it. I can hear Grace's voice. I can hear the grief and desperation and sorrow. Not in my ears, in my heart.

Voice, according to Miss Wilcox, is not just the sound that comes from your throat but the feeling that comes from your words. I hadn't understood that at first. "But Miss Wilcox, you use words to write a story, not your voice," I'd said.

"No, you use what's inside of you," she said. "That's your voice. Your real voice. It's what makes Austen sound like Austen and no one else. What makes Yeats sound like Yeats and Shelley like Shelley. It's what makes Mattie Gokey sound like Mattie Gokey. You have a wonderful voice, Mattie. I know you do, I've heard it. Use it."

"Just look where your voice got you, Miss Wilcox," I whisper. "And look where Grace Brown's got her."

I sit perfectly still for a long time, just holding the letters and looking out the window. In another hour or so, the sun will rise and Cook will barge in and wake us. We'll go downstairs and begin readying the dining room for breakfast. My pa will arrive with his milk and butter, and then Royal, with eggs and berries. I'll feed Hamlet and walk him. The guests will come down for breakfast. And then the men from Herkimer will arrive. Cook will badger and yell, and somehow, in all the commotion, I will try again to get down the cellar stairs to the furnace.

I look down at the bundle in my hands. At the pale blue ribbon. At the loopy handwriting, so like my own.

If I burn these letters, who will hear Grace Brown's voice? Who will read her story?

ter · gi · ver · sa · tion

"Would you like a cup of tea, Mattie? How about you, Weaver?" Emmie Hubbard asked. Her eyes were calm and smiling and not the least bit crazy looking.

"Yes, all right. Thank you," I said, putting the chocolate cream pie I was holding down on the table.

"Yes, please," Weaver said.

Emmie took a tin of tea and some cups and saucers down from a shelf. As she turned, I saw a flash of white. It was the nape of her neck, pale as milk above her collar. Her hair was coiled neatly at the back of her head. Usually it was down or caught in a loose messy braid. I realized I'd never seen the back of Emmie Hubbard's neck before. Her faded cotton dress hung crisply from her narrow shoulders. It had been pressed. Maybe even starched.

Weaver and I glanced at each other. I could tell from the expression on his face that he couldn't believe what we were seeing, either.

Emmie's house was tidy. The floor had been swept and the bed made. Her kids were clean—mostly. Myrton's nose still dripped, Billy's ears needed attention, and Lucius had sticky hands, but their faces were scrubbed and their clothes had been washed.

"Mattie, please tell Mrs. Hennessey thank you for the pie," Emmie said.

"I . . . I will," I said, embarrassed to find myself gawking.

Weaver and I had asked Mr. Sperry if we could take Demon to visit Weaver's mamma after the dinner service. He said we could, and Cook had given us a pie to take with us.

Weaver sat down on the bed next to his mother. She'd tried to get up to help Emmie with the tea, but Emmie had waved her away. "How are you feeling, Mamma?" he asked.

"My arm pains me some, but I'm all right," she said.

"I heard you got the pig back."

"That's right. The Loomis boys found her. They fixed her pen for me, too. I'm awful glad I didn't lose her."

The kettle whistled. Emmie leaned over the stove to get it. I remembered seeing her bent over the stove another time, for another reason. I had a feeling Frank Loomis wouldn't be fixing her stove again anytime soon. Not while Weaver's mamma was around. She was a righteous and upstanding woman. If she ever saw his bare ass in here, she'd tan it for him.

Emmie served the tea and cut slices of pie for everyone. The children loved the taste of chocolate. Even Lucius. He was too little to eat the crust, but Emmie gave him some whipped cream and filling and he smiled and clapped. We chatted for a while, and Weaver's mamma told us how Emmie was making fruit pies according to her recipe and selling every one down at the train station and how she, Weaver's mamma, minded Emmie's kids while Emmie was gone, but that was all she did, because Emmie didn't let her lift a finger. Emmie smiled and flushed and said it wasn't true—why, just the day before they'd both been over picking beans out of the Smiths' garden and at least the trappers hadn't managed to destroy that. Emmie's eyes darted to Weaver's mamma constantly as she spoke. It was like she was feeling for her, making sure she was there. Weaver's mamma nodded and smiled at her.

It was nice to sit in Emmie's neat house, watching her bustle about, seeing her kids smile as they ate Cook's pie. It was pleasant and peaceable and made a change from trying to haul her out from under the bed.

But then Weaver forgot himself and asked Emmie why she didn't plant a garden herself. It wasn't too late to get beans and greens out of one, he said, and then the whole room went quiet and I could see from the look on his face that he'd suddenly remembered about the auction. Nobody wanted to talk about it, though. Least of all me, knowing, as I did, who was going to buy it.

"But Mamma, we have to talk about it...," Weaver pressed.

"Hush, Weaver," she said, her eyes darting to Emmie. "I know, son. We will."

Emmie looked at us and bit her lip. She pulled at a tendril of hair.

"Where's Tommy?" I asked, anxious to change the subject.

"Over at your place. Helping your pa," Weaver's

mamma said. "They've got an arrangement now. Tom's to help with the plowing and clearing, and your pa will pay him for it in milk and butter."

"I like butter," Myrton said, sniffing a string of snot back up his nose.

"Myrton, honey, what did I tell you about using your handkerchief?" Weaver's mamma said.

"Oh yeah."

He dug a piece of calico out of his pocket, wiped his nose on it, and showed it to me. I mustered an admiring smile for him.

We stayed for a few more minutes, and then we had to get back to the Glenmore. Weaver was quiet on the drive. I was the one who spoke first. "Your mamma's one tough nut," I said.

"Don't I know it."

"I didn't think anybody could ever shape Emmie Hubbard up. God only knows how she did it. And with one arm broken, to boot."

Weaver smiled a sad smile. "You know, Matt," he said. "Sometimes I wish there really was such a thing as a happy ending."

"Sometimes there is. Depends on who's writing the story."

"I mean in real life. Not in stories."

Tergiversation, my word of the day, means fickleness of conduct, inconstancy, turning renegade. I felt like a renegade myself just then. I didn't believe in happy endings. Not in stories or real life. I knew better. But then I thought about Emmie's shabby little house and how it was warm and welcoming now. I imagined my pa showing Tommy how to handle a plow, and Tommy all manly and important as he brought home the milk and butter he'd earned. I thought about Weaver's mamma being looked after for once in her life. And Emmie's pride in doing the looking after.

And then I thought of Mrs. Loomis crying in the barn, and Jim and Will tormenting the Hubbards every chance they got, and the set of Royal's jaw when he talked about wanting them gone.

"Me, too, Weaver," I sighed. "Me, too."

lu · cif · er · ous

"Mattie Gokey, what's ailing you? You're slow as a mule tonight and every bit as stupid! Pick up for table eight. Pick up!" Cook yelled.

It was evening, right in the middle of the supper service. The dining room was full to bursting and Cook was in one of her tempers. I ran one order out and came right back in with a new one. John Denio was sitting at Cook's worktable as I called the order out, eating his supper.

"Henry?" I heard him say. He was staring at the bite of food on his fork.

"Vat?"

"You make your biscuits with pepper in 'em?"

Henry had cooked the help stew and biscuits for supper. We'd all finished eating an hour ago, but John had missed supper as he had to go meet an evening train. Henry had kept the leftovers warm for him.

"Vat pepper?"

"You know, black pepper. From peppercorns."

"I don't know vat you talk. I don't put any pepper in any biscuit."

John put his fork down. He covered his supper with

368

his napkin. "Then do me a favor, will you, Henry? Keep the damned mice out of the damned flour bin!"

Weaver laughed his head off. So did I.

"Don't know what you're laughing at. You et 'em, too," John growled.

We stopped laughing. I felt a little green. I didn't have long to dwell on it, though.

"Mattie, pick up for table seven. Pick up!" Cook barked.

I carried four bowls of soup to my table, sloshing them as I walked. I craned my neck trying to see the boathouse from the dining room windows. The boats were all in for the evening. The dock was empty.

"They must've gotten back," I said under my breath. "They must have. So where are they?"

There was cream of celery soup all around the rims of the bowls and down the sides, too, as I served them. The croutons had sunk. The guests at table seven did not look pleased.

"You got lead blocks for feet tonight?" Cook asked me, when I returned to the kitchen.

"No, ma'am."

"Look alive, then!'"

The kitchen doors flew open. "I need a pot of tea for room twelve, Mrs. Hennessey," Mrs. Morrison said, whirling by. "And a dish of milk toast. One of the Peterson boys is poorly."

"Am I running a dispensary now as well as a kitchen? Mattie, cut two slices of white bread—"

"Mrs. Peterson asked especially for you to make it, Mrs. Hennessey. She said your milk toast cured her little Teddy of his spastic bowel last summer."

"Give little Teddy some of Henry's mouse-shit biscuits. That'll cure him," John grumbled.

"Anything else I can do? Fluff Teddy's pillow? Sing him a lullaby?" Cook groused, pulling lamb chops from under the broiler. "Mattie, fix a pot of tea, will you? Or does Lady Peterson require that I boil the water, too?" she grumbled at Mrs. Morrison's back. "Eighty-five for supper, fifty of them in all at once, a special birthday meal for twelve, and now I'm a nursemaid as well..."

We were supposed to have eighty-seven for supper. Eighty-*seven*, not eighty-five. Two guests hadn't showed—rooms forty-two and forty-four. Carl Grahm and Grace Brown. They had table nine. I'd set it for them, but it was already eight o'clock and they still hadn't come in off the lake.

I'd waited on them earlier at dinner. They'd ordered soup and sandwiches, and they'd argued throughout the meal. I'd overheard them as I brought their food.

"...and there was a church right by the hotel in Utica," Grace Brown said. "We could have gone in and done it there."

"We can do it up here, Billy. We'll ask if there's a chapel," Carl Grahm said.

"Today, Chester. Please. You said you would. You promised me. I can't wait any longer. You mustn't expect me to."

"All right, don't get so upset. Let's take a boat ride first, why don't we? It's a beautiful day. We'll ask about a chapel right after."

"Chester, no! I don't want to go boating!"

I passed by a few more times to make sure that there was nothing they wanted. The man ate all of his lunch, then the girl's untouched soup, then he asked for dessert. He told me to charge the meal to his room. "Grahm," he said. "Carl Grahm. Room forty-two." I'd heard the name earlier from Mrs. Morrison. She'd told me a couple on vacation, a Mr. Grahm and Miss Brown, had come without any reservations and that she was putting them on the top floor and that I was to turn down their beds that night.

I cleared their plates when they were done. And then, later, I'd seen Grace on the porch and she'd given me her letters and I'd stuffed them under my mattress and forgotten about them, and about her and Carl Grahm, because Cook kept me busy all afternoon peeling potatoes.

I hadn't thought about them at all until the supper service started and I'd seen that their table was empty. Then I couldn't stop thinking about them.

"Mattie! Water's boiling!" Cook shouted now. "Get a tray ready for room twelve."

I grabbed a teapot and spooned leaves into it, careful to stay out of her way. I took the kettle off the flame and poured water into the pot. Just then Mr. Morrison came into the kitchen to get himself a cup of coffee.

"Didn't see you at supper tonight, Andy," Cook said. "You all right?"

"I missed it. Too busy waiting for a couple of darn fools to bring my boat back."

Cook snorted. "Which two fools? The Glenmore's full of 'em."

"Grahm. Room forty-two. Had a woman with him. Took a boat out after dinner and never came back."

I dropped the teapot. It shattered. Scalding water splashed all over.

"Look what you did!" Cook screeched. She whacked my behind with her wooden spoon. "What on earth's gotten into you? Get that mess cleaned up!"

I thought of my word of the day, *luciferous,* as I picked up the broken pieces of the teapot. It means bringing light. It has the name *Lucifer* in it. I knew all about Lucifer, thanks to my good friend John Milton. Lucifer was a beautiful angel whom God chucked out of heaven for being rebellious. He found himself banished to hell, but instead of being sorry for angering God and trying to make amends, he set about agitating again. He went to the Garden of Eden and wheedled Eve into eating from the Tree of Knowledge and got the whole of mankind kicked out of paradise forever.

It was a dreadful thing that he did, and he is not to be admired for it, but right then I felt I understood why he did it. I even felt a little sorry for him. He probably just wanted some company, for it is very lonely knowing things.

Quietly, I get out of bed, dress, put up my hair, and gather my belongings. I'm not sure of the time, but I would guess about five o'clock. When I am ready, I count out my savings. Between the money I started out with, and my wages and tips, and the extra money I made walking Hamlet, and the five dollars Miss Wilcox gave me, I have thirty-one dollars and twenty-five cents.

I leave the attic, careful to make no noise, and walk down the main stairs. I am in Mr. Morrison's office, my mamma's old carpetbag in my hand, just as the sky is starting to lighten. I place Grace's letters on his desk, then write him a note on Glenmore stationery, explaining how I got them.

I write three more notes, address them, and put them in the mail basket. The first is to my father. It has two dollars in it, the balance of what he owes on Licorice, the mule, and a promise that I will write. The second is to Weaver's mamma. It has twelve dollars and seventy cents in it and a note telling her to use the money to pay off Emmie's taxes. The third one has a ring in it—a small, dull ring with an opal and two garnets. It is addressed to Royal Loomis and says to see if Tuttle's will take it back and that I'm sorry and that I hope he gets his cheese factory someday.

I pass the coat tree on my way out of the office, the one made of twisted branches and deer hooves. In the gloom of the foyer, it looks like a dark, malevolent fairy-tale tree and for a few seconds I feel that it wants to catch me in its gnarled limbs and hold me fast. There's a woman's boater hanging on it. It's worn at the edges; its black ribbon is frayed. Grace Brown put it there when she and Chester arrived. I lift the shabby little hat off its hook and fight down the urge to crush it. I carry it into the parlor and place it next to Grace's body.

I take her hand. It is smooth and cold. I know it is a bad thing to break a promise, but I think now that it is a worse thing to let a promise break you.

"I'm not going to do it, Grace," I whisper to her. "Haunt me if you want to, but I'm not going to do it."

IN THE BACK of the Glenmore, a little ways into the woods, is a cottage where the male help sleeps. It is quiet and dark. I pick up a handful of pebbles and toss one at a window on the second floor. Nothing happens; no one comes, so I toss a second and a third, and finally the window opens and Mike Bouchard sticks his sleepy face out.

"That you, Mattie? What's up?"

"Get Weaver, Mike. I need to see him."

Mike yawns. "Huh?"

"Weaver!" I hiss. "Go get Weaver!"

He nods. His head disappears, and a few seconds later, Weaver's pops out.

"What do you want?" he asks me, looking cross.

"I'm leaving."

"What?"

"I'm leaving, Weaver."

He pulls his head in and then barely a minute later, the cottage door opens and he's outside, shrugging his suspenders up over a half-buttoned shirt.

"Where are you going?"

I reach into my skirt pocket instead and press seven dollars into his hand.

"What's this for?"

"For your train ticket to New York. Use the money you earn here to pay for a few months' room and board in the city. You'll have to get a job when it runs out, but it'll get you started."

Weaver shakes his head. "I don't want your money. I'm not taking it." He hands it back to me.

I throw it on the ground. "Better pick it up," I said. "Or someone else will."

"Mattie, it's not just train fare and rent. You know that. It's my mamma. You know I can't leave her."

"She'll be fine."

"No, she won't. She's got nowhere to go after Emmie's place is sold."

"Emmie's taxes have been paid. The auction's off. Didn't you hear?"

Weaver gave me a long look. "No, I didn't," he said.

"You will."

"Mattie—"

"Good-bye, Weaver. I've got to go. Now. Before Cook gets up."

Weaver bends down and picks up the money. Then he takes hold of me and hugs me so hard, I think he'll break me right in two. I hug him back, my arms tight around his neck, trying to draw some of his strength and fearlessness into me.

"Why, Matt? Why are you going *now*?" he asks me.

I look at the Glenmore. I can see a light glowing softly in a window in a little bedroom off the parlor. "Because Grace Brown can't," I tell him.

We let go of each other. His eyes are welling.

"Don't, Weaver. If you do, I'll never make it. I'll run right back inside and put my apron on and that will be the end of it."

He nods and swallows hard. He makes a gun of his hand and points it at me. "To the death, Mathilda Gokey," he says.

I smile and aim right back at him. "To the death, Weaver Smith."

It is just past ten o'clock. The dawn came and the sun rose on a flawless summer morning. I am standing, frightened but resolved, on the train platform in Old Forge.

Is there a word for that? Feeling scared of what's to come but eager for it, too? *Terricipatation? Joybodenous? Feager?* If there is, I mean to find it.

376

My carpetbag weighs heavy in my hand. I have most everything I own inside it. I also have my train ticket in there, an address for Miss Annabelle Wilcox of New York City, and two dollars and twenty-five cents. It is all I have left from the money I saved. It isn't very much at all. I will have to find a job right away.

It had only just gone light when I left the Glenmore, but I was able to get a ride into Eagle Bay from Bill Jarvis, who owns the Jarvis Hotel in Big Moose Station. He was on his way to see Dr. Wallace. He was suffering from a toothache and was not in a talkative mood. I was glad for that. I didn't want to answer any questions.

The *Clearwater* was still in dock when we arrived, and I was able to get a seat on its return run to Old Forge. I had decided not to take the train so I wouldn't have to explain myself to Mr. Pulling. The engineers change a lot on the steamers; I didn't know the one on the morning run. I was worried when I saw the pickle boat coming, but I just scrunched down in my seat and Charlie Eckler never saw me. I looked back once, just before Eagle Bay disappeared from sight, and I felt more lonely and frightened than I have ever felt in my life. I thought about turning around when I got to Old Forge, but I didn't. There's no going back once you're already gone.

Now, AS I WAIT for my train, Grace's words echo in my memory. *I have been bidding good-by to some places to-day. There are so many nooks, dear, and all of them so dear to me. I have lived here nearly all my life . . . Oh, dear, you don't realize what all of this is to me. I know I shall never see any of them again . . .*

A NORTHBOUND train pulls in. An express. There are only a few people on it. A handful of tourists and some workmen get off, followed by two men wearing jackets and ties.

"That's him. Austin Klock. He's the undersheriff," a man standing next to me says to his companion. "Told you this was more than some run-of-the-mill drowning." They pull out notepads. Reporters, I imagine.

"Who's the man with him?"

"County coroner. Isaac Coffin."

"*Coffin?* You're kidding me, right?"

"Brother, I am not. Come on. Let's see if we can get a statement before that guy from the Watertown paper does."

The undersheriff holds his hands up as they approach him. "Gentlemen, I know as much about it as you do. A girl drowned at the Glenmore. Her body's been recovered. Her companion's has not . . ."

Soon you'll know more, I think. A lot more. Soon you'll know that the girl was called Grace. And that she spent her last weeks on this earth pregnant and afraid, begging the man who'd made her so to come and take her away. But he'd had other ideas.

I close my eyes and I can see Chester Gillette. He's

signing the guest book at the Glenmore. And having his dinner, and going for a boat ride. I see him row all the way out to South Bay. Maybe he and Grace get out and sit on the bank for a while. He leaves his suitcase there. They row some more. He waits until he's sure there's no one else around, and then he hits Grace. He tips the boat and swims to shore. Grace can't swim. He knows that because she told him. She'd drown even if she wasn't unconscious, but it's quieter this way. She can't scream for help.

Later, when the boat is recovered, it will look to the searchers like Grace Brown and her companion both drowned. No one will ever find out that Grace was pregnant or that Chester Gillette was the father of her child. Her death will be Carl Grahm's fault, and Chester will be free to return to Cortland and have a good and dandy time.

I see Chester now, today. He's eating breakfast somewhere. Maybe up at Seventh Lake. Maybe at the Neodak in Inlet, or the Arrowhead. Swinging his tennis racket. Smiling. He's sure as hell not dead. Not him. I'd bet my last dollar on that.

I see Grace Brown, too. Stiff and cold in a room in the Glenmore with a tiny life that will never be, inside her.

And then I hear a whistle, shrill and piercing. I open my eyes and see the tracks, and the southbound train coming down them. The monstrous engine pulls in. Screeching and steaming, it comes to a halt. I cannot move. The conductor jumps down and helps passengers out. The porters unload trunks and luggage. People swirl

379

around me. Heavy canvas mailbags land on the platform beside me.

"All aboard!" the conductor yells. "This is the ten-fifteen New York Central for Utica, Herkimer, and all points south! Tickets, please! Have your tickets ready!"

People are boarding the train. Mothers and children. Businessmen. Holidaymakers on their way home. Couples. And still I cannot move.

I think of my family. Of Beth's songs. Of Lou's swagger. Of Abby's gentle voice. I can see Pa sitting by the fire. And Emmie and Weaver's mamma picking beans. I see Royal plowing his father's fields, gazing across them to my father's land with a look of love and longing he'd never shown me. I see Barney's blind eyes turned up to mine. And the poor dead robin at my mother's grave.

The conductor grabs the iron railing on the side of the car and climbs up its metal steps. "Last call! Last call! All aboard!" he bellows. The engine exhales. A huge cloud of steam billows up from under it. The wheels strain against the tracks.

"Wait!" I cry, stumbling forward.

The conductor sees me. "Come on, missy!" he yells. "Her bark's worse than her bite!" He reaches down for me. I look around myself wildly, my heart bursting with grief and fear and joy. I am leaving, but I will take this place and its stories with me wherever I go.

I reach for his hand and clasp it. He hoists me onto the 10:15 southbound. To Utica and Herkimer. And all points south. To Amsterdam and Albany and beyond. To New York City. To my future. My life.

AUTHOR'S NOTE

On July 12, 1906, the body of a young woman named Grace Brown was pulled from the waters of Big Moose Lake in the Adirondack Mountains. The boat she'd been in had been found capsized and floating in a secluded bay. There was no sign of her companion, a young man who'd rented the boat under the name of Carl Grahm. It was feared that he, too, had drowned. Grace Brown's death appeared to be an accident, and neither the men who dragged the lake nor the staff at the hotel where the couple had registered could have foreseen that they would soon be embroiled in one of the most sensational murder trials in New York's history. Grace Brown, they would soon discover, was unwed and pregnant, and the man who had taken her boating was the father of her child. His real name was Chester Gillette.

Grace and Chester had met in 1905 at the Gillette Skirt Factory in Cortland, New York—a place where they both worked, and which Chester's uncle owned. A romance blossomed between them and eventually Grace became pregnant. Shortly after realizing her condition, she left Cortland for her home in South Otselic—possibly at Chester's urging. There, she worried and wrote to Chester, pleading with him to come for her, threatening to return if he did not.

Eventually, he did. They met in DeRuyter, a town near

Grace's home, and from there traveled to Utica and on into the Adirondacks. They had little money and no set plan. Or rather, Grace had no plan, just a hope of marriage; Chester, his prosecutors claimed, did. Only a poor relation of the Cortland Gillettes and hungry for the society in which they moved, Chester hoped to improve his social standing by courting a girl from a prominent family. To do so, he first needed to rid himself of the factory girl he had once cared for but later came to regard as an obstacle.

There were no eyewitnesses to Grace Brown's death and no one knows for certain what happened on Big Moose Lake on July 11, 1906. Chester originally stated that Grace's death was an accident, then later claimed she'd committed suicide. George W. Ward, the district attorney who prosecuted the case, reconstructed Chester's activities before and after Grace's death—among them his use of an alias when registering at the Glenmore Hotel, the fact that he fled the scene and did not report Grace missing, and the fact that he was found enjoying himself at an Inlet hotel three days after her death—and argued that Chester had killed Grace. Instrumental to Ward's case were Grace's own letters.

In *A Gathering Light*, I've taken the liberty of having Grace give a fictional character—Mattie—all of the correspondence between herself and Chester. In reality, however, when Grace was in the Adirondacks, she had only the letters Chester had written to her packed among her things. The letters *she* had written to *him* were found by the police in Chester's room in Cortland after he was arrested.

Grace's letters had a profound effect upon those who attended Chester's trial. People sobbed openly as they were read. Everyone wept, it was said, except Gillette. Though the case was based solely on circumstantial evidence, the jury found for the prosecution. Chester Gillette was convicted of murder in the first degree and executed in Auburn Prison on March 30, 1908.

Nearly a century after her death, Grace Brown's words have the same effect on me that they had on the people who attended Chester Gillette's trial—they break my heart. I grieved for Grace Brown—a person I'd never known, a young woman long dead—when I first read them. There is so much fear and despair in those lines, but there is much else, too—a good heart, humor, intelligence, wit. Grace liked strawberries and roses and French toast. She had friends, and a brother who teased her about her cooking. She liked to go riding and shoot off firecrackers. Her letters remind me of what it was like to be nineteen, and I often wonder what she would have made of her life had she been allowed to live it. I'm glad that she helped Mattie live hers.

My grandmother, who worked as a waitress in a Big Moose camp in the twenties, says Grace Brown still haunts the lake.

Her letters will always haunt me.

Jennifer Donnelly
Brooklyn, New York
October 2002

ACKNOWLEDGMENTS

Though Mattie Gokey, her family, and her friends are fictional beings, some of the story's characters, like Dwight Sperry and John Denio, were real. Others, like Henry the underchef and Charlie Eckler the pickle boat captain, are fictional but drawn from descriptions of real people. Several area authors helped me put the flesh back on old bones. I would like to acknowledge my great debt to Marylee Armour; W. Donald Burnap; Matthew J. Conway, my granduncle; Harvey L. Dunham; Roy C. Higby; Herbert F. Keith; William R. Marleau; and Clara V. O'Brien. Their memoirs and histories allowed me to weave fact with fiction by providing names, dates, and events; accounts of area people and their daily lives; and chronologies of towns and resorts. A list of books by these authors, plus additional sources and suggestions for further reading, follows.

Jerold Pepper, director of the Adirondack Museum's library, allowed me access to a transcript of the Gillette murder trial and much else, including the diaries of Lucilla Arvilla Mills Clark—a Cranberry Lake farm wife—and ephemera from the great camps. The museum's exhibits provided me with information on logging and transportation. The Farmers' Museum in Cooperstown, New York, gave me valuable insight into earlier methods of farming and animal husbandry. I am obliged to the staff at both of these excellent museums. They could not have been more helpful, or more patient, with my endless questions.

I am also indebted to Peg Masters, Town of Webb historian and former director of the Town of Webb Historical Association, for allowing me to view the association's collection of photographs as well as its census and tax records. She also provided information on early Inlet businesses and the Inlet Common School. I would also like to thank the librarians at the Port Leyden Community Library, who gave me extended loans of out-of-print Adirondack titles.

My thanks, too, to Nancy Martin Pratt and her family for keeping the beautiful Waldheim just as it always was, and to the staff of the current Glenmore (originally the Glenmore store, now a pub) for letting me prowl the premises and play with their very own "Hamlet."

A very heartfelt thank-you goes to my mother, Wilfriede Donnelly, for introducing me to Grace Brown; my father, Matt Donnelly, for lessons in botany and the fine art of bug roping; my grandmother, Mary Donnelly, for telling me stories about her lumberjack father and her waitressing days at the Waldheim; and my uncle, Jack Bennett, for having more stories about the woods than the woods has trees. Lastly, I would like to express my deepest gratitude to Steven Malk, my agent; Michael Stearns, my editor; and Doug Dundas, my husband, for their unstinting encouragement, wisdom, and guidance.

SOURCES AND SUGGESTIONS FOR FURTHER READING

GRACE BROWN AND CHESTER GILLETTE

Brandon, Craig. *Murder in the Adirondacks: "An American Tragedy" Revisited*. Utica, N.Y.: North Country Books, 1986.

Brown, Grace. *Grace Brown's Love Letters*. Herkimer, N.Y.: Citizen Publishing Company, 1906.

People of New York v. *Chester Gillette*. Court transcript, Adirondack Museum, Blue Mountain Lake, N.Y.

EAGLE BAY, INLET, BIG MOOSE LAKE, BIG MOOSE STATION

Aber, Ted, and Stella King. *The History of Hamilton County*. New York: Great Wilderness Books, 1965.

Armour, Marylee. *Heartwood: The Adirondack Homestead Life of W. Donald Burnap*. New York: The Brown Newspapers, 1988.

Higby, Roy C. . . . *A Man from the Past*. Big Moose, N.Y.: Big Moose Press, 1974.

Marleau, William R. *Big Moose Station*. New York: Marleau Family Press, 1986.

O'Brien, Clara V. *God's Country: Eagle Bay Area—Fourth Lake/In the Heart of the Adirondacks*. Utica, N.Y.: North Country Books, 1982.

Scheffler, William L., and Frank Carey. *Big Moose Lake, New York in Vintage Postcards*. Charleston, S.C.: Arcadia Tempus Publishing Group, 2000.

ADIRONDACK GUIDES

Dunham, Harvey L. *Adirondack French Louie: Early Life in the North Woods*. Utica, N.Y.: North Country Books, 1953.

Keith, Herbert G. *Man of the Woods*. Syracuse, N.Y.: Syracuse University Press, 1972.

FARMING

Allen, Rev. Daisy Mavis Dalaba. *Ranger Bowback: An Adirondack Farmer*. West Virginia: Edwards Hill Press, 1997.

Clark, Lucilla Arvilla Mills. Diary entries of a Cranberry Lake farm wife, from 1897, Ms 87-18. Adirondack Museum Library, Blue Mountain Lake, N.Y.

Cutting, Edith E. *Whistling Girls and Jumping Sheep*. Cooperstown, N.Y.: Farmers' Museum, 1951.

Davidson, J. Brownlee, and Leon Wilson Chase. *Farm Machinery: Practical Hints for Handy-Men*. 1908. Reprint, New York: The Lyons Press, 1999.

Herbert, Henry William. *Horses, Mules, and Ponies and How to Keep Them: Practical Hints for Horse-Keepers*. 1859. Reprint, New York: The Lyons Press, 2000.

Myer, Ruth. *A Farm Girl in the Great Depression*. Ithaca, N.Y.: BUSCA, Inc., 1998.

LOGGING AND LUMBERJACKS

Bird, Barbara Kephart. *Calked Shoes: Life in Adirondack Lumber Camps*. Prospect, N.Y.: Prospect Books, 1952.

Hochschild, Harold K. *Lumberjacks and Rivermen in the Central Adirondacks (1850–1950)*. Blue Mountain Lake, N.Y.: Adirondack Museum, 1962.

Welsh, Peter C. *Jack, Jobbers and Kings: Logging the Adirondacks 1850–1950.* Utica, N.Y.: North Country Books, 1996.

GENERAL HISTORY

Beetle, David H. *Up Old Forge Way.* Utica, N.Y.: North Country Books, 1972. Originally printed in the *Utica Observer-Dispatch,* 1948.

Grady, Joseph F. *The Adirondacks: Fulton Chain–Big Moose Region: The Story of a Wilderness.* Little Falls, N.Y.: Press of the Journal & Courier Company, 1933.

Janos, Elisabeth. *Country Folk Medicine: Tales of Skunk Oil, Sassafras Tea, & Other Old-Time Remedies.* Guilford, Conn.: The Globe Pequot Press, 1990.

Kalinowski, Tom. *Adirondack Almanac: A Guide to the Natural Year.* Utica, N.Y.: North Country Books, 1999.

Milne, William J., Ph.D., Ll.D. *High School Algebra.* New York: American Book Company, 1892 and 1906.

Peterson's Magazine. Philadelphia, Pa.: 1860.

Teall, Edna West. *Adirondack Tales: A Girl Grows Up in the Adirondacks in the 1880s.* Jay, N.Y.: *Adirondack Life* magazine, 1970.

B
L
O
O
M
S
B
U
R
Y

21

JENNIFER DONNELLY
A Gathering Light

A READING GUIDE

ABOUT THE BOOK

In brief

Based on a real-life murder which shocked turn-of-the-century America, *A Gathering Light* is the story of the coming of age of a strong, selfless heroine. Mattie's dilemmas and choices are quietly reflected in the life of a young woman found drowned in a lake, a woman whom Mattie gets to know only through a bundle of letters left in her possession.

In detail

Inspired by the infamous case of the People vs. Chester Gillette, Jennifer Donnelly re-examines the story of the murder of Grace Brown, approaching it from the point of view of a local, North Woods girl.

It is July 1906, and sixteen-old Mattie Gokey is spending her first summer away from home. She is working the busy holiday season in an Adirondacks hotel, earning the money her family needs to maintain its run-down farm, and saving up to set up home with her fiancé. When a young woman is found drowned in the nearby lake, Mattie finds herself in possession of a secret that may prove impossible to keep: the day before, the woman gave her a bundle of letters which Mattie promised to burn.

As the local men search for the woman's partner and suspicions grow as to the circumstances of her death, Mattie recounts the previous four months of her own life: her attempts to care for her younger sisters and her sullen, violent father in the wake of her mother's death; and her struggle to turn her love of literature into a college career. But she has neither the funds nor the freedom to leave for New York. She also realises increasingly that her small farming town is built on the inter-dependence of broken families and the secrets they fail to hide.

As her tale unfolds, Mattie begins to read Grace Brown's letters and comes to see her own life reflected in that of the drowned young woman.

ABOUT THE AUTHOR

Jennifer Donnelly lives in Brooklyn, New York, and Tivoli, New York, with her husband and daughter. She grew up in New York State, in Lewis and Westchester counties, and attended the University of Rochester, where she graduated Magna Cum Laude in English Literature and European History. Living in England as a college student and after she graduated, she developed a lifelong love of London and its people. She credits London, the East End in particular, as the inspiration behind her desire to become a writer. Before becoming a novelist, Jennifer Donnelly worked as an antiques dealer, reporter and copywriter.

A Gathering Light was winner of the Carnegie Medal and was selected for Richard and Judy's Summer Reads in the UK. In the US it was awarded the *Los Angeles Times* Book Prize, a Michael Printz Honor and the Borders Original Voices prize.

FOR DISCUSSION

- What did you think of the use of Mattie's words of the day as chapter headings? To what extent do you think the author has played on the parallels between these headings and the action?

- Mattie tells us her sisters' ages when she introduces them; it is not until page 59 that we find out she is sixteen. Why might Mattie and/or the author have left us guessing for so long? Were you surprised when she revealed her age? What might have made her seem younger, or older?

- '... a few acres as a wedding gift from your pa, Mattie, and Royal's pa, too, would round it out nicely' (page 325). How accurate is Martha's reading of Royal's ulterior motives? Do you believe there are other reasons for his courting of Mattie?

- 'I know it is a bad thing to break a promise, but ... it is a worse thing to let a promise break you' (page 374). Is this always true? Mattie's promises to her mamma and Grace shortly before their deaths are the most prominent examples, but many other promises are made in the novel. How do these compare with Mattie's dilemmas, and her resolution of them?

- 'And if the many sayings of the wise / Teach of submission I will not submit...' In what ways is this epigram fitting to *A Gathering Light*?

- 'Dey be French girls, Michel. Dey be Guathiers ... not Gokey. Ba jeez, what da hell is Gokey?' (page 155). Is Uncle Fifty right: should the family have maintained their French identity?

- 'My heart suddenly turned traitor on me, and I wanted to take Miss Wilcox by the arm ... and tell her to leave my pa alone' (page 166). Do you ever share Mattie's pity for her father? If so, when and why? Does sympathy for Pa affect your opinion as to whether Lawton should have left home? Or Mattie?

- 'I took hold of the angel's head and snapped it off. And then I snapped one wing off, and then the other. I broke his arms off, too, and then I asked him how serene he was feeling now' (page 184). Did Mattie's act of vandalism surprise you in any way?

- What is the significance of the dead robin (first mentioned on page 211)? In what other ways do animals play a part in the novel?

- In the Author's Note (page 381), Jennifer Donnelly explains that Grace Brown was her inspiration for *A Gathering Light*, and makes it clear that her letters contained a full, rounded character. Why, then, is Mattie the novel's protagonist, rather than Grace?

- 'How exactly do you stand up like a man when you're a girl?' (page 33). How different are the difficulties confronting young women in the North Woods in 1906 from those faced by the men? And how different are the prospects of black men and women from those of the white people around them?

- It is clear from the book's end matter and from interviews with Jennifer Donnelly that research is extremely important to her writing. How successful is she at managing the relationship between historical detail and fiction, and avoiding its potential constraints?

- Many different authors, novels and poems are referenced in the novel. Does Mattie make you want to read any of these which you haven't? How does it affect your reading when she mentions books you do know?

- 'You're too interested in what Blueberry Finn and Oliver Dickens and all the rest of them made-up people are doing to see what's going on right around you' (page 330). Is there any truth in Royal's accusation? Does Mattie's reading sometimes blind her to her surroundings? Or could it be said rather to improve her insight and understanding?

- 'For I am good at telling myself lies' (page 1); '...a word in your dictionary for when people know the truth but pretend they don't' (page 336). What do you think of Weaver's temperament, and his relentlessness in saying things that may be better left unsaid? Do you agree that Mattie is good at telling herself lies?

- '... there are books that tell stories, and then there are books that tell truths' (page 201). Do you agree with Mattie's distinction?

- 'I didn't believe in happy endings. Not in stories or real life' (page 366); ' ... freedom is like Sloan's Liniment, always promising more than it delivers' (page 33). Does *A Gathering Light* have a happy ending? How fully will the freedom attained by some of the characters deliver them happiness?

- *A Gathering Light* was originally published in the USA as *A Northern Light*, and was renamed in the UK to avoid confusion with Philip Pullman's UK publications. To which things could the 'light' of the two titles refer? Which title do you prefer, and why?

OTHER BOOKS BY JENNIFER DONNELLY

Humble Pie – a picture book
The Tea Rose – a novel
The Winter Rose – a novel

SUGGESTED FURTHER READING

Fiction
I Capture the Castle by Dodie Smith
Little Women by Louisa May Alcott
To Kill a Mockingbird by Harper Lee
Tess of the D'Urbervilles by Thomas Hardy
The Adventures of Tom Sawyer by Mark Twain
Winter by John Marsden
Witch Child by Celia Rees

Background
See pages 387–9 for Jennifer Donnelly's sources and suggestions.
Adirondack Tragedy: The Gillette Murder Case of 1906
    by Joseph W. Brownell and Patricia W. Enos
An American Tragedy by Theodore Dreiser
A transcript of the trial of Chester Gillette is also available on
the web: http://www.courts.state.ny.us/history/gillette.htm

JENNIFER DONNELLY'S FAVOURITE BOOKS

Children's book/s

Oh, man. One favourite children's book? That's torture. It's impossible. How can you choose between Scout Finch (*To Kill a Mocking Bird* by Harper Lee) and Huck Finn (*The Adventures of Huckleberry Finn* by Mark Twain)? Between Meg and Charles Murry (novels by Madeleine L'Engle) and the Pevensie kids (*The Chronicles of Narnia* by C. S. Lewis)? Between *Harriet the Spy* (Louise Fitzhugh) and *Ramona the Pest* (Beverly Cleary)? The books of my childhood – and the characters in them – are more than favourites, they're friends and I can't imagine having navigated the wilds of childhood and adolescence without the guidance, companionship and courage they provided.

Classic/s

Oh, forget it. There are way too many. James Joyce's *Ulysses* for sure. I didn't read it until I was in college and I almost missed it. A few years of rotten books and uninspired teaching had nearly put me off literature for life. I was an English major, but thinking of changing to something else. Anything else. And then I found the moderns. Steinbeck. Fitzgerald. Eliot. Joyce. Especially Joyce. And his astonishing *Ulysses*. Can books really change lives? And how. This one changed mine. It showed me a man in Dublin on a June day in 1904, and in so doing, it showed me the world in all its boozy, shitty, gorgeous, tragic, raucous glory. It showed me human beings not as we would be, but as we are – weaselly, lying, generous, cheating, loving, funny, stanky, skanky, kidney-eating philosophers, heroes and bums. I read this book when I was nineteen years old. I've never been the same since. I never will be.

And then there's Graham Greene's *The Quiet American*. I crave Fowler's company these days. I keep the book on a shelf by my desk, only inches away. I need to hear his voice because it seems that Pyle and his insanity are everywhere again – reading his York Harding, doing good no matter what the cost, and never, ever seeing the blood on his shoes.

Contemporary book

Philip Pullman's *His Dark Materials* trilogy. For so many reasons. For Pullman's belief in the sanctity of a child's soul and for his condemnation of those who try to separate children from their souls. For the dizzying originality of the world he created in these books. For the dozens upon dozens of big themes he fearlessly tackles. And because it's such a wild ride of a story with shootouts and chases, terrifying bad guys, talking daemons, and a polar bear with a drink problem who comes good in the end.

Top 10

Well, *Ulysses* is Number One. Other than that, I'm all over the place. I grew up on a mixed diet of mass and class and I still love both. *The Quiet American* and *To Kill a Mockingbird*. F. Scott Fitzgerald's *The Great Gatsby*, John Steinbeck's *The Grapes of Wrath* and Emily Brontë's *Wuthering Heights*. *Last Orders* (Graham Swift). *The Shining* and *The Stand* and *It* (all Stephen King), the Wooster and Jeeves books (P. G. Wodehouse), *His Dark Materials* (Philip Pullman), *A Woman of Substance* (Barbara Taylor Bradford), *The Wind in the Willows* (Kenneth Grahame), *A Wrinkle in Time* (Madeleine L'Engle), *The Scarlet Letter* (Nathaniel Hawthorne), *Lord of the Flies* (William Golding), and the Nancy Drew books – and that's just novels, and is by no means a sane and comprehensive list. Let's not get started on poetry and history. Political commentary. Fairytales. And cookbooks.

B L O O M 21 S B U R Y

Cat's Eye	Margaret Atwood
A Prayer for Owen Meany	John Irving
The English Patient	Michael Ondaatje
Snow Falling on Cedars	David Guterson
Fugitive Pieces	Anne Michaels
Harry Potter and the Philosopher's Stone	J. K. Rowling
Easy Riders, Raging Bulls	Peter Biskind
The Map of Love	Ahdaf Soueif
Holes	Louis Sachar
Marrying the Mistress	Joanna Trollope
Kitchen Confidential	Anthony Bourdain
Witch Child	Celia Rees
If Nobody Speaks of Remarkable Things	Jon McGregor
Middlesex	Jeffrey Eugenides
The Little Friend	Donna Tartt
Frankie & Stankie	Barbara Trapido
A Gathering Light	Jennifer Donnelly
The Kite Runner	Khaled Hosseini
The Promise of Happiness	Justin Cartwright
Jonathan Strange & Mr Norrell	Susanna Clarke
The Two of Us	Sheila Hancock